WONDROUS

Travis M. Riddle

Cover design by Travis M. Riddle
Cover illustration by Aaron Griffin - AaronGriffinArt.com
Book Layout © 2014 BookDesignTemplates.com

Wondrous/Travis M. Riddle. -- 1st ed.
ISBN: 978-1539343677

For all of you.

"I speak of wondrous unfamiliar lessons from childhood,
make you remember how to smile good."

—CHANCE THE RAPPER, *COLORING BOOK*

CONTENTS

CHAPTER ONE

INTO BLACK

There were loud shouts. Angry noises. Things to make Miles' skin tingle and stomach flip. He was soothed with quick I Love Yous and goodnight forehead kisses, and then the room blackened into stillness.

Light from the hallway couldn't eke its way into his bedroom how he liked. His mother never closed the door all the way, just in case he needed something in the night and called out for her or his father. But tonight she had closed it.

He wanted to crawl out of bed and crack the door a little, but the angry noises had resumed. Better to remain under the snug safety of his fluffy Pokémon comforter. He shut his eyes but it was no different than what he saw with them open.

"I can't believe—"

The words were sucked away and Miles felt like his body was turning inside-out. He wanted to cry, he started to cry, clutching his comforter and pulling his legs up to his chest.

He felt anxious and uncomfortably warm. He suddenly wondered when his sheets had last been washed, and it made him even more restless. He needed to do one of his calming exercises. Deep breaths. In. Out. He was more than warm now. Hot. Too hot. He flung the comforter aside and opened his eyes.

The air was humid. Sticky. There was a bit of a breeze but it was fleeting, only briefly satisfying. Insects buzzed all around, and the scampering of woodland animals on branches above rustled the leaves.

It was a far cry from the twin-sized bed that Miles had been in moments before. The only similarity was that the grass was a similar shade as his sheets. He was still wearing his faded gray pajamas, which clung to his skinny legs from the moisture.

The first words he heard were a raspy *"Are you a spy?"*

This was especially unsettling for Miles because not only did he not have any idea who he could be a spy for, but the creature asking the question was not a human being.

It wasn't exactly an animal either. It was a cross between a man and a scorpion. It—he?—towered over Miles, his body thick and muscular, skin like sand. He was completely bald, with a neatly-trimmed jet black goatee that came to a fine point at the end of his defined chin. His eyes were black with white pupils that appeared to always be dilated. Three arms jutted out from his sides—two on his left and one on the right. The two left arms were normal, humanoid, but the right was an enormous pincer.

"Are you a spy?" the scorpion-man repeated.

Thunder crashed overhead, rattling the frightened boy's bones as he stood. His pants were dripping with wet mud. The moon shone a sickly green through slight cracks in the treetops.

From behind the stranger's back rose a segmented tail covered in crusted mud with a sharp stinger at its end. The tail slithered like a snake through the air around Miles and came to a stop pointed at the back of his head.

Miles was suddenly astutely aware of how close he was to the man. Monster. Whatever it was. His breathing became ragged and uneven, his warm tears coalescing with the bitter raindrops that pelted his face. *"Mom!"* he screamed. *"Dad!"*

The stranger leaned forward and their eyes locked. Miles could taste the creature's warm, rotten breath. "Don't toy with me," he said, his white eyes leering at Miles.

Miles felt the tip of the stinger lightly poke against the back of his head as a warning.

"Jericho? Sir?"

The call came from somewhere behind the seething creature. From the thicket of trees emerged a man similar to the one threatening Miles, though he only had two arms: one normal, one pincer. "What are you doing?" he asked, his voice lighter and calmer than Jericho's.

"Think I found one of the queen's spies," said Jericho, his eyes trained on the shivering kid. Rain came down harder and faster.

"That doesn't look like one of the queen's spies, sir. He's pink and small."

"Just go fetch some rope, Vinzent. Stop arguin'."

As Vinzent disappeared back into the forest, Jericho asked, "What's your name?"

The young boy had been taught to never talk to strangers, but Jericho took that moment to remind him that there was still an exceptionally sharp stinger aimed at the back of his head, so between sobs he whimpered, "Miles."

"Are you a servant of Queen Alys?"

Miles shook his head.

"If you're lying, I'll have you killed. Might even do it myself, if I'm feelin' like it. You understand?"

Miles nodded. Jericho pulled his tail back.

Vinzent returned with a length of rope and proceeded to tie Miles' hands behind his back, which was a considerable feat as he only had one real hand. He swiveled Miles around and asked, "Too tight?"

"No," Miles whispered. He sniffled as snot ran down his upper lip.

"Don't need to show him any courtesy," Jericho hissed.

Vinzent frowned, his tail drooping slightly. "He's small. Looks like he's just a child, Jericho."

"And we're in the middle of a war and we don't know who or, more importantly, *what* this thing is. There ain't no exceptions." Jericho turned on his heel and marched out of the glade. Vinzent pushed Miles along.

The trio trudged through the thick underbrush, Jericho clipping long branches that obstructed their path. Beetles scuttled along tree trunks and birds cawed high above their heads, seeking shelter from the storm. Flowers sprouted from many of the trees, their petals a faint bluish-purple that seemed to glow in the growing darkness. Long orange tendrils protruded from their centers, trailing down to the forest floor.

Rain fell heavier with each passing minute.

As he marched between the two hulking figures, Miles was finally able to regain a bit of composure. His mind was focused on how cold the rain was making him. A shiver coursed down his spine. He wished he was wearing his red hoodie, or at least had some slippers on.

Mud squished between his toes with every step and he tried not to think about the microscopic germs that were crawling all over his feet. His eyelids fluttered and he took a deep breath.

After almost half an hour of walking in tense silence, they approached a camp situated under a thick canopy of trees that for the most part shielded the area from rain.

In the clearing were four tents, one in each corner of the camp, with a large bonfire at its center. A small makeshift awning of fallen branches and leaves, tied together with rope, covered the fire to give it extra protection from the rainfall. Nestled between two of the tents, about ten feet from the fire, was an iron cage holding something vaguely human but bulbous and slimy green.

There were five other beings similar to Jericho and Vinzent traipsing around the campsite, tending to various tasks. Two were feeding broken sticks to the fire while two others were chopping a variety of meats and vegetables and tossing them into a pot. The fifth was conversing with the caged green man.

"What're we doing with this one?" Vinzent inquired, giving Miles a gentle shove toward the fire. The two humanoid scorpions that were preparing dinner looked up at their new prisoner.

Jericho said, "Throw him in with the Rompun. And don't forget to *lock it*," he added.

"The hell is that thing?" one of the scorpion-men asked as Vinzent and Miles passed the bonfire. "Looks like a forn, but it's got arms and legs."

"And it's a lot bigger than a forn, moron," said the other chef.

"It isn't a forn," Vinzent said. "We aren't sure what it is."

"We gonna eat it?" the second man asked, snipping a branch in half with his chipped pincer. He smacked his lips hungrily.

"No, no," Vinzent told them. "He's being locked up with the Rompun. C'mon, now," he said, pulling Miles along.

Vinzent fumbled for a ring of keys in his pocket, muttering softly. "Wish this rain would ease up just a toonce." The ring held three distinct keys: two silver, one larger than the other, and a dull golden one. Vinzent slipped the large silver key into the hole on the cage door and clicked it open.

"Some company for me, eh?" the large green man groaned, scratching his protruding belly. "He looks funny."

"I'll bring you two dinner in a while."

"*Merci*, chief."

Vinzent slammed the door shut as Miles shuffled in. Heeding Jericho's words, he made sure to lock up before departing.

Now that he was closer, Miles was struck by how frog-like the creature the others referred to as a "Rompun" appeared. He was much taller and fatter than Miles, his skin a grimy shade of green that glistened with fallen raindrops. His head was round and shiny, and his lower jaw jutted out in an impressive underbite. His nose was flat, with wide nostrils. The eyes were large and amphibious, a dirty yellow color with a black slit slicing vertically down the middle.

He wore a chunky brown jacket adorned with several pockets on top of a plain white t-shirt and baggy cargo shorts. It was an interesting look, topped off with flip-flops.

The Rompun smiled cordially and greeted Miles, patting him on the back. He only had three large fingers on each hand.

"Name's Mortimer," he said, extending a hand for Miles to shake. When the boy only shivered in response, Mortimer retracted and said, "You pretty cold, eh?"

"Yes, sir."

The frog-man burst out in deep-throated laughter. "*Sir*, he says! Ha-*ha*! Ain't been called 'sir' before. That's not necessary, kid."

"Okay."

Mortimer shrugged off his musky, muddy coat and placed it on Miles' shoulders. The boy nearly toppled from the weight.

"Um," Miles started, his voice barely above a whisper, "can you please take this off of me?"

"What for?"

"It's dirty."

Another laugh from the Rompun. "So? You in the middle of the Violet Woods, kid. Everything's dirty."

Miles felt his stomach begin to knot. It felt like an anchor had been tied to his waist and he was being dragged to the bottom of the ocean. "Please take it off me," he requested.

"You not a fan of dirt, huh?" Mortimer asked as he lifted the coat from the boy's back. "You know you just standing in the mud with your bare feet, don't you? Not too sanitary either, if that's your concern."

Miles shut his eyes, welcoming the dark. He steadied his breaths, half time in comparison to his heart. He was suddenly aware of the wet mud between his toes again. He tilted his head down, then looked back up and pictured his shoes tucked safely away in the hallway closet back at home.

"Yes." He opened his eyes. "As long as I don't think about it much, I'll be okay. I think," he amended.

Mortimer chuckled. "Alrighty. Good luck with that."

Miles could still smell his mother's lavender shampoo. He could feel her damp hair brush across his cheek as she leaned down to kiss him on the forehead. A sigh as she pulled away, a faint smile for her son. "Get to sleep, bug."

He was tucked soundly in his bed, his toes rustling against the soft sheets. His comforter was pulled up to his chin, and he reciprocated the smile.

His mother edged out of the bedroom, flicking the light switch. A sliver of the hallway's light crept into his room from the slightly open door, his mother's shadow passing through it. Miles could just barely make out his father's voice asking, "How is he?"

"You alright, kid?" Mortimer asked, dangling a burnt piece of meat above his gaping mouth. He dropped it in, gnashing away as Miles shook his head.

"I don't know how I got here," the boy said.

"Well, where you from? I never seen you around Trafier before, so I know it's not there. I would remember someone as goofy looking as you. You from Merrikar?"

"No," Miles replied, not knowing where that was.

"You from, uh…that town near Maulage? I can never remember its name." He tossed another slab of meat into his eager mouth.

"I'm from Austin."

Mortimer looked perplexed.

"Austin," Miles emphasized.

Mortimer let his plate drop to the ground carelessly and scratched his bald head. "Haven't ever heard of that one. Is it in Ruhig or something? I don't travel to Ruhig all that often. Too hot for my tastes."

"It's in Texas." Miles had never heard of Ruhig, but Texas shared its "too hot" characteristic.

The Rompun's grin wrinkled into a frown. "Texas, huh?" he murmured. "Never heard of a place called Texas." He cocked an eyebrow at the boy. "Kinda like…" but he let the thought trail off. It was replaced with, "How old are you, kid?"

"Nine," Miles answered. He tried taking a bite of his food, unable to identify what kind of animal it had come from. His was less burnt than Mortimer's, but the meat was still tough and hard to chew.

The Rompun's expression grew friendly again. "Only nine years old and lost out here in the woods? You must be scared outta your wits. Don't worry, Mortimer'll look out for you."

They shared silence while Mortimer studied Miles, who continued fighting his meal. He'd also been given a stale roll that he accidentally dropped on the ground. He offered to let Mortimer take it, which the Rompun happily did.

"My name's Miles."

"Miles, eh? Good name. Starts with an M. You know what they say about men whose names start with M, don't you?" He prodded Miles playfully and the boy shook his head. "Me neither," Mortimer laughed. "Hopefully it's something good, though."

The rain had not let up even the slightest bit. The ground under their feet was soft and they sunk half an inch into the soil, which made Miles' skin tingle.

"Do you know where my mom and dad are?" he decided to ask Mortimer. Now that he had been in the cage a little while, he had begun to calm down somewhat and his thoughts turned to his parents.

"Can't say I do. Never seen anything quite like you before. You one of a kind."

This worried Miles. He could only assume he was in one of the countries way on the other side of the world—the ones he could never pronounce or spell correctly. That could be the only explanation for all the unfamiliar types of people that surrounded him. But he had no idea how he got in bed and ended up here.

"Where are we?" he asked.

"In Rompu. In the Violet Woods, specifically."

Miles frowned. "I've never heard of Rompu," he said.

Mortimer blinked several times, his eyelids sliding together like the doors of a supermarket.

"Really? It's much bigger than Ruhig. Probably bigger than, uh...*Texas*, too," Mortimer said.

"I've never heard of Ruhig either," Miles admitted, feeling foolish.

Mortimer could read the uncomfortable expression on the boy's face. "What's wrong, kid?"

Miles slammed his eyes shut once again. He tried not thinking about the mud and the rain and the germs and the animals and the woods. He thought about laying in his bathtub, the soapy water rippling under his nose. Blowing bubbles with his mouth, wiggling his two big toes on the other end, near the faucet. His chest tightened, his breathing faltered.

"I can't stand in this mud," he choked out.

Without skipping a beat, Mortimer reached down to his own feet and removed his wooden sandals, presenting them to the kid. "Here, wear these."

Miles snatched them without a second thought and plopped them back onto the ground. He lifted his feet one at a time, delicately wiping mud off on the top of the wet grass, and placed them in the sandals that were three times too big.

Mortimer put his hand on Miles' shoulder, his bulky fingers stretching out across most of the boy's back.

"I don't think you gonna like Rompu much, kid."

Miles drummed his toes against the wood. "Why?"

"Because, like I said," Mortimer told him, "everything's dirty."

Time seemed to be crawling by. What was only three hours at the camp felt more like three days.

Mortimer had informed Miles that the scorpion creatures were a race called the Skyr. Miles had been able to surmise that Jericho was the leader of this pack, and Vinzent was his right-hand man.

Miles asked Mortimer, "Why are you here? Why did Jericho lock you up?" He had begun to feel less tense around him; there was a sort of warmth to the Rompun.

Mortimer laughed. It was a deep, guttural sound. "I was just in the wrong place at the wrong time, I suppose."

"Are you a spy?"

"What gave you that impression?" Mortimer asked, amused.

Miles shrugged. "That's what Jericho asked me when he found me. He asked if I was Queen Alys' spy. Why would a queen spy on him?"

Mortimer's eyebrows drooped, his face scrunched up in thought. "Well," he began, "the queen and the king aren't re-ally...fond of each other right now. And Queen Alys is a Rompun, so naturally the Rompuns sided with her, and...well, can you guess what the king is?"

Miles shook his head.

"Oh. The king is a Skyr. So they sided with him." Mortimer tossed his plate through the iron bars and the two watched it skid toward the bonfire, where three Skyr sat chatting. As the plate slid to a halt, they shot glares at the Rompun. "Most of them, anyway," he went on. "Some stayed loyal to the queen. They weren't really buyin' in to what the king was saying."

"So everyone's fighting?"

Mortimer nodded. "It's a civil war. You know what a civil war is?"

Miles had heard his grandfather refer to a civil war before, but he had never quite understood what it was. He knew that the United States had one a long time ago, but he wasn't sure why. He simply nodded in response to Mortimer's question.

The Rompun grinned. "Pretty smart kid, aren't you?"

One of the Skyr had stood and snatched up Mortimer's discarded plate. "Rompun!" he yelled, clutching the ceramic disc in his hand. His other arm was a fairly diminutive pincer, compared to Jericho's. "Done with dinner, are ya?"

"Yep. That's why I threw the plate."

Moving so swiftly that Miles could barely comprehend his motions, the Skyr let the plate fly like a frisbee. It shattered against the iron bars, bits exploding in every direction. Miles let out a short shriek as lightning flashed above their heads.

"Stop scaring the kid!" Mortimer placed his gigantic green hand on Miles' shoulder. Thunder rumbled in the clouds.

The Skyr grimaced. "Why's it been raining so much lately?" he wondered aloud. A light drizzle snuck through openings in their leafy ceiling. He approached the cage, licking rain from his curled lips.

As the Skyr grew closer, Miles took awkward steps back, nearly tripping over himself in Mortimer's large flip-flops.

"C'mere," the Skyr smiled, exposing jagged teeth. Miles noticed a long scar streaking across the creature's arm; with his runt of a pincer, he probably wasn't nearly as adept at combat as the others.

Mortimer stepped in front of Miles and firmly planted his hands on his hips. "Leave him alone."

The Skyr clenched his gut with laughter. "Look at the Rompun!" he called over to his comrades, doubling over. "Posing like a sassy housewife. A fat, blubberin' housewife."

In another motion that was too fast for Miles to register, Mortimer's bulky hand somehow shot between the cage's bars and wrapped its meaty fingers around the Skyr's neck. Mortimer yanked his arm back, slamming the man's head against the unflinching metal. His grip loosened and the Skyr collapsed on the forest floor. Miles' body began to tremble.

The others raced to their comrade's side, roaring that they were going to rip Mortimer to shreds. Miles didn't doubt they could do it, though Mortimer would put up a tough fight.

"Who do you think you are, Rompun?" one of them sneered.

Mortimer returned his hands to his hips. "I'm having a bit of an identity crisis at the moment," he said nonchalantly. "Why not open this cage up and we can figure it out?"

Miles did not want them to figure it out.

He wanted everybody to stop yelling and for everyone to just be quiet and happy. He rapped his toes against the wooden sandals, the raindrops pelting down harder and splashing against his face.

Vinzent stumbled out of his tent on Miles' right, looking quite irritated. "What in the world is going on out here?" he asked. "What's all this commotion?" It was then he noticed his ally lying motionless on the ground. Miles wondered where Jericho and the other two Skyr had gone.

"The tubby Rompun knocked Hale out," one of the remaining men explained. "Smacked his head straight into the metal. Lemme kill him, Vinzent. We don't need him, not *really*."

Vinzent shook his head adamantly. "Jericho has strict orders not to kill this one. We can't defy His Majesty."

The Skyr let out a menacing growl. "We can just say he escaped…"

"And make it seem like we're incompetent? Are you an idiot? Just back up. I need to bring the little one over to my tent."

Miles felt like he was shrinking in the corner of the cage. His arms began to shake more erratically. He wanted to be brave like his father always told him to be, but he couldn't muster up any courage.

"What you need him for?" Mortimer asked defensively, slinking toward the boy.

"I just need to ask him a few things," Vinzent said. "What're you gonna do, Mortimer? Bash my head in too? Stand aside. Make this easier on all of us."

Vinzent reached into his pocket, extracting the ring of keys. They swung on the thin silver circle.

The gray sky lit up with a fierce brightness that surged through the clouds and connected with one of the winding trees hanging over the camp. The dark brown of the branches gave way to vibrant orange that engulfed its purple leaves and bark. Thick branches snapped with a noise like a panicked shriek. They crashed into the glade only a few feet from Vinzent and the incapacitated Hale.

Vinzent was thrown off-balance by the impact, slipping on the slick grass. His head slammed into the cage just like Hale's had.

Rain was coming down in sheets now, breaking through the canopy, but it didn't quell the flames.

Vinzent didn't move.

The fire began to spread.

Miles closed his eyes and screamed. He began to cry. He tried to imagine his mother's voice, but it was overpowered by the frantic shouting of the two Skyr that were still conscious.

"Snap out of it!"

It was Mortimer.

"Kid, you gotta stay with me!"

Miles opened his right eye, his entire body shaking with fear. Mortimer was on his hands and knees, reaching between the iron bars for Vinzent's limp body. In the distance, the flames were creeping toward Jericho and Vinzent's tent. It wouldn't be long before it was nothing but ash.

Mortimer looked back at the child. "Miles," he said. "You gotta stay with me, yeah? Don't be scared. You gonna be alright. Mortimer's here."

The boy nodded. He had to be brave. He thought about his mother telling him, "There's nothing to be worried about." The lavender scent of her hair.

He had to be brave.

He wiped the tears from his eyes. They were replaced by more tears.

Mortimer strained to reach Vinzent, his fingers grazing the Skyr's tattered pants. He struggled to push his arm further, just half an inch, and he was able to grasp a pant leg. A look of relief washed over his face as he pulled Vinzent's body closer and plucked the key ring out of his hand.

"Okay," Mortimer said, facing Miles. "We gonna get outta here. Okay? First I gotta get something out of Vinzent's tent, then we run. Just stay close. You'll be fine. Nothing to be worried about. Yeah?"

Miles nodded. He watched the tent catch fire like a marshmallow over a campfire. Smoke billowed into the air, smothering them all as if it were a heavy blanket.

"Good. I need you to unlock the cage, though. I can fit my arm through, but I can't angle it right. I'm too fat." He smiled encouragingly. "Can you do that?"

"I don't know," Miles said, his voice hardly a whisper.

Somehow Mortimer was able to hear him. "You'll do great. Don't worry." He handed Miles the keys, singling out the large silver one. "No time to waste."

Miles stepped forward, the huge flat sandals slapping against the muck, sinking into it. The tips of his pajama pants grazed the mud and torn-up grass. Every step was a challenge. He stuck his thin arm through the cage, reaching to insert the key into its hole. He turned it and could feel the satisfying *click* of the lock shifting. The door opened with a push.

"Here we go," said Mortimer, rushing past Miles. The Rompun made a beeline for the tent to their right, which had not yet succumbed to the raging fires.

One of the remaining Skyr jumped through a cloud of smoke and landed a powerful blow on Mortimer, nearly knocking him over, but Mortimer landed an equally powerful punch on the Skyr's face.

The creature fell onto his back. His own stinger pierced the back of his head, emerging through his cheek. Miles screamed, but Mortimer said to him, "C'mon, kid! We gotta hurry!"

Miles couldn't spot the other Skyr anywhere. His dizziness was beginning to subside, but Mortimer's flip-flops were making it near impossible to move. They were too large and unwieldy to run in. He knew he would surely die if he didn't get moving.

He had to be brave.

He shut his eyes, tried to block out the sound of the fire burning away blades of grass and eating up the coarse bark of the trees.

He had to be brave.

He tried to not think about the beautiful bluish-purple flowers erupting in flame, the mud covering the ground.

He had to be brave.

He kicked his feet out of the sandals and ran.

Up ahead, Mortimer was already scrounging through the tent. Miles joined him inside, still wondering where the remaining Skyr had scurried off to.

Mortimer was in a frenzy, thrashing about, knocking over cabinets and scanning through loose sheets of paper. It was obvious he was searching for something specific, but Miles had no idea what. At last, under one of the two cots, hidden beneath a pile of ragged monochrome clothes, Mortimer found it: a large, locked chest of a deep red color.

"Hey!" came a gravelly voice.

In unison, Miles turned his head and Mortimer swung his arm, still holding on to the chest. His hand soared over the boy's head, crashing the chest into the Skyr's face.

The Skyr clutched his bloody mess of a face and fell over, his mouth agape. Blood dripped from his gums.

"I need the keys," Mortimer said, ignoring the Skyr's bloodied face. Miles stared at the unconscious Skyr, wondering if the man was going to die. "Miles. I need the keys. We have to hurry."

Miles snapped out of his daze and glanced up at Mortimer. "They're in the door," he said. His cheeks flushed, burning with embarrassment.

Without even a momentary thought, he took off toward the cage.

All he could see were the keys sticking out of the door that hung open, beating against the side of the cage with gusts of wind. Everything else blurred together, blue into green into orange into yellow into brown into red into black. He grabbed the keys. Ran. Vision nothing but black.

"Open your eyes, kid. Need you to be able to see me."

The world popped back into existence all at once. Miles realized that he was once again standing in front of Mortimer, who was inserting the tiny golden key into the chest's keyhole.

Its top popped open and Mortimer's shaky hands spilled its contents out all over the damp ground. Mortimer unfolded every scrap of paper, crumpling each one and tossing them over his shoulder until finally he found one that made him stop and smile. He folded it and stuffed it into his pocket, then fished through the chest and took all the coins inside as well.

"You ready?"

Miles nodded, so they ran.

Flames whipped at them from both sides, creating a bright tunnel that they shot through with haste. Mortimer's stride was much longer than Miles', but the boy made up for it in speed and trailed only a short distance behind the Rompun.

The boy pictured Vinzent's body idle and charred. A sudden, immense feeling of remorse enveloped him.

As they ran, tree branches and leaves fell from above. Some of the leaves were green, some were a muted purple, and many were burnt.

Mortimer zig-zagged through tree trunks, splashing through puddles and hopping over decayed logs. Miles wondered if his companion knew at all where they were going or if this was just some mad dash to freedom. He wondered if Vinzent had a son or daughter. Wondered if anyone was going to miss him.

"Just keep running!" Mortimer yelled up ahead.

A second later, the Rompun disappeared.

Miles wanted to stop but he had to be brave. He shouted after Mortimer, but the only response he received was the sound of a far-off splash.

And then there was no ground at his feet.

Three thoughts went through Miles' head as he careened through the air.

The first was: Am I going to die?

The second was: How will Mom and Dad know what happened to me?

The third was: I'm going to die.

He was only in the air for six seconds before breaking the surface of a spring below.

His entire body screamed out in agony. His bones were mashed potatoes. It took a few moments of floating underwater for Miles to understand what had transpired. He swam upward, joining the world again, and saw Mortimer treading water a few feet away.

"You alright?"

Kicking his feet underneath him, Miles moved his arms through the clear water and concluded he hadn't broken anything. "Yeah," he said.

The dark clouds began to give way to the moon, a luminous crescent. Mortimer swam to the spring's edge and pulled himself out. Miles followed suit, gliding jerkily through the water with each pained kick. Even aching all over, he was still a pretty good swimmer. His grandmother had always praised his swimming ability. He joined Mortimer on solid ground and the Rompun looked him over.

"Hey, where are my sandals?"

CHAPTER TWO

THE SPIRIT OF THE FLAMES

At the edge of the Violet Woods were the Screaming Crags, a mountain range that covered most of the northern kingdom of Ruhig and extended down into Rompu, where they currently were, as Mortimer had explained to Miles. They were traveling to Windheit, the capital city of Ruhig.

On the outskirts of the forest, Miles looked up at the purple leaves covering the tops of the trees. He wondered what the Violet Woods looked like from a bird's perspective.

After a day of hiking, the two had stopped to rest where the Crags met the treeline, at a waterfall that cascaded into a dingy lake filled with lily pads and mossy rocks. Long, orange fish slithered underneath the water's surface. Miles watched them glide through his reflection in the swaying mirror.

"I'm hungry," Miles said, peering into the lake.

Mortimer waded into it, wearing nothing but his undergarments. Tiny yellow berries speckled with orange were the only thing the two had eaten on their journey through the woods. Mortimer had called them fennberries.

The Rompun splashed about in the cool water with each step. His head rotated back and forth until suddenly he shot his hand forward, spraying water onto Miles. When the ripples settled, he was clutching one of the eel-like fish. He tossed it onto the shore, where it flopped helplessly at Miles' feet, gasping for water.

"There you go!"

Miles' brow furrowed as he hung his mouth open in disgust. "I can't eat that!"

"Why not?" Mortimer snatched another fish out of the water and shoved its head into his mouth. His chomp induced a yelp from Miles.

"That was alive! *This* is alive!" He pointed to the fish at his feet. "It has germs! You have to cook food before you eat it!"

Mortimer was too busy slurping the rest of the fish into his mouth to pay the boy any attention. "Gotta do the best with what you got," he said, "and what we got is raw fish. Just eat it, you'll be fine."

Miles kicked the fish back into its home. Mortimer shrugged.

A day later, the two were delving deeper into the Crags, moving closer to the Rompu-Ruhig border.

The mountains reached so high past the clouds above that Miles couldn't even see their peaks. They were taller than any skyscraper he had ever seen walking through downtown Austin. He almost asked Mortimer if the Frost Bank Tower was as tall as the mountains, but he realized it would be a stupid question.

They had not encountered any other Rompuns or Skyr. Near the middle of the day, though, Mortimer leapt behind a jagged rock twice his size and told Miles to "Shush, kid!" The boy did as he was told, ducking next to his guardian. His stomach gurgled.

With their own footsteps and conversation no longer filling Miles' ears, he was able to hear what Mortimer had picked up on: three voices. Low, gruff. Not far off. Miles' heart started to pound.

"We near a Skyr outpost," Mortimer said. "We must be close to the border crossing. Gonna have to go around."

"Where are we going?" Miles whispered back.

"There's a shortcut through the border. An underground passage. Don't worry, it's safe."

"But where are we *going*?"

"Back to Queen Alys."

"She lives in Ruhig?"

The question made Miles feel like a child. He was indeed a child, but it made him feel even younger asking so many questions. In school, he prided himself on almost always understanding what his teachers were explaining, and very rarely had to ask for clarification, unlike his classmates. In Rompu, nothing was familiar.

Mortimer held up his hand and waited a moment, listening for the voices. "No," he then answered quietly. "She lives in western Rompu. We in the east right now. We can't just cross Rompu, though. Not on our own. Takes too long and too many camps full of Skyr that're looking to give Rompuns a good pounding. The king of Ruhig is a pal; he'll help us get back."

He slowly rose and motioned for Miles to follow him back in the direction they had come from, tacking on an extra hour to their trip as they sought the alternate route.

"Will Queen Alys be able to help me get home?" Miles asked. "I really want to go home."

"I don't have a clue where you from, but if anyone might know how to help, it's the queen," Mortimer said. "She's very smart. But first we gotta get some transportation from the Ruhigans."

Miles nodded, feeling somewhat optimistic. "How do you know Queen Alys and the king of Ruhig?"

"I'm the queen's aide," Mortimer explained. "My wife and I both help her out with day-to-day stuff. Lately that's involved me traveling around to different cities, meeting with the king up in Ruhig, stuff like that, and reporting back to her."

The plan wasn't much, but it helped put Miles a little at ease. There wasn't a guarantee that Queen Alys could get him home, but at least it was a plan. Better than not having one at all.

The farther north they traveled, the more grass disappeared and gave way to desert sand. The air grew drier as well, chapping Miles' lips and making him thirstier than he already was. After four more hours of meandering through the relentless heat, they were stationed in front of a Rompun-sized boulder resting against the side of a mountain.

Most of the afternoon had been spent with Miles riding on Mortimer's back, his tiny feet red and sore from the scorching sand. Miles sat on a flattened rock, massaging his battered feet as he watched Mortimer place his giant green hands on the boulder.

"The mighty strength of Mortimer is about to be on display," the Rompun grinned through his underbite. You not gonna wanna miss this one. Count me down!"

Miles chuckled. "Three—two—one!"

Mortimer let out a vicious war cry as he gave the weathered boulder a single, forceful shove. It didn't budge.

"I underestimated this one," he frowned. Miles laughed.

He began pushing against the stone even harder, putting all of his weight into it, and finally it began to scrape against the grains of sand. As Mortimer moved it out of the way, a tunnel was revealed in the mountainside.

Mortimer slipped through the opening, beckoning Miles to join him. The boy hopped up off the rock and raced across the sand into the dark passage, welcoming the feel of cool ground on his feet. It was soothing despite the fact he wasn't enjoying walking around barefoot.

They set off down the secret pathway.

After a couple steps, Miles asked, "Don't you need to move the rock back? So the Skyr don't find us?"

Mortimer looked over his shoulder at the massive brown rock, letting out a lengthy sigh. He begrudgingly approached the boulder again.

"Dangit," he muttered.

Miles had been worried he wouldn't be able to see very well in the tunnels, but every thirty feet or so, lit torches hung from the walls. He began to imagine whose job it was to ensure all the torches were still burning. It made him think about his mother waking up in the morning and getting ready for her job. Had she gone into his bedroom and discovered an empty bed? It had already been a couple days since he'd appeared in Rompu, so surely his absence must have been noticed by now. The thought make his stomach tighten.

It was probably a Rompun who lit the torches, or some other friendly creature he had not yet met. Surely the Skyr wouldn't be helping anyone. Which prompted his question, "Is there anything besides Rompuns and Skyr? Other types of people, I mean."

The Rompun giggled. "Yep. In Ruhig, the kingdom up north we're goin' to, most of the people are, uh, Ruhigans. Then there's also Omnes, daft little fools."

So far there had only been one path for them to follow through the tunnels. The path had curved drastically to the right near the entrance, but since then it had mostly been a straight shot.

"Whose side are the Ruhigans on in the war?" asked Miles.

"The Ruhigans aren't really technically on anyone's side," said Mortimer. "They're pretty isolated up in their own country. Though they've been helping us Rompuns out a bit. There's a good history between us, except for a hiccup or two. Mostly they stay up in the mountains, though, flying from city to city and minding their own business as much as they can. All their cities are nestled up on the highest peaks, touching the clouds."

"They can fly?"

"Yep. Their arms are big, feathered wings."

Miles tried to picture a Ruhigan. All he could conjure up was the image of Big Bird. "So they're like huge birds that can talk?"

"Pretty much," Mortimer confirmed. "I wouldn't say that around them, though. They hate the comparison. They say birds are just flying rats."

"That's weird."

Mortimer laughed at the kid. "Yeah, it is, ain't it?"

"What about the Omnes?"

"Oh, they've all aligned themselves with King Mykael. Not that it's a huge loss. He offered them certain resources in exchange for their loyalty and they couldn't turn it down."

Miles was growing tired of all the walking they had done. He wanted to find a bed and sink into its sheets, get lost in a pillow, and sleep for days. He wanted to be wrapped in his mother's arms and held tight. He wanted to eat food from one of the countless Austin food trucks, something besides strange-looking berries. He wanted to be home.

"So a city might be above us right now?" Miles asked. He didn't like asking questions, but he liked learning, and talking with Mortimer was making the time go by faster.

"Probably not," said Mortimer, shaking his head. "I think we still technically in Rompu. Probably gonna be underground for…I think a day, day and a half. At the very least, we'll be in here all day today and finish early tomorrow."

The boy let out an exhausted groan. "Really?"

"Ha! Yes, really. Why? You tired of traveling with your old pal Mortimer already?" The Rompun patted him on the back, the force nearly causing him to fall on his face.

"No," said Miles. "I'm tired of walking. My feet hurt."

"My feet are aching too. Somebody lost my sandals," Mortimer smirked.

Miles frowned, assuming the sandals had probably caught on fire back in the camp. An image of Vinzent's scorched face flashed in his mind.

Up ahead was a fork in the path. Mortimer initially veered to the right as they approached, but stopped short where the two branches split. "Wait," he whispered to no one. "What was it Jaselle said…?"

Miles kept quiet as Mortimer murmured something else to himself, pointing back and forth to each path. He might've been playing eeny-meeny-miny-moe.

"This way," he eventually declared, pointing at the left tunnel.

"Are you sure?"

"Yep. Nope. Well, eighty to eighty-five percent sure." Mortimer started down the passageway and Miles trailed closely behind. The tunnel's ceiling was high above their heads.

The confined space of the tunnel reminded Miles of the buses back in Austin. He had only ridden on a bus a couple times, when his grandparents were visiting. His parents preferred to walk around the city rather than take the public transportation, but his grandmother couldn't handle so much walking in a single day.

Miles felt more comfortable here than he had on the bus, however. The dim lighting calmed him down. It wasn't as cramped and hectic as riding the bus, with its noisy passengers and constant jarring stops and starts. Both places smelled unpleasant.

What Miles loved most about riding the bus with his grandparents was that he got to sit in the special seats designated for old people. At first he had argued, "I can't sit there. I'm not old," but his grandmother assured him it would be fine. His parents sat in regular seats farther down at the back of the bus, talking about something he couldn't hear.

He heard a whimpering up ahead. "What's that noise?" he said aloud.

Mortimer didn't respond. He jogged forward, and Miles took off in a sprint after him. Miles quickly squeezed past the Rompun and skidded to a halt when he came upon a peculiar creature lying in the middle of the widening passage.

It had four legs and was as big as a medium-sized dog, covered entirely in black fur. Its ears were pointed sharply upward, flicking in Miles' direction. Smooth, rounded gray ridges poked up along the animal's spine, ending where the tail began. Its tail was skinny and long, with a tuft of fur at the end. The tail wrapped back around to almost reach its head. One of its paws was coated in dried blood, its four toes mangled. It let out another soft whimper as the two grew nearer.

"What is it?" Miles asked, kneeling down beside the animal. It flattened its ears down, looking up at him with sad eyes.

"It's a maylan," Mortimer said, taking another step forward. "He looks hurt pretty bad. Don't think he can walk."

"Can we help him?" Miles' stomach twisted at the idea of the helpless animal being left injured in the lonely tunnels.

Mortimer sighed. "I dunno, kid. We got a long ways to walk, and carrying a hurt animal won't make it easier…"

"But he's hurt," Miles objected. "We can't just leave him here."

The maylan licked at his bloody paw. Miles reached his hand out shakily, extending it toward the animal's snout. The maylan lifted his head up and sniffed Miles' fingers, assessing whether or not the boy could be trusted. His ears perked up. He licked Miles' index finger and the boy grinned.

"He's not mean," Miles said.

"Never said he was. Just said I don't wanna carry him, and we both know I'd be the one carrying him."

"Please, Mortimer! Clint needs our help!"

"Clint?"

"I named him Clint just now. Please?" Miles gently ran his hand along the maylan's ridges. They felt padded, like the bottom of a dog's paw. He counted twelve of them.

Mortimer got down on one knee next to Clint, hesitantly placing a finger on the maylan's paw. Clint jerked his leg back and emitted a high-pitched yelp.

"He can't walk on this thing at all."

"What can we do?" Miles asked, locked onto Clint's eyes. The animal looked nervous.

Mortimer shrugged. "I can't carry him all the way to Windheit, kid. I just can't."

"But I love him."

"You just met him."

"That doesn't mean I don't love him."

Mortimer rose and brushed his shorts off. "Hate to say it, but we can't take Clint with us. Sorry, kid." He frowned, scratching his chin. Stubble was starting to darken his green complexion. "Say bye to him and let's get a move on. Got a ways to go still."

Miles felt tears forming in his eyes. His lips began to quiver and he wanted to punch Mortimer in his fat gut but actually he didn't and he knew the Rompun was right anyway. Clint was too injured to walk. He placed his palm on Clint's bobbing stomach.

A bluish-green light very faintly emanated from the boy's hand, coupled with a barely noticeable vibration. The dry blood on the maylan's paw melted away, sliding off onto the ground. The tense, furry toes seemed to ease up as the open wound on the top of Clint's paw sealed itself shut. He jumped to his feet and wagged his tail joyfully.

"Mortimer," said Miles, beaming. "Look! Clint's better!"

His mouth hanging open in disbelief, Mortimer stared down at the boy. *"Jamais d'la vie..."* he muttered. "What'd you just do?"

"I didn't do anything."

"But you touched him and now the thing's all patched up. What'd you do?"

"I didn't do anything." Miles ran his hand down Clint's back, smiling at Mortimer. "So we can bring him with us?" The look on Mortimer's face clearly conveyed that he really did not want to bother with the maylan. "I'll take care of him," Miles assured the Rompun. "I don't know what they eat, though."

"Fine," Mortimer forfeited.

Miles hopped up and thanked Mortimer with a hug. Clint yipped and licked the boy's cheek with his slick, pink tongue.

"Never seen anything like that," Mortimer muttered.

"Maybe it was magic," Miles said dismissively.

Mortimer chortled. "You think?" Miles nodded and Mortimer went on, "I didn't actually think magic was real, but after what King Mykael did, I guess anything's possible. Maybe Cléoma ain't as crazy as I figured."

Miles ignored whatever Mortimer was saying and continued cheerily petting Clint.

"Did you have any pets back home?" Mortimer asked as they resumed their trek through the underground passage.

"I have a dog like Clint," Miles responded. "He's big and black and his name is Ollie."

"Why'd you name him that?"

"I think that was the name he already had when my mom got him from the shelter," Miles said. Clint was panting alongside him as they walked.

"No, I mean Clint."

"Oh. I named him after Clint Eastwood."

The Rompun shot a curious glance at Miles. "Clint Eastwood?"

"Clint Eastwood is the best actor ever!" said Miles excitedly. "He was in *Unforgiven*, and *The Good, the Bad and the Ugly*, and lots of cool stuff. But he's old now."

"I dunno what any of that is or means."

"They're movies."

"Never heard of any of them. I dunno what in the world you talkin' about."

Miles scoffed. "You're missing out. They're awesome." He scratched behind Clint's ear as they followed the curve of the path. Letting out a light chuckle, he said, "You're weird, Mortimer."

Ollie's fur was all black, short and soft. When he stood on his hind legs, he was almost as tall as Miles.

"His name is Ollie. He's three years old," his mother had said when she brought him home. "That's twenty-one in dog years."

"What are dog years?" Miles asked curiously. His mother was the only person he felt entirely comfortable asking questions. He smiled, rubbing Ollie on the top of his head. The dog licked up and down his cheek, tickling him. Miles was instantly in love. His mother grabbed a tissue off the counter by the door and wiped his cheek.

"It's hard to explain," she said. "It just means every year is like seven years to a dog." She placed her keys on the counter, joining her son and their new pet on the living room carpet.

"So does time move really fast for them?" Miles asked. He waved his hand back and forth in front of Ollie's face as fast as he could, the dog's eyes following as best they could. "Did he even see that?"

His mother laughed. "No, that's not what it means. It means, uh…" She looked for an explanation. "It means that their bodies age faster than ours. Do you know what I mean by that?"

"I think so," said Miles. "So Ollie is like a grown-up, not a baby? Even though he's only three? Does that mean he'll be old soon?"

"In a couple years, I guess."

"Does that mean he'll die soon?"

"No, bug," his mother said, shaking her head. "Ollie is going to live for a long time, and we're going to love him together. Do you like him?"

Miles tip-toed his fingertips down Ollie's spine. An even wider grin stretched across his face and he said, "I love him."

He was woken up by Mortimer's gigantic hand smothering his face. His breathing became more rapid as Mortimer whispered, "Keep quiet." He removed his hand.

Miles listened. From farther down the tunnel, he could hear footsteps and men's voices. Clint lifted his head, his ears at attention. The voices were croaky and strained.

The tunnel was just a single path. The last branch had been over an hour before they had decided to stop for the night. Miles didn't know what the plan was. They had nowhere to hide.

A low grumble started in Clint's throat, its volume increasing until it culminated in a series of fierce barks.

"Shh," Miles urged the maylan, clamping his mouth shut. The growling continued.

"Was that Klipse?" Miles could hear one of the voices ask. He held onto Clint.

"Don't worry," Mortimer whispered to him reassuringly. "Mortimer's here. We'll be alright."

The footsteps were brisk. Whoever it was had begun running. Miles could tell they were just around the bend. Then he saw them.

There were only two, accompanied by a maylan that had just four large ridges. The two creatures were short, barely taller than Miles. Their skin was gray and scaly, accentuated by bulging black eyes. Their faces came to a sharp point, like that of a lizard's. Miles presumed they must be Omnes.

"Don't even think about moving," the one in front shouted. A long, slimy tongue lashed out with every word he spit. He wore a patch loosely over his left eye.

"We aren't starting any trouble," Mortimer said, putting his hands up in a sign of peace. "We just passing through. Stopped for the night to rest. That's all."

"Hey, look," the other Omne yelped. "You were right. It's Klipse." He was pointing at Clint, who continued barking wildly at the duo, obviously incensed. "That ugly pink thing's got Klipse!"

The stocky lizard-man glared at Clint's foot, his tongue dangling out of his mouth.

"Hey," he said again. "How'd you two fix his foot? Look, Kricket, they fixed his foot." The Omne beckoned Clint, clicking his tongue rapidly, but the maylan remained unmoved, yapping at them.

"Go get him, Gryff," said Kricket, taking a pack of cigarettes out of his pocket. He smacked the carton against his palm and took one of the white sticks out, standing on the tips of his toes to hold it to a nearby torch to light.

"F'na," Gryff nodded, extracting a dagger from a sheath that hung from his belt. He waddled toward Clint and Miles.

Mortimer eyed the weapon and moved aside. "Give him Clint," he instructed Miles.

"No. He's mine."

"He's actually *mine*, if we're gettin' technical," Kricket said before taking a drag of his cigarette.

"Just let Clint go, Miles. Then these guys'll leave us be. Go on." He gestured toward the two Omnes.

But Miles shook his head as Gryff grew closer, fiddling with the dagger. "C'mere, Klipse," the ugly creature cooed.

"He's mine," Miles repeated, his body beginning to tremble. He didn't want to cry. He wanted to yell. "You don't even care about him! You left him back there when he got hurt!"

Gryff laughed. "Yeah, and now he's not hurt. Get away from the maylan, chump." Behind him, Kricket blew smoke into the air. It smelled of berries and burnt wood.

Miles flew into a frenzy as Gryff reached toward the ravenous Clint. Without thinking, Miles clenched his fist and flung his arm forward, smashing his insignificant knuckles into Gryff's chest. His hand let off a bright spark with the impact.

Gryff fell backwards, tripping over his own feet, scrambling to rip his brown leather vest off. It was covered in flames that licked at his face, burning his body with every second he kept it on.

"Help me, Kricket!" He kicked at the air, desperately trying to remove his vest. The fire spread to his thin, white shirt.

"How'd he do that?" Kricket demanded, wielding a knife of his own. His blade was considerably larger than Gryff's. "What the hell is this thing?" he asked, glaring at Miles.

Mortimer and Miles exchanged confused looks, trying to suss out what had just happened. Smoke rose from Miles' hand as well as Kricket's cigarette.

"He's the Spirit of the Flames," Mortimer blurted out.

"I'm what?" Miles wafted away the smoke from his hand. Clint's tail wagged at the sight of Gryff's flaming clothes.

The Omne finally managed to wrestle his shirt and vest off. He stood in the middle of the passage, stamping out the fire. Burns marked his chest and face.

"You two had better get going," Mortimer warned them, "or else he'll unleash a whole maelstrom on you."

Kricket looked exceptionally worried about this threat, but snarled as best as he could, exposing two rows of sharpened teeth. He bent his knees, said a swear word, and half a second later he was clinging to the ceiling. He scurried and dropped down behind Miles, grabbing him forcefully, raising his blade to the boy's throat.

Miles let out a screech that tore through the air.

Clint's fangs sunk into Kricket's leg, tugging, ripping flesh. Miles slipped through the Omne's loosened grip.

The boy ran toward Gryff with a hand encased in intense blue flames that flickered like the torches hanging on either side of the tunnel. He swung his arm, connecting with Gryff's lower jaw.

A blur of gray and black shot past. The crumpled mass skidded down the dirt pathway, kicking up dust. As it settled, Miles could see that it was Kricket with Clint still attached to his leg, gnawing away. Mortimer had thrown the pitiful Omne.

"Sorry, Clint," Mortimer apologized.

Miles turned, saw the other maylan charging at him. He stumbled backward and the beast pounced.

It was knocked out of the air by Clint, who took its neck in his mouth. The two collided with the wall.

There was a shout behind Miles. He swiveled around to see Gryff tumbling through the air toward Kricket, courtesy of Mortimer. Their heads bashed together as he landed on top of his ally.

"Get Clint and let's go!" Mortimer bellowed.

Miles called for Clint as they raced down the tunnel. Clint stopped chewing on the other maylan's neck and followed his new owner.

"Remember the Spirit of Fire! Spread his legend!" Mortimer yelled back at their attackers.

"You said 'Spirit of the Flames' last time," Miles pointed out.

"Oh. *I meant Spirit of the Flames!*" the Rompun roared.

The three of them ran, twisting and turning through the tunnels, which grew taller and wider as they continued on, the ceiling reaching up twice as tall as Miles' house was. Mortimer led the pack. Miles struggled to keep up with his long strides and Clint's agility. They made one final turn and found themselves facing a dead end.

In front of them was the biggest, most horrifying monster Miles had ever seen.

"Alright, we definitely went the wrong way," Mortimer mumbled, backing up slowly. Clint began to bark again.

The hulking beast turned to face them. It was purple and muscular, its posture like that of a gorilla's. Its face was rough and weathered with many sharp edges. It had thick horns that jutted from the sides of its head, and Miles could make out folded leathery black wings sprouting from its back. A long tail lashed at the tunnel's walls. Its head bumped up against the ceiling.

Mortimer uttered a couple words Miles' mother had told him never to say then took off back the way they'd come, scooping the kid up in his arms. Clint dashed ahead of them.

As the beast pursued them, its bulky shoulders scraped against the tunnel walls, sending cracks rippling through the foundation. Tiny bits of rock fell from the ceiling. Soon the tunnel would be too small for it to navigate through.

If they could outrun it for that long.

It reached out a dirty claw, just barely missing Mortimer's large frame as they rounded a corner.

Miles had no idea Mortimer was capable of such speed. Clint was far ahead of them, running back toward where Kricket and Gryff were incapacitated.

"Clint!" Mortimer yelled, turning right, down a fork they hadn't taken before. "This way, boy!"

They couldn't stop to wait for the maylan to catch up. Mortimer raced down the passageway, the colossal beast slamming into a wall behind them as it tried to follow them down the new path. Miles could feel the tunnel shake as fractures appeared in the ceiling.

Glancing back, he couldn't see Clint. All he saw was the monster's horned face lumbering after them, charging on all fours, its blue-veined purple hands smashing into the ground. Miles immensely regretted looking back.

"Almost out," Mortimer said, tightening his hold on Miles. "Almost out. We gonna make it." It was as if he said it to reassure himself.

The boy kept his eyes focused on the monster behind them, calling after Clint. Suddenly the maylan zig-zagged between the creature's legs, yelping as he sped up, dodging the purple limbs crashing into the ground.

In an instant, the darkness of the tunnel gave way to the light of outside. An orange sunset rose behind the rocky opening of the passage.

Thunder crashed overhead as Mortimer ran, his feet slapping against wet grass.

The gigantic beast reached forward, its claw wrapping around Clint's meager black body. The maylan howled and wriggled frantically.

With another whip of its tail against the tunnel's wall, the passageway had taken more abuse than it could handle. Miles saw the tunnel begin to collapse behind the creature as lightning lit the sky.

Miles screamed Clint's name so loud, it felt like someone poured nails down his throat. The maylan bit and clawed at the monster's hand, but it was no use. It didn't even cause the creature to flinch.

A roar permeated the air as dirt and rock fell on the monster's tail, then its back, and its hand shot open in pain. Clint tumbled to the ground, quickly standing back up and sprinting toward the exit. He scampered through the tunnel's opening just as it collapsed with debris, crushing the beast's head.

They didn't stop running.

CHAPTER THREE

LIKE RICKETY CRESCENT MOONS

"There's something you not telling me."

By nightfall, the trio had found a secluded spot tucked between two low mountains in which they could set up a campsite. As far as they could tell, Kricket and Gryff—and more importantly, the monstrous abomination—were not in pursuit. Despite this, Mortimer insisted they stay hidden for the time being, just in case.

"What do you mean?" Miles tossed a rock the size of his fist, smiling feebly as Clint fetched it in a mad dash. He had thrown up several times after their encounter this morning and he was still feeling a bit shaky, though much more calm.

"Back there in the tunnels, you did something to Clint and those Omnes. What was that?"

"I really don't know. Magic, I guess," Miles offered again.

Clint returned the rock, dropping it at Miles' tired feet. He snatched it up and closed his eyes to block out the sight of his blistered feet and stubby toes covered in dirt and scrapes. An image of the monster's maw flashed in his mind. He took a deep breath and threw the rock again, his eyelids popping open.

Mortimer had been able to scrounge up only a few fallen branches in their vicinity. While they did have some patches of grass, the Screaming Crags were distinctly lacking in other greenery. He had stacked them up against each other, surrounded by a circle of small stones.

"Okay. If you can do magic, then light these branches on fire. We gotta eat sometime." He stepped back to give the kid more space.

Miles picked up Clint's rock and asked, "Won't the monster see the smoke?"

Mortimer shook his head. "Nah, I don't think we gotta worry about that thing right now. Don't even think about it. Just try making us a fire."

As Clint chased after the rock, Miles examined the animals Mortimer had caught and killed while he had been off collecting the firewood. They looked remarkably similar to squirrels, but they had no arms, legs, or tails. They simply consisted of a small, furry head and torso with long, thinly webbed wings.

Clint placed the rock on the ground near Miles once again, panting eagerly. Miles ignored him, concentrating on the dead branches that were snapped in half, leaning against each other like a miniature wooden teepee. His mind wandered to thoughts of school, learning about Native Americans eating the first Thanksgiving feast with pilgrims. It sounded like a pleasant evening.

He held his arms up. That must be step one of spellcasting, he figured. He hesitantly pointed his index fingers at the wood, repeating the word *fire* in his head.

Nothing.

"I can't."

"Why not?"

"I dunno."

"You don't know much, do you?" Mortimer teased.

"That isn't nice."

"Sorry. What if you tried touching them? You were touching Clint when you healed him, and you were punching that Omne when you set the ugly little bugger on fire. Maybe that's the key."

It was a fair suggestion. Miles bent down and placed his open palm on one of the sticks, thinking *fire, fire, fire,* but still nothing happened. Not one spark.

He hadn't even tried back in the tunnels. It had just come naturally.

"Well," said Mortimer, "I know you won't eat these zol raw. I'll get the fire burning." He picked up two of the branches and struck the thinner of the two against the other like a match. A small flame ignited, which he spread across the rest of the pile.

"How'd you do that?"

"Just an old trick my folks taught me. Works every time, most of the time." He skewered one of the limp zol on another stick and held it out over the fire. "This will probably take longer than I'd like."

Miles picked up the rock and chucked it into the distance to satiate the hyper maylan. Clint sped off, his four legs a dark blur as he kicked up a cloud of dust.

"Here you go," Mortimer said, handing over another speared zol. There were only two left, but Miles did not suspect he would maintain his appetite long enough to want seconds. He thanked Mortimer and began to roast the lifeless animal.

The maylan raced back, slobber-drenched rock in tow. "Good boy, Clint," Miles praised him. "I have to make my dinner now. We can play later." He scratched behind one of Clint's pointed ears.

Miles had never cooked his own food before. Being nine years old, his parents generally handled that task. It was strange, but kind of fun. When his father had told him about Cub Scouts, he had mentioned going on camping trips with the troop and how they would have to prepare their dinner over a fire like this. He said they would cook hotdogs and eat s'mores for dessert.

It was the first time since arriving in Rompu that things had finally settled down enough for Miles to realize how bad of a situation he was in. He'd never heard of this place before, and he wasn't sure if his parents had either. Even if they knew where Rompu and Ruhig were, what were the chances they'd think to look for him there?

He started to grow anxious again and had to calm himself down. Deep breaths. In. Out. At least there was a plan. As long as he and Mortimer stuck together, they would reach Queen Alys and she would be able to help him get home. He hadn't known him long, but he trusted Mortimer. The Rompun would keep him safe.

Embers danced in the silent air above the sizzling meat. Orange and yellow orbs of light floated upward gracefully before dissipating.

"So," began Mortimer, "tell me about Clint Eastwood."

"He's the best," Miles said. "His movies are the best. My favorite movie is *The Wild Bunch*, and he's not in that, but my favorite Clint Eastwood movie is *Unforgiven*."

"What's *Unforgiven* about?" Mortimer rotated his zol, cooking its underside. Miles mimicked his action.

"Clint Eastwood is this guy named Will Munny and he has to kill a bunch of people, pretty much."

"Sounds violent," Mortimer frowned.

"All westerns are," Miles said.

"Westerns?"

"A western is a movie in the wild west with lots of sand and stuff. Clint Eastwood is in a lot of them. You don't have any westerns either?"

A shake of the head was Mortimer's response. Then, "Western Rompu ain't got much sand. It's pretty hilly. A little swampy."

Miles continued, "They're my favorite kind of movie. My dad and I watch them together all the time. Mom doesn't like when I watch them."

"I don't blame her, from the sound of it."

"But I love them! Besides, that's really the only time Dad and I get to hang out. He's busy a lot." The tail end of his zol caught on fire, and he hastily huffed and puffed the flames out. He resumed cooking.

"What's the last one you two watched?" Mortimer asked after a few quiet moments. He turned his zol back over, as did Miles.

"The Wild Bunch," Miles answered.

"Ah. Your favorite."

"Mhmm. A lot of people die in that one too, though. And there's one part I don't like."

Mortimer looked up from the fire at the boy's face. "What part?"

Miles frowned at the thought of it. "There's a part at the very beginning where a bunch of kids put a scorpion in the middle of a bunch of fire ants," he told Mortimer. "And all the ants attack the scorpion and he can't do anything about it because there's so many ants and just one of him. The whole time the kids are just laughing at the scorpion. Then the kids set the ants and the scorpion on fire and they all die." Miles shrugged. "I don't get it," he said. "My dad said it was a metaphor or something but I don't know what that means. I don't understand why the scorpion had to be hurt."

"Other people are hurt in the movie, though, I'd wager," Mortimer said. "Why's the scorpion special?"

"Everyone else had a reason to hurt each other, even if it wasn't a very good reason," Miles explained. "But the kids had no reason to hurt the scorpion. They did it just because."

Mortimer nodded and said, "Sometimes people just...do bad things. And they don't have any reason to. Sometimes they don't even think about it. They just do it."

"But why?"

"Dunno, kid. Wish I could give you a better answer than that." He pulled his zol closer and pinched its skin between his fingers. "Yours should be pretty crispy by now," he told Miles. "Unless you want it to get crispier."

Miles took his food out of the fire as well and took an over-zealous bite into it. He hadn't realized before how hungry he actually was. The heat of the zol instantly burned his tongue and he let out a meager yelp. He desperately wished they had something to drink.

A deep laugh escaped Mortimer. He plunged the kebab into his gullet and bit down, sliding the stick between his teeth to let the zol drop onto his tongue. He began to gnash at it, swallowing after a couple hearty chews.

"If only we had some seasonings," he lamented, clearing his throat. "My wife is a master of seasonings." He stuck another zol on the end of his stick.

"Do you have any kids?" Miles asked, his tongue still stinging. He tried taking another bite, this time much slower and smaller. The meat was tough and dry, a lot of its flavor coming from the smoke but with a hint of sweetness, like green apple candy.

Mortimer appeared apprehensive, but his mouth curled into a half-smile. "A son," he replied. "His name's Kiko."

"How old is he?"

The Rompun looked to his right toward Miles, running his eyes up and down the boy's frail frame. "About your age," he said. "A year younger, though. But his birthday's in a couple days."

"And you won't be able to see him on his birthday?"

"Nope," Mortimer said after a long breath. "I'm *en d'oeuille*." He wagged his stick, slapping the dangling zol against charred wood.

"What's that mean?" Miles asked.

"Nothin'. Just means I'm sad." With his free hand, Mortimer reached into his pocket and took out the piece of paper he had obtained from the chest in Jericho and Vinzent's tent a few days prior. The page was fragile, all limp and wrinkled after being soaked in the spring they had jumped—or rather, fallen—into. He carefully unfolded the yellowing paper and handed it over to Miles.

On it was a crude drawing done in green, red, and blue crayon. It depicted three Rompuns, two big and one small, swimming in shallow water. One of the Rompuns had flowing red hair and a necklace with a blue pendant on its end. They all wore wide smiles on their faces like rickety crescent moons.

"Kiko drew me that," Mortimer explained, focusing again on roasting his meal. "We'd spent all day lounging in his favorite marsh and right when we got home, the little guy drew that. 'So you'll always remember,' he said."

Miles handed the picture back to Mortimer. "Why'd Vinzent take that from you?"

"Jericho just took everything I had on me and told Vinzent to lock 'em up. I guess even a crayon drawing is too risky for a prisoner to have," he joked. He cautiously folded up the paper and returned it to his pocket. He removed the second zol from the campfire and ate it whole, like before. The explosive burp that followed made Clint perk his ears up.

Miles no longer had anything to say. Clint's eyelids fluttered shut, being carried to sleep by the warmth of the fire. He noticed Mortimer staring into the flame, grinding the tip of his skewer in the dirt absentmindedly.

"Want my other zol?" he asked Mortimer. He then took another bite into the tiny animal he had not yet finished eating.

The Rompun was knocked out of his daze. "Huh? Oh, no. You should eat it. You need the protein and whatever other stuff." He stabbed the stick straight through the remaining zol and stuck it in the fire. "I'll cook it for you."

After a couple minutes, Mortimer said, "I know how much your parents must miss you. We gonna get you back home. I promise." His voice cracked.

Hearing Mortimer say it was a huge relief. "Thanks," Miles smiled.

Mortimer smiled back.

An hour later, the two got ready for bed. Clint was still fast asleep near the ashes, snoring loudly and absorbing the leftover heat.

Mortimer lay on his side, facing away from Miles, who was on top of Mortimer's coat and looking up at the stars. Half the moon was obscured in black, the other half letting off a faint luminosity that bathed them in a silvery green glow, giving them the appearance of spirits floating through the world.

Miles didn't enjoy being on top of Mortimer's filthy coat, but it was better than lying directly on the ground. He imagined himself lying on his couch back home, his head on a pillow in his father's lap and Ollie at their feet as they basked in the glow of the massive television screen. They watched as a rough-looking man muttered, *"What I like and what I need are two different things."*

Raindrops began to fall softly, washing Miles' dirty cheeks. He closed his eyes and felt the water hit his eyelids, his arms, his feet. He pictured the repulsive winged giant chasing them through the tunnels, its sharp tail whipping back and forth. His thoughts soon drifted to the dark clouds traveling lethargically above him, covering up the moon, hiding the stars.

CHAPTER FOUR

PEPPERS

The troupe embarked not long after the sun had risen, and Miles' feet were already aching. He badly wanted a pair of shoes and regretted leaving Mortimer's flip-flops behind in the Skyr camp. His skin was ill-equipped for traveling such long distances on rough terrain, unlike Mortimer's, which was thick and resilient.

They navigated away from the mountain range that covered over three-fourths of Ruhig and were now traveling through the grassy plains that made up the rest of the country. They had come to a stop at the bank of an immensely wide river. Miles was in awe of it.

Mortimer slouched his shoulders. "I...forgot about this," he muttered.

"About what?" asked Miles, watching the water rush by.

"The Third River. It's the widest river in the kingdom."

"How did you forget about the widest river in the kingdom?"

"Not sure."

The river looked more like a raging ocean. Vicious waves crashed against each other and Miles secretly wondered what types of hideous creatures might lurk in its depths.

"It's more that I forgot it'd be along our route," said Mortimer. "We have to cross it, though." There was some hesitation in his voice.

Miles shot him a harsh look. Clint's tongue lapped up the clear water that washed up onto the bank. "Are you sure?"

Mortimer looked to their left, far past Miles' short body. The boy looked with him. Miles followed his gaze back across the Third River, trying to analyze the twisted expression Mortimer was sporting. He had no idea what it meant.

"Yeah," Mortimer finally let out, nodding. "We definitely have to."

"Why?"

"Because we just need to, kid. Gotta get where we're goin' in time."

Miles nodded as well. It felt like the thing to do, despite his uneasiness. He trusted Mortimer. "Okay," he said. "How?"

"Not sure," Mortimer repeated. "There should be a canoe around here somewhere, tied to a dock..."

They began marching toward what Mortimer claimed was east, staying close to the riverside. Mortimer kept murmuring something under his breath while Miles pictured himself eating a Chicago-style hotdog back in Austin.

He could taste the mustard and sweet relish mixing together, a stark contrast against the pickle and tomatoes. He always threw away the peppers and hated how the poppy seeds stuck to his fingers after he was finished eating it.

"Why do you take your peppers off?" his father asked one chilly day. He bit into his own hotdog, walking by his son's side. They had just spent the afternoon visiting a local museum called the Thinkery that Miles loved and decided to drive downtown to get some food from one of his father's favorite food trucks.

Miles shrugged. "There's no reason to have them," he said simply.

"Why not?"

"Because they're too hot. They just make eating it harder. There's no point."

His father laughed. "Eat your hotdog," he grinned.

"When are we eating?" Miles asked Mortimer.

"I dunno," the Rompun replied from up ahead.

"*What* are we eating?" Miles hoped the modification would net him a more solid answer.

"Whatever we can find. Maybe we can catch a fish while crossing the river. It's pretty choppy though, so we might have to just wait until we've gotten to the other side."

"I'm hungry *now*, though."

"Me too. We'll eat as soon as we can," Mortimer said. He scratched the top of his head.

Miles thought about Kiko. He wondered what activities Mortimer and Kiko did together besides hanging out in marshes, which sounded disgusting to him. He wanted to know more about Kiko's mother.

"Is Jaselle your wife?" he asked.

"How do you know Jaselle?" Mortimer craned his thick neck back to look at the boy. Clint was leading the pack.

"You said her name in the tunnels," Miles said. "You couldn't remember which way she told you to go."

"Oh. Yeah, she is."

Miles smiled. "Where is she?"

"Back in Trafier," Mortimer replied. "That's where we live. In the capital, where Queen Alys is."

"So you wanna get back to Trafier pretty badly, huh? To see Jaselle and Kiko?" His stomach grumbled discontentedly. He was surprised to find he was actually at the point where he wanted another zol for lunch.

"Yep," Mortimer said, softer this time.

A ways in the distance, Miles could make out the wooden dock with a canoe tied to one of its posts. The mid-sized vessel was being violently knocked about in the water. It slammed against the dock, bits of wood chipping away. Both the canoe and dock looked battered.

"C'mon," Mortimer said, breaking into a jog. He passed up Clint, who interpreted this as a challenge to race. The maylan sprinted toward the dock, his tongue flapping in the arid wind.

Miles followed as fast as he could manage, but his short legs could not carry him at nearly the same pace. Mortimer was already pulling the boat toward the dock by the time Miles arrived breathless at his side. Clint had plopped himself down on the wooden planks, panting happily.

"Thank goodness there's a boat on this side," Mortimer said to himself. "Hop in," he told Miles, doing his best to steady the rocking canoe. Clint barked as Miles stepped near the dock's edge.

"It's okay, boy," Miles assured the animal. "Right?" he asked Mortimer.

"Right." He sounded impatient.

Miles inched toward the canoe and lifted one foot into the air, guiding it down gently into the boat. Thunder crashed overhead, startling him; his other foot slipped and he crashed face-first into the floor of the canoe. Mortimer asked if he was alright. His nose ached, to match his worn-out feet. Tears ran down his cheeks, but he didn't want Mortimer to see. "Yeah," he lied, sitting up.

Mortimer turned and picked up Clint, placing him in the boat next to Miles. The canoe shifted a bit with the added weight of the maylan Suddenly Mortimer's size and what it was about to mean for their voyage dawned on Miles.

"Are you sure we have to cross?" he asked one last time, hoping he and Clint could get back out and continue walking until they reached the end of the river and just walk around it, even if it meant walking on his mangled feet. He saw lightning strike, and thunder followed it moments later.

"Yes, we have to cross," Mortimer said hurriedly. "Don't have time to waste. Don't have the days, kid. This is the quickest way." He readied himself for boarding.

Miles wished the Rompun was not so extraordinarily rotund.

Mortimer stepped into the boat, which almost capsized instantly. He yelled out incomprehensibly then grabbed the paddle resting on the floorboard.

Clint whimpered, jerking his head around in every direction, trying to make sense of his current surroundings.

Mortimer reached up toward the slanted wooden post and untied the rope that tethered them to the dock. He bundled up the fraying rope and dropped it onto the floor by Miles' feet and shouted, *"Here we go!"*

No longer bound to its home, the boat was tossed into the air effortlessly. It slammed back down onto the water's surface with a ferocious whack that Miles could feel deep in his gut.

He gripped the side of the canoe with his right hand and wrapped his other arm around Clint, who was shivering uncontrollably. The maylan was frightened out of his mind.

Lightning struck closer.

Thunder boomed like an explosion.

Water sprayed against Miles like bullets, dampening his pajamas.

Mortimer tore into the water with the bulky oar, but it felt like they were moving more *down* the river than *across* it. Miles imagined the purple behemoth from the tunnel ripping its claw through the waves and snatching him out of the canoe, dragging him to the bottom of the Third River as he screamed and water filled his body. He held Clint closer.

The thin line of Miles' mouth dipped into a frown as the boat cut its uneven path across the river. Clint licked his hand and stared up at him with shimmering, hopeless eyes.

They somehow reached the middle of the river, where the waves intensified as if they had something to prove. Mortimer tried, in vain, to match the power of his rowing to the waves. He gritted his teeth, blinking away the droplets of rain that splattered against his face.

Miles attempted to focus on anything besides their situation. Anything to calm himself down.

He thought about the zol they had eaten last night, then went back even further to the Chicago hotdog.

He tried naming its ingredients in his head: poppy seed bun, peppers, wiener, relish, peppers, mustard, pickle, peppers, peppers, peppers—

"Hang on!" Mortimer yelled over the roaring waves. His voice was barely audible as the boat was cast into the air.

And then Miles was in the water.

He wasn't sure how it happened.

The green bulk of Mortimer had suddenly turned into darkness and his entire body felt frozen.

His arms were being thrashed by the current.

He closed his eyes.

He imagined the peppers.

Something tightened around his ankle.

He opened his mouth to scream and bubbles rushed out.

The canoe's rope was tangled around his leg.

All he could hear was the rushing of water beating against him and thunder rumbling.

More bubbles escaped.

There was a pounding in his chest.

In his head.

He started kicking his leg wildly.

The rope's fierce grip grew stronger.

He thrust his arms, propelling himself toward what he thought was up. What he hoped was up.

"—are you?" Mortimer's voice screamed as Miles' head broke through the water's surface.

"Mortimer!" Miles gasped. He was drifting a couple feet away from the canoe.

"Miles! Grab my—"

He was sucked back underwater, like a piece of lint into a vacuum cleaner.

He thought of his father telling him, "Be brave, Miles."

He pictured the monster's fanged mouth emerging from the murky darkness below and devouring him whole.

He created bubbles.

He assumed he was crying.

His feet felt refreshed.

He had to be brave.

Peppers.

He crashed through the surface of the river once more and tried shouting "Mortimer, help me," but all that made it out was "Mor—" before he was choking on icy water.

He was pulled under.

He tugged at the rope with more force than he ever thought he could exert.

He remembered his mother telling him, "You're a strong boy. I'm so proud of you."

His hands balled up into fists.

The thunder mocked him.

He could feel it in his chest.

The water bullied him.

It beat against him.

The rope felt sympathy and gave way after a final, desperate kick, and Miles fought his way upward.

"—ver here!"

"Mortimer!"

"Miles!"

Clint howled.

"Help!" He struggled to stay above water. Now that the rope was no longer attached to him, he was floating away from the canoe at an alarming rate.

He had to be strong.

He had to make his mother and father proud.

He had to see them again.

The thunder seemed to taunt him, telling him he wouldn't.

Mortimer's oar ripped into the river, trying to close the gap between the boat and the boy.

Miles swam against the relentless current, hoping that he was at the very least staying in place and not drifting farther away.

Mortimer hollered something else at him.

Miles' eyes and forearms bulged. His face was stained with tears or river water or both. He couldn't see Clint and his heart started to beat even faster at the prospect of Clint going overboard.

"Clint!" he managed to scream hoarsely.

He could hear a yip from the maylan amidst the madness. Clint poked his furry head up from behind Mortimer's round and frantic figure.

Lightning flashed and illuminated the sky in a dizzying white, and with that flash Mortimer was in the river.

Within a few powerful strokes, he was at Miles' side, cradling the boy in his arm, hugging him to his chest. Clint barked madly as Mortimer brought himself and Miles back to the boat. He tossed Miles in before hoisting himself up. The side dipped, filling the canoe with a shallow layer of cold water.

"Lay down," Mortimer ordered him. Miles did as he was told without the slightest hesitation despite the freezing water covering the bottom of their boat. He could hardly move his body anyway. Clint mirrored his actions, flattening his ears against his head and letting out a tinny whine.

He thought of his father's words: "Be brave, Miles."

He thought of his mother's: "You're a strong boy."

He thought of peppers.

He began to cough, his throat scratchy, as if he had swallowed steel wool. His eyelids were too heavy to keep open and he gave in to them.

The darkness accentuated every terrible noise that clashed around them.

More than anything, Miles wanted to open his weary eyes and find himself back in Austin, nestled up cozily in his bed with the comforter pulled all the way up to his chin. With Ollie at the foot of his bed, curled up into a fuzzy ball, sleeping soundly. With his parents in the next room, in case he needed them.

And right now, he needed them.

But what he had was Clint and Mortimer and a cold, shaky boat. He wouldn't have a Chicago hotdog to eat later on, either. He wouldn't have peppers to take off and toss aside. All he had was a zol or an ugly eel-thing or berries or any other weird thing they would happen upon.

He might never find his way back home, and that filled him with dread.

Mortimer's three-fingered hand shot into Miles' view and yanked the rope out of the angry river. A few anxious moments later, the meaty hands clutched Miles and threw him through the air. Miles landed on his back on a cracked wooden pier, shouting out in pain. After a couple seconds, Clint landed nearby, yelping in discomfort as well.

Miles sat up groggily and watched Mortimer climb up out of the canoe, which was now secured to one of the pier's poles. Beside it was another, larger canoe that it brushed up against.

Clint trotted away, sniffing at grass at the end of the dock. The sky was clearing up.

Mortimer dropped to his knees and draped his arms around Miles.

"I'm so sorry, kid," he sputtered. "I'm so, so sorry."

"It's okay," Miles told him. "It wasn't your fault." But after he said the words out loud, they felt false.

The two of them sat there for a moment, tightly clutching each other. Miles could feel phantom waves passing through his body. He felt uneasy. He felt tired. But at least he was no longer in that boat.

They separated and Mortimer inhaled deeply. Heavy tears fell from his yellow eyes. A smile flickered on his face. "Are you still hungry?" he asked.

Miles nodded.

A strained laugh. "Good," Mortimer sighed. "Me too. Let's find something to eat. Maybe Clint is onto something." He gently patted Miles on the back.

As the two of them ambled down the pier, Miles could not help but think about the peppers on the Chicago hotdog again. He hoped getting something in his belly would push the thoughts away, but he was unsure it would.

CHAPTER FIVE

EVERYTHING WILL ALWAYS BE OKAY

Mortimer had not spoken since they broke down their camp. The trio had been walking for three hours, and the silence was starting to dig into Miles.

The landscape was hilly, the grass faded tufts of soft blades. There were no trees and no wildlife in sight. Just the Screaming Crags visible in every direction, an immovable fence. With no trees anywhere, Miles had an itching thought.

"Where do zol live?" He was growing more and more comfortable asking Mortimer questions about Rompu.

"Hmm?" Mortimer mumbled. His mind seemed to be wandering.

"I said where do zol live?" he repeated. "They have wings like birds, but there aren't any trees for them to make nests in. But they're kinda like slugs anyway so I dunno how they would do that. So where do they live?"

"They burrow underground," said Mortimer. His gaze had not shifted.

"Like moles? Or snakes?"

Mortimer only grunted. Miles frowned, thinking back to the zol he had eaten a few days before. His stomach dropped when he imagined all the dirt that might have still been on the animal from having to dig itself out of the ground before Mortimer had caught it.

He looked ahead where Mortimer's eyes were transfixed and squinted, trying to see what the Rompun saw. All he could make out were more hills that seemed to waver like a reflection in water.

Clint's tongue dangled from his mouth. A dopey grin decorated his long face. He trotted alongside Miles, glancing over at the boy every couple of minutes. Miles reached down and rubbed his hand along the ridges on Clint's back.

"What are these for?" he asked as his hand reached the last smooth bump.

Mortimer shrugged.

Miles had no idea why Mortimer didn't want to talk to him. The Rompun had been unusually quiet ever since the incident at the Third River, and even more so the past twenty-four hours. Miles was growing more at ease around Mortimer, but it seemed that for the Rompun, the opposite was true.

"Are you mad at me?"

"What?"

Clint yipped. Miles ran his hand along the maylan's back again. "You're not talking," he said. "That usually means a person's mad."

Mortimer did not look at him when he responded. "It don't always mean that, kid. I'm not mad at you."

They kept walking. Clint's tail slithered through the air. The fluffy ball of hair at its end tickled Miles' knee. He wondered if Clint's tail had ever brushed against Kricket like that.

"I'm not mad at you. I'm sorry," Miles' mother said to him the day his grandmother, her mother, had passed away. "It's just hard. It's really hard. I didn't mean to yell."

Tears were flowing down her face like murky waterfalls. They fell onto Miles' comforter, creating dark splotches on Pikachu and Charmander. They made his eyes well up and his splotches mixed with hers and they sat on his bed weeping together. Ollie curled up on the floor, staring up at the two of them with confused but sympathetic eyes.

"Why now?" his mother asked nobody, pulling her son to her chest. Miles desperately wanted her to stop crying, wanted the sadness to go away and never come back. She had been crying so often lately. He wanted to say something, but he couldn't find any words. There were no words.

He wanted his grandmother to appear in the doorway and say, "Look, you guys, I was joking! I'm fine! Everything will always be okay!"

But she didn't appear, and she wasn't fine, and nothing was okay.

Ollie let out a hushed whine. Miles' tears came harder and faster.

Rain crashed down on Miles, Mortimer, and Clint, but Mortimer's pace had not quickened. Miles shivered, his filthy pajama shirt sticking to his body.

"Mortimer, how far away is Windheit? I'm tired of walking. I really want shoes."

"I'm tired too," Mortimer replied. "Gotta make a stop somewhere before we go to Windheit, though. And we gotta get there today."

"Where do we have to go?" He was glad Mortimer was opening up a little more now.

"The Lake of Remembrance." Mortimer sounded exasperated. "We almost there."

Clint's ears were drooping. His tail was no longer wagging and his fur was soaked with rain.

"What's the Lake of Remembrance?"

Mortimer bit his lower lip before speaking. "It's, uh…it's where you go to remember loved ones," he said. "To honor them, I guess."

"Loved ones that are dead?"

Mortimer nodded.

Silence filled the awkward space between them as they continued walking.

"My grandma died," Miles said.

Mortimer finally twisted his head around to look at the boy. His bulbous yellow eyes appeared as if they were carrying a huge burden. His face glistened. "I'm sorry."

Miles didn't say anything. Mortimer faced forward. The only sound shared by the group for a long while was that of raindrops pelting the ground and their skin.

"Is the lake pretty?" Miles eventually asked.

It took Mortimer a few moments to find an answer. "In its own way, yeah," he said. "Calling it a lake is more of a metaphor, I guess. Like the scorpion and the kids in that movie."

Miles had to admit he was relieved the lake wasn't actually a lake and that they wouldn't have to deal with any more bodies of water after their recent incident. A metaphorical lake sounded weird, but at least he wouldn't drown in it.

The outfit Miles' mother had picked out for him for the funeral was drab and fit uncomfortably. He wore a dark blue button-up shirt tucked into tight black pants, which made him squirm in the pew. He hated dressing up, and the circumstance for doing so did nothing to ease his mind.

The family dropped off Ollie at a friend's house to be watched for a couple days and made the one-hour drive to Killeen for the service. It was a somber car ride, devoid of conversation. His father played a country music station on the radio.

His mother opted out of giving a eulogy. Instead, those duties fell to her brother and father. Afterwards, as people milled about the church lobby, Miles sipped from a plastic cup of water and stood in the corner watching everyone.

Everybody was dressed in dark, boring colors, which Miles thought made the whole affair seem even dourer than it already was. He wished people would wear happy, brighter colors at funerals so that everything would be less sad.

His uncle approached him and placed a hand on his shoulder. "How you doin', bud?" he asked absently. Before Miles could even answer, he asked, "D'you know where your mom is?"

Miles pointed at the door leading outside.

"Thanks." His uncle gave his shoulder a squeeze before leaving.

Miles finished his water and entered the sanctuary where the service had been held. He stared at the other side of the room where there was a large photo of his grandmother propped up on an easel. She looked happy being surrounded by beautiful wreaths and bouquets. He started toward the picture.

After almost another half hour of walking, the trio finally reached an enormous crater that stretched for hundreds of feet. Clint stayed behind as Miles and Mortimer stepped carefully to its edge.

Inside the hole were hundreds of thousands of trinkets piled on top of each other that varied in color, size, and shape.

There were golden lockets hanging off of thin chains, popped open to reveal photographs of aged Rompuns and Skyr. There were old wind-up music boxes with ballerinas and horses on them, like the kind Miles' grandmother always showed him when he would visit her. He saw muted dead flowers on top of vibrant blooming flowers on top of cracked vinyl records. There were sullied shoes and bent bottle caps and torn t-shirts. There were damp quilts and silver watches with immobile hands and moleskin journals with their ripped pages flapping in the wind.

The entire lake was filled with these items, with these memories, and the relentless rain attacked them with no empathy.

If he'd had the opportunity, Miles would have thrown a mug into the lake for his grandmother. She always loved drinking tea.

Both Miles and Mortimer were shaking in the cold, and Miles momentarily wished he was wearing the Rompun's jacket. Mortimer dug his hand into one of his coat pockets and extracted Kiko's drawing.

He unfolded it, and Miles watched the messily-drawn Rompuns being assaulted by dark, angry splotches.

Mortimer held the page up to his face, his eyes closed. His face contorted as he tightened his grip. He whispered something that Miles couldn't hear over the loudening patter of rain, then kissed the paper and let it go.

The two of them watched it float away in an unbearable silence.

Pellets of water crashed into it on its way down into the Lake of Remembrance to join the rest of the keepsakes.

As it came to rest, surrounded by all the other memories of the lost, Miles' body felt like it was about to collapse. He looked at Mortimer's round face, scrunched up and weary. It seemed like Mortimer was about to collapse too.

Miles wanted to scream and jump down into the hole and retrieve the drawing to return it to Mortimer. If he could just get it out, maybe Kiko would appear and tell his father, "I'm okay now!"

And he could throw more things out, like wallets and stuffed animals and blankets and rings and photos and perfume bottles and Mortimer and Kiko could assist him, and eventually they would be surrounded by everyone anybody had ever lost and sadness would finally be forced to leave everyone alone for good.

But he knew it wouldn't work, and so he wanted to scream until his lungs leapt out of him. He wanted to tell Mortimer that everything would be okay but he didn't know how to tell somebody that because he wasn't sure if it was true.

And he thought about being on his bed back at home with his mother crying and telling him she was sorry and how he wanted her to stop, just stop, and he wished he could tell her that Grandma was okay and he was okay and she was going to be okay but if she wasn't sure of that then how could he be? There were no words that would reassure his mother of those things and so he screamed.

The scream startled Mortimer, who nearly slipped and tumbled into the lake himself. "You okay, kid?" His voice was weak and it trembled.

Miles sat down on the ground, pulling his knees up to his chest. He felt like a baby for screaming. He also felt incredibly guilty for inadvertently making the moment about him, making

Mortimer feel concerned about him when really it was Mortimer who should have been allowed to scream. Miles didn't even know Kiko.

He shook his head and let the tears fall as he clenched clumps of grass in his fists.

Mortimer knelt down beside him and placed a hand on Miles. "Hush, now. Don't cry. We don't need to both be crying, do we? That's too many tears for one day."

Miles' breathing slowly started to settle and the rain began to ease up. He could not stop looking at the drawing that now rested on top of the pile of items.

He imagined Kiko, just a smaller version of Mortimer, with his green crayon in hand, placing its tip on a blank sheet of paper and moving it in a circle to create what would eventually form his father.

"I'm sorry," Miles told Mortimer. He loosened his grip on the earth. "I'm sorry about Kiko."

Mortimer said nothing but tried putting on a feeble smile.

"I wish I could've met him," Miles blurted out. He looked away from Mortimer.

"Me too."

Clint cautiously approached the two and licked Miles' face. He smiled, scratching the maylan behind his ears.

Mortimer stood and Miles did the same. They both stared into the lake and Miles heard Mortimer mutter, "Happy birthday."

Miles realized that was the reason why Mortimer had been so determined to cross the Third River rather than taking the long way around. He wanted to arrive in time for his son's birthday. It nearly crushed Miles all over again. He looked up

into the sky, and though it was still sprinkling, the sun was beginning to peek out from behind the clouds.

"Happy birthday," he said too.

CHAPTER SIX

HEAVY THINGS

For the week following his grandmother's funeral, Miles refused to speak to anybody. Every night before bed, his mother would try to get him to open up, but he wouldn't budge.

One night as she was tucking him in, he finally asked her, "Why did Grandma die?"

His mother looked away, down at Ollie, who was curled up by his feet at the end of the bed. "She got sick."

"I know. She said it was because of germs."

His mother sighed and directed her gaze toward him again. "Well, Miles, Grandma was really old. She actually got the flu, and her body couldn't handle it very well."

"The flu?"

"It's kind of like a cold, but worse," his mother explained. "Her body was too weak to fight it. Remember I told you the other night she was coming to town to see better doctors? It was too much even for them to help."

Miles began to shift anxiously under the covers. "You just get colds from germs, though, right?" he asked. "Just germs that are everywhere? They can kill you?"

He had already not been a fan of germs ever since his mother had explained why it was good to wash his hands before eating, so he always tried to avoid them as much as possible. This was alarming.

His mother leaned forward and held him close. "Miles, don't worry. You're fine. Grandma was old—you're young and healthy. Your body can fight anything off. You're strong. You don't have anything to worry about, bug."

"Yes I do. If Grandma can get sick from that, so can I."

Ollie lifted his head up to see what the fuss was about. He stood and walked gingerly over to Miles, licking up and down the boy's face.

Miles pushed the dog away and wiped away the slobber. "Stop, Ollie!"

His mother pulled Ollie away and said, "Miles, *you're okay*. Calm down. You're alright." His lip was trembling. "Just go to sleep, bug. Everything will be better tomorrow."

A few hours after commencing the day's walk, Miles could make out some sort of wooden outpost in the distance, at the base of a mountain. "That's where we headed," Mortimer told him, pointing at the structure.

"To the mountains?"

"Well, to be more specific, up *into* the mountains, where Windheit is," Mortimer said, moving at a quickened pace. Clint trotted alongside him as Miles attempted to catch up.

"So we finally made it to Windheit? And the Ruhigans are gonna help us get back to the queen in Rompu?"

Clint looked back at him. His tongue hung out goofily.

"I need to speak to King Al-dir about some important things, but yeah, I'm assuming he can get us back to Trafier as well.

That's what I've kinda been banking on. They've got big, flying animals called Carriers that can transport us across the country pretty quick."

Miles thought back to the winged creature that had chased them through the claustrophobic tunnels almost a week before. He imagined its jagged teeth tearing through his skin, ripping apart his organs. He heard his mother tell him, *"You're alright."*

The wooden outpost was deceptively far away. They walked for almost another hour before reaching it. It consisted of two thick, looming poles with wires attached to the tops that ran off into the misty distance, high into the mountains. Attached to the wires was a gondola that sat atop a large, sturdy platform between the two towers.

It was manned by two creatures that had full bodies like men, but the heads of falcons. Their bodies were covered in elegant white feathers, adorned with blue web-like designs. Their arms were long, slender wings with clawed hands. Beady eyes sat perched on either side of sharp, golden beaks. They had to be Ruhigans.

"Bonjour, gentlemen! *Comment les affaires?"* Mortimer greeted the two of them, waving enthusiastically. It was a stark contrast to how he had been acting since their visit to the Lake of Remembrance.

"State your name, please," one of the bird-men ordered. His voice was gruffer than Miles had expected.

"Couple of travelers from Rompu, here. Name's Mortimer Mouton."

"What is that?" the other Ruhigan asked, gesturing toward Miles. "Looks like an oversized forn wearing raggedy pajamas."

"He ain't a forn," Mortimer retorted. "He's…what'd you say you were, again?" he asked Miles.

"A human."

"He's a human child. He's with me."

"What in the hell is a human?" the Ruhigan asked.

"Look, I don't know. But he ain't no bloodthirsty monster, is he? He ain't no soul-suckin' demon with pointy horns and scaly wings. He's fine."

"Calm down, you made your point. State your business in Windheit," the first Ruhigan demanded, unamused. He appeared to be the one in charge.

Mortimer was displeased. "Security was never this tight before. What's going on? What happened?"

The second Ruhigan's feathers ruffled up. "The Skyr have been a lot more mobile recently, trying to make their way into the kingdom. Extra security is a must. If you aren't willing to cooperate, you can leave."

"Well that's fine, though I think it's pretty obvious I'm no Skyr," Mortimer said, grasping his considerable gut. "I'm here to speak with King Al-dir about the Veratt's whereabouts and the Omne-Skyr relations. I'm the aide to Queen Alys of Rompu. I'd also appreciate some safe travel back to Trafier, if it's in the cards."

"The Veratt's whereabouts?" The Ruhigan's voice got higher in pitch. "You've seen it recently?"

"A couple days ago. I really need to see King Al-dir," Mortimer said.

Both of the Ruhigans' demeanor changed noticeably with this admission. "Right away, Sir Mouton," the second one said. "Please, follow me."

Miles chuckled at the Ruhigan calling Mortimer "sir." The Rompun cast a knowing glance back at him and grinned.

They followed the Ruhigan around the side of the left-hand tower, where there was an iron door that he promptly unlocked before ushering them inside. Mortimer stepped in first and Clint rushed to his side. The maylan had really taken to him. Miles was next, and the Ruhigan came in last, shutting the door behind them all.

"What's your name, chief?" Mortimer asked. He leaned his large body against the wall and crossed his meaty arms. Clint sat down by Miles.

There was a small keypad on the wall by the door that only had two buttons: an up arrow and a down arrow. "Byrn Valamir," the Ruhigan replied, pressing a sharp claw against the up arrow.

"Oh-ho!" Mortimer chortled. "You an Amir boy, are you? You must be related to Marron Khrys-amir."

"Marron is my uncle, yes."

Suddenly the room lurched upward, and Miles realized they were standing in an elevator. It was more spacious than any of the elevators he had ridden at his father's office.

"Marron's a good man," said Mortimer. "Heck of a shoemaker. He special-made my sandals for me. Lost 'em back in the Violet Woods, unfortunately." Miles' face burned a bright red. "Got captured by some Skyr on my way up here. Nasty sort they are, these days. Didn't used to be."

Byrn faced the trio. "Where did they pick you up?"

"They set up a new outpost near the coast, on the edge of the Claire River. Do you know when that happened?"

"I believe they established it a month or so ago," said Byrn. "How did you escape?" The elevator rattled as they slowly climbed higher.

"Bit of good luck, really. Some lightning struck a tree and started a fire. We managed to get out in the middle of the chaos."

"What did the Skyr want with *you*?" Byrn's question was pointed at Miles. The boy shrugged as the elevator came to a halt and they left it at that.

Byrn pushed the door open. Angry sunlight bled into the elevator. The group exited onto the platform that connected the two wooden towers. Mortimer placed his hand on Miles' shoulder and gripped tightly. "Don't look down," he said softly. Louder, he said, "Clint, stay close." The maylan whimpered and huddled by Mortimer's leg.

Byrn undid the latch on the gondola and swung its door open. He took a step back to allow everyone else to enter first. When they were all situated inside, Mortimer let go of Miles.

The Ruhigan pulled a lever and the gondola began to crawl toward the clouds.

"So," he started, "you said you encountered the Veratt? Where was it?"

Mortimer let out a tired sigh before answering. "I assume you know the underground passage below the border?"

"You're not serious."

"Yep. No idea what it was doing down there, but there it was." He huffed.

Byrn ruffled his feathers. "I can't believe it was so close to Ruhig. I thought King Al-dir was monitoring its movements; I don't know why we wouldn't have been informed." He smoothed himself out, but in his eyes he looked concerned.

"Might've just slipped by him," Mortimer suggested. "Hard to track something underground when you folks are so high in the sky," he laughed. Byrn cracked a smile, which Miles could just barely register by the small shift of the bird's feathers around his beak.

Miles finally decided to ask the question he had been avoiding ever since they stumbled into the beast. "What is the Veratt?"

Mortimer eyed the boy. "The Veratt's that purple monster we saw back in the tunnels." To Byrn, he said, "Don't worry, chief. The tunnels collapsed on the ugly brute."

This news seemed to grant Byrn some relief.

Miles asked, "Where did it come from? Why did it attack us?" Clouds and blue sky inched by the window as the gondola crept along.

A strained expression swept across Mortimer's face as he searched for a response. "It's a complicated situation," he said.

"The king of Rompu summoned it," Byrn answered. "The madman set it free, and it's been ravaging Rompu ever since with seemingly no motivation except for the fact that it's a moronic beast that can cause some damage. And now it's starting to toy with Ruhig, too."

The answer caused more confusion than clarity for Miles. "Why would the king want the Veratt around?"

"Who the hell knows?" Byrn snapped, letting out an uncontrollable cluck.

"Is that why Rompu's king and queen are fighting?" Miles asked.

Mortimer nodded and Byrn tapped his foot on the floor irritably. Clint stared at the Ruhigan's rapidly-moving foot with widely-rounded eyes and intense concentration.

"King Mykael accidentally"—Byrn scoffed at Mortimer's word choice—"set the Veratt loose. He was trying to control it, but it didn't really work out. No idea where he found it, but it didn't take no time at all before it started tearin' up Rompu. The town of Creeyan was completely wiped out. No survivors." He looked out the window. "Some of the plains in the north were pretty much destroyed. But the king still wouldn't send the monster back to wherever he brought it from."

This piqued Miles' curiosity. "What do you mean? It's not from Rompu?"

"Course not," Mortimer replied. "Came from another world."

"Just like me," Miles whispered, low enough so that Byrn didn't hear.

"Anyway," Mortimer went on, "Queen Alys couldn't take it anymore. Called it treason. Had him exiled. He's been livin' in hiding ever since."

They rode in silence for a long while. Miles peered out of the gondola's window. He wasn't the only thing here to have come from another world. Surely Queen Alys would know how to send him back, if her husband had experience with other worlds. He felt relieved, lighter than he had before. He smiled at the various shapes the clouds made.

"Look at that one," his mother said one day while they sat on a bench in Zilker Park. She sipped from her vanilla chai latte, drumming her index and middle fingers on the green Starbucks logo garnishing the cup. Steam rose from it in the cool fall air.

He looked up and squinted, trying to find the cloud his mother had pointed at.

"The one that looks like an elephant," she said.

Finally he spotted the one she meant. "It looks like a hippo to me," he told her.

"A hippo? Then why does he have such a long nose?"

"That's his tail."

She laughed and took another drink.

"How many Carriers do you guys have in the stable right now?" Mortimer asked Byrn.

"Plenty. Probably a dozen or so. You said you need transportation back to Trafier?"

"Indeed. I haven't had any contact with our queen in weeks. She's probably worried sick about me. Not to mention my wife, too," he chuckled. "Look," he then said, nudging Miles. He pointed out the gondola's rear window.

They were steadily approaching a magnificent castle that rested on a sizeable plateau near the mountain's peak. It had numerous spires that stretched high up into the sky, disappearing in the clouds that surrounded it. At the base of the castle was a small community with a collection of homes, a marketplace, and an area carved out in the side of a mountain with a beautiful fountain that shot water up out of the mouth of two winged fish.

"There's Windheit," Mortimer said. Clint stood up on his hind legs but was still too short to see out the window. Miles had to stand on his tip-toes.

"Do they sell shoes there?" Miles asked. "I would really like some shoes."

"Of course! Byrn's uncle can surely hook us up with something, right Byrn?"

The Ruhigan shook his head. His beak gleamed in the sunlight that trickled through the dusty windows. "Marron passed away recently," he said.

This struck Mortimer. "Oh, no. Sorry to hear that," he said. He cleared his throat. "Your uncle...he wasn't part of the Seventh Unit, was he?"

Byrn only nodded.

Mortimer sighed. "Jeez. I've lost family to this thing too. I'm sorry, chief."

"No need to apologize," Byrn said, shaking his head. "I just want that purple abomination dead."

Miles lay sprawled out on the king-sized bed, clenching the soft, red comforter in his small hands. He felt like he was going to sink into the mattress and vanish from the world, wrapped in the gentle embrace of the silk shirt and pants Cordelia had dropped off for him to wear while their clothes were being washed. Clint was curled up on a pillow, sound asleep.

Cordelia Val-vyn was the name of the Ruhigan that had escorted him and Mortimer to the suite, which housed two of the enormous beds. "Wait here, get settled in," Cordelia had said. "I'll come get you shortly." Her feathers were flourished with pretty pink dots.

Mortimer stepped out of the bathroom, steam creeping out of the doorway and filling the room. A fuzzy blue towel was wrapped around his waist, with another smaller one covering his bald head. "Ahh," he moaned, a wide grin stretching out across his green face. "That was like a dream. I don't remember the last time I got to shower."

"Gross," Miles giggled.

The Rompun plopped himself down on his own bed, wiping the tiny towel on his shiny scalp. "You ought to take one yourself, kid. Gotta get nice and tidy for the king, don't you?"

"I guess so," Miles agreed, hopping up off the mattress.

But he skipped over to the window instead, savoring the feeling of plush carpet between his toes. The curtains were thick and velvety, with gold and blue embroidery on its edges depicting beautiful clouds and stars.

Miles opened them up to look outside. He observed Ruhigans soaring past, landing on balconies of storefronts and perching on toothed edges of mountains, drinking cups of tea and conversing with each other.

The buildings of Windheit all jutted out from the sides of mountains. They were built from white-painted brick with sturdy red shingles that looked weather-worn, like they had not been replaced in several years. Miles was reminded of the buildings in photos of Germany his uncle had shown him.

"This is where I stayed with my friend Benni," his uncle told him, pointing at a picture of a dingy apartment complex with a modest vegetable garden growing outside. "Every morning, after we had a cup of coffee, we'd walk to the grocery store and buy some fresh bread with cold meat and cheese for breakfast."

Most of the buildings in Windheit were small, one-story places with patios for Ruhigans to land on and rectangular windows with brown frames.

Others, however, were as tall as any skyscraper Miles had seen in Austin. He wondered how long it took the Ruhigans to build such an extravagant city so high in the clouds. It was even more impressive knowing that all of Ruhig's cities were constructed this way.

"This place is amazing," Miles whispered.

"Isn't it?" Mortimer called out behind him. "I love Trafier and all, don't get me wrong, but Windheit puts it to shame for sure. I wanted to come here for my honeymoon, but Jaselle laid that idea to rest pretty fast. *'Windheit is so busy and you go there for work all the time!'"* he said in a high-pitched voice, wiggling his fingers about mockingly. *"'I wanna go to stay at a nice bed and breakfast in Vidliés!'"* He started to laugh at his own obviously exaggerated impression.

Sitting back down on his bed, Miles asked, "Mortimer, what's the Seventh Unit?"

"The Seventh Unit?" Mortimer mumbled, holding up the complimentary pair of pants to his waist. "These are not gonna fit me. No sir."

"Byrn said that his uncle Marron was in it."

Mortimer carried the pants to the bathroom and shut the door. He yelled out to Miles, "A few months ago, that big monster—the Veratt—attacked a Ruhigan city called Crenn. Big, nasty, awful attack. The king—*jeez, these pants are tight*—King Al-dir gathered as many troops as he could muster to kill the stupid beast, but as you can gather, they weren't very successful."

He stepped out of the bathroom, his legs choked by the ridiculous purple pants he had been given.

"If my shirt is this small too," he said, "Al-dir is gonna get an earful. These things are choking the life outta me."

"What happened to the Seventh Unit?" Miles asked, ignoring the Rompun's wardrobe issues, despite how comical he looked. Though he couldn't suppress his chuckles.

Mortimer struggled to bend his knees to simply sit back down on the bed. "Well," he exhaled, "the king's troops—six units in all—were getting their behinds kicked by the Veratt, and Al-dir had no choice but to recruit a bunch of citizens to form a makeshift seventh unit to help fight. That's how a shoemaker like Marron wound up battling the Veratt. Not exactly a fair fight."

Miles frowned at the story, petting Clint. The maylan twitched in his sleep.

"Obviously, the Seventh Unit didn't fare too well against the Veratt. Considering the real army did miserably against it, no one expected them to, but Al-dir didn't really have a choice. Shortly after, though, the thing just up and flew away. No reason it attacked, no reason it left. It's just out for blood. No purpose."

Miles was having trouble wrapping his mind around the entire situation.

"I still don't get it," he said, his voice shaky. "I don't understand why the king of Rompu summoned the Veratt in the first place. What was he trying to do?"

Mortimer shrugged. "I don't really know, kid. The only person who could tell you that is King Mykael himself, I'd wager." He picked up his purple shirt and held it to his body, groaning. "You shouldn't worry about such heavy things, though," he then said. "You just worry about getting that shower."

Navigation in Windheit was not easy for non-Ruhigans.

The city had implemented a public transportation system for non-winged visitors, but it was fairly rudimentary and lacking. It consisted of trolley cars attached by cables to various platforms etched out of the mountains that rode back and forth on a set schedule.

Riding the trolleys was helpful, but it still left people with a lot of walking to do since they did not connect all of Windheit, just the major areas: the castle, the marketplace, and a relatively small neighborhood. Otherwise, for shorter distances between platforms and buildings, there were wooden bridges with thin railings or steep trails going up and down the mountainside.

Once he had finished showering, Miles followed Mortimer to the trolley platform in the castle courtyard and took the next one over to the marketplace. They were in search of Marron Khrys-amir's old shoe shop to see if someone else had taken over.

From the marketplace platform, they had to travel across three bridges that seemed far too precarious for Miles' liking before finally reaching the square that held Marron's old store as well as a candy shop, an antiques store, and a café.

Mortimer bought a cup of coffee before they entered the shoe shop, which was indeed still up and running. The owner was an older Ruhigan with faded blue feathers and striking red markings. "Welcome," he greeted them. "How may I help you gentlemen today?" The Ruhigan eyed Miles curiously but said nothing, which he appreciated.

"Just looking for some footwear," Mortimer smiled. "I'm thinking sandals for the both of us. Something sturdy but light, something good to travel in."

"I believe I can certainly help you out with that," the shop-keeper said. "The name's Kyren Khrys-bala, if you need it."

"Mortimer," the Rompun said.

"Miles," said the boy, now feeling it was expected of him.

It took the Ruhigan only a couple minutes to find a nice pair of sandals that fit Miles. They were made of a thin, solid wood and slid onto his feet comfortably, with soft padding for his soles to sink into. What ate up a majority of their time was searching for a pair that would fit Mortimer's enormous feet, which were considerably larger than a Ruhigan's. Miles could see now why Marron had to specially craft Mortimer's old pair.

Mortimer paid Kyren for his services and asked how he had come to own the shoe shop.

"The previous owner was my brother-in-law," the Ruhigan explained. "Unfortunately he is no longer with us."

"That's what I heard. Marron was a friend," said Mortimer. The two shared a few jovial stories about the late Ruhigan before saying their goodbyes.

Outside, Miles and Mortimer went to the edge of the square and leaned against the metal railing that stopped tourists from tumbling over the side. More accurately, Mortimer leaned against the railing while Miles stood a foot or so away from it. Just seeing someone else so close to the edge made him uneasy.

Across the sizeable gap was another area carved out with several other stores, but Miles could not make out what any of their signs read. Many Ruhigans milled about from store to store, but Miles didn't see any Rompuns or Skyr.

"They not traveling much these days," Mortimer said after the boy asked why that was. "Too dangerous out on the roads now, with the war going on."

"Are the king's Skyr killing a lot of people?"

"Not when they can help it. They actually avoid it, most times. But a Rompun can receive a good beating if they run into one of their groups; even worse beatings for the few Skyr who didn't follow the king during the split. Then they rob 'em. It's mostly that and setting up camps around Rompu, trying to establish dominance or something. Ain't gonna work, though. Try as he might, Mykael is still an outcast and way outnumbered."

Miles dropped the subject. It was too depressing for him to think about. They window-shopped at a few stores while Mortimer finished his coffee.

"The king should be ready for us soon," Mortimer said as he tossed his cup in a recycling bin. They began to head back toward the castle.

"Nothing interest you today?" a shopkeeper called to them from her doorway, disappointment evident in her voice.

"Oh, plenty," Mortimer told her, "but I just blew all our money on these enormous shoes."

The king's quarters were not quite what Miles had been anticipating. He had prepared himself to walk into a massive chamber, with light pouring in through wall-sized windows behind the king, who would be decked out in long, shimmering robes and sitting in an iron throne, stroking his beard—if Ruhigans could grow beards—as they approached and bowed.

Instead, Cordelia directed them to a spacious office filled with bookshelves that overflowed with books. The floors were glossy wooden planks, and there was an oaken desk where King Al-dir sat as they entered. Behind him was a windowed doorway that led to a stone balcony.

He was scribbling something on a piece of parchment as Cordelia said, "Your Majesty, your guests have arrived."

"Thank you, Cordelia," Al-dir smiled as Mortimer and Miles stepped inside. He rose from his chair and approached the two while Cordelia showed herself out. His talons click-clacked on the wooden panels as he extended his hand toward Mortimer.

"How are you, Mortimer?" he asked, shaking the Rompun's hand.

"Been better, truthfully," Mortimer answered. "But I guess I can't complain. I'm alive, ain't I? Though maybe not for long with these clothes on. You need to get a size XL."

"Those are XXL, my friend. And who is this?" Al-dir asked, shifting his attention to Miles.

The king did not in fact have a beard, but his feathers were a mesmerizing lavender that Miles had not seen on any other Ruhigan so far. His beak was a vibrant scarlet with a black tip.

He knelt down to look Miles in the eye and stuck out his hand for the boy to shake. "I'm King Al-dir," he greeted him warmly.

"I'm Miles." They shook, and Al-dir stood to return to his chair.

"I don't mean to sound rude, Miles, so please don't take offense, but what are you?" Al-dir asked, rounding his desk.

"I'm a human," Miles replied. He was growing weary of explaining this to people. If he could accept bird-people and scorpion-people and everything else he'd seen, why did everyone have so much trouble with such a normal-looking kid?

"I'm afraid I've never heard of a human," Al-dir said.

"He gets that a lot," Mortimer grinned.

Al-dir stretched out his wings, motioning toward the piles of books flanking them. "In all of these textbooks and novels I've read, I have never once read about a human. Peculiar, isn't it?" He welcomed them to take a seat, gesturing toward the two cushioned chairs positioned before his desk.

"Thanks, Majesty," Mortimer said, shuffling into the chair on the left. Miles sat in the other, looking past Al-dir at the clouds floating by outside. He had never before been so high up. It was fascinating.

Al-dir wasted no time. "I hear you've got some news about the Veratt," he said.

"Yep," Mortimer nodded. "But first, I've got some troubling news about the Skyr."

The king sighed and urged him on.

"Well, first of all, they captured me on my way here, which was unpleasant in most, if not all, ways. That explains my tardiness. Sorry. Second of all, they somehow found out about the underground route between Rompu and Ruhig."

"Damn," Al-dir cursed.

"Mhmm. We were passing through and a couple of Omnes were scouting the tunnels, probably mapping it. Not sure how long they've been there, or how often they report to the Skyr, but they were there. We knocked 'em out while we were in there, and then the Veratt collapsed part of the tunnels, so I'm not sure but they might be dead. Regardless, the tunnel is pretty much unusable now."

"That's where you ran into the Veratt? In the tunnels? What in the world was it doing down there?"

"Beats me," said Mortimer. "It can fly, so I dunno what it was doing underground. Maybe it was trying to get some dirt to eat. Does it eat dirt? I dunno."

Al-dir let out another sigh. "Come with me," he said, standing. He slid open the door behind him and stepped out onto the balcony. Mortimer and Miles followed, the cool breeze sweeping over them.

Miles ventured as close to the railing as he dared and peered over its edge. The balcony overlooked a small, grassy plateau on the mountainside that included a pond with numerous colorful fish lazily swimming in it.

"The pond's not natural," Al-dir said, standing next to him. "Have you ever heard of the Claire River, Miles the Human?"

The only time he had was earlier in the day when Mortimer briefly mentioned it in conversation with Byrn, but it was easier to just shake his head no.

"I didn't figure you had. The Claire River is a river in southern Rompu, spreading across the land from the Jesieu Marshes all the way to the Gulf of Lasir, which is a pretty impressive length." The king tapped his claws on the stone railing, smiling. "What's interesting about the river, though, is that it's artificial. One of the old kings of Rompu, one of the few romantic Skyr, decided to dig it out as a show of affection for his wife. When it was completed, he named it after her."

"Forever setting an impossible standard for the rest of the kingdom's husbands to live up to," Mortimer grumbled.

Al-dir laughed, then continued. "So that pond is kind of like my Claire River. I had it made in memory of my wife, who passed away many years ago. It's in the perfect place, don't you think? Right near my office. It always calms me down when I'm stressed."

Miles nodded. "That was sweet of you," he said.

"I think she would've liked it," Al-dir said fondly. "I tried to get species of fish that were her favorite colors. It was tricky finding ones that could live at this altitude. And then, after that, it was hard to find ones that wouldn't kill each other," he laughed again.

"What was your wife's name?" Miles asked, still looking down at the fishes. There had to be a dozen of them, varying in color from blue to yellow to orange to pink.

"Maggie," said Al-dir.

Miles looked to the king. "Did she have purple feathers like you?"

"No, she had *beautiful* silver feathers. The first time I ever met her, I couldn't believe how gorgeous she was. Have you ever met someone like that? Someone who just floored you the first time you saw them?"

Miles shook his head and the king chuckled.

"I didn't assume so. You will one day, Miles the Human. And I assure you, it is a fantastic and peculiar feeling." To Mortimer, Al-dir asked, "I take it you'll need to get back to Trafier?"

"As soon as possible."

"Of course. I'm sure Jaselle is quite worried about you."

"I'd imagine so. This trip was supposed to be a quick one, just checking in on everything with you then going back home. The Skyr really screwed that up."

"Right. Well, I can arrange some Carriers and escorts to take you two back to Trafier in the morning. The sun will be setting soon and, as you know, their eyesight is not the best."

"That sounds fine to me. We got a maylan with us too, is that a problem? Do the Carriers get along with them?"

"It should be okay, as long as the maylan refrains from provoking them."

"He won't," Miles chimed in. "Clint's a good boy."

Al-dir asked, "How did a maylan end up in the company of you two anyway?"

"That's another strange story," Mortimer began. He told the king about how they had discovered Clint in the tunnels with an injured paw, which was healed simply by Miles' touch. "Never seen anything like it."

"Neither have I." King Al-dir gave Miles a puzzled look. "My, my, Miles the Human," he said, clicking his beak a couple times. "You're an interesting little fellow, aren't you?"

Lying in bed that night, Miles was having trouble falling asleep. He stared up at the ceiling fan, watching its blades slice the air with ferocity. Clint was at the foot of the bed, asleep on his back with his paws in the air.

"Mortimer?"

"Yeah, kid?" came the quiet reply from across the room.

Miles ran his fingers through his hair, still keeping his eyes locked on the fan as it spun and spun. "The Veratt came from somewhere else, just like me," he said. He let that hang in the air for a moment, not sure where he was going with this train of thought. "Maybe that's why I can make fire and heal things."

"Maybe," said Mortimer.

Miles blinked in the dark. "Do you think my powers might be a bad thing, then?"

He could hear Mortimer shifting his position in his bed. He could tell the Rompun was struggling to conjure up an answer.

"I'm not sure," he finally replied. "That's another one of those heavy things you shouldn't try to worry too much about right now. We'll get all that sorted out later, when we're back in Trafier."

"Okay."

"Just try to get some rest."

"Okay."

"Goodnight, Miles."

"Goodnight."

The blades spun and they spun and they spun.

CHAPTER SEVEN

A LITTLE WINDY

Equipped with a brand new pair of sandals and a full stomach after a bowl of fresh fruit, the group was ready to depart from Windheit before noon. They had changed back into their newly-washed old clothes and were brought from their suite to a stable located on the west end of the castle's courtyard where the Carriers were housed.

There were six of them: hulking beasts roughly the same size as a truck. Each was covered in shaggy, turquoise fur with tusks of varying length protruding from the sides of their heads in front of floppy ears. They had long, reptilian tails that whipped at flies buzzing around their thick bodies. Large wings, at least six feet long each, were folded at their sides.

In front of the Carriers were Ruhigans dressed in golden armor, awaiting their arrival.

"Hey there, Felix," Mortimer waved to the Ruhigan stationed in front of the Carrier that boasted the longest and most impressive tusks. It whinnied gruffly behind him.

Felix returned the greeting before inquiring, "Who's this with you?"

"This is Miles, and this is Clint," Mortimer introduced the two of them. The maylan barked excitedly at the boy's side. "How the skies looking this morning?"

"Seem to be clear," Felix responded, still eyeing Miles quizzically. "Might be a little windy, but that shouldn't be an issue."

Mortimer grinned and asked, "Remember the turbulence that one time?"

"How could I forget? It took a solid hour of bathing Callisto in those marshes to get your puke out of his fur," Felix laughed wholeheartedly. Callisto grunted behind him.

"Sorry, Callisto," Mortimer apologized. "I get seasick easily. Or airsick, I guess. Whatever you wanna call it, I get it." He neared the Carrier and rubbed his nose. A gentle purr began to emit from the animal.

"Guess you're riding with me, then," one of the other Ruhigans said to Miles. His Carrier was somewhat smaller than Callisto, with shorter but more curved horns.

"What's your Carrier's name?" Miles asked.

The Ruhigan smiled. "Her name's Io. She's Callisto's sister, actually," he said, stroking Io's back. "She's got a bit of a tummy ache this morning, but she'll be fine for the flight. It's not gonna be too strenuous. My name is Sahen Cal-rhys. What's your maylan's name?"

"Clint."

"That's an interesting name."

"He's named after Clint Eastwood."

"I have no idea who that is."

Mortimer planted his hands firmly at his hips. "Four escorts this time?" he boomed, observing the troupe that would be accompanying them on their journey. "Seems a bit excessive, don't you think?"

"King's orders," Felix shrugged. "You three must be valuable cargo."

Mortimer smirked and said, "You already knew that, Felix, my boy!"

After the Ruhigans loaded a few more supplies onto the backs of their Carriers, which hung in huge sacks strapped to their backs, they were ready to take off. Io yawned and stretched out her wings, purring contentedly.

"Ready, kid?" Mortimer asked Miles. "I sent a letter with a messenger last night explaining everything. I bet they real excited to meet you over there."

Miles couldn't help but grin. "I'm ready," he said.

Mortimer and Felix hoisted themselves up onto their Carrier's back, as did the other Ruhigans. Sahen reached his hand down and offered to help Miles up.

The boy grabbed Clint around the waist, barely able to lift him. He took Sahen's hand with his free one and the Ruhigan pulled him onto Io's with relative ease.

"Okay, keep Clint between your legs and hold on tight," Sahen instructed. "Then grab a great big wad of Io's fur in both of your hands and *don't let go*, alright? Don't worry, you won't hurt her. She's a tough gal, aren't you?" He gave the animal a couple strong pats on the neck. Miles did as he was told.

"We'll be in Trafier before you know it, munching on a hefty bowl of gumbo!" Mortimer shouted from behind them.

"Ready?" Sahen asked.

"I don't know."

"Well, we're going," Sahen said, digging his claws into the Carrier's back. *"Up-up!"*

Io's wings expanded to their full length and began flapping furiously, sending them soaring off into the skies. Miles held on tighter to the animal's fur and Clint began barking madly, the wind whipping his wet tongue. Clouds surrounded them, a calming and ethereal whiteness in every direction. Io let loose an excited howl that Clint reciprocated with glee.

Miles was going to be sick. His eyes began to tear up with the cool air lashing against his face so powerfully. He yelled, *"Can we slow down a little?"* but Sahen evidently couldn't hear him over the rush of wind.

As they ascended, Io's nose began to dip, and they soon arced into a sharp descent.

"Hang on!" Miles could barely hear Sahen shout as Io accelerated.

Suddenly the Carrier broke through a layer of clouds and harsh green filled Miles' vision as he cautiously peeked over Io's side. They were diving straight toward the ground for several agonizing moments before Io tilted upward, evening herself out. Miles breathed a relieved sigh.

"Wasn't that fun?" Sahen asked giddily.

The group cruised at that altitude for over an hour, heading southwest in the direction of the Jesieu Marshes, where the Rompu capital of Trafier was located. While they rode, Sahen explained that Carriers were capable of much speedier flight, but they slowed them down to accommodate guests that were not accustomed to traveling with the animals.

Miles wondered how Trafier would differ from Windheit. He hoped he would be able to sleep in as big a bed as he did in the suite Al-dir had arranged for them. Clint rested his head on Io's fluffy back and shut his eyes as Miles scratched behind his ears.

Miles loved lying in bed and scratching behind Ollie's ears. One of Ollie's back legs would always start to twitch and then kick in the air and Miles could never stop himself from giggling at the sight.

Eventually, the sound from his parents in the other room got too loud and angry and Miles had to think up distractions to calm himself down. This was happening more and more often lately, so Miles had decided to teach Ollie every single trick he could think up.

"Okay, here's what you need to do for this one: when I say 'shake,' put your paw in my hand, like this," he instructed the dog, lifting his paw and dropping it into his own hand to demonstrate. *"Shake,"* he said slowly, grasping Ollie's paw and moving it up and down.

He let go and Ollie stared straight ahead at him, unflinching.

He could hear his mother yelling something about "the past three months" and his father shouting desperately that he "didn't mean it" and then his mother responded with bad words.

"Shake," Miles said, raising his voice to drown out his parents. Their words were like a rumbling in his head. The dog didn't move. "Ollie, it's easy," he grumbled, snatching the dog's paw and yanking it in aggravation.

Ollie let out a sharp yelp and retracted his arm, scooting away from Miles.

A few seconds later, his bedroom door was pushed open and the shadow of his father crept along the carpet. "What happened?" his stern voice asked, seeming to fill the entire room with its force. Sounding tired and frustrated, he asked, "Is everything alright?"

"Something's wrong," Sahen muttered to himself. "Why are you shivering, Io?"

Sahen craned his neck around and looked behind them. Miles saw the Ruhigan's dark eyes widen before he quickly turned back around, letting out a hurried *"Go, Io!"* His right arm shot into the air and he formed a symbol with his fingers that was lost on Miles.

Miles couldn't bring himself to shift his position even the slightest bit to check out what Sahen had seen. "What is it?" he asked apprehensively.

"Just hold on extra tight, alright?" Sahen said. He sounded worried, and that made Miles' stomach do gymnastics.

Suddenly Callisto, with Felix and Mortimer on his back, darted past them, and Sahen screamed his command a second time.

In an instant, the blue of the sky gave way to a harsh purple from above, and Miles realized what the problem was.

The Veratt had tracked them down.

Clint sat up and began to bark wildly at the beast that was cutting through the air in front of them, gaining on their companions. Miles clamped the maylan's mouth shut but hastily let go again, figuring he should probably dedicate both hands to clenching Io's fur. His mind raced, trying to think up how the creature had been able to not only survive but free itself from the tunnel's collapse. He thought of its claws ripping through him. His breaths began quickening.

Ahead, the Veratt let out a high-pitched shriek that Miles had never heard it unleash before. It swung one of its muscular arms, which appeared to be covered in fresh wounds, and sunk its sharp claws into the torso of one escort's Carrier. With its other hand, it snatched the rider off his mount and threw him downward, knocking loose some of the supplies strapped to the Carrier's back in the process.

The Ruhigan reacted swiftly and began flapping his wings fervently, rocketing himself back toward the monster.

But the Veratt held his Carrier on both ends and pulled, ripping the poor creature in two. It began to devour the front half of the Carrier and casually discarded the other half, which tumbled limply toward the earth. Sahen whispered something Miles couldn't hear while the other Ruhigan screamed in rage and flew toward the Veratt, which was still snacking on his fallen comrade.

He landed on the beast's back, digging his talons into its shoulder blade. The Veratt roared in what sounded more like annoyance than pain and dropped the other half of the Carrier. The Ruhigan screamed hoarse curses at the Veratt before it proceeded to deal with him the same way it had his Carrier.

Miles screamed and had to shield his eyes behind Sahen, who let out a pained yell. He tugged on Io's fur and shouted, *"Hold on, Miles!"*

Io dipped down with great speed, slowing once she was even with the Veratt, matching its pace. Thunder rolled high above them, the clouds transforming into a muted gray, and Sahen swore under his breath. "Where is this storm coming from?" he wondered aloud.

The Veratt flapped its wings to push itself upward and the gust of wind crashed forcefully into Io. Miles squeezed Clint tighter between his legs, his grip on Io's fur tightening, as the Carrier was shoved farther down. The other four Carriers began to descend as well, but Miles was not sure what their plan was to escape the Veratt. The two escorts still behind them were keeping their distance, while Io and the third escort zig-zagged through the sky.

Their maneuvers were not enough to avoid the Veratt, though. Having finished with its meal, it wrapped its cut-up hand around the escort and his Carrier. Without hesitation, it ripped off the Carrier's wings, pulled back, and hurled the bleeding body at Callisto.

The two Carriers collided, sending Mortimer smashing into Felix's back, who then tumbled forward over Callisto's head, holding on to one of his horns. He let go and hovered beneath him, but the Veratt swooped underneath and came to Callisto's front, sending the Carrier slamming into its chest. It let out what sounded like a cackle that blended in with the thunder, pinching Callisto's left wing in between two of its fingers and tearing it off with ease.

Callisto immediately lost his balance and plummeted, smashing straight into Felix, and Mortimer flailed through the air along with Callisto, now one wing short and unable to fly.

Miles could not muster a sound as he watched the green blur that was Mortimer plunge toward the hilly green landscape below.

When he finally could, it was nothing more than a ragged scream. He could feel his throat tearing. The limp green shape that had been Mortimer couldn't even be seen anymore through the mist and clouds.

As they fell, the Veratt seized the other wingless Carrier mid-air and drifted higher while it consumed the screaming creature.

Rain fell lightly as Io gained speed, putting a great amount of space between them and the Veratt that was still floating in the air, playing with its food. One of the remaining escorts managed to get away and joined at Io's side, but the other was not so fortunate.

Miles' body trembled, his eyes clasped tightly shut, listening to the horrible beast's wings slice through the air, roaring as it gnashed its yellowed teeth on the bodies of their friends.

With the Veratt distracted, Io and the other Carrier managed to make their way to the Jesieu Marshes with great haste. Sahen had not been lying about their speed. They flew close to the wet treetops that shaded marsh's murky waters, toward a dark blue spire that peeked out from the foliage.

The Carriers gently pushed through the thick leaves as they grew closer to the spire, meekly touching down on a large patch of damp grass surrounded by shadowy waters that were alight with glowing pink orbs beneath their surface. Up ahead were several Rompuns awaiting their arrival.

The first Rompun to reach them, a muscular man, asked, "Where are the others? Your messenger said six were coming."

A female Rompun with flowing auburn hair approached them. Out of breath, she gasped, "Where's Mortimer?" She had a silver chain around her neck, which held a blue gem. Miles could not place why, but she looked familiar to him.

Sahen slid off Callisto's back then helped Miles and Clint. The exhausted Carrier plopped herself down and shut her eyes, exhaling heavily. She let out a booming, mournful howl. The other Carrier did the same.

"It was the Veratt," Sahen said hesitantly.

The woman put a hand to her mouth, backing away. "Oh, no," she whispered. "No, no…"

Then Miles remembered the picture Mortimer had thrown into the Lake of Remembrance, the one Kiko had drawn. She was Jaselle.

The rain began to come down harder, but they were protected by the thick layer of leaves and branches above them.

Miles listened to the muffled sound of raindrops hitting against leaves mix with the sorrowful howls of the Carriers.

CHAPTER EIGHT

A LIE

Miles didn't remember being ushered into the palace as the storm began to pick up. All he could remember were the incandescent pink lights in the dark waters on either side of the trail as he marched toward the looming doors. Little rosy blobs drifted underneath the water's surface.

He thought he had heard Jaselle say, "He's staying with me," but he wasn't sure if it was she who had said it or if he was just thinking of his mother.

She led him through decadent hallways decorated with rich purples and blues that all blended together. His vision was fuzzy. His body was numb.

The image of Mortimer tumbling through the sky flashed in his mind as Jaselle navigated him through twists and turns to a cypress wood door three times his height. Above what Miles presumed to be a mailbox—a wooden cylinder protruding from the wall, draped in slick vines—was a placard that read Mouton.

Jaselle unlocked the door and stepped aside to allow him entry. She smiled weakly at him, trying her best to look inviting in spite of what had transpired. He hesitantly stepped forward into the living room.

The only modicum of light in the room came through the windows with their curtains half-drawn. Gray clouds were ornamented by streaks of lightning as rain poured.

Jaselle flicked on a light switch that dimly lit up the room as Clint snuck past them and hopped onto the couch, which was made of plush, dark blue velvet. He circled around a few times before laying down, staring over at the two figures who still stood in the doorway. The maylan shivered.

"Makes himself at home, doesn't he?" Jaselle chuckled meekly. Her voice was strained.

Miles only nodded and took a seat next to the maylan. He began to scratch behind Clint's ears, but it didn't stop them both from shaking.

The living room was roughly the same size as Miles' back in Austin, though it had bookshelves along the wall by the sofa instead of a television. Multicolored spines of novels and textbooks lined the shelves. On the bottom shelf was a short stack of picture books. The one on top was titled "The Boy, the Zol, and the Cherry Pie." All three subjects adorned its cover, painted simply but beautifully with pastel colors.

Crisscrossed vines covered the entire ceiling and snaked midway down the purple, gold-trimmed walls. A kitchen was directly connected to the room, and that was where Jaselle headed first, opening a wooden cabinet and removing a teapot with unsteady hands.

"Would you like some tea?" she asked Miles.

"Okay," he replied, tapping his feet on the red shag rug that took up most of the floor space.

He was not quite sure what to say to this woman, whose husband he had grown so close to over the past week and probably witnessed dying in order to protect him. He felt like "sorry" would not be sufficient, and so he said nothing.

"You can take your shoes off if you want," Jaselle offered from the kitchen. Her voice was muffled by the sound of running water filling the pot.

Miles slid the sandals off his tired feet, which he then pressed into the fluffy rug. He wanted to sleep for a month. He leaned over and rested his head on Clint's stomach. A few tears ran down his cheeks, but he wiped them away so that Jaselle wouldn't see.

A few long minutes passed and she came to him with a steaming ceramic bowl, green with yellow smiley faces painted on. She handed him the bowl and he cautiously took it. The water inside was colored by thick orange leaves that floated on its surface.

"What kind of tea is this?" asked Miles, wanting to fill the silence between them with something, no matter how insubstantial.

"Endalain," Jaselle answered. "I hope that's alright. I didn't even think to ask. We don't have any other kind right now."

"It's okay," Miles said, even though he'd never heard of it. He brought the bowl to his lips and blew before taking an apprehensive sip. The taste was very citrusy and sweet, with only a hint of bitterness to it. He was glad he wouldn't have to awkwardly ask for sugar. Drinking tea reminded Miles of his grandmother.

He noticed Jaselle was not looking at him in the same manner most people in Rompu and Ruhig had. Her eyes were not asking *"What are you?"* Whether it was because he had been described to her in Mortimer's letter or because she simply didn't care, Miles appreciated it all the same.

They each took another sip of tea. The prickly surface of the leaves tickled Miles' lip as he drank. Clint was already asleep by his side; the trip had taken a huge toll on the animal. On both of them. On everyone.

Jaselle set her bowl down on the table, still half full, and said, "I'm going to get in bed now, I think."

"Okay," Miles said again, suddenly exceedingly conscious of how often he was saying the word. The rest of his vocabulary must have fallen off the side of the Carrier.

Jaselle stood and left the room, leaving Miles and Clint alone on the couch. He licked tea from his lips.

It wasn't long before he retired for the night as well, trying to settle in on the sofa. It felt weird being in Rompu without Mortimer. It wasn't natural. He spent a long time crying before he finally drifted off to sleep.

Time inched by in Trafier. Miles spent most of his days wandering the grounds of the palace with Clint as his companion. At first he felt uneasy about walking around a swamp, but Jaselle promised him it was safe.

He would wake up early every morning to the clatter of Jaselle making breakfast shortly after the sun rose. She had told him he could sleep in Kiko's old room, but he'd been unable to bring himself to sleep in the child's bed. It didn't feel right, occupying the same space as Mortimer's son. It made him feel like an imposter. He opted for the couch instead.

Jaselle would greet him each morning with a groggy hello and the question of whether he would like some food and tea.

He always said yes, and she always had a plate prepared for him within minutes.

It seemed the only thing Rompuns ate for breakfast, as far as Miles could tell, was scrambled eggs with chopped green bell peppers and a spicy blue sauce mixed in. He didn't like the sauce at first, but he was growing accustomed to it as he ate more meals there. Rompuns doused most of their food in it.

After breakfast, Jaselle would depart to work with the queen, leaving behind a spare key in case Miles decided to go exploring.

He never strayed too far from the palace doors; there was a small enclosure a short distance down a trail that he usually visited and occupied all day. It had two iron benches and a fountain with a statue of a chubby fish built in the middle of a pond that was filled with the glowing pink blobs he had seen in the water before.

Each day, he sat and thought about Mortimer and cried. He always tried to stop himself, but couldn't help it. Clint would sit at his feet and whine, wanting to help but unable. At first he would try to conjure pleasant memories, like their campfire conversation about westerns or walking around Windheit, but invariably it turned to the image of Mortimer falling through the open air.

On her lunch break one day, Jaselle stopped by and explained to Miles that the pink blobs were actually called forn. They were tiny, gelatinous animals that lived exclusively in the Jesieu Marshes. Rompuns often ate forn as snacks, which was a fact Miles had learned when Jaselle snatched one straight out of the murky pond and casually tossed it in her mouth.

"Wanna try one?" she asked his mortified face. He politely declined.

The pond was surrounded by smooth, crystalline stones with a blue sheen. Miles would often take one of the rocks and throw it as far as he could, grinning halfheartedly as Clint chased after it. The maylan would trot back to the pond, rock in mouth, and drop it into the pond rather than return it to Miles. They both enjoyed the *plop!* of it hitting the water. Clint also enjoyed splashing about in the shallow ponds to cool himself off in the humid weather.

At sundown, the duo would return to Jaselle's apartment inside the palace and wait for her to finish cooking dinner. Miles took pleasure in sitting at the kitchen table and watching her cook. She reminded him of his mother, humming songs he never recognized as she sprinkled spices and oil on slabs of meat.

In the center of the kitchen was a small pit dug out in the floor and filled with ash. Jaselle would build a fire there each night while preparing the food. Four metal bars encircled the pit, coming together above it like a teepee. Where the bars met was a sturdy hook that she used to hang whatever it was she needed—a pot of water, a cauldron for stews, or an iron rack designed to suspend meat and vegetables. There were also two smaller fire pits dug into the marble kitchen counter, covered by similar iron racks akin to a stovetop, which is where she would place the teapot to make their endalain tea and eggs each morning.

Afterwards, Miles would help Jaselle wash the dishes. Then he would spend an hour or two looking through the books on her shelf. He had started with "The Boy, the Zol, and the Cherry Pie," which he had not found very compelling at all.

"What kind of books do you like?" Jaselle asked him one night as he scanned the spines. "Do you like stories? Or books that teach you things?"

"Stories."

"We have lots of those," she smiled. She skimmed a few titles then pulled one out. It was a skinny red book. Stitched in purple yarn on its cover was the title "The New King: A Novella by Bernard Cranteg."

"Does this look good?" she asked.

"What's it about?"

"The very first Skyr king in Rompu. It's pretty interesting. Almost all kids in Rompu read this one. Some of the events are a little melodramatic to make it more interesting, but it's mostly true." She handed the book to him.

"Thanks," he said, flipping through its pages. They were discolored, with worn edges.

He read the short book over the course of that night and the next, settling in on the couch with a blanket wrapped snugly around him after he and Jaselle finished cleaning up. Clint was curled around his feet, falling asleep almost instantly. His furry belly warmed Miles.

It told the story of Nuntara, a Rompun princess that lived many, many years before. Back then, not many Skyr had emigrated from their home kingdom to Rompu, and many who did ended up living in the Violet Woods to the east or near the Juene Gulf in the northwest, primarily working as fishermen or farmers.

On a chilly late autumn day, Princess Nuntara accompanied her mother and father to the eastern port town of Merrikar. The town rested on the edge of the Violet Woods, on the coast of the Gulf of Lasir. She had always read the leaves on the trees were a breathtaking purple hue, and she desperately ached to see them for herself.

The journey took several days. When the royal Rompun family finally arrived in Merrikar, Nuntara was dismayed to discover her father had no plans to show her the Violet Woods.

"We are here for business," he told her, his expression stern and unmoving. "I do not have time for a listless errand such as that."

"Fine," Nuntara conceded. "I will just go by myself, then."

"My foot!" her father exclaimed. The trip from Merrikar to the woods was not particularly long or arduous, but he still knew it was unwise to let the princess wander off on her own in an unfamiliar area.

"Co faire?" Nuntara begged.

Her father grew exasperated. "Because, my dear," he began, "you are a princess. You cannot go gallivanting around the forest on your own. You will get hurt. You may encounter ruffians. I will simply not allow it, and that is final. Do not make a big bahbin about it. Stay in town; your mother and I will not be long."

With that, he departed for the docks with his queen and assistants in tow.

Miles read about Nuntara growing anxious in Merrikar and eventually deciding to disobey her father's wishes and seek out the trees she so longed to see. After his own experience in the Violet Woods, he had to admit the leaves were quite dazzling.

Once there, Nuntara met a young Skyr who was picking apples to carry to his father's fruit stand in town.

> *The Skyr hopped down from the branch he had been sitting on and brushed his hands off on his shirt, which stuck to his body with sweat. He held it out for her to shake.*
> *"My name is Kieran," he said.*
> *"I am Nuntara."*
> *"Nuntara? What a simply gorgeous name."*
> *She could not stop herself from blushing.*

The book went on like this for several pages, detailing the two love interests chatting with each other. Miles found it to be dreadfully boring. He didn't care about a fruit stand or Nuntara's issues with her father. He wanted to get to a fight scene, but he began to suspect "The New King" would not have any.

When the novella turned into a straightforward romance, Miles grew to dislike it even more. He had no idea how every child in Rompu was able to stomach such a mind-numbing tale. Princess Nuntara and Kieran continued to see each other every day while she was in Merrikar. They were sad when she had to leave, and he kissed her right before she departed, which did not please her father one bit. The Skyr followed her back to Trafier and confessed his love for her. She reciprocated. They married. When Nuntara's father passed away, since she had no brothers, Nuntara became queen and Kieran became the first ever Skyr king of Rompu.

"I didn't like it," Miles told Jaselle as he placed the book back in its place on the shelf.

"Really? Why not? It's an important aspect of Rompu's history. It was the moment our kingdom and the Skyr's came together as one. They flocked here in droves after that."

"It's just a bunch of people talking and falling in love and stuff," said Miles. "It's boring. I like stories with fights and stuff."

"Oh, yeah?" Jaselle giggled. "Like what? What sort of *action-packed* adventures are you into?"

"*Unforgiven* and *The Wild Bunch*," Miles replied before remembering the Rompuns had no idea what those movies were. "They're so exciting! All Nuntara and Kieran did was talk about apples and oceans."

"I guess real life just isn't all that crazy for everyone," Jaselle said.

"Maybe," Miles shrugged, returning to the couch and sitting by her side. His own life was exciting enough for the time being while he was stuck in Rompu, still completely unaware of how he could possibly get back home. That recurring thought made his stomach feel unsettled.

Jaselle grew quiet. She was staring down at her hands, cracking her knuckles. Looking anxious. Her red hair hung past her shoulders, twisted in loose braids. She never had much conversation in her before growing quiet.

"Can I ask you something?" she then asked. The question was apprehensive, as was Miles' nod. She continued, "What exactly happened to Mortimer? With the Veratt, I mean."

Miles tore his gaze from her and fixed it on the floor, scrunching his face in thought. He couldn't look her in the eye. Mortimer's scream as he fell through the air crashed through Miles' skull and he had to make an effort to push it out. He lay down on the sofa, pulling a blanket up to his chin. The softness of the couch's fabric put him at ease, but only slightly.

She looked frustrated. She opened her mouth to say something, but stopped. Then, "It's okay if you don't want to talk about it right now," she said, though her disappointment was evident in both her face and wavering voice. "But…I know it's hard to understand, but I need you to tell me. Eventually. I have to know, and you are the only person who can tell me."

Miles nodded. Clint lifted his head up to see what all the fuss was about.

"I'll see you in the morning." She said it so softly, Miles thought he could even hear the tears forming in her eyes.

As she walked to her bedroom, he didn't think she heard him wishing her a good night.

The next day, Miles decided to take a new book with him to the fountain. After much deliberation, he decided on "The Skyward War," which sounded like the thrilling adventure he had found himself craving.

Unfortunately, he was left extremely disappointed when it turned out that "The Skyward War" was actually a textbook, written by who Miles believed had to be the dullest Skyr to ever live. His name was Nyles Veenan, and his photograph on the book's back flap showed him dressed in a wrinkled suit and a skinny tie. While he was indeed the most boring, he was at least also the fanciest Skyr that Miles had seen yet. Regardless, it was still an even more tedious read than "The New King" had been, which the boy had not believed possible.

A Prelude to War

With Rompu's increased taxation on sugar, coal, and other everyday exports, many Ruhigans took to developing new methods of obtaining such products.

The most obvious solution proposed was simply to fly across the Rompu-Ruhig border, steal the goods, and fly away. The Rompuns would have no way of catching the thieves in time.

This plan had one small issue: the Ruhigans would either have to fly in enormous troupes or take many trips in order to steal any worthwhile amount of goods from the Rompuns. They would need to devise a way to transport larger quantities in the same amount of time and with the same amount of speed.

A Ruhigan by the name of Ferris Khrys-dahn, a fisherman from Crenn, came up with the idea to tame the wild flying beasts that lived in the Screaming Crags in order to make them accompany Ruhigans over the border.

Miles set the hardcover down on the bench, having already decided not to press on. If there were any perks at all to being away from home, it was that he didn't have to attend school here.

For dinner, Jaselle cooked small creatures called vandats that she had caught herself around the marshes. Vandats had long, shelled bodies like shrimp but didn't have eyes. The tips of two thin, lengthy feelers on their foreheads helped them navigate underwater. Miles made sure to watch that the vandats were peeled and cleaned thoroughly before being thrown into the pot with the rest of the vegetables and broth.

"Do you like gumbo?" Jaselle asked, stirring the contents of the pot. She moved to one of the kitchen cabinets and fished out a container of mahogany-colored seasoning. She gently tapped some into the mixture. She had grown more distant since their short conversation on the couch.

"Yes," Miles responded. "My mom used to make it a lot. I don't like it too spicy, though."

"I won't put much myre, then," she said, referring to the spicy blue sauce. Clint lapped up water from a bowl nearby. Jaselle asked, "What's your mom like?"

The boy shrugged. It was hard to describe her. "She's really pretty," he said. "And she's nice, too. Sometimes she gets mad at me for dumb things, but I think it's just because she's upset about other stuff. My grandma died."

"I'm sorry," Jaselle frowned.

"It's okay," Miles said, even though it wasn't true. He immediately felt awkward bringing up death, with the shadow of Mortimer looming between them. He sat at the kitchen table, watching Jaselle intermittently stir the pot. Steam rose and fogged the lightbulb that hung motionless from the ceiling. "She was my mom's mom, though, so she was really sad. She and my dad are fighting a lot now because she's in such a bad mood."

Jaselle remained silent. She poured just a splash of myre sauce into the gumbo, mixing it in with the thickening broth.

"I miss her," Miles then said. And after a moment, "I miss Dad too. And Ollie. And my house." He looked to Clint, who looked back at him. Jaselle didn't say anything.

Miles drummed his fingertips on the tabletop, his long nails clicking against the finished wood. He could hear his mother and father engaged in another shouting match, their voices harsh but hushed, trying to mask their frustration from their son. His fingers began to move faster.

"Let's stop talking about such unpleasant things and eat some dinner, yeah?" Jaselle offered, grabbing them a bowl each. "How much do you want?" Clint made his way over to the pot of gumbo in the middle of the kitchen and sniffed at it.

"Just half a bowl, I guess," Miles replied. His stomach was already in knots after thinking about his parents and Mortimer. "I'm not too hungry."

Every time Clint snapped up a forn from one of the ponds near the fountain, he would spend a solid minute afterward staring ahead and licking his lips with his tail lowered and eyes widened. Miles always got a kick out of it. It was a much-needed relief from his heavy thoughts, however brief.

He had told Jaselle about the mishap with the textbook the previous day, and she recommended him a different book called "Candlelight," which was a collection of poetry written by her grandmother about growing up in the Jesieu Marshes. Miles had never been interested in poetry when he was forced to read it in school, but he figured he should give it a chance since someone in Jaselle's family had written it.

Thoughts in Claire River

*He and I often walked
many miles through the marshes*

to the one isolated spot where
the Claire River could be accessed,
and we could swim.

At the edge of the dirty swamp,
the full moon smothered us
in its ghostly glow as we broke
the water's surface. "What do you think
old King Waryn would say
if he was alive to see us here?"

Watching him float languidly on his back
in that unnatural river
ushered in half-thoughts of my father.

I tried to picture him.
Is he fat?
Does he have any hair?
What is his favorite food?
Does he blink quickly when he lies?
Does his jaw click when he speaks?
Is he unhappy?

I wondered if he had ever given my mother a gift
(besides me)
when he was around. A golden necklace,
or a floral dress with light blues and pinks,
or even just a nice dinner at a restaurant.

I wondered why he had not felt the impulse
to dig out a river for her.

Miles read a couple more poems, but each one made him frown. This was just another book about love, except all the poems had sad endings instead of happy ones. He closed the book and ran the pads of his fingers along its cover. It was made of blue felt, with the title "Candlelight: A Collection of Poems by Vahna Abshire" centered near the top. In the middle of the cover was a minimalist drawing of a candle, with its wax nearly completely melted.

The poems reminded Miles of sitting in his bedroom in Austin. He would scratch Ollie's neck, which would cause the metal tags on his collar to jangle.

"I can't even look at you," he could hear his mother seethe, angrily slamming cabinet doors as she stowed away clean dishes.

"Let me just talk," his father would attempt to interject, but she never allowed him.

"I don't know *what* the hell you were thinking. I don't even *want* to know," she yelled, her voice cracking.

Miles stopped petting Ollie, and the dog turned to face him with a confused look. His father tried to say something again, but was almost instantly cut off by his mother's shouts. Something inside Miles snapped, and he leapt from his bed.

He raced over to his shelf and started yanking books off the top and middle shelves, throwing them across the room. Some smashed into the walls, a few crashed into the blinds on his window, and others bounced onto the bed. Ollie jumped out of the way and retreated into the hallway.

Miles then grabbed the few CD cases he had scattered across the bottom shelf and tossed those as well, some popping open upon impact with the wall, their jewel cases fracturing. He ran back to his bed and tore the comforter away, flinging books and stray CDs across the room again, letting the comforter fall into a crumpled heap on the carpet. He proceeded to rip the sheets off, dragging them across the room. His pillows were jettisoned into the air and knocked away by the rotating ceiling fan. He was about to throw an empty glass from his bedside table when his parents stormed into the room.

"What the hell are you doing?" his father demanded, hastily snatching the glass away. "What in the hell has gotten into you?"

Miles didn't speak. He planted himself firmly on the floor, arms crossed. His gaze was locked on his own feet, despite his mother's constant orders to look up at her.

"Miles."

His heart was racing. He could feel his cheeks and hands heating up.

And then his hands exploded into flames. He jumped off the iron bench and pointed them straight ahead, out of instinct more than anything. "Candlelight" fell to the ground, the blue cover tainted by scorch marks. Two fireballs, one from each palm, shot out and arced into the pond just below the fountain. Squeals came from the tiny forn trying to swim to safety.

Miles was ready to dart toward the fountain and plunge his hands into the cloudy water, but he realized they weren't hurting. He felt no pain whatsoever. Red and blue flames danced around his fingertips, just as they had back in the tunnel when he and Mortimer had encountered Kricket and Gryff.

"Young man?"

Just as he whipped his head around to see who the voice belonged to, the fires died out. Standing a few feet away, accompanied by Jaselle and two armed guards, was Queen Alys.

"Can you come here, please?" It was more a command than a question.

He obeyed. Clint followed.

"How did you do that?" the queen asked him.

"I don't know," Miles said truthfully.

Alys looked to Jaselle. "So this is what Mortimer meant."

"I suppose so," she replied. "He hadn't done anything like that at home yet. I was waiting to see." She stared at Miles with awe.

Queen Alys faced Miles once more. After a few moments, she said, "Jaselle, take him home. You're dismissed for the day. But tomorrow at noon I want you to take him to see Cléoma in the courtyard. I'll let her know to meet you two there."

"Yes, Your Majesty," Jaselle said. "Come on, Miles."

She took him by the hand, but quickly pulled away. It was scalding hot to her touch. She whispered something under her breath.

"Miles," his mother repeated.

"Stop yelling at me and just go yell at each other some more," Miles said to her. He was starting to cool down, but he was still filled with frustration.

"Can you give me a second?" his father asked. As his mother reluctantly left the room, his father sat down on the floor next to him. "Hey," he said softly. "Look at me."

Miles did so but was not happy about it.

"I'm sorry you had to hear all that. Your mom and I are just having a disagreement, that's all."

"You're having them all the time," Miles said. He knew he was about to start crying and it made him feel stupid.

"I know, buddy. I'm sorry. Listen, why don't we go watch a movie? What do you say?"

The boy shook his head. Behind his father, he saw Ollie peeking in through the doorway.

"C'mon. You can pick whichever one you want."

"I don't want to."

His father sighed. "Alright," he resigned.

Ollie found the courage to enter the tense room, cautiously making his way toward Miles. He rubbed the back of the dog's neck. He felt a great pressure escape his chest.

"I understand you're upset," his father said, placing a hand on his shoulder. "You can't react this way, though. You have to control yourself."

"It's hard sometimes."

"I know it is. But it's what you have to do."

Miles nodded. "I'll try," he said. His heart pumped rapidly in his chest, like it was trying to break free. He felt hot again.

His mother came back a minute later with a glass of water in hand. She kneeled down to pet Ollie with him.

"Are you okay?"

Miles wasn't sure if it was his mother who had asked or if it was Jaselle. "Yeah," he told her, or both of them—he wasn't sure which it was—but either way, it was a lie.

He reached down and picked up the damaged poetry book Jaselle had lent him, the title now obscured by harsh black markings.

"I'm sorry I ruined your book."

She took it from him and looked it over, frowning deeply. "It's alright," she said weakly, in the way where he could tell it was not actually alright.

"Can you buy another one?" Miles asked hopefully. The book was still readable, but the cover was marred. He felt bad about her having to return such an ugly thing to her shelf, especially since it was her grandmother's writing.

"No," said Jaselle. "These are out of print now. It's a pretty old book."

"I'm sorry," he apologized again. He felt crushed.

They walked back to the apartment together but did not exchange another word.

CHAPTER NINE

GET ANGRY

Cléoma was shorter than other Rompuns Miles had previously met, barely standing an inch taller than him. Her skin had a tinge of grey, like it was starting to fade. She wore purple silk robes adorned with silvery blue designs that decorated her sleeves, with sandals fashioned out of thick, dark red wood. Her face was also impressively wrinkled, with her eyes seemingly half-shut at all times; it was not hard to guess she was probably one of the oldest Rompuns living in the Jesieu Marshes. Miles had no idea why Queen Alys wanted him to meet this elderly woman.

When Jaselle dropped him off at the courtyard that morning, they found Cléoma was already there, lackadaisically dipping her fingers in the water of a fountain that stood in the middle of the damp clearing, spewing jets of water out of the mouth of an unfamiliar beast. The courtyard was a ten-minute walk from the apartment and fairly close to Miles' usual spot in the swamp. Trees still trickled leftover raindrops from the previous night.

Jaselle explained to the aged Rompun what had happened the day before, as well as mentioning it had been raining the day Miles arrived, which he thought was an odd thing to bring up. But he was still just a child, so he assumed the adults knew what they were doing. Shortly after, Miles and the old woman were left on their own.

Miles stared at Cléoma. Her left hand was still submerged in the murky waters of the cracked fountain. He couldn't help but wish Clint were there with him to make him feel less nervous and awkward.

"Hello, dear," Cléoma croaked, removing her hand from the water. She flicked tiny droplets from her fingertips onto the grass at her petite feet.

Miles waved meekly in return.

"Not much of a talker, are you?" she asked, edging nearer.

He shook his head.

"That's alright," said the old woman. "Can you show me your fireball trick?"

But Miles shook his head again. "I don't know how to do it," he admitted. "It just happens."

Cléoma nodded. "That's alright," she repeated. "We'll figure it out together, won't we, *peeshwank*?"

She wandered over to a nearby stone bench as Miles tried and failed to decipher what the nickname meant. The bench was still wet with rain from the night before, but she motioned for Miles to join her.

The bench was cold and he hated it. He wished he had the ability to conjure the fire whenever he wanted so that he could warm himself up. Also, if he were able to do that, he probably wouldn't have to spend time with Cléoma, so that would be another plus.

"I take it you're not from Rompu," Cléoma said jokingly, looking him over. "Where are you from?"

"Texas."

"I've never heard of Texas."

"No one here has."

Cléoma smiled. "Well, dear, do they have magic in Texas?"

Miles knew that magic wasn't real, even though he always wished it was. He and his father sometimes watched a man named David Blaine do tricks on television, and his father would proclaim, "That's amazing. I don't have a damn clue how he does it." Miles hoped to one day do something that made people say the same thing about him.

"Well, no one believed there was any magic in Rompu either, until recently," said Cléoma. "The Veratt is only here because of magic. Did you know that?"

The kid stared at his feet, which swayed just above the ground. His legs were not quite long enough to reach it. He didn't really feel like conversing with this woman and he still didn't understand why the queen was forcing him to.

"It's true," Cléoma said, not at all bothered by his lack of communication. "King Mykael brought it here from another world. Used some bad magic he found in a dusty, forgotten book. Nobody thought it would work, but it did. That was the first time in a long time anyone saw real magic rather than just reading about it in novels. And then you did it yesterday."

"I didn't do anything like the king did," Miles said, somewhat offended. "I just made some fire, that's all. I didn't make a monster."

"I know," Cléoma assured him. "But it sounds like you came from another world too, and I suspect you've done more than just make fire."

Miles turned to her instinctively, but looked back down at his feet before he spoke. "What do you mean?" he asked.

"I think you made water, too."

Miles stayed quiet, rocking his feet back and forth. He had nothing to say.

"I've always believed magic was possible," she went on. "I experienced it when I was a young woman. I believe I brought a terrible storm to Rompu, just like you did when you flew in here a week ago. Mine was much more severe than yours, of course. I've been trying to recreate the conditions since then, but I haven't been able to. I've only read theories. But the skies were clear and sunny the day you came here; you literally brought the rain with you, and I don't think it was a coincidence."

Miles shrugged. He didn't know what she was blabbering about. There was no way he could bring rain with him anywhere, there was too much of it. Maybe the adults didn't know what they were doing after all.

He was reminded of an older woman he used to visit back in school. She always wore dark, wrinkled suits and her graying hair was usually put up in a bun. She had black-rimmed glasses that made her eyes look small and beady. Miles automatically disliked her because he would be taken out of recess to go see her in an office. He was torn away from his classmates who were getting fun a break from their tiring day while he went to talk to a woman with crinkled clothes and tiny eyes named Mrs. Mendol.

"Hel*looooo*, Miles," she greeted him annoyingly that first day, trying her hardest to come across as warm and inviting in spite of her shrill and grating voice. "How are you today?"

Miles did not want to answer any of this weird woman's questions, but he thought he would get in trouble if he refused, so he said, "Alright."

"Sorry I had to sneak you in here during recess," Mrs. Mendol frowned. "It's just that I can't take you out during your classes, now, can I?"

"Maybe during math," Miles suggested.

That made Mrs. Mendol laugh, though Miles found nothing humorous about the remark.

"Take a seat," she urged him, gesturing toward a small red chair that sat in front of her nearly-spotless desk. All that lay on top of the desk was a lamp, a purple pen, a piece of paper with some writing that Miles couldn't make out, and a picture frame that faced away from him. He did as he was told.

The rest of the office was just as spotless and sanitary as her desk. Everything had a certain sheen to it, like it had just been plucked out of a furniture catalog and placed in the room. It wouldn't have surprised Miles if she started dusting the place the moment he left. The air conditioner also seemed to be on full blast, injecting an unfaltering coldness in him, adding to the weird sensation of the office feeling like a hospital room.

"Do you know why you're here?" Mrs. Mendol asked. "I'm what's called a *therapist*. Do you know what that is, Miles?" He shook his head. "Well, what a *therapist* does is talk to people about their problems and try to help them understand their feelings. Does that make sense?"

"I guess so." Miles had no idea what was going on or why.

"Good. Well, Miles, I've been hearing that you're having some trouble at home. Your mom wanted me to talk with you and see if we can't straighten some stuff out."

"Okay." He did not like this woman.

"What was going on yesterday when your little incident happened?" Cléoma asked.

Miles shrugged. "I dunno," he answered. "I was just thinking about home." He hesitated before divulging, "About my parents yelling."

"Has this happened before? Creating fire when thinking about your family?"

"No," he answered. "It only happened one other time. It happened when I hit an Omne who was trying to steal my dog—my maylan," he corrected himself.

"I see," she nodded, the words trickling out of her mouth softly. "What about when you came here? When you brought the rain. What happened then?"

Suddenly Miles could hear Mortimer's scream again. He could see the large green body grow smaller and smaller as he plummeted through the grey clouds. His body grew stiff and he fought back the urge to cry.

"Nothing," he said coldly.

Cléoma sighed, but put on a smile for the boy. "Alright," she said warmly. He thought she sounded disappointed by his response, but he didn't particularly care. "I think you have a gift, Miles," she said to him as she scratched her sagging chin with a crooked and chipped nail. "I don't believe what's been happening to you is an accident. You're special."

Miles frowned and said, "No I'm not. I couldn't make fire back home. No one can except magicians, and I'm not a magician, and anyway my dad says that what they do is fake."

"We can try to make sense of it together."

Mrs. Mendol said that last sentence to him as well. He didn't believe her, and he did not have much confidence in Cléoma either. "How?" he asked anyway.

Cléoma stepped away from the fountain and stood opposite Miles with her hands on her hips. "Right now, I simply want you to try making fire."

"That doesn't work," Miles said irritably. "I tried forcing it before and I couldn't. It just happens on its own."

"What are you usually thinking about when it happens?" Cléoma asked. "Maybe concentrate on that; see if that works for you."

He knew that the day before, he had been thinking about tearing his room apart when the fireballs shot out of his hands. But when he punched the Omne back in the tunnels, no real thoughts had been circling his mind except for how mad he was at Kricket and Gryff for trying to steal Clint away from him.

"But it's been different," he said, explaining each scenario to her. "So which one should I think about?"

Cléoma thought about it for a second, her eyelids drooping heavily. She finally muttered, "Get angry." When Miles failed to react to this, she said, "Get angry about something and let's see what happens."

So Miles tried.

He thought about all the villains in the movies he loved, shooting innocent people and trying to get away with their schemes.

He thought about the time Kyle Titten from his second grade class shoved him off one of the swings at recess and called him a baby. When he got home that afternoon, he had secretly applied band-aids on his knees where they had bled. He didn't tell his parents.

He thought about being taken out of recess every other day even though all he wanted to do was play.

He thought about Mrs. Mendol tapping her mint-green fingernails on her desk, staring at him intently, waiting for him to say something about his grandmother's death. How was he feeling? Did he still think about her?

He thought about his mother and father.

"Nothing's happening," he said to Cléoma.

Her brow furrowed and her face contorted, like an old avocado. "Just keep trying."

The more Cléoma acted like Mrs. Mendol, the more Miles grew to dislike the old Rompun. Mrs. Mendol would always push him to answer her inane questions, asking the same things over and over even though he told her he didn't want to discuss those things.

"You have to talk to *somebody*," Mrs. Mendol sighed. "I'm here to *help you*, Miles. It's safe here."

"My grandma's dead," Miles finally spat out. He could feel his face burning red. "She got kind of sick and then she got even sicker and then she couldn't walk anymore and then she died and now I wish I could see her but she's dead so I can't."

His eyes bore into the backside of the picture frame on Mrs. Mendol's desk.

"Does that make you sad?" Mrs. Mendol asked him, not skipping a beat.

"Yes."

"Good, good." She scribbled something down on her piece of paper but Miles did not see how that was good at all.

"Do you have any nice memories with your grandma?" she asked. "Sometimes when we're missing somebody, it helps to think about good times we had with them. Tell me about one of those times."

His mouth felt dry but he tried to speak anyway, if that was what it took to get him out of that office. "Whenever she came over to babysit me, she made me hotdogs," he said. "She put them in really hot water and after a couple minutes she'd take them out and cut one end of them, halfway down, a bunch of times, so they looked like octopuses. Then she put them on a plate with macaroni and I'd dip the legs in ketchup and bite those off before I ate anything else."

Mrs. Mendol was smiling. "Does your mom ever cook hotdogs for you like that?"

"No," Miles said. "Only my grandma."

Mrs. Mendol's dim office fizzled away as raindrops began to pelt Miles' face. Cléoma let out a soft grumble that at first sounded like annoyance, but after a second Miles realized it was satisfaction. He knew what question was about to come.

"How are you feeling?" Cléoma asked.

After a moment, "Sad."

Cléoma grinned. "Good," she said.

Miles still didn't understand how being sad could be good, but as the chilly raindrops trickled down his face and sprinkled onto the damp earth, he began to think that maybe Cléoma knew more than he did.

The next day, Miles tried to get angry again. He wanted to feel the heat in his palms. He wanted to feel his heart pounding inside of him, begging to break out and scream. But nothing happened.

"It's not working," he told Cléoma once more. "I keep trying, but nothing is working." Rather than disappointed, he felt irritated at the fact that she kept making him drudge up old memories for the sole purpose of making himself mad. He only wanted to feel the heat so that he wouldn't have to anymore.

He told Mrs. Mendol, "Some of the kids pick on me."

"Why? Who?" She prepared to write names down on her paper. Her pen was silver with black ink today.

But he didn't want to name names. "They think I'm crazy."

"What do they say?"

Miles took a deep breath before speaking. "They say I'm a baby because I'm scared to play in the dirt or touch the chains on the swing."

Images of recess the day before slithered back into his mind, of him scrambling to get up off the ground after Kyle Titten knocked him off the swing. He swiped the dirt off his pants and dug a hand into his pocket to take out a miniature Purell bottle.

The kids swinging and standing around nearby giggled at what Kyle had done.

Mrs. Mendol frowned worriedly. "Who picks on you, Miles?"

"Most of them."

"Why are you so anxious about those things?" she asked, veering away from the topic of the children's names.

"The germs," Miles responded quickly. He wanted to see Ollie. Feel the dog's warmth while they sat on the couch together, watching a movie. He knew Mrs. Mendol was going to ask why germs made him nervous, but he hoped she would instead say that he could leave now.

"Why do germs scare you?"

"Because they kill people."

"Really bad germs can, but not most," Mrs. Mendol said.

"My grandma was really sick," Miles told her. "I don't want to get sick like she did."

Mrs. Mendol put down her pen and said with sincerity, "You won't, Miles. You'll be fine."

"Maybe I won't be."

"No, you will. I promise." She continued staring at the boy. He knew what was going to come next. She asked again, "Who picks on you?"

"I don't know," he said to Cléoma. "It just doesn't work. I don't know why." He was growing increasingly frustrated with this whole exercise.

Cléoma stroked her floppy chin some more. It sent an uncomfortable shiver down Miles' short spine. "You just have to keep trying. Keep pushing yourself," she instructed him, tugging at a stray hair.

"I don't want to!" he said, raising his voice at her. "I'm tired of it. I'm tired of thinking bad things that make me feel worse. I don't care about the fire."

"But you have an amazing gift, Miles. That rain yesterday? *You* made that happen. I know you did." Confidence rang in her voice.

"I don't care," he said again. "Just thinking about stuff isn't working." He was becoming more frustrated by the second. Even the mere sight of Cléoma was beginning to set him off.

The old Rompun looked upset. "Do not shout at me," she said sternly. "All I'm doing is trying to help you. You have a lot of potential. I had a lot of potential too, once, and some people tracked me down and wanted to help me realize it, but I refused. And now I've lost any abilities I might have had. Don't squander your potential, *peeshwank*."

Miles didn't want to hear about potential. He wanted to go home. He wanted annoying old people that he didn't like to stop talking to him. He wanted to see his dog, or his maylan, or whichever one was around. But he was unable to. His cheeks flushed, his body trembled. He could feel the heat rising. He clenched his fists. He wanted to go home. He wanted everything to stop. He wanted to scream but couldn't so the scream filled up his body.

And that is when his entire body erupted in flames.

All he could see was blue and white blinding his vision. The Jesieu Marshes and Cléoma were distorted blurs, morphing with the swirling colors.

The heat subsided after less than a minute, maybe less than ten seconds. He wasn't sure.

Miles found himself standing before Cléoma with his clothes nothing but a pile of ash at his feet. He covered his naked body with his hands and blushed harder than he could remember ever blushing.

"My goodness," Cléoma muttered. "I think you just about gave me a heart attack."

CHAPTER TEN

LIKE A MAGIC TRICK

The next two days blended together, just like they had in Mrs. Mendol's too-clean office. In the same manner Mrs. Mendol had asked Miles the same questions over and over, trying to catch a glimpse at how his mind was processing everything, Cléoma was giving him the same instructions with very little variation, yet was still surprised when the results never changed.

Miles hadn't been able to replicate the explosive outburst he'd incited before. This was greatly frustrating, which in turn he thought would help summon the fire, but unfortunately that wasn't the case. Instead he continually disappointed Cléoma and himself.

After too many failed attempts for him to count, Miles was finally given some time off to enjoy the marshes and Clint's company. The maylan trotted alongside him as they explored the winding, narrow strips of land that wove through foggy green waters eliciting a faint pink glow from the forn swimming about. Benches made of either stone or iron were arbitrarily scattered throughout the trails.

It was hard to truly enjoy himself with his mind so burdened by Mortimer and finding a way home, but he tried. He decided to stop and take a rest on a particularly thick stone bench since they had been walking aimlessly for almost half an hour. Clint was not yet tired, so he kept sniffing around the area, making sure to stay relatively close to where the boy sat.

Miles let out a sigh. He was exhausted. Not just from the walk, but from the demanding week with Cléoma that had been thrust upon him. If he never had to see her again, he wouldn't mind it. A small part of him felt compelled to understand his supposed "gift," but a larger part wanted to just relax on benches and explore the outdoors while he tried to work out some way to return home.

The problem with getting back home—with getting things back to normal—was that Miles had absolutely no idea how he had ended up in Rompu in the first place. If he could uncover this one vital piece of information, he might be able to concoct a plan to reverse it.

But until then, he was stuck.

Stuck without Mortimer.

Held captive in the Skyr camp, Mortimer had said to him, "You must be scared out of your wits," and he was totally correct.

An unexpectedly chilly breeze blew through the marsh, sending a violent shiver coursing through Miles. The image of Vinzent's limp—more accurately, probably dead—body lying in the dirt infiltrated his mind.

"Don't worry, Mortimer'll look out for you," the Rompun had assured him. He had also promised they'd figure out a way to send Miles home whenever they arrived in Trafier. With everything that had been going on, he'd completely forgotten about talking to Queen Alys about the rift her husband had opened. He made a note to ask Jaselle if they could go visit the queen soon to discuss finding a way to open a portal for him.

He suddenly felt anger at Mortimer for being gone, but felt guilty for doing so. It wasn't Mortimer's fault things had turned out so terrible. There was no use blaming anyone besides the Veratt.

The Veratt and the king.

At a certain point, Miles had become fed up with Mrs. Mendol's repetitive questions and chose to simply sit in silence with his arms defiantly crossed.

She asked him questions about his grandmother, but he would just shrug.

She asked him how his mother was coping. More shrugs.

This had gone on for a couple sessions. Mrs. Mendol made Miles want to use the bad words from the westerns.

"Your mom tells me the doctor diagnosed you with a mild case of mysophobia," Mrs. Mendol said. "Do you understand what that is?"

Miles shrugged once more in response, but truthfully he did know what the word meant. He even knew how to spell it: M-Y-S-O-P-H-O-B-I-A. He had requested the doctor say it numerous times and write it down for him so he could practice writing and saying it.

Miles had filled a page of a notebook with his scribbles:

mysophobia, mysophobia

"It means that you have a fear of germs and getting sick. That's what *phobia* means—*fear*," Mrs. Mendol explained. He shrugged again even though she had not asked him anything.

Clint got bored of whatever he had been smelling and meandered over to the bench where Miles was resting and hopped up, placing his front paws on the bench. He licked Miles' arm, which the boy hastily wiped away on his pants. Clint's hind legs sunk slightly into the softened soil.

With all these memories clogging his brain, Miles began to spell the word aloud. "M-Y-S-O-P-H-O-B-I-A," he said to the animal. He sighed before saying it again. "M-Y-S-O-P-H-O-B-I-A." He had a perfectly clear visual of his notebook, which helped him recall the spelling.

He also remembered Mrs. Mendol asking, "Why are you afraid of germs?"

Then he remembered Mortimer saying, "Everything's dirty."

Then he remembered Mortimer hurtling through the sky.

Then he remembered the dark, cracked skin of the Veratt.

He didn't respond to Mrs. Mendol.

So she tapped the end of her pen on her desk, glancing down at the notes she had written about him.

"There's something else bothering you, isn't there?"

Shrug.

"You can talk to me, Miles," Mrs. Mendol assured him. He didn't believe her. "This is a safe space." He hated that she kept using that phrase, "safe space."

Miles scratched behind Clint's ear, moving down the maylan's neck, then to the soft ridges on his backside. Clint maneuvered himself down to the ground and rolled onto his back, presenting his stomach to Miles. He scooted off the bench and obliged, rubbing his hand up and down Clint's belly, which bobbed up and down in sync with the maylan's panting. But the petting was cut short as Clint jumped to his feet at the sound of a nearby splash.

"What was it?" Miles asked the animal as he stood.

The two walked over to the small pond where the sound had originated and looked beneath the grimy surface of the water. Bright pink forn shone underneath, jetting back and forth past each other, occasionally leaping out and back into the water like tiny vibrant dolphins.

"It's just the forn, buddy," Miles told Clint, who yipped at the little creatures. Then he remembered Jaselle slipping her hand into a pond, extracting a forn, and popping it into her mouth.

It felt like his mysophobia had been somewhat tempered ever since coming to Rompu. It was definitely still present, but Miles found himself feeling less anxious and worried about every little thing. He was spending his days hanging out in a marsh, after all, and it hadn't killed him yet. He wasn't even sick.

So he made a decision. Without much thought, Miles plunged his hand into the water and clenched one of the forn in his fist. The others scurried away in fear.

Water dripped from his fingers as he stuffed the animal in his mouth and began to chew.

At first, he felt nauseous. Closing his eyes helped.

The forn was chewy and tasted surprisingly sweet, like an orange gummy bear. When he finally swallowed, he opened his eyes and saw Clint staring at him with his furry black head cocked.

He felt dizzy, but that and the nausea began to subside after only a few seconds.

"What did I just do?" he asked. The maylan remained quiet and looked at the boy quizzically. Miles asked the question one or two more times. He returned to the bench. It was all he could think to do now. It was the only action that made sense.

The letters flashed in his mind: M-Y-S-O-P-H-O-B-I-A.

Shockingly, he did not feel horrible.

Clint was still at the pond's edge when Miles decided to do something else with very little thought put into it. He held his hand out in front of him, palm facing upward, and concentrated on one simple image.

There was one spark, and then a couple more.

Then fire.

His fingers impulsively squeezed shut, dousing the meager flame. Miles stared wide-eyed at his hand and noticed that Clint had retreated. He stood a few feet away now, shaking with fright.

Miles slowly unfurled his fingers and the fireball blossomed again. It licked at the cool air, hovering just above his sweating palm. It didn't burn or even lightly singe his skin.

It didn't take the two long to get back to Jaselle's apartment. She hadn't gone to work that day, so she was still there, preparing herself some lunch.

"Oh, hi Miles," she greeted him as he burst through the door. "I didn't know you were gonna be here for lunch. Want some food?" She held a bowl full of steaming tea in her hand.

"No. Well, maybe. Yes. In a minute," Miles said hurriedly. Clint sauntered into the den and got cozy on a pile of pillows he had arranged for himself in the corner.

"What's wrong?"

"I just ate a forn out of the pond and also I made fire again," Miles said, out of breath. It felt like everything he uttered was slurred, merging into a single incomprehensible word.

Jaselle's eyebrows sloped downward. "I'll go get Cléoma," she said.

"No!" Miles yelped, startling Clint in his secluded corner. "I don't want Cléoma," he said, this time quieter. "I just want to talk to you."

Jaselle nodded and set her bowl down on the countertop. With its vivid scent invading his nostrils, Miles could almost taste its sweetness.

"I met Mortimer because we both got captured by Skyr," Miles began. He told her about how the two of them had escaped the camp as it burned to the ground. He told her about finding Clint abandoned and injured in the tunnels, where they had escaped the Veratt. He told her about visiting the Lake of Remembrance, and how small that place had made him feel, and that he was deeply sorry about Kiko. He told her about how beautiful Windheit was and how fancy their room had been. Then he told her about their flight to Trafier.

He told her about the image that kept repeating in his head. About Mortimer's body flailing through the open air.

Falling, plummeting.

Disappearing beneath thick clouds like a magic trick.

When he finished, it felt like hours had passed but in reality it was only a few minutes. He wasn't sure how long, exactly, but he did notice the tea was no longer steaming. He was in the middle of apologizing once more when Jaselle began to sob.

Miles blinked. He didn't feel comfortable seeing a grown-up cry. It was too foreign; he had no idea how to react.

Her shoulders heaved up and down as she covered her face with one hand. Her cries were an ugly, personal sound, like something Miles wasn't supposed to witness. She then edged forward and wrapped her bulky arms around him, squeezing him tight. He hugged her back as tightly as he could, and he began to cry too. The distance that had hung between them ever since he arrived evaporated in that moment.

They stayed like that for a while, finally grieving the loss of a man they both loved. When Jaselle finally pulled away from him, she said, "Thank you for telling me."

"I'm sorry it happened," he said, wiping at his eyes.

"It wasn't your fault," she told him, smiling faintly. She hugged him again, and whispered once more, "Thank you."

They ate lunch together after settling down a bit more. They shared stories about Mortimer, and Jaselle got a kick out of hearing how tightly his clothes had fit him in Al-dir's castle.

"I made him a robe like that once," Jaselle told Miles. "It was my first—and last—time trying to make some sort of clothing. It ended up being so small on him, he looked like a true fool strutting around the apartment in it. I begged him to just throw it away, but he said he wanted to keep it. The man was an idiot." They both laughed heartily.

There was still an emotional current coursing between them. A question had been biting at Miles for several weeks, but only now did he feel somewhat safe asking it. After their laughter quieted, Miles ventured, "What happened to Kiko?"

Jaselle's smile faltered, but she pressed onward. "It was the Veratt," she started. "It was...well, right when King Mykael summoned it. He did so right here in Trafier, of course. The thing just went wild, started attacking. Killed a lot of people, knocked down one of the palace towers." Her eyes began to well up again. "Kiko was one of those people."

Seeing her cry made Miles tear up as well. "I liked his picture he drew Mortimer," he said. At the mention of her husband's name, Jaselle broke down even further. "I like his room, too. I bet he was a really cool kid."

"He would've liked you," Jaselle smiled. "He was a little younger, but you would've been great pals, I bet."

"I bet so too," said Miles.

This seemed to be too much for Jaselle for one afternoon. She stood and placed their empty bowls and plates in the sink before returning to her bedroom.

Miles watched her shut the door behind her, and his eyes trailed off to Kiko's open doorway. He felt like taking a closer look inside. He wanted to get to know Mortimer's son. On his way over to Kiko's room, he grabbed the family's copy of "The New King" off the bookshelf.

He entered the room and sat down cross-legged on the bed. He ran a finger along the title's purple stitching before opening it to the first chapter. After a few pages, Clint joined him, hopping up and resting by his side.

CHAPTER ELEVEN

SAY BYE

Miles sighed before answering the question. He had come to the conclusion that Mrs. Mendol was going to persistently ask it every time they met until he finally caved and offered a real response. It was as good a day as any to cave.

"I visited her in the hospital," he said, thinking about his grandmother. Even in the cramped elementary school office, he could smell the sickness and feel the stillness of the cold hospital air.

His mother had brought him along even though he'd made it abundantly clear he had no desire to go. She told him he had no reason to be scared, and he had lied by telling her he wasn't and just didn't feel like going.

So he had stood at his grandmother's bedside, watching her sleep. The thin, crisp blanket was pulled halfway up her stomach, her thick arms resting at her sides on top of it. He had made note of her left index finger twitching. She hadn't woken up until after his mother already left to buy lunch at the cafeteria downstairs.

Spittle stuck to her lips as she spoke.

"How are you?" She hadn't sounded like herself. It was more like an alien, or a frog.

"Good," Miles had told her.

"Better than me, it looks like." A feeble smile etched onto her face as the words tumbled out.

Mrs. Mendol nodded supportively, urging him to continue the retelling.

His grandmother had gestured for him to sit in the chair on the other side of her bed. It rested near a small table that held a turquoise vase with wilting pink orchids.

Miles had shaken his head. He didn't want to stay in the hospital long enough to warrant getting comfortable. He had been preoccupied with thoughts about french fries from the cafeteria when his grandmother sputtered, "Do you know what's going on?"

"You're sick."

Another attempt at a smile. "*Really* sick," she had corrected him.

Mrs. Mendol asked, "Were you scared?"

Miles let out another sigh and then nodded.

"That sounds pretty scary," Mrs. Mendol said.

He told her how weak his grandmother looked that day. She had always been a large woman, but for some reason that day she seemed so frail. As if simply tapping her arm would've shattered the bone.

"She couldn't get up," Miles told Mrs. Mendol.

"Are you sure you don't wanna sit down?" his grandmother had asked him. He told her he was fine standing. Her arm had ferociously shaken when she reached over to the bedside table to pick up her glasses. "That's better," she'd said as she put them on. "Now I can see your handsome face."

Miles had shifted back and forth awkwardly without anything to say. Suddenly he started craving her octopus hotdogs.

"When are you going home?" he had asked.

She had let out a soft chuckle, but Miles understood it as different from the kind of laugh people make when they think something is funny. It was like when the men in his westerns were about to deliver bad news to somebody. Or pull out their pistols and shoot them.

"I'm probably not going home, Miles," she had then said.

"Your grandma told you that?" Mrs. Mendol interrupted, hastily writing something down on her paper. Miles told her yes.

He had asked his grandmother, "Why not?" Knots started to form in his stomach, due either to what his grandmother was saying or to hunger. Or both.

"I'm really sick. Too sick to go home again. The doctors don't think they can fix me."

The room had felt even colder then. "What's wrong?" he'd asked.

Her eyes never left his. "Lots of things," she'd said. "Stuff that's too complex for you to understand, bug. Just germs and things like that." She then scratched her head, her fingers tangling up in wiry white hair.

"Germs?"

Barely more than a week later, a doctor would write the word *mysophobia* for him.

He had silently begged for his mother to return.

His grandmother frowned then. Miles didn't think he had ever seen her do that before.

"I'm sorry," she had apologized. "I don't mean to scare you."

He hadn't reacted.

"I love you," she'd said.

"I love you too." It was almost inaudible. He would have thought she hadn't heard him if not for the frown curling into a smile.

"I'm very proud of you, you know."

Miles told Mrs. Mendol how his grandmother had grabbed his hand in hers, which took him by surprise. Her bony, wrinkled fingers wrapped around his palm. He could see tears forming behind the thick lenses of her glasses. Then she had smiled.

At that point, his mother had finally returned to the cold room with a tray of faded food in hand. She set the tray down on a table and handed Miles the blue Jell-O cup she had brought along with her. By the unappealing look of the food his grandmother was given, he was glad he didn't get any french fries from that cafeteria.

"Your dad isn't here yet?" his mother had grumbled. He shook his head. "How are you feeling, Mom?"

Miles had peeled back the lid on his Jell-O and jiggled it, watching the reflection of the dim fluorescent lights shift in the gelatinous half-cylinder. His father then appeared in the doorway, offering a weak hello before entering the room.

"There you are," he'd said, smiling at Miles.

His mother had wasted no time in asking, "So are you still taking him to Thinkery?"

Miles had asked what Thinkery was. "It's that museum we went to, remember? The one you liked so much. Wanna go back?"

"His stuff's still in my car," his mother had interrupted before he could answer. "I'll go down with you two and get it. Say bye to Grandma, Miles."

He had looked at the old woman sitting up in her bed. Her smile was small but firm. "Bye, bug," she had said to him.

"Bye. See you soon."

But he wouldn't.

Cléoma sat idly, taking in Miles' story about the previous day. She licked her chapped lips. Miniscule droplets of saliva filled the shallow cracks around her graying mouth.

"That's it," Miles said, in case the elderly Rompun was unclear about the story's ending.

"How'd you get rid of the fireball? Did it evaporate?" Cléoma asked.

"I threw it."

"Why the hell would you do *that*? What if it had hit a tree and set the whole swamp on fire?"

"There's water all over the place anyway! And I threw it into a pond!"

"Where forn—*living creatures*—are?"

"You guys eat those alive!"

"Still," she said, "that was irresponsible. Don't do that again." She dipped her hand in the waters of the courtyard fountain and swirled it around, sending ripples through the surface. "Could you do it again?"

"I haven't tried," the boy confessed.

"Well, try."

Fists clenched, he shut his eyes and began to focus. To focus. To focus. To focus on one image, one idea. To focus on—

—his right hand erupted in a blaze of fire before he even realized what was happening. Cléoma jumped a bit, accidentally splashing some water onto Miles' shirt. He unclenched his fist, palm facing up, and opened his eyes to watch the fireball float in inch above the lines on his palm.

"I guess I can do it again," he said.

"You certainly can." Cléoma rose and wiped her hand off on her mauve robe that draped down to the ground. She took a step closer to him as the light of the flame began to flicker.

"I don't want you to get hurt," Miles said, edging backward.

The Rompun told him not to fret and continued forward. She held her wrinkled hands up to the fire, feeling its warmth emanate. "Incredible," she whispered. She swiped her hand through the fireball, earning a yelp from the boy. "You can put it out now," she told him.

"I don't know how," he reminded her.

Cléoma sighed. "Fine," she conceded.

He lobbed the flaming ball at one of the nearby ponds. It dissipated into steam that floated up into the cypress tree leaves.

"We really need to work out a better way for you to get rid of these things," Cléoma muttered, "but I guess that'll do for now." She reassumed her position on the fountain's edge, running her fingertips along the water. "You said that all it takes is focusing on an image. What do you think of?"

"My dad," he answered.

She didn't know what to make of this response. "Well, if you can craft fire, we need to start focusing on the other elements now. We'll refine them all later."

"Like what?"

Cléoma grinned, exposing a row of lopsided and yellowed teeth. "I already told you I suspect you can summon water. You might even be able to create lightning and manipulate the earth. Those are what the old theory books mention, anyway."

Miles reluctantly nodded. He held his palm open again and a tiny flame coughed into existence, which he then tossed from hand to hand. Cléoma praised his skill.

"I'm very proud of you for opening up to me," Mrs. Mendol said to him. "I know it's hard and scary sometimes. You're a brave kid."

He thought of his father telling him, "Be brave, Miles."

Mrs. Mendol then asked, "Was Thinkery a fun place to visit with your dad?"

In the car that day, his father had asked Miles if he was doing okay. "No," he had answered. "Grandma said she's not coming home."

His father had lightly pressed his foot down on the brakes, easing behind the row of cars ahead of them on the highway. Miles stared at an exit sign that read TEXAS FARM TO MARKET RD 1325 and wondered what it would be like to raise a goat.

"She didn't mean that," his father tried to assure him while the car inched forward.

"Yes she did."

"Miles, Grandma is just tired. She didn't mean to say something so silly. You shouldn't bother worrying about stuff like that."

But Miles had ignored him and continued looking out the window at the rectangular green sign, thinking about who it was that painted the white letters onto it. They didn't speak to each other for several minutes after that. Miles had started to imagine his baby goat munching on his stupid math homework.

"Yes," he said to Mrs. Mendol. "Thinkery was fun. They have a place where you can build cool stuff. My dad helped me make a tiny airplane there. It was called the Spark Shop."

Cléoma said, "Let's work on lightning first. Maybe think about your dad again, but focus on trying to form a lightning bolt."

"Where am I supposed to make it strike?" Miles asked.

"That's a good question, actually."

"Wouldn't it be dangerous to make it strike near us?"

"Probably, yes."

"I don't want to do lightning."

"Just make it hit one of the ponds, like you did with your fireballs."

"Won't that electrocute the forn?"

"*Now* you're concerned about the forn?"

"It's just too dangerous!"

"It's fine."

"I'm scared."

Cléoma frowned a deep frown. "Sometimes you've gotta face your fears, *peeshwank*. Not a whole lot is gonna get done if you don't."

He thought of his father's words: "Be brave, Miles."

He thought of his mother's: "You're a strong boy."

He thought of the Third River, being dragged beneath the crashing waves as Mortimer's voice called out for him from their unimpressive boat and lightning flashed above.

He thought of Mortimer's body careening toward the earth as the Veratt chased them through the storm on the backs of the Ruhigans' Carriers.

He had to be brave.

"Okay," he said begrudgingly. "I'll try."

Cléoma smiled her toothy smile, which quickly disappeared as she took a few steps back. "Just to be safe," she said with her hands up. Her words were not encouraging.

Miles held his hands up high, palms toward the sky, assuming that if he were to conjure a lightning bolt it would either be crashing down from above or shooting straight into the clouds from his hands. He closed his eyes like last time and drew his father into his mind, trying to see every contour and imperfection on his face. He continued to focus. To focus. To focus on that image, the idea, that—

—but nothing came.

No fire, no lightning, nothing.

The elderly Rompun was still eyeing him from a few feet away.

"Ca viens?" her voice broke through his concentration. "Are you alright?"

He opened his eyes and threw his arms to his sides. "It's not working," he said, defeated. "I did the same thing as before, but it doesn't work."

Cléoma pondered for a couple moments. Then she suggested, "Maybe you need to think of something else besides your father."

"Like what?"

"I don't know," she admitted. She stepped closer to him and said, "Start with a time when you remember there being a storm and see where your mind wanders."

Miles could picture lightning flashing overhead as he struggled in the rough waters of the Third River. He could perfectly hear Mortimer's shrieks asking where he was, attempting to navigate the vast river and reach him.

Then his mind flashed back to the hospital room as his dad walked in and said, "There you are."

He thought of his grandmother's words: "The doctors don't think they can fix me."

"Too sick to go home again."

"I'm really sick."

His body was trembling. He rubbed his fingertips together. He was mad at Cléoma for forcing these thoughts into his head, and he hated Mrs. Mendol for making him talk about them in the first place.

"I think I can do it," he said.

"So do it."

Miles replayed the image several times in his head: "The doctors don't think they can fix me."

"The doctors don't think they can fix me."

"The doctors don't—"

A yellow streak lit up the sky, and a few seconds later a distant rumble filled their ears.

Cléoma was looking up at the cloudless, light blue sky. There was no storm approaching.

"Did you do that?" she asked. "You must have. The sky's clear." She clapped her hands together. "Great job!" she congratulated him.

"Thanks," he whispered uneasily. He took a seat on the edge of the fountain, the same way he had found Cléoma positioned a while before.

"How are you feeling? Are you up to doing it again?" She was exuberant.

Miles pierced the reflection of his nose with a finger and swirled it around, distorting his wavy face. "Not really," he said.

"Are you sure? We're making a lot of progress today. You're on a roll."

But he was too tired. He felt like going back to Jaselle's apartment so he could pet Clint, eat a snack, and read a bit. Cléoma told him she understood, so they agreed to meet at the same time tomorrow.

On his walk back through the marsh to the palace entrance, Miles glanced upward and noticed dark rainclouds starting to move in on Trafier even though the backdrop of the sky was still bright and sunny. Rain began to fall just after he got inside.

CHAPTER TWELVE

THREE DEAD FLOWERS

The next day, Miles awoke to the now-familiar smell of endalain tea and honey coming to a boil, the sticky yellow goo dissolving and mixing in with the hot water.

He stumbled out of bed and into the den where he greeted Jaselle. She motioned for him to take a seat as she grabbed two small bowls from the cupboard. "You slept in Kiko's room?" she asked.

He had. He didn't even realize it until Jaselle said it aloud. It had been an accident; he must have fallen asleep at some point late at night—or, rather, early in the morning. He had been too depleted to get up and walk to the sofa. "Yeah," he said.

"Was it comfortable?"

"Yeah."

They left it at that. "I'll start the eggs soon."

Miles nodded even though he wasn't feeling hungry yet. He watched her pour the steaming liquid into his favorite orange bowl as he told her, "I read 'The New King' again."

"Did you?" She set his bowl down on the kitchen table and took a seat across from him. "What'd you think? Still too boring for you?"

"Yeah," Miles said honestly. "I liked it a little more this time, though. I like the part when Kieran tells Nuntara how he got his scar in that fight against the ryrrell."

She smiled. "That's a pretty exciting part," she concurred.

"Yeah. But what's a ryrrell?"

Jaselle laughed before sipping her tea. "I think Bernard Cranteg is pretty lousy with descriptions too. A ryrrell is an animal that lives mainly on the eastern coast, at the beaches on the edge of the Violet Woods. They go back and forth between living on land and dipping into the Lasir Gulf. Nasty things, if you get them riled up."

"What do they look like?"

"They're about four feet long and a foot or so wide, and their legs can retract into their bodies when they go underwater. Let's see…their bodies are cylindrical, which helps them swim. And they're completely covered in a bright yellow shell, which they use to blend into the sand on the beach."

Miles could paint a pretty good picture of the animal in his head. "So they're kinda like vandats?"

"Sort of, except bigger and meaner."

Miles did not want to meet a ryrrell. He drank from his bowl, appreciative of the sweetness honey lent the tea. Endalain was already naturally sweet, but he enjoyed the extra boost every once in a while.

"There's something I don't get, though," he said. "If the Skyr and the Rompuns coming together was such a big deal that they wrote a whole boring book about it, why are you separated now? Why'd everyone give up so easily? I read it again because I wanted to understand and thought that maybe I missed a part but I didn't miss any parts."

Jaselle looked troubled by his question. Her eyes glanced over at Clint, who slunk into the living room and made his way over to Miles, sniffing the air.

"It wasn't easy," she said.

Miles waited for her to elaborate. He put the orange bowl to his lips and slurped.

It was obvious she had been hoping this answer would suffice. But she continued: "What King Mykael did was difficult for everyone—Rompuns and Skyr alike—to accept. Especially because no one really knows for sure why he summoned the Veratt in the first place. The thing is such a terrible beast, it seems like the only possible reason could be for it to destroy something. I'm sure Queen Alys knows the reasoning behind it, but she hasn't confided in anybody. Anyway, she and the king kept fighting and fighting about what to do about the creature and eventually, she banished him."

"That's it?"

Jaselle frowned. "Well, of course it was much more complicated than that," she said. "But her anger over what he'd done was the catalyst. And he was somehow...different after it all went down."

"Different how?" Miles asked.

"It's hard to explain. He just wasn't himself anymore. He wasn't who she had fallen in love with. It wasn't an easy decision for her to make by any means, but she knew it'd be best for the kingdom if he was gone."

"Where'd he go?"

Jaselle shrugged. "We're not entirely sure," she replied. "The Skyr have camps set up all over the eastern side of the kingdom. They also have one right at the entrance of the marshes, so our usual trade route's been shut down a while. We can't figure out where the king has actually gone, but his troops are definitely staying active. Some people think he's laying low in Merrikar."

Miles remembered reading in "The New King" that Merrikar was located near the Violet Woods, where he and Mortimer were first held captive. He asked, "If King Mykael was kicked out anyway, then why does everyone care where he is? And why are the Skyr fighting for him?"

She tried to divert the two of them away from the topic by asking if Miles wanted his eggs now, but he declined. So she said, "Not all of the Skyr sided with him. Some are squarely against him. I think the ones that remained loyal to him did so because he promised he would reclaim Rompu in the name of the Skyr, and they're his people, so they want to support that, however unrealistic it is. I suppose it helps that he has that horrid creature running around too, so they wanna be on his good side."

"I haven't met any of the good Skyr yet," Miles sighed. Clint had since lain down on the floor and rested his head on the boy's bare feet. It was warm.

"Why are you so curious about all this?" Jaselle asked. "This isn't really stuff a nine-year-old should be worrying about."

"I just wanna know," Miles said. "Since I haven't been able to talk to Queen Alys about a way home yet, I thought I should know more about Rompu." He had broached the subject of meeting with her the day before, but Jaselle had told him the queen was too busy with other matters right now, and wanted him to focus on his training with Cléoma.

He watched as Jaselle prepared their breakfast. She cracked six eggs into a cast iron skillet and held it over the open flame in one of the pits on the countertop. He asked, "Why are the Omnes helping the Skyr? Mortimer said it was because of 're-sources.'"

This drew out a chuckle from Jaselle. "Probably because they're a bunch of idiots," she said. "They're helping because the Skyr have what they want, and they have a huge supply of it."

"What do they want?"

"Eggs."

Miles stared at her. "Eggs?"

"Hichin eggs. Tiny little eggs laid by ugly little bugs in some caves on the northern border of the Violet Woods, where a lot of their camps are located. Since the Omnes can't readily access the caves, they rely on the Skyr for those eggs. Omnes grind them up and mix them with their tobacco. Gives it a richer flavor, they say."

The kid grimaced. "So they do all these bad things just so their cigarettes taste better?"

"Afraid so."

"Can you eat the eggs too?"

"Not really. They're very small, my dear. Remember, they're bug eggs."

"That's stupid." It seemed too simplistic an answer, but the two Omnes he had encountered had certainly seemed like simplistic individuals.

"No one ever said Omnes were smart." She sprinkled pepper into the beaten eggs that were starting to solidify on the bottom. "Do you want any cheese?"

A few minutes later, Jaselle set two plates on the table and they began to eat. Clint had woken up and now sat by them, wagging his tail as he tried to detect what food was being served. "Can I ask you something?" Miles asked apprehensively. Jaselle nodded, so he ventured on. "What was Kiko like?"

She played with her eggs on the plate as if she hadn't heard his question. She blinked her larges, yellow eyes. Her fiery hair was pulled back in a ponytail this morning. It shone vibrantly against her pale green skin.

Miles promptly backtracked. "You don't have to answer." They had grown closer since bonding over stories about Mortimer, but he knew Kiko was still a sore subject, especially with Miles now occupying the space.

"It's okay," she said, taking a bite of egg. She swallowed and said, "Kiko was really energetic. Always running around the apartment, always asking Mortimer to take him out into the marshes to catch forn and swim."

"I would never want to swim in that water," Miles said before stabbing some eggs with the end of his fork. Clint sniffed the air, pleading for some scraps.

"Aw, it's not that bad," Jaselle grinned. "I bet you'd have fun splashing around in there."

"No way," Miles laughed. He set his fork down, which seemed to intrigue Clint.

Jaselle raised a hand to her cheek and scratched her rubbery skin with dull nails. "That kind of stuff never bothered Kiko."

"I'm getting better about it," he told her.

Jaselle got out of her chair and picked up both plates then brought them over to the sink. "Would you like some more tea?"

Miles' reply was interrupted by a heavy knocking at the door. Jaselle started running hot water over the plates before she walked across the room to answer. She pulled open the slab of dark wood and on the other side was Mortimer.

Jaselle screamed, which in turn made Clint bark.

Miles stood up and stared at the doorway, letting his mouth hang open despite how dumb he knew he looked. His heart thumped wildly in his chest and his entire body felt like it was vibrating. His eyebrows lifted.

Mortimer's stubble had now become a full-fledged beard. Black, curly hair covered his face, and his mouth was barely visible amongst the bushiness. The Rompun no longer sported the plain white t-shirt and cargo shorts he'd been wearing when Miles last saw him. Now he had baggy black pants with a leather belt strapped around his belly and an untucked red flannel shirt. He had kept the enormous flip-flops and dirty brown jacket.

With a dopey smile stretched across his face, Mortimer held a bouquet of three large flowers in his hand, each one standing almost as tall as him. They each had what must have been fifty petals, which alternated between a faded red and dark blue. They were wilting.

"I got you some of those flowers you loved so much from our honeymoon," Mortimer smiled, his voice raspy. "They kinda died, though. I mean, Vidliés is a long ways away. Sorry. Well, I mean, I'm sorry, but there's not really anything I could've done, so…"

Jaselle cried out and threw her arms around him as he continued to sputter out nonsense. After several moments, they shared a kiss.

Clint ran over to the two and jumped up on Mortimer's legs, his tail wagging violently. It was about to fly right off of him. "Hey, Clint!" Mortimer greeted the animal. "Thought your old pal Mortimer was long gone, did you?"

He looked over Jaselle's shoulder and saw Miles standing by the kitchen table. Tears rolled down the boy's cheeks, which were burning intensely.

"What you crying about, kid?" Mortimer asked him, grinning widely. "I can smell some endalain, so it don't seem to me like there's anything to be sad about here."

"I thought you were dead," Miles said.

"I know."

"I saw you falling."

"I know."

"I saw—"

"I know, kid, I was there," Mortimer joked. "Come give me a hug, why don't ya?"

Miles raced across the room and did just that. His face pressed up against Mortimer's plump belly. The Rompun patted him on the back as Clint yelped in unrestrained excitement.

"You need a bath," Miles said.

"Jeez, thanks, kid," Mortimer laughed at him. He squeezed even tighter and asked Jaselle, "Can I get some of that tea?"

"Let me make a new pot," she said. "I made this one with honey."

"Ech! Why would you do that?"

"I like it with honey!" said Miles defensively, pushing himself away from Mortimer. His teardrops had stained the Rompun's shirt.

"That's kinda foolish, kid," Mortimer shrugged. "Also, can I get a vase for these things?" he asked, holding up the dead flowers. "I'm really tired of carryin' 'em."

CHAPTER THIRTEEN

ONLY SECOND CHANCE

The three spent the rest of the day enjoying each other's company, not indulging in much more than just sitting around the apartment, sharing food and stories from the past two weeks.

Mortimer told them about how he had landed in the middle of the Vidliés Plains, which apparently were full of even taller and thicker flowers than the ones he'd brought back with him. He explained to Miles that they were called cerylians, and that they grow to the heights of trees, sometimes even reaching higher. Being so tall and with such sturdy stems, the cerylians were able to cushion Mortimer's considerable fall as he navigated from one massive petal to the next, making his way down to the ground.

"My arm was pretty banged up, though," he told them. "I had to do some walking, but I managed to find that village— what's it called?—and get myself patched up. Had to rest there for a few days, of course."

Jaselle reminded him the name of the village was Heriin. He thanked her, then spoke of the villagers' hospitality. They offered him a sling for his arm and all the food he required to nurse himself back to health. He confided in the two that perhaps he'd partaken in more of their food than was necessary.

For several days, Mortimer had gorged on the village's specialty dish, which included some kind of cherry and maple-glazed bird with a side of sweet bread and mashed-up black beans with green chilis. He then had to travel from Heriin down south toward Trafier, making his way around the Juene Gulf, which had taken a formidable amount of time, given his walking pace. "Tossed my sling in the Allier River," he said. "Didn't take long for my arm to heal."

"Allier?" Jaselle piped up. "Do you mean Verte?"

"Don't think so. Unless I got my geography mixed up."

"So that means you went near that Skyr outpost at the northern entrance of the marsh?" Her voice was a higher pitch than Miles had ever heard it. "Why in the world would you do that? Why not just cross Verte, you oaf?"

"Allier is easier to cross!" Mortimer objected. "I ain't afraid of no Skyr enough to make me swim across that wide, filthy strip of water!" He assured them that he snuck into the marshes undetected, far removed from any outposts. Even though she was visibly annoyed with her husband for doing something so reckless, it was also plain to see how extremely grateful she was for his safe return home.

Miles spent most of their lunchtime detailing his sessions with Cléoma, which endlessly amused Mortimer. The Rompun would cackle at the idea of Miles interacting with the elderly woman, an interruption which lengthened the time it took to relay the story.

He explained how he was now able to conjure fire, the same way he had accidentally done so back in the tunnels when they battled the two Omnes. Jaselle hastily shut down Mortimer's requests for a live demonstration of these newfound abilities. He also talked about his experiments with lightning, which Mortimer was not as anxious to see in his own home.

What interested Mortimer the most was exactly how Miles was able to do these things at all. "I've never seen anything like it," he said. "What do you do? What's the process?"

"I just think of certain things," Miles replied. "Imagining my dad helps with the fire. I was able to make lightning when I thought about my grandma. It just depends on what I'm trying to do." He still didn't fully understand how the memories correlated with his magic, but he was at least aware of what was effective. It was a start.

It was one of the best days Miles had experienced in a long time, possibly the best since arriving in Rompu. A day of good food, relaxation, and stories. And best of all, Mortimer was safe.

They ended the day dining with Queen Alys, who was relieved to discover her aide had safely made his way back to Trafier.

It was the first time Miles had seen the queen since she'd witnessed him accidentally conjuring the fire. Before dinner, Mortimer and Jaselle both assured him that they would speak to her about King Mykael's portal and whether she had any idea how to replicate it. It was obviously a touchy subject, though, so they'd need to build up to it.

"The trek from Heriin must have been tough," Queen Alys said sympathetically. "I'm sure you'll welcome a lot of rest in the coming days."

"It wasn't too bad," Mortimer told her. "A trader traveling from Feryn-lac toward Garn and Merrikar picked me up and gave me a ride in his cart until we got to the Allier River. He had a lot of interesting knick-knacks in that thing. Some shell necklaces, sand dollars, dried kyrfish encrusted with jewels and such. And some of the best chili shrimp with rice I've ever tasted."

Miles had read about Feryn-lac in one of Jaselle's books. It was a coastal town, built almost entirely on docks, which stretched out into the Juene Gulf in the west. He wanted to ask what a kyrfish was, but Queen Alys had a question of her own.

"Why would you go to Allier? It is much safer to cross at Verte. The Skyr could have spotted you."

But Mortimer brushed off the question as their food arrived. In the center of the table, near where the queen sat and far from Miles' reach, was a stunning golden plate with a plump creature that had been browned in the oven. A thick blue glaze dripped down its sides. It had a snout like a pig, but the animal was a round, misshapen sphere, and Miles could see where two legs had been chopped off underneath its body. It was held in place on the plate by a ring of skinned and roasted zol with thick slices of zucchini and yellow squash on top.

Closer to Miles were two bowls, one filled with freshly-baked bread and the other with jellied forn. He assumed the forn were meant to be spread over the bread like jam. In addition, there were many other plates and bowls filled with side dishes. Some looked familiar to Miles, such as a plate of boudin that smelled exactly like the kind his mother made in Austin: smoky, with just the right amount of spice to tickle his nose.

Other foods were foreign to him, like a bowl of black paste and a plate with some sort of spindly fried meat drizzled with the spicy blue myre sauce.

Everyone at the table drank glasses of red wine except for Miles, whose glass was filled with water. He didn't particularly enjoy the scent of wine anyway.

Mortimer sliced a thick cut of the pig-ball creature for Miles and plopped it down on his plate, as well as some of the black mush and boudin. Miles declined the fried meat, but served himself some crispy green beans and bread.

"This stuff is great on the meat," Mortimer said, pointing at the black substance on his plate. Miles had planned on leaving that portion of his plate untouched.

Conversation at dinner was light, which Miles appreciated because it meant he could actually follow along. No one was discussing anything too serious or confusing, though he hoped the subject of his return home would crop up soon. The only slightly serious topic they touched on was his progress with Cléoma, which he summarized for the queen as concisely as he could manage.

Alys was quite impressed with what he had accomplished already. "What are you going to attempt next?" she asked him. The queen had large, earnest eyes and a sweet smile. Her voice was warm and inviting.

"I guess we'll just try to do lightning better," he answered. "But then I dunno. Maybe water?"

The rest of the time was spent reminiscing about the landscapes Mortimer had seen on his journey, the trips everyone had taken to Feryn-lac throughout their lives to see the kyr-fish—which Miles still could not find an empty moment to ask about—and the Jesieu Marshes cooling down as winter approached.

Miles greatly enjoyed the feast even though the pig-ball, which he had learned was called a kreer, had a smokier flavor than he usually liked. When he finally relented and tasted the black paste, he found out it was just mashed black beans with lime juice squirted in.

Eventually, as the evening began winding down, the adults called for a servant to escort Miles back to the apartment so they could discuss heftier issues.

"But—" Miles began to object.

"Don't worry," Jaselle shushed him. "We know. We'll talk about it."

"But I—"

"Let us handle it," Mortimer told him. "We gotta talk about some other stuff too, kid."

"You do not need to be troubled with thoughts of war," Alys said, evidently unaware that such thoughts were constantly on Miles' mind. He considered resisting more, but decided things would be okay in Mortimer and Jaselle's hands.

An unexpectedly skinny Rompun escorted him through the maze-like hallways of the palace until they reached the immense wooden door of Mortimer and Jaselle's apartment. Miles smiled at the Mouton placard.

"Do you need anything else, sir?" the Rompun asked. It took Miles a moment to register that he was the "sir" being addressed.

"No, thanks," he responded awkwardly. The Rompun gave a curt bow before rushing off. Miles stuck the key Jaselle had given him into the keyhole and unlocked the door, slipped into the apartment, and shut the door.

Clint was eager to greet him. He jumped up on Miles the moment the boy entered the room, pawing at his chest. He made his way into Kiko's room with Clint nipping at his heels after retrieving a new book from the den's bookshelf.

A book with a bright red spine had caught his eye. He had seen it before, of course, but never pulled it off the shelf. Its cover was a picture of two young Rompun men sitting around a campfire, each holding live vandats in their hands. The sky behind them was navy blue with bolts of purple. A dark storm was brewing. Its title was "The Scarlett Ruins," and Miles was surprised to see its author was Bernard Cranteg. The man liked his red spines. Miles opened it to its first page and hoped it would prove to be more immediately engaging than Cranteg's other novella.

Miles had not even gotten to the end of the prologue before he heard the apartment door open, which took him by surprise. He thought surely the Rompuns would be talking well into the night, long after he'd already tucked himself into bed. But he had to admit he was excited to hear what the queen had said about the rift. Clint darted out into the living room to say hello and instantly started yapping.

"Well, look who it is!" a familiar voice slithered down the hall. "How are ya, Klipse?"

It felt like Miles' stomach had fallen out.

He had forgotten to lock the front door. He guiltily let out a swear word and inched backward into the corner of the room, not having anywhere else to go.

In the doorway two figures appeared, one twice the height of the other. It was Jericho and Kricket.

"There you are, you little runt," Kricket grinned devilishly, peering at Miles with his one good eye. The Omne's sneer was just as ugly as Miles remembered it from the tunnels. He appeared to have a new, tighter-fitting eye patch covering the left one. The stench of his berry cigarettes was already seeping into the room.

"I had no idea you were such trouble when we first met," Jericho seethed, taking a step into the bedroom. His jet-black goatee looked unkempt and his enormous pincer was caked in dried mud. They must have had to crawl through some portions of the marshes so as to not be spotted. The scene was not dissimilar from Miles' first meeting with the intimidating Skyr when he first arrived in Rompu. "I don't appreciate what you did to Vinzent or my men."

"I didn't do anything," Miles protested, not sure if he was lying or not. In retrospect, it was entirely possible he had been responsible for the storm at that camp nearly a month ago.

As Jericho ventured further into the room, his bulky tail rose up from behind his head and swung back and forth as if it were inspecting the surroundings. It was at that moment Miles realized that Clint had stopped barking almost half a minute earlier. His stomach sunk with fear for the maylan as he imagined Jericho snapping his pincer closed around Clint's neck.

Jericho held out a callused hand and motioned for Miles to come. "If you cooperate with us," he said, "I won't have to get my pal Kricket here to hurt you."

"We're pals?" Kricket asked hopefully.

Miles cast a glance at the Omne. "I already beat him up once before," he said quietly.

The Skyr stopped moving. He turned to look at Kricket.

"What?"

"What?" Kricket asked.

"Is he serious?"

"About what?"

"About beatin' you up."

"Uh, yeah. I guess so. I mean, c'mon, Jericho, he's the Spirit of the Flames. What do you expect from me?"

Jericho only stared down at his companion. Then he asked, "What the hell are you talkin' about? Spirit of the Flames? I swear to—" The Skyr cut himself off and faced Miles again, taking another step forward. "Whatever. Cooperate, and *I* won't have to hurt you."

Miles was really starting to regret not learning how to dissolve his fireballs. He knew he could possibly ward off Jericho and Kricket with them, but the cost was too high. He would probably set the entire room ablaze, getting himself killed anyway in addition to burning down the whole apartment and a section of the palace. Of course, there was also the option of trying a flaming punch like he had done to Kricket before, but he didn't know for sure how to replicate that and it ran the same risks. There was no way he could do that to these Rompuns that had given him so much. He had to cooperate.

He stood and got off the bed, cautiously nearing Jericho.

"No tricks," the Skyr scowled, edging closer. He scooped Miles up and held him to his chest. "Don't make a single peep," he warned. "You won't want me to have to squeeze any tighter."

Miles nodded.

Kricket led the way back to the front door, his stout body waddling around the sizable Rompun furniture. Slung over Jericho's shoulder, Miles could make out Clint's unmoving body slumped against one of the chair legs in the dining room.

The Omne was looking at Clint too. "Hey, Jericho, can we bring Klipse along?"

"No." Jericho sounded like he was at the end of his rope. It was apparent this pairing had been appointed by a higher authority rather than by choice.

"C'mon! He was my maylan first!"

"No," Jericho hissed, straining not to raise his voice.

Miles was glad that Clint wouldn't be falling into Kricket's hands again, and the fact that the Omne wanted to bring the animal along at all meant that he wasn't dead, just unconscious. Miles sighed deeply, pressure escaping from his chest. Jaselle would nurse Clint back to health in no time. Though Miles' touch would probably be much faster and more effective...

Defeated, Kricket peeked into the hallway to make sure nobody was patrolling or passing through. "We're clear," he said, exiting the apartment. Jericho followed, his bald head nearly scraping against the top of the doorframe.

"So what's the plan?" Kricket whispered.

"The plan is to get out of these disgusting marshes," Jericho said, "which will be tricky. Do as I say."

Kricket nodded and they set off down the hall. Miles' chin bumped against the rough fabric of Jericho's vest. The palace's exit was not very far from the apartment, but it would be foolish for a Skyr and an Omne to attempt strolling out the front door with so many guards posted right outside.

The halls were quiet, with not a single servant in sight. It was likely that many of them were off duty by now, and the ones who had night shifts were busy attending to Queen Alys and her guests at the dinner table. As they slunk toward a large metal door, Jericho whispered to the boy, "Remember what I said: not a peep."

Kricket produced a tiny watch from one of his pockets. It was a wristwatch with a faded brown face and a missing band. Satisfied with the current time, he returned it to his pocket. With a small, gray, scaly hand, he gently pushed the door open, reaching his jagged head inside to inspect the room. "Looks fine," he said to his accomplice.

They hurried inside, being sure not to make too much noise and arouse suspicion as they closed the door. It clicked shut.

The room was darkly lit and packed with machines that Miles couldn't identify. Some looked like washing machines and dryers; others were tall cylinders that reached to the ceiling. They set off across the room to a door on the other side. The wristwatch had been to ensure they arrived at this room when nobody was inside it. The whirring of the machines' inner workings buzzed through his brain as he tried to take his mind off what was happening.

A symphony of bugs greeted them as Kricket hastily swung the door open. The night air was thick and uncomfortable.

"What a relief," Kricket sighed, scratching his rough nape. From the same pocket that held his watch, he produced a cigarette carton and slid out one of the thin rolls of paper. Miles grimaced.

Jericho glared at the stocky Omne. "What are you doing?"

"...smoking," Kricket answered after a confused moment.

"We are in the middle of the Jesieu Marshes, in case you forgot," Jericho said. "Do you truly think it's the best idea to light up a cigarette and have the foul stink of those stupid eggs driftin' through the air so that everyone knows we're here?"

The cigarette dangled from Kricket's lips. He put it back in its carton with great resignation.

It was hard to determine their location in the dark. All of the trails in the marshes looked the same anyway, so in the black of night it was nearly impossible for Miles to tell where they were. Even if he managed to escape somehow, he wouldn't know where to run. That is, if he let Jericho carry him any farther away.

If he could manage to burn Jericho here, he could race back through the door and lock his kidnappers outside and then go warn the queen. This was his only chance.

His hands burned through the Skyr's vest almost instantly, scalding the smooth, tan skin underneath. Jericho screamed and dropped Miles to the ground, impulsively kicking the boy in the stomach. The remains of his tattered vest fluttered to the ground.

Miles threw a small fireball toward Jericho, which flew past his head and arced into a shallow pond several feet away, where it dissolved into steam. But the Omne was already at his side, holding a knife to his throat, just like the last time they'd met.

"That was stupid, kid," Kricket growled. After a second, he was swatted away by Jericho's gleaming pincer. Bits of crusty mud chipped off and bit at Miles' face. The Skyr kicked Miles onto his back, then opened his claw wide and dug it into the dirt around the boy's throat, pinning him to the ground.

"I told you no tricks," Jericho said, his breathing heavy and uneven. "That really hurt, by the way. I didn't wanna have to hurt you, but *damn* that really hurt."

The Skyr's pincer was so tight around Miles' neck, he could barely turn his head. He felt the dirt in his hair, on his neck. His staggered breaths matched Jericho's.

"I *did* tell you he's the Spirit of the Flames," Kricket said, lifting himself up. The knife had nicked his other arm and blood dripped down to his palm.

"Shut up!" Jericho barked in flagrant disregard of his own rule for keeping quiet. To Miles, he said, "Ain't time here, but don't think for even a second that I won't be makin' you regret pullin' that stunt."

Miles stared into Jericho's eyes for several agonizing moments, taking note of the arches of his eyebrows as he glowered in rage and discomfort. The burns on his back would take a long time to heal and possibly even scar.

"What are you gonna do to him, though?" Kricket asked curiously, breaking the tense silence. Jericho looked up at the Omne. Kricket stared back, patiently waiting for an answer.

"I hate you," Jericho told him.

"Well, that's hurtful."

The Skyr lifted his pincer, loose dirt splattering onto Miles' face. They both were still panting, but Jericho seemed to have not lost any of his strength. He lifted Miles off the ground with ease and stood him upright.

Miles saw an opportunity. He would have to act faster than he had the last time, though. This was his only second chance.

And then Jericho swung his meaty claw, smashing it into Miles' head, and everything went black.

It was still night when Miles came to.

With the moon's light obscured by the treetops, trying to make out the details of anything in the darkness was a waste of time. Miles was being carried by Jericho's two normal arms like a limp rug in front of the Skyr's body so that he would not bump up against the burns. Kricket was in the lead.

Miles had no idea how long he'd been knocked out and how far they had traveled. Considering he had flown to Trafier rather than walked through the swamp, he also didn't know how deep the city was nestled inside. It was equally likely that they were minutes from reaching the marsh's edge as they were hours. Or days.

Given his situation, it wouldn't do Miles any good to alert Jericho to the fact that he had woken up. If he did end up needing to attack, he would be better off having the element of surprise. But if that were to happen, he'd likely get lost trying to navigate back to the palace and eventually starve. He wanted to cry.

He wanted to scream.

He had to be brave.

He heard his mother's words: "It's alright."

But her words sounded like a lie. They bounced around in his head, distorting, buzzing like bees. It felt like bugs were sneaking down his spine. He tried to steady his breathing and hoped that Jericho would assume he was just having a nightmare.

Kricket and Jericho had been bickering about something, and finally the words were starting to come into focus. "You're wrong, though," Kricket said up ahead.

"No I'm not," Jericho grumbled. "There's absolutely no way a resort ticket for *one* person is less than a hundred bucks, let alone *two* people. You're insane."

"No I'm—"

"You're an idiot."

"No I'm—trust me, I've been to that lake plenty of times! My brother and I always went on vacations there before all this junk with the king and queen kicked off. It's a great place to meet ladies. All laid up lakeside, drinkin' their drinks…"

"I went there all the time. My camp was near the treeline of the woods. Only half a day's walk to Maulage, at most. My boys and I would stop by there for a few hours whenever we gathered supplies from Garn."

"Fine," Kricket muttered. "I'd believe you paid over a hundred for a group of you."

"Oh, we didn't pay anything. I threatened to tear the place down if that plump little fool of an Omne running the joint didn't let us in for free. But I saw the prices posted."

Fortunately, Kricket dropped the argument after that. Miles feared Jericho losing his temper and tearing the Omne apart if he pushed it any further. As little as Miles cared for Kricket, he did not want to see that.

As they trudged through the muck, Miles tried his hardest to figure out where they were, but everything looked the same as every other part of the marsh. Creepy trees, gross water, mossy boulders. All he knew for sure was that they were a good distance from the palace, since there appeared to be no distinguishable pathways, streetlights, or benches. Jericho's legs sloshed through murky water, ripping through lily pads and stomping the defenseless forn that swam like mad to escape the pillars crashing down. Kricket's body was much less destructive with the water level up to his chest and his tiny feet not raising up high enough to squash anything.

"Are we gonna set up camp?" Kricket inquired. "My legs are getting tired. They've been tired for a while now, if I'm being honest."

"No," Jericho replied, and Miles could feel him shake his head. "Too much risk of the child escaping. We need to keep goin' and walk through the night so we can get to the outpost."

The Omne let out an exasperated sigh. "I may die here," he declared. "Die of exhaustion."

"I can live with that," said Jericho.

"Can I at least smoke now? We're as far away from the city as we're gonna get."

"That ain't remotely true since we're still walking away from it, but go ahead."

Kricket gleefully muttered something in a different language as he pulled out his carton of cigarettes and lit one up. The berry-and-wood scent tickled Miles' nostrils and he had to stop himself from sneezing or coughing.

"Want one?" Kricket asked. The Skyr declined with ruder words than were necessary. Kricket scoffed and blew mediocre smoke rings.

Time inched by as Miles tried to devise a solution to his current predicament.

"I know it's hard, and weird," his mother told him, "but it'll be fun."

He was standing in the entryway to their house, his mother crouching down to look him in the eye. Squeaks from Ollie's new rubber ball came from the living room as the dog swatted and chewed it.

"But I don't want to," he told her.

"I'm just so tired," Kricket groaned. Miles heard the click of his lighter as he lit another cigarette. Miles did not think the Omne's safety was guaranteed if he continued to complain about their voyage; Jericho's temper was easy to ignite. For the moment, however, the Skyr remained silent and focused on his task of transporting the boy.

Suddenly Miles began to wonder whether Mortimer and Jaselle had returned to their apartment yet, only to discover Clint knocked out and him missing. If so, did that mean a search party was already combing through the marshes, seeking him out? Assuming that was the case, Miles suspected he had a fairly good chance of being tracked down by a friendly Rompun guard if he happened to elude his captors.

It was worth a shot.

He had to decide what type of magic would be most effective. Jericho had already shown that burns hardly fazed him, but using a lightning bolt had a much higher chance of harming himself. He would have to try fire again.

His mother smiled faintly at him in the entryway. The doorbell rang and Miles answered it, greeting his father.

"Hey, buddy," his father said in return.

Miles' whole body burst into flames at the thought. Jericho immediately tossed him away in panic, letting out a feral yelp as he did so.

Landing in the water extinguished the flames, but it hadn't done any damage to Miles' skin anyway. His clothes are charred and a bit ragged, but the water had put out the fire before they were completely burned away. As he stood, with the water up to his chest, he saw Jericho frantically splashing a couple feet away in an effort to soothe his fresh burns. Kricket was a short ways ahead of them and had swiveled around to investigate the commotion.

"You alright?" the Omne called back cluelessly. "What happened?"

"The boy!" Jericho shouted. "Grab him!"

It took that long for Kricket to even notice Miles was no longer in Jericho's possession. He made his way toward the child with as much haste as his weary body could muster.

"Don't make this any harder on yourself than it needs to be," Kricket said as he approached, his lip curled into a nasty snarl. Miles lifted his hands above his head and produced another fireball, which he threw at Kricket. The Omne ducked underwater, narrowly avoiding it.

Miles turned and sped away as fast as possible, but his progress was impeded by the surprising thickness of the water and the mud at its bottom. He brushed lily pads aside, nearly tangling his legs in their wiry web of stems. From the sounds of the splashing, Jericho had recovered and was now advancing toward Miles as well.

Kricket was already out of breath. "Just stop!" he pleaded.

But Miles conjured two more fireballs, one in each hand, pleased with himself at how effortless the magic was coming to him. He blindly lobbed them backwards, hoping at least one would hit its target. It was a disappointment when, instead of pained shouts, he heard the flames dissipate at the water's surface.

"Let's go," his father said.

The strip of muddy, grassy land was only a few feet away now, but so was Jericho. Miles could feel a breeze whip the back of his neck as Jericho swiped at him, just barely out of reach. It was probably safe to assume Kricket had given up.

Miles quickly lifted himself out of the water, the Skyr's blistered hand only inches from his foot as he climbed onto land. He swung his body around, fist already engulfed in flame, and connected with Jericho's face just as the Skyr reached the edge of the pond.

It wasn't much, since his weak punches didn't carry a lot of force, but it bought him a few precious moments. He turned and began running as fast as he could, following the curve of the path, trusting that it would bring him back to Trafier and Mortimer. Miles had a lot of energy pent up, and with an arduous trek already under his belt and mild-to-severe burns covering his upper body, there might actually be a good chance of Jericho wearing out first.

"Come on!" Miles heard the Skyr scream at Kricket, who was presumably not even on dry land yet.

Up ahead, the path forked; one branch led straight while the other veered to the right. Miles speedily processed which direction he had been running in relation to where he wanted to go, and came to the conclusion he should turn. He really hoped Jericho was too far back to see which way he'd chosen.

The path he had picked was already splitting in two again. He chose the left branch, and only a couple feet further was a tiny pond with a massive boulder submerged in its center, surrounded by lily pads and cattails. Without thinking, he dipped into the pond and waded through to the other side of the boulder, squatting down slightly so that his nose hovered just above the surface. He eyed the pathway and waited to see if Jericho had tracked him.

Swear words growing less and less faint indicated that the Skyr had indeed been on his trail. It only took a few seconds for him to appear before Miles, but he darted past the pond and continued down the path. Kricket was nowhere to be seen, but Miles wasn't sure if the Omne was bringing up the rear or not. It would be best not to get out of the water yet, especially if Jericho decided to double back and look down another pathway.

As expected, Kricket did not show up, but after only two or three minutes, Jericho returned. This time he was walking slowly and deliberately, meticulously eyeing the ground with each step. He came to a halt in front of the pond, staring down at his own feet.

Miles kept his body perfectly still, taking care not to send any ripples out through the pond that would give his location away.

"Believe it or not," Jericho said suddenly, a grin carved on his sharp face, "you're not as clever as you think you are."

The Skyr leapt into the air and crashed down into the pond next to Miles. Water exploded everywhere. He grabbed Miles' wrists and held them together with one of his hands. With the other, he held the boy by the neck and wove his stinger around to touch its tip to the back of Miles' head. It was a regrettably familiar scenario.

"You leave footprints in the mud, brat," Jericho laughed.

Miles struggled to free his arms, but it was no use. Jericho was too much stronger. He had tried and failed once again.

"You set us back a bit, but not by much," Jericho said, sliding his hand from Miles' throat to his ribs in order to lift the boy. He slung him over his shoulder once more, but this time he was sure to keep a firm grip on the kid's wrists. Miles could tell as Jericho sifted through the muddy water that the Skyr was physically drained.

"We'll find Kricket then move on. He's probably just standing in the same spot I left him." He stepped up out of the pond and grumbled, "Let's go."

They returned to Kricket's location and found the Omne laying on the ground, staring up at the cypress trees and smoking another cigarette.

"Get up."

Kricket scrambled to his feet and puffed on the white, rolled-up paper. "Hey," he said to them. "You found him. Good job."

Jericho allowed the group to rest for almost an hour before their journey continued. The burns and pursuit had tired him, and they were all well aware of how desperately Kricket longed to relax. It didn't take much time for the Omne to fall asleep, but Jericho kept his eyes on Miles even after tying the boy's hands together.

Once his captors felt properly rejuvenated, they set off again, sticking to their route through the water rather than on designated paths. Miles knew that at a certain point, the paths were controlled by the Skyr stationed at the entrance of the marshes, so maybe they weren't as far from Trafier as he originally thought. Maybe he would have made it back, if he hadn't tried to hide.

His mind went back to the image of Clint lying motionless in the kitchen. Tears welled in his eyes and raindrops slipped through the tree leaves above.

It was mid-afternoon the following day when they at last reached their destination.

There had only been one stop, hours before, so that Jericho and Kricket could eat breakfast. Miles had been allowed one piece of bread while the other two consumed various slices of meats and cheeses. The meat Jericho greedily stuffed in his mouth carried the same odor as the kreer Miles had eaten the night before, and the smell was intoxicating. His stomach gurgled with jealousy.

The Skyr camp they came to was a much larger operation than the one Miles had seen in the Violet Woods. It covered at least a square mile, if not more, with heavy fortifications surrounding its perimeter and several guards posted at the gate.

"Step aside," Jericho ordered the male and female Skyr guarding the entrance. "I'm tired and angry and I wanna get this nuisance off my hands."

Someone set in motion the machinations for opening the gate and the tall, iron doors lethargically crept open to reveal the inside of the camp, which had more in common with a small village than any campsite Miles had ever seen.

Numerous buildings had been erected throughout the area, some of them two or three stories tall and all built with what looked like high-quality materials. The fire pit, located in the center of the outpost, was easily three times the size of the one in the other camp, so even more men were able to circle around it and roast their food.

Far off in the distance, against the back wall, Miles saw cages just like the one he'd been imprisoned in. They held three Rompuns and two Ruhigans, whom Miles recognized as Felix and Sahen. They would be relieved to learn that Mortimer had survived the Veratt's attack, if Miles ever got the chance to speak with them, which he doubted. It took Miles a second to notice that Felix was missing an arm. He would never be able to fly on his own again. The realization pained Miles and he felt hatred toward King Mykael and the Veratt all over again.

Jericho lugged Miles past the fire pit toward a building near the back of the camp. Kricket still followed closely behind them, waving to a young, bearded Omne who was sitting by the fire and cooking a kebab.

As they neared the tallest building in the camp, its door swung open and a shorter Skyr with just one normal arm beckoned them inside. His other arm had been severed at the elbow. "Welcome back, sir," he said to Jericho, who returned the salutation.

"Do you have the room prepared?" Jericho asked. "The kid is just as irritating as this idiot described," he said, gesturing toward Kricket, who stared blankly at a clock hanging from the wall.

"Yes, sir," the one-armed Skyr responded. "Did you have any trouble entering Trafier?"

"No, it was pretty simple," Jericho told him. "We actually followed some jackass Rompun through a hidden entrance. I'll talk to you and Nyre about how we can best launch an invasion on the city. Come to the meeting room after dinner."

The other Skyr nodded then led them deeper into the building. They came to a brightly-lit room painted white that held a cage with thick iron walls. There was no way to see inside except for one glass windowpane on its door. Miles' stomach twisted.

"Good," Jericho said, examining the iron cube that would confine the boy. "He's capable of more than I expected. I thought the Omne had been exaggerating in his reports, but he wasn't." He tightened his grip, digging his nails into Miles' wrists.

"He can really make fire outta nothing but his bare hands?" the other Skyr asked, casting doubtful eyes upon Miles.

"Yep," Jericho confirmed. "Got the burns to prove it. Open the door."

Jericho's comrade did as he was told, pulling open the heavy door to reveal there was absolutely nothing on the other side. Not a pillow, a blanket, a metal slab. Just nothing.

Miles was thrust forward violently and the door slammed shut behind him.

"Get some rest tonight," he could barely hear Jericho tell him through the thick walls. "We're settin' off again in the morning. Dinner's in four hours."

The door locked with a click. Miles stood in the middle of the iron box with nothing to look at or do.

So he sat down and waited.

CHAPTER FOURTEEN

RIDE

There was a rumbling in Miles' stomach, an ache from hunger that he had never experienced in his nine years. The dinner the Skyr had provided for him was nothing but half a leftover zol, two dried forn, and some sort of leaf to wrap it all up in. The leaf appeared to have been cleaned, so he ate it and then wished he hadn't after experiencing its bitter taste. When the door to his cell creaked open the next morning, he hoped it would be an Omne with a tray of fresh fruits. Instead, he got the one-armed Skyr.

"Get up."

"I'm hungry."

The scorpion-man laughed, his tail peeking over his left shoulder. Its stinger was pinpointed at Miles. "Don't care," he said. "Get up. You've got a long walk ahead of you."

Miles knew there was no point in arguing. He did as he was told and followed the Skyr through the halls and back into the lobby of the building, where Jericho was waiting for them. He was hunched over a table and scribbling something down on a yellowed piece of paper.

"Sir."

Jericho looked up and smirked, eyeing Miles. "Thank you, Risath. How you doin', kid?"

"I'm hungry," Miles repeated.

The one-armed Skyr, Risath, chuckled. It was a weird sound. "You want me to get him something to eat, sir? I don't particularly care if the kid's stomach wails all day, but he might be a better companion if his belly's full. Won't complain the entire way there."

Jericho nodded in agreement and commanded one of the Omnes milling about the office to fetch some food. Turning his attention back to Miles, he grinned and reached for a length of rope that rested on the table beside him. "I ain't gonna deal with your nonsense today," he said. He instructed Miles to hold his arms out.

Miles complied and Jericho looped the rope around his wrists, tightening it until Miles was sure his hands would snap off. The Skyr tied a neat knot and checked his handiwork.

"Seems like he's less able to do any of his magic when he's constrained," Jericho explained to Risath. "It all comes out of his hands or something." He got back to writing on his paper.

As Miles gave it a closer look, it appeared to be a map of the Jesieu Marshes. Numerous squiggly lines originated at a black box marked Camp and trailed through various sections of the swamp, all of them colliding at a rectangle labeled Trafier.

Miles swallowed.

Jericho folded the weathered parchment in half and handed it to another Omne, the bearded one Miles had seen the night before.

"Bring this to Yoren. Tell him to hold off initiating the plan until after I've sent word back. Got it?"

The Omne affirmed and left the three of them alone.

"The carts should be nearly ready," Risath said. "The Carriers have all been fed and washed. They're ready for the trip. And I made sure to stock your cart with plenty of liquor and kreer. Need anything else?"

"No, that'll be fine. Go get ready to leave. We'll be headin' out as soon as this pest is finished eating."

Risath took his leave. A sliver of sunlight crept onto Miles' arm for a brief moment as the door opened and closed. He daydreamed about the kreer meat in Jericho's cart; its aroma was probably already filling all the holes and cracks in the wood. Though he figured it wasn't likely they'd be sharing a cart, and even less likely that the Skyr would share his food anyway.

The first Omne returned with a few grapes and roasted cherry tomatoes on a cracked ceramic plate. "It was all I could find," the Omne shrugged. "I guess the guys were hungry this morning."

Jericho sighed. "It's fine. I'll give him some of my food," he resigned. "Better that than hear him whine all day. You can go now." Alone again, Jericho set the plate down on the table and motioned for Miles to eat. "We're in a hurry."

With limited mobility, Miles slowly maneuvered the food into his mouth. He wasn't really a fan of tomatoes, but had reached the point where he would eat anything if it meant satiating his demanding stomach. Chewing a mouthful of the soft, juicy tomatoes, he asked, "Where are we going?"

"To see King Mykael," Jericho answered. "He's interested in meeting you."

This puzzled Miles. Most of all, he was stunned that the Skyr king even knew who he was in the first place. "Why?"

Jericho scoffed at the question. "Are you joking? Did you see the trouble you put me through yesterday?" He yanked on the collar of his shirt, revealing the burns that marred his chest. "The king is *very* interested in meeting you."

Miles mulled over the Skyr's words. He also decided to see if he would enjoy the tomatoes more if he ate one in conjunction with a grape, and discovered it tasted even worse and was also a waste of a grape.

Once Miles cleared his plate, Jericho told him to leave it on the table and ushered him outside. The sun was blinding after so much time stuck indoors. The camp was bustling, with Skyr and Omnes alike rushing about. Miles understood why all the grass underfoot had died and given way to dirt. Near the entrance of the outpost were three wooden carts, each hitched to a separate Carrier. Miles gasped as he passed by the animals.

They had all been mutilated. Their impressive wings had been amputated, leaving nothing but scabbed stumps on their backs.

The middle Carrier began to huff as he walked by, and upon closer examination Miles realized it was Io, the Carrier he had ridden to Trafier. He shuddered to think that the creature would never cut through the skies again. Io's tusks were also pared down, made duller. The poor animal had to be miserable.

"You'll ride with me until our first break," Jericho told Miles, coming to a stop beside the door of the front wagon. "That way you can eat some of my food and get your strength up a toonce. Can't have you keelin' over before you even reach the king."

An Omne sat atop a short bench at the front of the cart. At his side were a canteen and a whip, awaiting use. The stout, gray lizard-person drummed his cracked fingernails on the wood.

While Jericho and Miles made themselves as comfortable as possible inside the body of the cart, Kricket's face suddenly appeared in the window. "Can I come?" his floating head asked.

"I'd rather you didn't," Jericho replied.

"I know, but I really want to."

"I'd rather you didn't," Jericho said again.

"C'mon!" Kricket begged, disregarding the authority Jericho held over him. Miles would have never guessed Jericho was the outfit's leader based on how casual and sometimes flippant Kricket had acted toward him in the swamp. "I won't even stay in your wagon. I'll ride in the next one. You won't even know I'm here."

Jericho sighed. "Will agreeing to this shut you up?"

"Yes. Probably."

"Fine. Go ride with Risath."

"Thank you!" Kricket smiled gleefully. His face vanished and Miles heard him scamper away.

Jericho exhaled loudly and reached above their heads, where two shelves held several containers and sacks. He pulled down a thick, silver container and popped off its lid.

"What do you want?" he asked.

"What is there?"

"Slices of kreer, cubes of white cheese, a few apples, crackers, uh…a lot of other stuff. What do you want?" he asked again.

"Some kreer," Miles said. He took two slices and ate them before the Carriers had even commenced their slow march to wherever their destination was.

The wagon creaked with their weight and bounced on the uneven paths they followed. Every couple of minutes, the silence was interrupted by the cracking of the Omne's whip. Miles frowned at the thought of Io being so cruelly thrashed.

As he bit down on one of the crisp, chilled apples, Miles was reminded of riding in his father's car down the highway in the nighttime. Lights from cars up ahead blurred into fuzzy circles, abstract red and orange brightening then dimming. Rain beat against the windshield and the air conditioner blew too-cold air on his face.

"You'll like it," his father said.

"Okay." His voice barely audible above the pellets of rain hitting the car. He didn't feel much like talking. He dug his hand into the Ziploc bag of apple slices his mother had packed him.

"Is everything okay?"

"Yeah." Miles tried reading the highway signs, but he was too sleepy. He missed Ollie already. Then he said, "I don't understand where we're going."

"We're heading toward the Eastern Sea. That's all you need to know," Jericho told him.

"Are we going to the Violet Woods?"

"You're more talkative than when we first met. I don't like it. But no, we ain't. Especially not after you burned down my whole camp and made me have to go fetch you in that disgusting swamp. Just shut up and eat your apple." He popped a cube of cheese into his mouth, smacking his lips as he chewed. He had trimmed his goatee at some point the night before.

Another crack of the whip.

The Omne at the head of their carriage shrieked, *"Hurry on, you tubby beast!"*

Miles wondered how Io was doing. He began to suspect that the other two Carriers were also with their party when the Veratt had struck. The lucky few that survived now had to suffer the indignity and agony of having their wings clipped.

"Why did you cut off the Carriers' wings?" Miles asked.

Jericho rolled his eyes. "What's it matter? Nothin' you can do about it."

"I just wanna know why," Miles said. "I knew these Carriers. They brought me to Trafier."

The Skyr laughed, leaning forward. His breath was warm and sour. "We cut them off so they couldn't fly away. Now they're ours. They won't be flyin' back up to the Ruhigans in their little mountain huts." He chomped down on another piece of cheese and leaned back.

The small caravan didn't stop until mid-afternoon. Jericho allowed Miles to step outside and stretch his legs, joining the other Skyr and Omnes that accompanied them. Risath looked shaken as he meandered toward Jericho.

"Did I piss you off?" Risath asked, his breaths short.

"Nope," said Jericho.

"Then why would you do something so awful to me?"

Both Jericho and Miles were confused until they spotted Kricket ambling out of the cart. Jericho laughed heartily.

"Well I couldn't have him stuck in my wagon, could I?"

"Very funny."

While everybody else ate outdoors, Jericho consumed his meal concealed inside the cart while he toiled away on something, jotting down notes on a pad full of crinkled pages. Miles sat leaning against Io's side while the Carrier lay in the grassy field, resting her legs. Her breaths heaved Miles forward and back while she slept. It was strangely soothing.

Risath and some low-ranking Skyr soldier sat nearby, talking and eating while ensuring Miles didn't try to escape. He could see Kricket sitting cross-legged in the distance, eating a sandwich by himself. Judging by the people he'd seen during their lunch break, the wagon bringing up the rear held three Skyr, which made Kricket the only Omne in the group besides the drivers.

When it was time for everyone to load back up, Miles was herded into the cart Risath and Kricket occupied. Jericho would be on his own for the duration of the trip. Miles felt a sort of comfort in knowing that it would be Io pulling him along now.

Miles felt uncomfortable sitting on the bench next to Kricket, but Risath refused to sit beside either of them.

"Hey there," Kricket greeted Risath.

"Don't start," the Skyr snarled.

The hours that passed were tense and tedious. Miles didn't open his mouth once. Kricket rarely did so, but when he did, his comments were always met with derision from Risath. The Skyr's response to the simple, innocent question of whether or not he had ever visited the Maulage Lakeside Resort was an affirmation followed by a curt insult. After that, Kricket kept quiet for a long while.

Miles remained silent as he sat in the car with his father. He knew the trip was not as long as it felt, because the clock on the dashboard had only changed from 8:02 to 8:25 when his father announced, "We're almost there."

He would be glad to get out of the car and turn the television on. If there was even a television to watch yet. "Is there a TV?" he decided to ask.

His father snickered. "Yeah, I hooked the TV up, don't worry. Is something you like on tonight? We can watch it together."

"Not really," Miles said. "I was just gonna flip through." Another thought suddenly popped into his head. "Are pets allowed?"

"Oh, yeah, I made sure of that," his father replied. "Ollie will definitely be coming. The place has Ollie and television, so you should be good to go."

Miles feigned a smile.

A shiver went down his spine as he heard their Omne driver lash out at Io. Miles had thought he'd feel better being with Io, but hearing the whips was much harder on him now.

A light drizzle had begun to fall and thunder rumbled overhead, which was making the Carriers nervous, presumably because they were accustomed to avoiding flight during such conditions. Thinking that he might be the cause of the rain made Miles feel guilty.

"Come on, it's just a bit o' rain!" the chubby Omne shouted. The smoke from his cigarette wafted into the wagon.

"I could really use a cigarette," Kricket declared, his snout pointing up and sniffing the smoke. Risath had already banned smoking inside, which Miles was grateful for.

Miles decided to pass the time by sleeping, but unluckily for him that meant by the time the group was ready to stop for the night and pitch a campsite, he wasn't the least bit tired. Four tents were set up near each other, surrounded by the wagons and slumbering Carriers. The animals wore chain leashes that were linked to a metal contraption pinned securely into the ground to ensure they couldn't escape.

Jericho had his own sleeping arrangements while Risath and Kricket were clumped together in one tent, with the three other Skyr in another tent and the three Omne drivers bunking together in the last one. Miles, who was not trusted enough to stay in an easily-opened tent while everybody slept, was locked inside their carriage for the night with no pillow and one thin blanket. It was more like a napkin than a blanket, and it did a poor job of keeping the night's cool breeze from chilling the young boy. He lay on the stiff wooden bench with the red blanket draped over him, dreaming about Clint and Ollie's warmth.

The next day brought much of the same.

The rope wrapped snugly around Miles' wrists was starting to irritate his skin, producing a light red rash that itched incessantly. He tried to concentrate and burn the rope away, but he was unsuccessful. For some reason, he was unable to use his magic when he couldn't move his arms freely. If Cléoma was correct about the extent of his powers, though, and he was able to create water, then his hands being tied had seemingly no effect on that ability, seeing as rain continued to fall throughout the day. He was under the assumption that it was his own doing, rather than a natural occurrence.

He spent lunchtime laying against Io again while she fed on some grass. Kricket waddled over to where he sat with two plates of food in hand. "Here," he said, handing one to Miles. It contained a piece of hardened bread, a charred zol—evidently the most common creature to find and kill in Rompu—and some grapes.

The grapes were the first thing Miles reached for. "Thanks," he said to the Omne. To his surprise, Kricket took the token of appreciation as an invitation to join him. His own plate was a lot fuller than Miles'.

Kricket grabbed the handful of grapes rolling around on his plate and dropped them onto the boy's. "I don't like fruit much," he said, grabbing his cooked zol. "I don't like getting seeds stuck in my teeth. Irritates me. Hurts my gums. I've got sensitive gums, y'know."

"Most grapes don't have seeds," Miles told him.

This painted astonishment on Kricket's reptilian face. "Where'd you hear that?" he asked incredulously.

"My parents told me. And also, I've eaten them."

"Hmph." Kricket pierced the skin of one of the purple ovals with his long fingernail and cautiously slid it into his mouth. He gnashed the piece of fruit with his sharp teeth. Nodding, he said, "Not bad."

"Do you want your grapes back?"

"Nah, the taste ain't great neither. You can have 'em."

Miles thanked him again. The rain had started to let up. Io was enjoying the dewy grass.

They sat side by side, chewing their meat and bread methodically, with Miles timing it so that he would be putting a new piece of food into his mouth as Kricket was swallowing so that they wouldn't have to converse. The strategy only worked for half the meal before Kricket decided to pipe up.

"Are there any other fruits without seeds in 'em?" he asked. His voice was low. "Maybe I'll try 'em out."

"Bananas," Miles answered after thinking it over. "I dunno if there are any others. Sorry."

"That's alright," Kricket said. "I'll try to find a banana somewhere. Maybe they've got some at the Maulage resort.

Never seen them there before, but who knows? Maybe they're just now in season."

Miles nodded then asked, "Is that where we're going? The resort you keep talking about?" He couldn't stop himself from staring at the Omne's eye patch as he spoke.

"Nah, I just like it. The place we're going is near it, though. Only half a day's walk, I'd guess."

"Oh. Is that why you wanted to come with us? So you can go to the resort?"

Kricket laughed. "No, though I wouldn't mind checkin' out their prices to see if that know-it-all Jericho is right or not. But nah, my buddy Gryff is at the outpost we're going to." He tore off a large chunk of bread and gulped it down without chewing. "You remember Gryff, I'm sure," he said, spitting out crumbs.

Miles did indeed remember him from the mountain tunnels. Gryff was the first person Miles had ever used his fire magic against, which had been a shock to the both of them when his vest was lit on fire. Miles nodded meekly.

"He's still a little banged up," Kricket said. "Not from your fire or anything, though that did leave some scars. But your big Rompun pal throwin' him around like a doll and some dang rocks collapsin' on his legs didn't do him any favors either. Still can't walk."

Miles almost instinctively gave an apology, but caught himself. Then he realized he really was sorry, so he said it. He took a bite of his bread, which tasted like herbs and was tough to chew. He nearly spit it out, but didn't want to offend any Skyr that might be watching. Behind him, Io let loose the groan of a full belly and placed her head down on the grass, rubbing her shaggy face in it. Her stubby tusks kicked up some dirt.

"Why don't you eat with the other Omnes?" Miles asked, setting his plate down. He had eaten all the grapes and a good portion of the zol and was still mildly hungry, but he couldn't take much more of the food. He was tired of receiving everyone's leftovers.

Kricket shrugged, vigorously chewing his last piece of meat. "Don't care for them, and the Skyr don't care for me. Risath, especially." They both chuckled.

The Omne who drove their wagon kicked Io in the side to wake her up. She woke with a yelp, startled but not hurt. Her hide was too thick for the petite creature's boot to do any real damage.

Once again, Miles sat across from Risath while Kricket lounged by his side, staring out the window.

Outside, Miles watched infrequent cars speed past as his father merged into the right-hand lane. He flicked his blinker on.

"See that building?" he asked, pointing ahead. Miles nodded absentmindedly. "That's it."

"Cool," Miles said, attempting to muster up the appropriate amount of enthusiasm. The word sounded frail and unconvincing.

They pulled into the parking lot of the apartment complex, passing an illuminated sign with letters that Miles couldn't make out in the dark. He didn't really care what the place was called anyway. His father parked in a spot under an awning that protected them from the rain as they stepped out. Miles' backpack was slung over his shoulder. It was a swift jaunt from the car to the stairwell.

"We got lucky with a space on the first floor," his father said, wiping raindrops from his hair. He led his son down the short hallway to a red door on the left.

Before sticking his key in the door, he wiped his shoes off on the welcome mat. Miles' face scrunched up, noticing it was nothing like their old doormat.

His father pushed open the door and gestured for Miles to go inside. "We have arrived," he said. "Welcome to our new abode."

It was another half a day of travel before the caravan reached its destination, which was the rim of a cluster of hills that surrounded a village called Garn, which bordered Lake Maulage.

The hills were like something out of a painting. They didn't seem real. Too perfect to exist. The grass was a delightful shade of green and it swayed peacefully in the gentle breeze. The sun peeked out from behind some of Garn's taller buildings in the distance, igniting the sky in rich purple and orange hues as it gave way to the moon.

But Miles was confused. There wasn't really anything in sight except for grassy hills and smoke rising from chimneys far away. This place was no different from the other featureless fields they had slept in the night before.

Then Risath marched forward, his gait confident and purposeful. He stopped about ten or fifteen feet ahead, bent down, and lifted up a square patch of land. Miles' brow furrowed. There was a secret passageway.

Risath began to climb down a ladder affixed to the side of the tunnel that burrowed underground. The Skyr followed suit, with Kricket, Jericho, and Miles bringing up the rear. Jericho ordered the Omne drivers to take their Carriers to the stables, and the stocky lizard-men led the animals away through the hills.

As Kricket made his way down the rungs of the ladder, Jericho picked Miles up and draped him over his shoulder like he had in the Jesieu Marshes. Evidently he still couldn't be trusted with the full use of his arms. Jericho pulled down the square of earth and locked the latch before beginning their descent.

Nearly four or five full minutes of climbing took place before they finally reached the bottom, and Miles couldn't even venture a guess as to how deep in the ground they were now.

The air was hot and stuffy, and the walls felt like they were closing in. Miles followed Kricket through a tunnel with Jericho not far behind. The pathway was largely a straight shot, with only a slight bend to the left after about ten minutes. When they reached the expansive opening at the end of their path, Miles was amazed by how similar the layout of the underground camp was to the one stationed outside the swamp. They were nearly identical.

"Go on," said Jericho, shoving Miles forward.

They walked toward the building that looked exactly the same as the one where Miles had been kept in the metal cell overnight.

"It's time for you to meet the king."

CHAPTER FIFTEEN

SPLIT APART

The first time Miles set foot in the new apartment, he was taken aback by how empty it was.

The entryway led straight into the living room, which contained nothing but an entertainment center with a wide-screen television resting on top. There was no sofa, coffee table, or any other kind of furniture in the room. It was barren.

"I haven't quite gotten everything moved in yet," his father said, locking the door. He placed his keys on a countertop that granted a view into the kitchen. "Want anything to drink?" he asked, heading for the fridge. Miles declined.

He wandered into the center of the room and sat down on the floor, gazing up at the television. He blinked at himself in the dark reflection, moving his arm up and down and watching his mirror self do the same.

"Wanna watch something?" His father didn't wait for a response before switching the television on. The mirrored Miles evaporated into an image of a glass being filled with orange juice. They watched the screen together for only a couple minutes before Miles stood and asked where his room was.

"This way. Pick up the pace," Jericho growled, leading Miles up several flights of stairs then down a narrow hallway. The boy's arms were still tied together and his fingers were turning a light shade of purple.

At the end of the hall was a dark brown door, crafted from the same material as the wagons they had rode to the camp in. It was worn down, marred with deep scratches and discoloration. Jericho loudly knocked twice with his pincer. The claw looked a lot scarier without mud obscuring it.

There was a muffled shout from inside. "Jericho, Your Majesty," Jericho responded to the faint words. After another syllable Miles couldn't understand, Jericho turned the gold handle and opened the door.

Miles was not expecting the infamous King of the Skyr to be so plain.

The man was dressed like every other Skyr Miles had encountered, which was perhaps understandable given the fact that he was in hiding and not sitting on a throne. He didn't really have a need for fancy attire. He stood behind a mahogany desk, with ink-black hair that fell down to his square shoulders. He had a thicker beard than Miles had seen on a Skyr, but it was well-groomed and gave the man an air of wisdom and authority that neither Jericho nor Risath possessed. Of his four arms, two had pincers; both sides of his torso had one of each, with the clawed arms above his normal ones. This, coupled with his ordinary clothing, made him appear to be combat-ready at a moment's notice.

"Jericho," he said in greeting.

The Skyr bowed. Miles stood motionless. When Jericho rose, he shot a venomous glance at the boy.

A vintage record player rested on a small side table in the corner of the room with a stack of vinyl on the floor beside it. Nothing was playing.

"So," the king said, circumventing his desk to approach them, "this is him. The 'Spirit of the Flames,' as Kricket and Gryff called him."

"Yes, King Mykael—"

Within a flash, the king was upon Jericho, slamming the Skyr's body into the wall and holding him by the throat.

"I did not ask you anything, and you will not open your mouth unless I explicitly tell you to," Mykael exploded with a rage in his voice and features that was not so much as hinted at the second before.

Jericho said nothing.

"Is that clear? Or do I need to snap your neck?"

"Yes, Majesty, it's clear," Jericho sputtered. Mykael released him, and he began to massage his throat. He glared at Miles.

The boy couldn't piece together what had just happened or why. There must have been some tension between the two that he hadn't been privy to. The king took a step toward Miles, his tail swinging back and forth, stinger pointed upward at the ceiling.

"I want to see it," King Mykael said.

Without hesitation, Jericho untied the knot that bound Miles' arms together. As the rope dropped to the floor with a thud, Miles hurriedly rubbed his sore wrists.

"Go on," the towering Skyr urged him. The stinger was now pointed directly at Miles.

Taking a gulp, Miles shakily raised his hands. Jericho slanted his eyes as if to say, *Don't even think about attacking us.* Miles had absolutely no desire to attempt such a feat, especially after seeing how violently the king had reacted to Jericho for no discernible reason.

Miles said softly, "I don't know how to make it go away once I make it. I usually just threw it in a pond. I think I'd set the room on fire."

The king shrugged. "Just punch Jericho, then."

Jericho's eyes widened, darting back and forth between his king and the young boy standing before them. Miles hoped Jericho recognized the apprehension in his face.

"Go on," Mykael motioned toward Jericho. "I want to see it."

Miles' father brought him down a short hallway and into a cramped bedroom. "Here it is," he said.

The room was more furnished than the den, at least, which Miles was thankful for. It had a bed tucked in the corner, a dresser near the closet, and a small bookshelf on the wall opposite the bed with a lone DVD resting on the middle shelf. Miles went over to investigate.

The case was shorter than a regular DVD and had a blue border. The picture had a background the color of sand, with nine brown silhouettes under the title The Wild Bunch. He looked to his father.

"It's a blu-ray," he said, scratching his beard. "It looks and sounds better than a normal movie. I already hooked up the blu-ray player in the living room, if you wanna watch that with me. Sound fun?"

Miles shrugged. "Okay," he conceded, balling one of his hands into a fist. He was nervous; he didn't want to upset the king. He swung and it connected with Jericho's abdomen, burning through the measly cotton shirt and singeing the tanned flesh. Miles had to admit he felt a pang of satisfaction in the act.

Jericho coughed up obscenities while he patted the small flame away. King Mykael clapped and laughed manically.

"Wow," he said, looking down at Miles. "That was impressive. Really. Those Omnes weren't exaggerating at all."

Jericho bared his teeth as if to comment, but decided against it. After all, Miles had been under strict orders to throw the punch. It would have been foolish to refuse.

"Hit him again," the king then said.

But this made Miles uneasy. He looked over at Jericho, who held a hand to the burned flesh on his chest. The Skyr had already taken a good beating from the kid over the past few days.

"Do it!" Mykael screamed, and Miles obeyed without a second thought.

He slammed his fist into Jericho's left arm. They both yelled out in pain. As the flames subsided, Miles rubbed his aching knuckles. Some of them had started to bleed.

"Again!" the king clapped with mad glee. "In the jaw, this time! C'mon!"

"I can't," Miles objected. It didn't feel right.

"Do it." The same booming pitch.

So he did it.

Jericho's body was littered with scorch marks as the kid continued to pound him at the king's behest. When he was finally allowed to stop, Jericho slumped down in the corner of the room, his breaths staccato. Each strike had elicited a boisterous laugh from King Mykael, who now returned to sit behind his desk. "Jericho," he said to the weary Skyr, "you can leave."

Struggling to stand, Jericho asked, "Do you want me to take the boy, Your Majesty?"

"No, he's staying for now. I wanna talk to him."

"Yes, Majesty." Jericho left the room without even a passing glance at Miles.

The door clicked shut. "That was fun," Mykael sighed merrily.

Miles didn't speak. He frowned, feeling vulnerable and uncomfortable about being left alone in a room with the psychotic king. It was no wonder he and Queen Alys hadn't been getting along.

"This is fun, right?" Miles' father asked, passing the bowl of popcorn to his son.

Miles nodded, his attention more focused on the movie than what his father was saying. The two of them were seated on the carpet, leaning their backs against stacks of pillows with a large blanket thrown over their legs.

On the screen, children laughed and smiled as they poked at a scorpion that had been rolled around in a swarm of fire ants. Names of men Miles didn't know flashed across the screen as he watched the tiny red insects crawl all over the scorpion's body, biting at it as it swung its tail around hopelessly, trying desperately to pierce them with its stinger and flee. The kids giggled at its worthless attempts. Miles was glad this scene came at the start of the film so that they could move past it quickly and he could enjoy himself more, but the image of the scorpion struggling beneath a perpetually bustling red mass would stay imprinted in his mind throughout the entirety of the movie. He didn't care if it was a metaphor.

"Sorry," Mykael said. "Let's get right to it: you're gonna use your magic to capture the Veratt for me."

"I thought the Veratt was yours," Miles sputtered. "You summoned it."

"I summoned it, yes, but does it really seem like I control that thing? It's too volatile, too powerful. I don't have any more control over it than that numbskull Kricket does. I haven't had a grasp on it for even one second since I brought it here.

"But you have power. Power no one else has. I sent Jericho and Kricket to fetch you as soon as I saw those scorch marks all over Gryff. You're somethin' special."

Miles shook his head. "I don't wanna help you."

Mykael groaned. "I don't care if you want to or not. You're going to. That's that. I'm not gonna threaten to kill you, because it'd be a false threat and we both know that. Instead, let's talk about some good, old-fashioned bribery. What do you want?"

"I wanna go home," Miles blurted out. He immediately felt foolish and wanted to take it back. He didn't want to make a deal.

"Home. Great. Where's home for a weird little pink thing like you?"

"...Austin," Miles answered reluctantly. "It's in Texas. I think I'm from another world, like the Veratt." The words felt strange on his lips.

The king brightened. "Well, if I ripped the Veratt from some other dimension, I'm sure I could toss your scrawny self into another one."

"How did you get it here?" Miles asked, hoping the answer would shed some light on how he had appeared in the middle of the Violet Woods.

King Mykael's face hardened. He was growing weary of this conversation. "Found an old text on the subject of other worlds and the rifts that can be opened to connect them," he replied coldly. "A bunch of stuff my wife deemed 'nonsense,' stuff she was afraid of. Wanted me to stop researching, thought I was obsessing. But I didn't listen." His mouth curled into a harsh grin, exposing sharp teeth. "So after countless hours of research and fruitless attempts, I finally succeeded."

"But why would you even want it here?"

There was a noticeable shift in the king's expression, a softening of his features. His eyebrows sloped downward and his mouth curved in a slight frown. He breathed heavily, as if he had just run a mile.

"It was an accident. Honest. I just wanted to open a rift, see if I could do it. See what was on the other side. But that *thing* came through, and I couldn't stop it. I couldn't stop the massacres."

The words were meek and regretful. Mykael sat back down and placed his hands on his desk, waiting a moment before grabbing a pen and sketching aimlessly in a notebook.

"So why do you want to capture it?" Miles asked, his voice soft. This shift in the king's attitude definitely made him more approachable, but he couldn't help feeling like the man was unhinged. He had turned on Jericho almost instantly, and Miles wouldn't be surprised if the same thing happened again in a moment.

"Capture it?" Mykael muttered, looking up. "I want it dead. I believe your magic is the only thing strong enough to destroy it."

"But a minute ago you said—"

"Forget what I said a minute ago," the king interrupted. His voice grew frantic. "Listen *right now*, this is all that matters.

No matter what else I say or ask, please kill the Veratt. *Kill*. It's hard for me to push through sometimes, but *this* is me."

The king set his pen down, looking dejectedly at the picture he had drawn. It was a rough sketch of the Veratt with its wings outstretched, mouth agape in a terrible screech. He crumpled up the paper and threw it into a plastic trash can.

"Opening a rift, it...takes a toll on a person. They can affect you in extraordinary ways. A side effect of being too close, maybe. When I cast that spell, it—I don't know, it ripped me apart. My head is always filled with a thick fog now."

"What do you mean it ripped you apart?" Miles asked, though he had a suspicion. Based on the king's behavior, it was as if there were two men trapped in that same body, like his mind had been torn in two when he opened the rift.

"Nevermind what I meant," the king snarled, his eyes once again piercing. "Point is, you and I were both changed by those rifts. So if you use your new talents to subdue the Veratt for me, help tame the thing, then I'll tear open another portal and send you home. You can go up above ground to train, to harness your skills, if you want. You'll be supervised, of course. Can't have you runnin' off back to Trafier. We got a deal?"

The conflicting requests clearly demonstrated what Mykael said about being split apart. Two personalities were warring inside his mind, struggling for full control of the broken man. He was far too erratic for Miles' comfort. But killing the Veratt was a much more appealing goal than handing it over to the insane king. If opening the rift was the cause of the king's severe mental damage, perhaps eliminating the Veratt would reverse the effects, or at least begin to repair his mind. Then maybe he could return to Queen Alys and Rompu could stop the war with itself. Everything would go back to how it was before.

Miles still felt uncomfortable with the agreement, and he couldn't be entirely sure which side of the king he was talking to at any given moment, but he was aware of the opportunity being presented to him. "So if I help you with the Veratt," he clarified, "you'll open a rift back to Austin?"

Mykael nodded. "If that's what you want."

"I just wanna go back to where everything's normal," Miles sighed.

"I know you do, buddy," his father said, tucking the boy into bed. He ruffled his hair before moving to the doorway. "See you in the morning," he said. "Love you. Goodnight."

"Goodnight," Miles said back.

As his father closed the door, all light vanished from the room. Only a sliver remained in the thin space between the carpet and door. A peek into the outside world.

It took Miles over an hour to fall asleep.

CHAPTER SIXTEEN

THEORIES

The hills above ground were a light, unnatural green, a shade that Miles had never seen before except in a box of crayons. In the distance, smoke rose from brick chimneys behind the humps of grass.

Miles was only allowed outside under the supervision of Risath, who always remained no more than five feet away at most. Other Skyr and Omnes usually accompanied them in case Miles tried to make a run for it. Kricket was a member of the revolving cast of watchers more often than not, but Gryff was never with him. Perhaps he didn't particularly care to see the child that had given him such a lashing, or maybe it was just too much effort to climb the extremely long ladder with extremely broken legs.

But now that Miles was finally attempting to craft lightning, he was having absolutely no luck. It wasn't coming as naturally to him as the fire had. It was necessary to tap into a different part of himself for each type of magic, and he was unable to pinpoint exactly what he needed for lightning. In the meantime, he continued to work on the magic he already knew how to cast, honing his skills in preparation for a battle with the Veratt. The prospect terrified him.

Every day around noon, Risath would ask if Miles wanted to go back down into the camp for lunch or stay outside. Miles always chose to stay, since the darkness and dirt made him feel claustrophobic. The sun was always at its apex at that point in the day, but the fall air made it bearable and even enjoyable. The lounging Omnes were always ordered to go fetch the group something to eat.

On the fifth day of Miles' training, the unfamiliar Omnes brought up rectangular red and blue bento boxes for Miles and Risath filled with cheeses, apple slices, and cubes of meat. The company of Omnes had a large cardboard box of food that they split amongst themselves.

Miles found a spot to eat near a patch of pink flowers with seemingly hundreds of tiny petals on each of them. In the past it would've bothered him to be sitting on grass without a blanket or towel underneath, but now the thought barely even crossed his mind. He opened the blue bento box and picked the largest piece of cheese from the side compartment and popped the yellow square into his mouth. It was soft and flavorful.

A couple minutes later, after all his cheese had been consumed, Kricket hobbled over and sat down next to him, accidentally tearing up some of the grass with his shoes. "Hey, kid," he said to Miles.

"Hi."

"Ate all your cheese already?"

Miles nodded.

"I don't much care for cheese."

"Does it hurt your sensitive gums?"

"No, I just think it tastes crummy," Kricket replied, picking out a piece of meat from the handful he had carried over.

"You're a picky eater," Miles chuckled.

"I just really like meat," the Omne shrugged. "What can I say? You must have some kind of food you like more than others."

"French fries," Miles grinned. "I still eat other stuff, though. But I used to only eat chicken nuggets all the time. At every restaurant I just wanted chicken nuggets. I think it annoyed my mom, so I stopped, and now I eat a lot more things."

They continued to talk through lunchtime, and when they finished, Miles resumed work on the lightning. He successfully created a small spark between his thumb and index finger, but that was his only accomplishment for the day.

As everyone began milling toward the hatch to go back to camp, Miles tugged on Risath's shirt to ask a question.

"Do not do that again," the Skyr grumbled. "What do you want?"

"I wanna see the king," Miles said.

"What for?"

"To ask him something."

"Ask me."

"Can I see the king?"

Risath sighed melodramatically and Miles knew it was an affirmation. They made the tedious climb down the ladder and Risath escorted him to the king's room.

"Majesty," Risath said, bowing as they entered. "The boy wishes to speak with you."

"Thank you, Risath. You may go."

The Skyr turned and grumpily marched out of the room to wait for Miles in the hallway. Miles took a step forward and waved shyly.

"What do you want, boy?" Mykael asked, his voice low and weary. He sat behind a messy desk. A record was spinning and bluesy rock music drifted from the record player's speakers.

"You said you read about how to summon the Veratt in a textbook."

"Okay," Mykael said, growing irritated. Miles knew he needed to get to the point quickly before the man erupted.

"Can I see it? The magic book?" Miles asked.

The king cocked his eyebrow. "What for?" he asked suspiciously.

"Just to see what's in there," Miles said. "I'm having trouble creating lightning, so I wanna see if the book says anything about how to, uh…do magic easier."

Mykael scratched his beard, contemplating the request.

"I think it might have a section on that," he said. "I haven't read through the book in a while, but it sounds familiar. Would've given it to you right off the bat, but I guess it slipped my mind."

He stood and shuffled over to his bookshelf, running a long and cracked fingernail across the leather spines of the books, muttering their titles as he passed them over. He finally stopped on a blue book and pulled it out. "Here it is," he said, opening the book to its table of contents. "Yep, there's a chapter called 'Theories of Elemental Magic.' Sounds right. Though I guess you're proof that 'theories' is an understatement." He closed the text and handed it to Miles.

"Thanks," Miles said. Then he asked, "Did you try to do magic and use it on the Veratt?"

"Of course I did," Mykael hissed, his nostrils flaring. "It pains me to say it, but you're the only person in this damned kingdom I know who can pull off these spells."

Miles knew it was time to end the conversation before things got ugly. "I'll start reading this tonight," he said.

"Get out," the king seethed, sitting back down at his desk. "I expect to see results in the next day or two."

Miles knew not to say anything and evoke an unwanted response. He left the room, clicking the door shut behind him. Risath furtively glanced over the book's cover.

"That's what you wanted?" he asked.

"Yeah."

"You dragged me all the way here for a book?"

"Yeah."

The room where Miles was staying—or kept, rather—was in a building located near the entrance to the camp, a three-story dormitory filled with enough cramped rooms to house the vast majority of the Skyr and Omnes occupying the outpost. Only a select few higher-ups, such as Jericho, had their own private cabins.

Risath unlocked Miles' door and locked it again once the boy was inside. His room included a bathroom and a refrigerator stocked with cheese, meat, and bottles of water. He was allowed to come out again around dinnertime, and then not again until the next day when it was time to train. The arrangement was not ideal, but there was nothing to be done about it. The first night he had felt like sobbing, and he did cry for a little bit, but he hardened and told himself he needed to be brave. All he could do here was practice his magic, so that's what he would do, and hopefully he would be able to get rid of the Veratt and go home.

The room was small, but it was enough for Miles. It was cozy, in its own way. Next to the refrigerator was his bed, which perfectly fit his short body. The dorm had obviously been designed for an Omne. There was a desk by the doorway, as well as a two-drawer dresser near the bathroom.

Miles got comfortable on top of his sheets. Before turning the blue textbook open to the page for Elemental Magic, he ran a finger over his knuckles. They had started to scab over from the beating he'd given Jericho.

He skimmed through the chapter's introduction, but had to reread it a few times to fully grasp what it was communicating. He sighed, realizing it would probably be necessary to read the entire chapter at least twice in order to fully comprehend it.

Throughout the years, very few individuals have ever been capable of manipulating the elements of the world, and those who have succeeded largely kept their abilities a guarded secret. For this reason, many doubt the existence of such powers, but Elemental Magic is indeed possible, and it is undoubtedly one of the most unstoppable forces in the world.

There are four types of Elemental Magic: Water, Fire, Lightning, and Earth. It has also been heartily debated whether or not Healing is a possible fifth type of magic, but due to scholars' inability to lock down any definitive evidence of such occurrences, it will not be discussed within this chapter.

Tapping into each of these four classes takes extreme focus, and each element requires a different form of energy from within the user. In this chapter, we will explore what it takes to conjure the four elements and how one can most easily unlock their potential.

Cléoma had known about Miles' ability to craft fire and water, and she had suspected lightning as well, but she had never mentioned earth to him. He reread the line about healing. Cléoma hadn't mentioned that to him either. It wasn't exactly an element, though, so it was possible Cléoma wasn't even aware of it, or maybe she didn't believe it was possible. But it would explain what had happened in the tunnels when he had first met Clint. The maylan had been seriously injured, to the point where Mortimer had thought the easiest course of action would be to leave the animal behind, but after one touch—a weird, blue-green glowy touch—the maylan's paw was mended.

Miles could heal. He had no doubt about that.

His face bunched up in a frown, displeased by the fact the author wasn't going to go over healing. It was indeed possible, and Miles wanted to tell the author so and order them to do more research and rewrite the chapter so he could better understand his powers. He'd have to settle for experimenting with the ability on his own if he got the chance.

He continued reading the next section, which primarily concerned water. The book talked about accessing one's emotions, becoming in tune with them, and other concepts that Miles thought seemed out of place in a scholarly text. Its style and tone was unlike any textbook he had read in school, but while it was unexpected, he was able to connect with it more easily and better understand the ideas the author was conveying.

Because magic is such an unpredictable power not often discussed or taught, many of those who possess the ability to conjure it are sometimes oblivious to moments when they are casting.

When it comes to Water Magic, this can occur in the form of rain. When users experience a deep, sad emotional response to an event or individual that they cannot control, this energy is oftentimes released through anything as simple as a quiet sprinkle to a torrential downpour, depending on the severity of their reaction and ability to restrain themselves.

In history, the most well-known example of such an occurrence is the 33-Day Storm. While not acknowledged as a magical event, the storm has never been explained by researchers or scientists, who simply chalked it up as a freak natural phenomenon. In actuality, the 33-Day Storm can be traced back to a Rompun* who resided in Trafier.

On the first morning of the storm, the Rompun received news that caused her to delve into profound mourning. The emotional reaction to this news manifested itself in Rompu first as a light drizzle in the Jesieu Marshes, but it quickly spread throughout the entire kingdom and came down harder with each passing day, flooding many areas. The second and third weeks of the storm even produced hail in some cities.

This Rompun had not been aware of her powers until a group of magic users determined the initial location of the storm and tracked down who they believed to be the source several years after the incident. They informed her of their theory, which she had trouble believing, and demanded the group let her continue living her life in peace.

The 33-Day Storm is an extreme example of what can happen if a magic user allows their power to go unchecked.

With the proper training and determination, however, one can harness their energies into a nearly unstoppable force.

The last sentence irked Miles. If this group of people was "nearly unstoppable," why did they never attempt anything like King Mykael had with the Veratt? Why did they never forcefully take over Rompu, if they were so much stronger than everyone else? It didn't make sense to him why these spellcasters wouldn't get cocky and try to overtake the king and queen. He shrugged it off and continued reading:

When mastered, Water can be manipulated in various ways. The user can create a harsh storm to flood cities, or they can shape it into a fluid whip to attack their enemies on a more personal level.

This paragraph further confused Miles. If this entire book was about how one could use their magic as a weapon, why did nobody do it? It made no sense. Maybe it really was too difficult for any Rompuns or Skyr to truly control, and these writings actually were just theories, as far as the author was concerned.

But Miles had trouble believing that he, of all people, was the first to successfully harness magic. His eyes glanced down to the bottom of the page where a footnote was written underneath a thick black line.

*due to the delicate nature of the tragedy, the Rompun requested that her name and the details of the tragedy be left unmentioned.

The chapter had proven to be somewhat beneficial so far, though, despite the reservations Miles felt about believing no magic users ever having attempted to stage rebellions. It had revealed to him that sadness was the key to conquering water magic; it wasn't exactly an emotion he wanted to confront, but at least he now knew what was necessary.

He skipped ahead to the other sections, bouncing around every other word until he found what emotion was tied to each element.

Water :: Sadness

Fire :: Anger

Lightning :: Fear

Earth :: Guilt

As he finished reading a short paragraph about earth, there was a brisk knock on his door. "You decent?" Risath's voice slithered through the thin wood.

"Yes," Miles answered, folding down the corner of the page. He left the book on his bed as he stood and moved toward the door, which Risath unlocked from the other side. Miles wondered how much time had passed if dinner was already prepared.

He followed Risath outside to the fire pit in the center of camp where a large number of Skyr were gathered, chatting with each other and scooping up bowls of stew that they spooned messily into their mouths. Due to their large numbers, the Skyr ate in shifts so as to not overwhelm the chefs. Risath was in the second shift, so that was when Miles ate as well.

Unfortunately, Miles didn't know which group Kricket ate with. Despite their violent prior meetings, Kricket had grown to be the closest thing Miles had to a friend here in the underground camp. He spent a majority of his time around Risath, but knew the one-armed Skyr didn't care for him in the slightest. Miles felt oddly comfortable around the Kricket, though. At least he could joke around with him.

Miles was instructed to sit next to Risath, who would either discuss the army's future plans or share crude anecdotes with his pals. There was one particular story the night before about a female Skyr Risath had met in Garn's tavern that Miles knew his mother would not have appreciated him hearing.

The stew comprised of chopped carrots, green onions, and kreer—which seemed to be the meat of choice amongst Skyr—all swimming in a thick, dark broth that bubbled in Miles' bowl. He shoveled the mixture into his mouth with unexpected intensity once it had cooled enough. He hadn't realized how hungry he was until smelling the cooked meat as steam rose into his face.

After dinner, it was another silent walk back to the dormitories with Risath. Miles refrained from staring at the Skyr's stump of an arm.

When Miles returned to his room, he climbed into bed and pulled the sheets over his body, nestling in comfortably. Or as comfortable as he could be, having to wear the same stiff, bland outfit he'd worn the past week rather than his favorite gray pajamas. He didn't even know what the Skyr had done with his old clothes.

He opened the blue book to the page he had dog-eared and scanned it until he found the sentence he'd stopped on. Satisfied, he turned back a few pages and returned to the section on lightning.

There was studying to be done.

CHAPTER SEVENTEEN

THERE IS PLENTY
YOU CAN DO

Miles picked up the book, his mouth a slight slant as he looked at its cover for what felt like the hundredth time.

"Did the book help?"

His gazed moved from the flimsy cover to Mrs. Mendol, who sat behind her desk looking awfully proud of herself. The black-rimmed glasses sat at the tip of her nose while she peered over them and her hair was hanging down to her shoulders for once. Her red lipstick was glaring against pale, crinkled skin.

"Yes," he said, flipping the book to a random page.

It was page six. There were four illustrations, one in each corner of the large page. Fluffy dogs wearing human clothing expressed their emotions in exceptionally unsubtle ways.

In the top right was a boy dog sporting a frown and drooping eyelids. Below the picture was a caption that read, SAD.

Next to it was a girl that appeared to be shouting fiercely. ANGER.

Below the boy was a dog with a blanket pulled to his chin, trembling, and a stuffed animal by his side. AFRAID.

Finally, beside him was a dog wearing a collared shirt with both hands behind his back, eyes averted to the floor. GUILTY.

At the top of the page, it read, IT'S OKAY IF YOU FEEL…

"Good," Mrs. Mendol smiled. "I'm glad to hear that. I've found that this book is really great at helping kids like you understand what's going on at home and how they can express what they're feeling."

"Okay."

The seventh page said, YOU WON'T ALWAYS FEEL THIS WAY, AND THERE IS PLENTY YOU CAN DO TO HELP YOURSELF COPE WITH THESE FEELINGS.

Mrs. Mendol peered over her desk to inspect what page he had turned to. "Oh," she said, reaching out and turning the page for him. He felt a shiver run up his spine. She pointed at the text on top of page eight and asked, "Did you read this part?"

"Yes," he said again, not planning to give Mrs. Mendol more than one-word answers. There was still a residual feeling of discomfort from the meeting when they had talked at length about his grandmother.

"The part about how it's good to talk about your feelings?"

"Yes." He had read the entire book several times. It wasn't long.

"So what did you learn?" Risath asked, using his nails to pick something from between his teeth. The sun was shining bright and the heat bore down on the lot of them. There wasn't a cloud in sight. Miles had brought the blue book outside with him in case he needed to consult it.

"Stuff," he replied.

That was evidently a sufficient answer for Risath. The Skyr continued to pick at his jagged teeth. The company had eaten scrambled eggs with pepper and some kind of leafy green mixed in, which was what Risath currently had problems with.

Miles was still planning to work on lightning, since he had shown mild progress with it back in Trafier. He held up his hands and pictured his grandmother's face, leaning back in her hospital bed, just like last time.

"The doctors don't think they can fix me," he imagined her saying again.

He could feel his chest begin to tighten as he looked straight ahead and focused on the task at hand.

But his focus dissipated with the smacking of Risath's lips.

"Finally," he heard the Skyr mutter a few feet behind him. The boy shot back a disapproving look, which Risath did not acknowledge, before looking forward again and starting anew.

"The doctors don't think they can fix me."

Her skin sagging and cold.

Her eyes cloudy.

"I don't mean to scare you."

Thunder crashed overhead. The wind was picking up.

"I don't mean to scare you."

"The doctors don't think they can fix me."

"I love you."

Her uncomfortable laugh.

"I'm probably not going home, Miles."

A thin yellow line rocketed across the empty sky, hardly visible against the pale blue backdrop.

Risath looked up from examining his nail and scoffed, impressed. Kricket pushed open the hidden hatch door just in time to view the spectacle. He clambered over to where Risath stood and observed Miles.

The boy collapsed to the ground, physically and mentally exhausted.

"I don't mean to scare you."

"The doctors don't think they can fix me."

He worked to push the thoughts of his grandmother away. He needed to take a break. The memories had taken an unanticipated toll on him.

Against his will, his mind began painting pictures of the germs he imagined killed his grandmother. Hulking beasts with green, plated bodies and arms that extended over five feet long, pincers dripping with acid. Their blood-red eyes blinked rapidly, the clicking of razorblade teeth putting Miles on edge.

A lightning bolt crashed into the earth no more than fifteen feet from where Miles sat with his knees pulled to his chest. Risath and Kricket both yelped, and suddenly the small group accompanying them paid close attention to the child.

"*Hey!*" Risath yelled, his voice cracking. "Watch what you're doin' over there!"

The words were hollow and distant in Miles' ears. His eyes were glued to the spot where the lightning had struck. The grass was charred and smoking. He shivered, nausea building up.

"Have you talked to your mom at all about how you're feeling?" Mrs. Mendol asked. He shook his head in response. "How about your dad?"

"No," Miles said.

"Well, if you won't talk to them, I think it'd be good to talk to me. Remember how we had that conversation about your grandma? Didn't it feel good talking about that?"

"I don't want to," he said. "I don't wanna talk to anyone. I don't need to." He didn't know how many words he had stuffed into that sentence, but regrettably it was more than one.

Mrs. Mendol let out a curt sigh. "Miles," she said impatiently, "you need to talk about this stuff. It's unhealthy to keep it bottled up inside. Remember what the book said?" She gestured toward the thin paperback he still held in his hands.

On page eight, a stout dog child stood in between her parents in a living room. White text floated above their heads.

IF YOU ARE AFRAID OR SAD ABOUT THE CHANGES IN YOUR FAMILY, LET YOUR PARENTS KNOW HOW YOU'RE FEELING AND ASK THEM QUESTIONS.

"Yes," Miles said. "I remember."

"It's good to ask questions. It's natural. Everyone has these feelings sometimes, and it's *okay* to let them out and let people know what you're thinking."

"I know," Miles said. "I just don't want to."

"Why not?"

"Because I don't like thinking about that stuff so I don't like talking about it either," he said, anger slipping into his tone.

"I know it's hard," Mrs. Mendol said unhelpfully.

"I can't do it," Miles whispered to himself, still looking at the burnt grass in front of him. Staring at the grass helped him to forget about his grandmother's words. Her face. The sterile smell of that hospital room.

"You don't have to be afraid," Mrs. Mendol told him. Her words frustrated him.

"Do it again!" Kricket cheered, clapping his scaly hands together.

Miles closed his eyes and everything vanished.

Not just the sight of the dead grass, but also the thoughts of his grandmother, of his parents, of Mrs. Mendol, of the germs, of all his fears and anxieties.

He took a deep breath.

A soft, simple melody played through his head. The tune was familiar.

It was the song that played from his grandmother's music box. The one she'd wind up and play for him when they sat down to drink tea at her house. *Greensleeves*. A peace flowed through him. The lilting piano was the only thing that existed anymore. His head felt heavy, then light, then he couldn't feel it at all.

He let the sun's heat sink into his skin and ran his fingers through the grass. He didn't need to be afraid.

He thought of his father's words: "Be brave, Miles."

He thought of his mother's: "You're a strong boy."

They disappeared again.

Then his grandmother appeared. She said, "I love you." She said, "The doctors don't think they can fix me."

The song continued, floating through the air as if it were a physical thing, wrapping itself around his body like a cocoon.

The piano's final notes rang in his ears as he opened his eyes. He blinked once, twice, still facing the blackened grass several feet away. Kricket continued to egg him on.

"Okay," Miles said.

"Good," Mrs. Mendol said. "Go ahead. Whatever's on your mind."

Miles shifted in his seat and closed the book he was still holding. He placed it on Mrs. Mendol's desk next to the picture frame and tried figuring out what to say. Nothing felt right.

"I went to the new apartment a few times," he started. "With my dad."

"How was that?"

"Weird."

"Weird isn't always bad."

"It was bad."

"I'm sorry," Mrs. Mendol frowned. "What made it bad?" Her lipstick was no longer as distracting as it had been when Miles arrived.

The boy shrugged. "It's different," he said. "It's just weird. I dunno."

"Did you and your dad do anything fun while you were there?"

"We watched a movie the first time."

"What movie?"

"*The Wild Bunch*. It's one of my favorites." Judging by her reaction, Miles could tell Mrs. Mendol knew what the film was and agreed with his mother that he should not have seen it.

"That sounds like fun," she said anyway.

He nodded. "It was."

"So it wasn't all bad."

"I guess not," he confessed.

What he did not want to admit was that telling Mrs. Mendol did in fact make him feel somewhat better. It felt like a weight was being lifted. Like everything was disappearing, making him lighter. It was kind of a relief.

"It wasn't all bad," he echoed her. "The next time I went, we ordered a pizza. He also hooked up his old video game console that he had when he was younger. We played Mario Kart on it."

A toothy grin was plastered over Mrs. Mendol's face. It did not suit her. "That sounds great," she said. "Did you enjoy that?"

"All the characters looked blocky but it was fun. I didn't win, but I didn't get last place either."

"That's good. I bet you'll beat him next time."

"Maybe," Miles said. "I always pick Toad. He's the one with a mushroom on his head." This time he could tell by her expression that Mrs. Mendol had no clue what he was blabbering about. "My dad usually picks Yoshi." He was feeling good now. He said, "I kinda like it there, I guess."

"You do? That's great, Miles. Really, it is."

The dog on the book's cover was wearing a green shirt with blue shorts, riding a yellow bicycle while thought bubbles protruded from his head with images of his mother and father. Miles couldn't help but think it must be painful sitting on a bicycle seat with a tail.

"It's still kinda weird having another apartment, but I don't feel scared or worried about it anymore," he said, surprising himself. He hadn't been fully aware of his feelings until he said them aloud.

Mrs. Mendol flashed her unnaturally white teeth again. "I'm thrilled to hear that," she said. "That's a fantastic step forward."

"I guess so."

"No, Miles, it is. See? Don't you feel better, having all this out in the open?"

He acted nonchalant, but the conversation had improved his mood. He was also feeling less animosity toward Mrs. Mendol, which was an unexpected yet welcome change.

"It's great to know you're not feeling so afraid anymore," she said. "It's completely fine that you were, though. That's nothing to be ashamed of, by any means. But I'm glad that feeling is going away and being replaced by something happier."

Miles nodded. He stood, raising his hands once more. Kricket yippee'd somewhere behind him, followed shortly by Risath telling the Omne to shut up.

"I'm just excited," Kricket grunted. "Don't be a dang sourpuss."

"Actually," Miles called back, "could you keep quiet, please? I need to focus."

"Oh."

Miles closed his eyes. Darkness flooded his senses.

Then darkness was replaced by the hospital room. The smell returned, his grandmother's face returned, his grandmother's words returned.

Her uncomfortable laugh.

Her cloudy eyes.

Her skin sagging and cold.

Her words echoed and echoed and echoed.

"I'm really sick."

"I'm probably not going home, Miles."

"I love you."

"I don't mean to scare you."

"The doctors don't think they can fix me."

"The doctors don't think they can fix me. The doctors don't think they can fix me. The doctors don't think they can fix me. The doctors don't think they can fix me. The doctors—"

Thunder.

Miles' hands began to shake, at first just a minor vibration which quickly turned violent and overwhelming. Energy shot up from his feet through his legs—his vision blurred—his chest—teeth gritted—his arms—the song's melody—

Lightning burst from his palms like rockets, shooting into the hillside fifty feet in front of him, igniting two small fires.

"Hell," Risath cursed. "I guess that's why we're babysittin'. Fetch some water!" he barked at his men. "Be quick about it!" A few of the Skyr leapt down the hatch, their longer legs able to carry them farther and at a faster pace than the stocky Omnes.

"Wow," was all Kricket managed to say.

Miles still held his hands in front of his face as the tremors died down. His body felt less constricted after releasing the pent-up energy. He watched as the fire licked the sky, embers floating upward.

He pointed one hand skyward and fired off another blast of lightning toward the sun, smiling as it disappeared in the distance. He shot off another, switching hands after numerous successful attempts, all of which elicited roars of victory from Kricket.

The other Skyr returned with buckets of water and raced over to the fires, which had merged and begun to spread, though they hadn't crept toward the hatch at all. They tossed the water onto the flames, hastily putting them out.

"Work on water next so you can put your own fires out," Risath grumbled.

But Miles ignored him, casting lightning bolts into the empty blue sky, a sense of calm washing over him.

CHAPTER EIGHTEEN

CHURN

A scream of *"Get up!"* coupled with the slamming of his door jumpstarted Miles. He sat straight up in his bed, blinking his eyes to cast away the grogginess. Risath stood before him, yanking the sheets off the bed. "Come on," the Skyr demanded.

"What time is it?"

"Come *on*," Risath repeated, tugging the boy's arm. "We don't have time to waste right now."

Miles was suddenly aware of the sounds of fighting outside. Loud shouts. Angry noises. Gunfire, along with the smell of smoke. Something had obviously gone wrong.

"What's happening?" Miles asked.

Ignoring him, Risath continued dragging Miles toward the doorway where several other Skyr darted past, heading toward the battle. The ones who had normal hands held pistols; some had shotguns. A window shattered somewhere nearby.

"What's going on?" Miles asked again, though he already suspected he knew the answer.

"Rompuns," was all Risath said. "Come on."

Holding him by the wrist, Risath led Miles through the corridors and out the back entrance of the dormitory. They shoved past Skyr running in the opposite direction, their meaty claws slapping against Miles' chest as they moved along.

It was pandemonium outside.

Even though the door they'd gone through had them facing nothing but a dirt wall, numerous bodies—both Skyr and Rompun—were strewn about the area. Several yards to their right, a crate that had previously been full of prepackaged hay for the Carriers was on fire. He could hear screams around the corner of the building. Guns blasting.

Risath pulled him to the left. They raced past a hulking Skyr and a scarred, grizzled Rompun who were engaged in a fist-fight, yelping with each punch thrown. The Rompun was struggling to keep the Skyr's two pincers away from his neck, holding onto the creature's wrists while a third, normal hand repeatedly punched him in the gut. Miles didn't like the Rompun's odds.

A couple seconds after passing the two, Miles heard the forceful *snap* of pincers clamping together, followed by a heavy *thud*.

The Rompuns had tracked him down. He wasn't sure how they'd done it, but they had. It was possible Mortimer was amongst the warriors here, fighting to reclaim Miles and escort him back to safety. Miles shuddered and hoped Mortimer wasn't caught up in this madness just for his sake.

Risath brought Miles to the building that housed King Mykael's office. The Skyr had set up a barricade in front of the building. The king was still inside, so the majority of their man-power was putting forth a defense there. It was simultaneously the safest and most dangerous place in the camp.

"Up you go," Risath grunted, suddenly lifting Miles and tossing him over the crates and barrels that comprised the makeshift wall.

Miles landed hard on his left arm. A sharp pain flared up as he tried to stand and he let out a weak whimper, trying not to cry. The pain won, though, and a few tears snuck out.

Risath hopped over the barricade and looked at the weeping boy. "What's your problem?" he asked as he kneeled down, yelling over the gunfire behind him.

"You hurt my arm," Miles said through clenched teeth.

"Did not," Risath spat. His half-arm hung limply at his side.

He tapped another Skyr's shoulder, and the Skyr hastily handed over a hefty pistol. It looked identical to the gun Clint Eastwood's character used in the *Man With No Name* trilogy; Miles recognized the rattlesnake on its grip. The barrel was long, thick, and black. There was no doubt it could pack a wallop. Miles had seen it do so plenty of times in the movies. Assuming Risath was as good a shot as Clint Eastwood, anyway.

And as it turned out, he was. It was hard to see, vision obscured by tears and smoke, but Miles was still able to make out the massive green blobs dropping in the distance as Risath fired his weapon. Rompuns were dying all around him. Just to rescue him.

One of those green blobs might have been Mortimer.

Miles wanted to knock Risath out along with all the other Skyr who were shooting at his friends, but that was a foolish wish. His meek punch probably wouldn't even faze Risath, let alone neutralize thirty soldiers. All he could do was wait.

Or use his magic and run.

Wiping away tears, Miles played out the latter scenario in his head. He could light up Risath first, then throw fireballs at the other Skyr until they were eliminated or fled. Their initial confusion would benefit him greatly. After that, he would need to run somewhere and find a Rompun he could trust to get him out of there. That would be the difficult part. Navigating the battlefield wasn't something Miles felt he was presently equipped to handle, and even if he found a helpful Rompun, there was no guarantee they'd make it out alive. If the Skyr caught him trying to escape, there would surely be horrific consequences.

Picturing himself burning their flesh made Miles nauseous. Suddenly the plan sounded extremely unappealing. These might not be the most upstanding people he had ever met, but they still had souls. Lives. Families. Miles knew with unflinching certainty that he didn't have it in him to go so far as killing them. Just the thought nearly made him puke.

Miles scooted up against the barricade, leaning his back against it. He squirmed, all the sounds of combat making his skin crawl. It felt like he was about to leap out of it.

"Get back!" Risath roared, firing off another round. "If a bullet goes through there, you're done!"

The boy nodded and crawled away to the midpoint between the crates and the building's exterior. His anxiety was not subsiding. He threw up. A Skyr that had witnessed the grotesque event uttered a curse word and continued shooting. Miles wiped away the bile from his mouth and coughed.

The prospect of leaving began to seem less and less tempting. Risath was momentarily distracted, and Miles could easily slip away into the chaos, but instead he stayed put, edging away from the puddle of vomit he had produced. It would be much easier for him to face the Veratt if he stayed with the Skyr. As much as he wished it were untrue, Miles knew he had to eventually fight the Veratt, and given King Mykael's history with the monster, it would probably be more likely for the band of Skyr to succeed in tracking it down than the Rompuns.

So staying had its advantages.

That is, if having a better chance to challenge an enormous, bloodthirsty killing machine could be considered an advantage.

Miles peered out over the barricade at the bedlam. He looked up just in time to see a hole appear in the back of a Skyr's head, the one who had commented on his unfortunate nausea. The Skyr's body flung backward and his skull slammed into the dirt floor with a wet crack.

"Stay down," Risath ordered, not bothering to check whether Miles was even poking his head out or not. The Skyr ducked down as bullets whizzed by, lodging into the building.

A Skyr a couple feet away began to shout orders at the others. Blood was smeared all over her scalp and cheek. "Go inside and make sure things are secure," she said, pointing at two particularly muscular Skyr. Things must have been going pretty well if the commander was willing to give up two of her men. Either that or things were so dire, she was more concerned with the king's well-being. The two Skyr grunted a confirmation and entered the building with haste, disappearing into a haze of smoke as the door creaked open.

Risath continued to fire upon the incoming Rompuns, whose numbers seemed to be multiplying somehow. It was as if Queen Alys had sent her entire army to retrieve Miles. Risath let out a laugh, squeezing off two more shots. The unfettered violence made Miles' stomach churn.

The bloody Skyr giving orders suddenly noticed the boy's presence. "Hey!" she shouted over to Risath. "What the hell are you doin' bringin' him here?" She cocked her head in Miles' direction.

"Need to keep him and the king together," Risath yelled over the gunfire as he squatted, his back to the crude wooden wall. "Jericho's orders."

"Well get him inside, then," the Skyr demanded. At the end of her four limbs were two pincers and two hands. A useful combination in situations such as these.

"Is it safe in there?"

"Sure, safer than out here. For now."

One of the soldiers behind her was blown backward, his head skidding into the dirt, creating a small mound at the edge of his skull.

"They're makin' headway," Miles heard one of the soldiers bellow.

"Get him inside *now*," the woman roared.

Risath nodded and stood, grabbing Miles by the arm again. He dragged the boy toward the doorway and instructed him to hold his breath.

Inside the building, smoke filled the halls from floor to ceiling that stung Miles' eyes. He closed them and let Risath pull him through the halls.

The busy noise of the battle taking place outside contrasted with the simple darkness. He breathed a short, relieved sigh, thankful that no one had forced him to use his magic against the Rompuns.

With his eyes closed, he pictured Mortimer falling through the sky.

He couldn't help opening his eyes as he was swung around a corner and into a nondescript room. Risath hastily slammed the door shut behind them.

The room was unfamiliar. It contained three desks and a bookcase against each wall. Documents and pencils were scattered across each desk, abandoned in light of the raging battle. They looked like maps drawn on parchment paper.

"Get under the desk," Risath ordered the kid.

"Which one?"

Risath didn't acknowledge the question and instead stood against the wall the door opened toward, his one good arm raised. It would have looked like surrender if not for the pistol he gripped. His sandy knuckles were turning white.

Miles crawled under the nearest desk, rotating his body to face the doorway. He heard shouting from the other side of the wall.

"In here," a voice said. It was deep, guttural. Rompun.

The door creaked open, hiding Risath behind it. Two large Rompuns trudged into the room, one holding a machete while the other wielded a shotgun. The one with the machete had a hole in his shoulder with a line of dried blood leading down to his wrist.

It took them hardly any time at all to spot Miles cowering on the floor.

"There," Shotgun said, pointing. "Grab him."

"Wait, what about the Skyr that—"

But Machete hadn't been fast enough. On cue, Risath kicked the door away before the sentence was completed and blew a hole in the back of Shotgun's head.

The Rompun toppled over like a fallen tree, crashing into the floor. His face impacted with the tile and sent a web of cracks shattering across it. Miles lay flat against the ground, his body chilled as he tried focusing on anything other than the corpse now less than a foot from his face.

Machete's reflexes were well-honed, and he was instantly swinging at the attacker. Risath ducked below the blade and fired off a round into the Rompun's kneecap. He let out a cry of pain as he fell to his knees, weapon still in hand. Another slash, which cut into Risath's thigh.

That proved to be the Rompun's final action before Risath put a bullet in Machete's forehead. His bulky green body slumped forward, smashing face-first into his late companion's calf.

It was all over in less than ten seconds.

Miles shut his eyes again, partially to avoid the violence and partially because they were irritated by the smoke that had crept into the room.

"Dammit," Risath swore, inspecting his injury. Deciding it was nothing worth worrying about, he told Miles for the second time that night, "Get up."

"I can't," said Miles, petrified by the two lifeless bodies lying in their own pooling blood. Images of lightning lit up the darkness of his vision as he pictured himself struggling to stay afloat in the Third River.

"Yes, you can," Risath groaned, exhausted. "Get up before I make it so you *really* can't."

The threat was enough to get Miles out from under the desk. He brushed the dust from his plain, tan clothes and looked into Risath's eyes, purposefully not letting his own wander down to the floor. In his peripherals, he could still see the hump of Shotgun's backside.

Miles sidestepped the bodies, his stomach churning again, and followed the limping Risath back into the hallway.

Risath brought Miles to a closet at the end of the hall that contained supplies such as ropes, empty boxes, screws, and other assorted objects. The Skyr knocked it all out of the way and felt around on the floor, finally uncovering a concealed latch that he pulled on, revealing a ladder that went even further underground. Risath ushered Miles down, shutting the hidden door behind him to remain entrenched in the battle. The ladder was only about ten feet tall, and Miles reached the bottom quickly.

"Hello," came a voice from the back of the surprisingly spacious room.

Miles looked at the king, who sat at a table with a plate of grapes. A novel rested on the table, opened to somewhere near the middle.

"Hi," Miles said.

"It's a bit messy down here," Mykael said, sweeping his hands toward the various books and bags that littered the linoleum floor. "This room isn't really frequented by anyone, and it's kind of a secret, so it's never cleaned. And I'm too lazy to do it myself."

Miles didn't say anything as he sat down at the table opposite Mykael. Without asking, he reached forward and plucked a plump grape off its stem. It was sour.

"Watch yourself," the king glared.

Miles nodded as he chewed, mentally chastising himself. Mykael's behavior was too unpredictable to pull a stunt like that.

"I wanted Risath to get you here sooner, but I guess he got distracted. He's a good fighter, but he gets a little bloodthirsty sometimes. Though maybe that's why he's as good as he is."

Mykael tried to feign a smile, but they both felt the tension between them. The fear Miles felt was revealed in his eyes, his body language, everything.

"We'll be safe down here," the king said, eschewing small talk. "I assure you."

"Okay," Miles said. "Can I have another grape?" he asked. The clatter upstairs was blocked by the thick walls and ceiling. The quiet calmed him.

Mykael nodded and picked one for himself as well. Miles popped another in his mouth. This one was crisp and sweet.

They sat in their awkward silence for almost half an hour, not sure what to say to each other, just shoveling grapes into their mouths to fill the gaps between weak conversation. Miles was grateful that Mykael was in one of his better moods, but he felt more at ease once the king continued reading his novel.

Miles walked around the room, checking out the books that lay on the floor, hoping that one might pique his curiosity.

"Don't touch anything," Mykael barked as Miles leaned over to grab one.

All the books were either about history or novels that took place a long time ago, so they didn't really interest him anyway. He slumped against the wall and dozed off.

The curdling screams of Rompuns and Skyr were faint that far below ground. Nearly inaudible.

"What's the situation?"

The words jolted Miles awake. To his right, Jericho was climbing down the ladder as he answered the king's question.

His face and arms were still covered in burns from the last time he had seen Miles. The boy felt a pang of guilt.

"They're retreating," Jericho said. "Their numbers've been dwindlin' for the past two hours. Must be thirty or less left out there. Some are delusional and stayed to finish what they started, but for the most part they're gettin' the hell out."

"Great." Mykael stood and closed his book. Miles remained on the floor with his legs stretched out in front of him.

"How the hell did they find us?" Mykael wanted to know, his voice turning dark. He clenched the back of the chair so tightly, Miles thought it was going to splinter. "Was it one of your damn caravans? Did they spy you migrating between here and the Jesieu outpost?" His voice grew louder with each sentence. "I told you to separate the Carriers so they don't see a big group of Skyr beelining for the same place, Jericho."

"No, Majesty," Jericho said, remaining near the exit. Miles had never seen Jericho afraid except for in the presence of King Mykael. "We...have a theory."

"Well, I'm dyin' to hear it," the king said, his words sharp.

"We think it was *him*," Jericho said, pointing a finger toward Miles.

"You're gonna have to elaborate."

Jericho explained, "We think his lightning attracted them to the area. Lightning striking overhead in a place where there's no real sign of a storm must've made them suspicious." He paused for the king to respond. When he failed to do so, Jericho continued. "The hatch leading down here is perfectly well-hidden to anyone passin' by, but if you're specifically tryin' to find something like this, it can be found."

"Sounds like a design flaw to me," said the king, letting go of the chair and moving toward his soldier. Miles thought he saw Jericho gulp.

"I agree, Your Majesty."

Mykael stopped short less than a foot away from Jericho.

"We should head to the new base," Jericho went on. "It ain't safe to say here, and construction is mostly finished."

"You think?" the king asked sarcastically, baring his teeth like a wolf. "Start planning the move. Take some men to Garn after you get some sleep so we can stock up on supplies. I wanna leave no later than midnight. That clear?"

"Yes, Your Majesty."

"Go."

Jericho nodded and returned up the ladder to the wrecked hallway. King Mykael looked down at Miles, who had pulled his knees to his chest. Their eyes locked.

"Seems you're the most likely cause for so many of my men dyin'," Mykael hissed.

And for so many Rompuns, too. Miles' stomach was no longer churning. It felt like it had dropped out of his body completely. He looked into the king's empty eyes.

"Let's hope you're worth it," the king said. His tail slinked through the air, its stinger pointed at the young boy.

CHAPTER NINETEEN

KYRFISH GLIDING

The Rompuns that had narrowly managed to escape were gone by sunrise. Jericho ordered a band of Skyr to track them down on their Carriers, and unless the Rompuns possessed winged Carriers to fly away on, there was no way they'd make it back to Trafier.

The next day was one of recovery for the camp.

King Mykael remained cooped up in his panic room. Miles was ordered to stay there for a few hours as well until they were able to confirm there were no Rompun stragglers. Miles and the king each read silently on opposite sides of the room.

"It's clear," Jericho finally announced, calling from the top of the ladder. Miles could have gotten whiplash from how quickly he raced out of the room.

Ever since the king's threat, Miles had felt even more nervous around the man and it was a relief to be out of the isolated room. He had tried to concentrate on devising a strategy to defeat the Veratt, but his eyes always wandered over to Mykael sitting at his table, slowly turning the yellowed pages of his book with a smug smile.

Outside, the surviving Skyr shuffled about, repairing the damage the Rompuns had inflicted. Some were dragging limp corpses to a platform attached to a pulley at the hatch's opening, while others picked up debris and threw it into a fire burning in the center of the camp.

Behind his mask of scars and blisters, Jericho looked like he was near the end of his rope. "Can you get back to your room on your own?" he asked Miles. "I've gotta get to Garn and I ain't got the time or patience to babysit you."

Miles nodded, but then asked, "Can I go to Garn?"

"Didn't you just hear me say I don't wanna babysit you?"

"You don't have to babysit me," Miles assured him. "I can look after myself."

Jericho rolled his eyes. "Wait here," he said.

The Skyr re-entered the building and then emerged two minutes later. Miles had not moved from his spot, fearful of Jericho finally exacting the revenge he'd promised on their trip through the marshes. The king's need of his powers was likely the only reason he'd been spared a thrashing thus far.

"I ain't happy about it, but the king says you can come," Jericho grimaced.

Miles smiled. "Thanks."

"Just stay outta my hair," Jericho said. "You can stick with Kricket. He'll keep an eye on you."

Miles was excited. It felt like forever since he had gotten a chance to see Kricket. He was still weirded out by how fond he had become of the Omne.

As the company of Skyr gathered above ground at the hatch's opening, Miles was able to ascertain that the entire camp was going to be moving with them to the new outpost before the Rompuns had the opportunity to regroup, so they needed to obtain a huge amount of traveling supplies from Garn.

Miles stood by Kricket at the edge of the congregation. He noticed he had grown slightly taller than the stocky lizard.

"I think I'm taller than you," he said.

"What? No way," Kricket objected. His eye patch had grown loose and was almost falling off his eye. Miles was morbidly curious and tried to catch a peek of what was underneath, but he was unable.

"Yeah I am," the boy said. "Stand back-to-back."

Kricket did so, and Miles placed his palm flat on his own head. He steadily moved it backward toward Kricket and then stepped away, leaving it hovering an inch or two above the Omne's head.

"Told you!"

"When did that happen?" Kricket growled in dismay. He took out a cigarette and lit it, taking a long drag. The familiar, nasty scent of dirty berries filled the air.

Miles then asked him, "Where are we going?"

"To Garn," Kricket replied. "What are you, dense?"

"I mean after that," Miles clarified. "Where's the new camp?"

"Oh. I dunno, somewhere west," Kricket said. "There's another outpost somewhere out there that the king's had people building for a while, just in case something like this happened. A back-up plan." He blew smoke rings that broke apart on Miles' face.

The young boy coughed and waved away the smoke. "I wonder how far it is," he said.

"Well, it ain't close."

They started north toward Garn ten minutes later. The group was divided into three carts and consisted mostly of Skyr, a handful of Omnes, then Kricket and Miles, who were bringing up the rear along with a Skyr who was in charge of making sure Miles didn't try to escape. Not a lot of faith had been put in Kricket.

The countryside was gorgeous. Miles had never taken the time to admire it before. During all his other trips, there had been something stressing him out and distracting him from how beautiful Rompu actually was.

"What are these hills called?" Miles asked.

"I dunno," Kricket said. "Who cares?"

Time didn't matter. The hills rolled by, and eventually the group reached the outskirts of Garn sooner than Miles would've liked.

The village was fairly small but covered a greater area than the Skyr encampment. All of its buildings were short and wide, constructed from brick with thatch roofs. They looked silly to Miles.

Omnes milled about town; crossing the roads to enter shops, stopping to converse with each other, buying food from street vendors. There were no resident Rompuns or Skyr that the boy could spot.

They parked their wagons outside the grocery store and Jericho instructed one of his men to keep watch of the Carriers, promising to bring out some vegetables for them to eat before the short journey back.

Miles stepped out of his cart and stretched, letting out a deep yawn. Kricket did the same, followed by the Skyr chaperoning them.

"Where should we go?" Kricket asked.

"Nowhere," the Skyr said gruffly. "Just stay with the group. You being allowed to come is a courtesy."

"I dunno what's here," Miles said.

"Plenty of stuff," Kricket said, blatantly disregarding their babysitter. "Grocery store, street food, clothes—"

"I don't have any money to spend," Miles interrupted.

"Oh. That's a limiting factor."

"So is the fact that you aren't going anywhere," said the Skyr.

Kricket shrugged. "That's fine," he said to Miles. "We can just walk around a bit." He started down the street, his arms crossed inconspicuously behind his back. "C'mon," he beckoned Miles.

The boy followed, with the Skyr trailing close behind.

"Let's head up to Lake Maulage and check out the resort," Kricket suggested under his breath so that only Miles could hear him. "I wanna see the prices and tell Jericho he's wrong and stupid. Really rub it in his face."

"What about him?" Miles asked, nodding back at the irate Skyr no more than a few steps behind them. "I don't think he'll like that plan."

"On three, follow my lead," Kricket instructed.

"What?"

"One—*three!*" The Omne darted into an alleyway between two shops on their right.

Miles ducked into the alley behind Kricket, following him around the corner to the back of the building. They could hear the Skyr shout obscenities as they ran around to the other side of the building and back out onto the street.

Kricket was already winded and transitioned into a jog then a walk. "He won't think to look for us on the street," he said.

"Makes sense that we'd keep hiding back there, right?" Miles laughed at him. "Wanna check out that resort now?"

"Okay," Miles grinned. He was excited to check the place out after hearing about it so many times.

Kricket led the way through the streets of Garn, stopping by a shabby stand to purchase a box of fresh meatballs.

"These are the best meatballs in Rompu," he told Miles as they continued their walk to the resort. "They're a blend of beef and kreer, with some locally-grown herbs. Kinda moist too, so there's some sort of sauce mixed in, but I never remember to ask what it is." He stabbed his wooden fork into a meatball and let Miles take a bite.

"It's spicy," the kid sputtered, choking it down.

"That's the cayenne," Kricket grinned before popping a meatball into his slender mouth. The quick flash of his slimy tongue reminded Miles just how lizard-like he was. "Love me some cayenne."

"Did you used to live here?" Miles asked him.

"What? No," Kricket said. "Why?"

"It's the only Omne town I've seen since I came here. I didn't know if there were any others or not."

Kricket ate another meatball before responding. "Well, it might be the only village in Rompu that has exclusively Omne inhabitants and no one else. Not many places are like that; generally everyone's mixing in with everyone. I grew up in Ferynlac, though."

"I've heard of that place," Miles said, thinking of Mortimer's journey back to Trafier. "What's a kyrfish?" He was ecstatic about finally finding a chance to ask the question.

"Just an ugly little red fish that everyone eats. It's good when you season it with cayenne."

The answer was anticlimactic.

As they passed through the marketplace, Miles peered into shop windows and examined the items on display.

One store, called Yillfrem's Designs, had a stout lavender dress hanging on a mannequin. It had thin frills at the end of its sleeves and a slight glimmer that sparkled in the sunlight as they passed. Two Omnes stood by the window fawning over the dress.

Next door, Toy Depot had a multitude of products prominently featured in the window, including wooden train sets, alien-looking action figures, and puzzles of scenes such as a meadow within the Violet Woods and Carriers soaring through the Screaming Crags. The shop was full of Omne children, so Miles assumed it must currently be a weekend in Rompu.

Kricket finished his meatballs and tossed the empty box into a trash can at the edge of the market, where stores were beginning to give way to houses.

"Do you have any friends that live here?" Miles asked. "Since you visit so often?"

"I don't really visit that often," Kricket said, "but nah. I'm a pretty solitary guy. I like Gryff, though."

They walked down the village's red stone pathway in silence. Miles simply absorbed his surroundings, watching Omnes walk in and out of their homes and children playing with maylans in the small patches of grass on the side of each house. He yearned for Clint and Ollie.

"See it?" Kricket asked, pointing a scaly finger straight ahead. A ways away, Miles could make out a large building at the top of a hill. Smoke puffed from its chimney. "It's a bit of a walk from here, but the solitude is what makes it so relaxing."

It took another twenty minutes to reach the resort. Outside was an enormous, beautifully-carved stone fountain with water shooting up ten feet into the air. Specks of water blown by the wind sprayed Miles' face. Immaculately-trimmed hedges lined the walkway leading to double red doors stationed under a hanging sign that read MAULAGE LAKESIDE RESORT. The building was three stories high, built with smooth yellow stone and dark brown shingles that matched the lining of the window frames, which bordered five-foot-wide windows, two on each floor. Miles couldn't imagine how huge the rooms must be if the windows alone were that size.

"Maybe we can squeeze in some swim time," Kricket suggested.

"I don't have a bathing suit. I don't have any other clothes, actually."

Kricket ignored him and pulled open the doors.

Miles followed the Omne inside, which was just as impressive as the outside. The inn's furnishings were old-fashioned, but undeniably very nice. It had the feel of an upscale log cabin, with stained wooden furniture and thick, colorful rugs. A fireplace crackled happily on the far side of the room.

Behind the counter sat an overweight Omne with a short, messy white beard. He fixed a convincing smile on his face and greeted the two visitors. "What can I do for ya?"

Kricket's eyes narrowed as he scanned the numerous words scribbled messily on a chalkboard behind the innkeeper.

"What can I do for ya?" the Omne repeated, his throat sounding congested. Each word was thick and wet.

"I'm lookin' for your prices," Kricket told him. "How much is it for a full day and one night? Less than a hundred bucks, right?"

The old Omne smiled cordially. "For one full day and night, it would be one-hundred and ten dollars. Check-out is at noon."

"I was ten measly dollars off," Kricket grumbled. He looked at Miles and pointed a filthy, crooked fingernail at the boy. "You can't tell Jericho," he said. Miles agreed.

"Two-hundred twenty for the both of you," the chunky Omne said. "Should I ring it up?"

"No, no, don't have time for that," Kricket said, waving the man away. "I'd like to take a quick dip in the lake, though. How much for that?" He tapped his foot impatiently on the rug beneath his feet, but it wasn't audible with all the extra padding.

"Thirty dollars each."

"*Each?*"

The Omne nodded.

"To be in water?"

Another curt nod.

"Well, he can't even pay for a bathing suit, so we'll just take one. He'll sit in the grass or something. Or is there a sitting fee too?"

"There is not a sitting fee."

Kricket begrudgingly paid the Omne thirty dollars after complaining a bit more. Miles then noticed a bowl of fruits sitting on the other end of the table. It held apples, pears, and bananas. He tapped Kricket on the shoulder and pointed at the bowl, telling him the yellow fruit was a banana.

"The thing you said has no seeds?" Kricket asked. Miles confirmed, so Kricket grabbed one and told the innkeeper, "I'm taking one of these, too. I feel I am owed."

The old, weary Omne just grunted and shrugged.

After showing Kricket how to peel the banana, the Omne bit off a chunk of the soft, mushy fruit and smacked his lips as he ate it.

"Not bad," he nodded, swallowing. "Not bad."

Miles followed Kricket through some hallways and out a door into a stunningly beautiful fenced-off area. The lake was massive and shimmering, surrounded by bushes adorned with blooming flowers. Petals blew off and danced through the air before landing on the water's surface. It seemed like a perfect honeymoon spot, which made the fact that Kricket was so enamored by it all the stranger.

Miles dipped his feet into the cool water, sitting at the edge of a short dock that extended out from a nice area with benches and a picnic table. Kricket had entered a nearby shack to change into the complimentary bathing suit provided by the bearded Omne. He returned minutes later, sporting bright red shorts that barely reached his knees and clung tightly to his skinny legs. A white MLR logo was emblazoned on the left-hand side near the waistband. He hastily dove off the pier where Miles was sitting.

Kricket surfaced and wiped water from his eye, letting out a long whistle. "Feels great in this heat," he said, swiveling around to get a 360-degree look at the lake. The only other people in sight were a great distance away, lounging in a canoe. "Must be their slow season."

Miles splashed his feet, breaking his reflection. Kricket apologized for not buying him a ticket to swim, but Miles said it was alright. He watched the water settle, his face reforming and growing tranquil.

"If you wanna slip in for a minute, I won't tell that old sack o' bones," Kricket said.

"I don't wanna get wet anyway."

"Suit yourself." Kricket inhaled deeply and torpedoed underwater.

The water was so clear, Miles could watch Kricket swim around underneath, brushing aside the stalks of plant life that tangled around his arms. When he resurfaced, his scales glittered with a wet sheen in the sunlight.

"What was Feryn-lac like?" Miles asked.

Kricket floated on his back, shutting his good eye to block out the sun. "It's a neat town, for sure," he replied. "I used to swim all the time, since it's coastal and all. Whole town's built on docks. Swimming's what I miss the most, probably. I can only ever swim now when I make the time to come up here."

"You said you used to visit here a lot with your brother," Miles remembered.

"Yep. Every spring we'd make the trip and spend a week loafing and chattin' up girls. My brother was always more of a ladies man than me, though. But then he got married and had a kid and moved to Heriin. I don't get a whole lot of chances to come here anymore," he sighed. "Not with everything that's going on in this kingdom lately."

"And the Veratt," Miles added.

"That too." He floated in silence, drifting closer to Miles, toward the shore. He asked, "What's it like where you're from?"

It was a big question, and Miles wasn't sure how to answer. So he said, "Big. There are lots of really tall buildings. There's a lot of cool nature too, though."

"What's it called?"

"Austin."

"Weird name."

"I guess so."

Kricket dipped into the water and came back up near the wooden dock. "It's got cool nature, though?" he asked.

"Yeah," Miles beamed. "My dad took me to this place where there were a lot of really smooth rocks and cliffs by a creek, and there was a little waterfall running down them. People were running and jumping off the cliffs and they would grab a rope swing or cannonball into the water."

"That sounds pretty fun," Kricket said. He squirted lake water out of his mouth and blew bubbles.

"I never did it." He was still watching himself rippling in the water. "I didn't go in the water much. I mostly just ate lunch on the towel my dad brought."

Kricket frowned. "Well that's lame," he said. "Why not?"

Miles shrugged. "I was just worried, I guess."

"About water?"

"About germs. My grandma died because she got too many germs in her body and doctors couldn't save her."

The Omne didn't offer any condolences. Instead, he positioned himself on his back once more and looked up at the sky.

"I'm better about it now, though," Miles said, kicking his reflection again. Water splashed onto Kricket's face, but he didn't react.

Then Kricket said, "Austin sounds weird."

"I like it."

All of a sudden Miles realized how long it had been since he'd really thought about his hometown or his parents. Things had been such a whirlwind lately, he had somehow not even stopped to consider what his parents would do if they discovered he had died in some strange world. Or just that he'd died at all.

They probably wouldn't find out. They would just go on thinking their son had vanished without a trace, never to return. It had been just over a month since Miles had found himself in the Violet Woods rather than his cozy bed.

The thought made him shiver, so he stopped himself from thinking about it.

"I used to watch westerns with my dad," he said to fill the silence.

"What are westerns?"

Miles kept forgetting that people here had never heard of westerns. "Stories about guys killing each other in old, dusty towns," he explained. "There's always a lot of dirt and it's really hot. That's why they're called westerns."

"Killin' each other, huh? Sounds neat," Kricket grinned, slapping his palms on the surface of the lake. His eye patch was damp and clung to his eye. "Do you remember any of them?" he asked. "Can you tell me one?"

"You don't really tell them. They're movies," Miles said.

"Oh."

Miles thought about the cover art of the *Man With No Name* trilogy blu-ray that his father had bought for them to watch together. The bright yellow sand juxtaposed with blood-red mountains against a white sky, with the collection's title in bold print next to the image of a pistol in its holster and Clint Eastwood's hand creeping toward it.

His father told him that *A Fistful of Dollars* was based on some other movie called *Yojimbo*, which was about a samurai in Japan. They tried to watch it, but it bored Miles with its black-and-white imagery and the text on the bottom of the screen disappeared too quickly for him to read it all. He preferred movies in English. Eventually, they switched over to

Samurai Jack, which was a much more vibrant and palatable samurai story.

Even the cover art for *Yojimbo* bugged him; it just looked like yellow parchment paper with the movie's title on top of a faded blue symbol. It was nonsense. It surprised him how clear the image was in his head.

"Can't you just tell me what happens in one?" asked Kricket, obviously disappointed.

"It's hard to explain," Miles said, not in the mood to elaborate. But he did so anyway, for the sake of avoiding another lull in the conversation. "One of the stories is about a guy trying to get lots of gold from these two families that are fighting with each other. All he wants is money."

"All anyone wants is money," Kricket interjected. "What's this guy's name?"

"I dunno."

"How do you not know his name?"

"It never says his name. That's the point," Miles said.

"The point is you don't find out his name? What kind of garbage is that?" Kricket asked, his interest waning.

After arguing over the merit of westerns for several minutes, Kricket waded out of the lake and wandered into the shack again. He threw open the door a moment later and stepped out, rubbing the top of his bald head with a red, cottony towel that matched his bathing suit.

But Kricket's expression soured almost instantly, and when Miles turned to see what he was staring at, the boy understood why.

Their Skyr babysitter had tracked them down and was approaching the dock where Miles sat. He pointed at Miles and merely said, "Up." To Kricket, he growled, "Jericho isn't gonna be pleased."

Conversation was nonexistent on the walk back, which didn't bother Miles much. He was content simply looking in the storefronts they hadn't passed on the way to the resort. Kricket, however, looked nervous, like he was about to melt away in the heat.

When they reached the rest of the group, Jericho was shockingly reserved.

"Went to the resort, did you?" he asked, towering above the Omne's short frame.

"Yep," said Kricket.

"Take a look at the prices?"

"Yep."

"I was right, wasn't I?"

"Nah," Kricket shook his head.

Jericho glanced at the Skyr that had brought them back.

"I checked them like you asked," the Skyr said. "You were right."

Jericho grinned and Kricket cursed.

"Costs thirty bucks to swim, too," the Omne muttered dourly.

"Really?" Jericho sounded genuinely surprised. "That's gone up since the last time I was there."

Kricket shrugged. "Worth it, though."

Jericho pointed both a pincer and a finger at the cart that had carried Miles and Kricket. He didn't say anything, but they understood. They quietly boarded, along with the still-nameless Skyr, and awaited the journey back to camp.

"Do one more inventory check," Jericho shouted to the rest of his men. "Confirm the count, then we're headin' out."

Miles looked at Kricket, who sat across from him and whose gaze was transfixed out the window, staring toward the hills in the distance. His eye patch was still wet, dragged down slightly by the added weight, and Miles could barely see the top of a scar where his eyeball should have been.

He looked away from the Omne and imagined himself swimming in the waters of Feryn-lac. He tried to picture kyrfish gliding under the sea.

CHAPTER TWENTY

THE SWORD AND THE STAR

Miles woke up groggy and nauseated. He stumbled to the dormitory door and knocked three times then waited for the guard to address him. He forcefully rubbed his eyes and coughed. The heavy door swung open and Miles was surprised to find Risath standing before him.

"Yeah?" the Skyr grunted, casting an exasperated look at the boy. He had dark bags under his eyes.

"I don't feel good," Miles said, his voice raspy from sleep.

"Okay," Risath replied. He scratched under his chin.

"Do you have any tea?" Miles asked after a few moments, realizing wasn't going to say anything else. "My grandma always made me tea when I felt sick."

Risath's eyelids drooped. "Tea?" he echoed.

Miles nodded and cleared his throat. It stung.

Without a word, Risath slammed the door and locked it. If he listened closely, Miles could hear the sound of Risath's footsteps growing fainter as he ambled down the hall. He was banking on getting special treatment on account of his importance to King Mykael.

Miles lay back down on his bed to wait and found himself unable to stop his eyelids from fluttering. Risath returned some time later with a steaming mug in his hand from which an unfamiliar scent drifted. He placed the tea on Miles' desk then promptly departed. "Be ready to leave in about an hour," Risath said before closing the door. "Don't wanna waste more daylight than we have to." He disappeared behind the grey slab.

Right away Miles could tell the tea wasn't endalain, or if it was, it was not brewed nearly as well as Jaselle's. The flavor was bitter and dark, like he was chewing on the leaves themselves. And surely Risath had not bothered to pour in any honey. The honey would've helped his throat, but at least its warmth momentarily made him feel better.

Getting ready was simple, considering Miles had no possessions aside from the clothes he currently wore. Ten minutes after gulping down the last of his tea, the door flew open without warning and Risath stood waiting impatiently. The weary expression on the Skyr's face said far more than words could.

Outside the hatch, a dozen wagons were loaded up with boxes of food, clothing, and other supplies strapped to their roofs and shelves that were attached on their backs. The de-winged Carriers were already hitched up to the carts. Miles sought out Io and found her grazing.

Skyr and Omnes milled about amongst the carts, conversing with each other and figuring out who they would ride with. The packing was already complete; they had been killing time until Miles arrived. It made him feel important.

Based on the chatter, Miles surmised that the caravan would be split into a multitude of groups—no more than three wagons per group—in order to avoid any suspicions from spying Rompuns. Each group would take a drastically different route so that it didn't look like a huge collection of Skyr were moving to one specific area. Some caravans were even stopping in other towns for a few nights.

Risath ushered Miles toward the middle of the convoy to one of the more barren carts hitched to a Carrier that Miles didn't recognize.

"Climb aboard," Risath said.

Miles pulled open the door and hoisted himself into the cart, knowing that it would be pointless to argue in favor of riding with Io instead. Risath probably couldn't even tell the animals apart. Miles took a seat on the bench across from King Mykael.

"Hi," he said softly, unsure which version of the frightening Skyr he was speaking to.

"Hello," Mykael responded absently, more interested in the piece of paper he was reading than the child.

Risath had the door halfway shut before Miles addressed him. "Can Kricket ride with us?"

The Skyr chuckled. "Nope," he said. And that was that.

Looking out the window, Miles watched the creatures pile into their respective carriages. Many squeezed in two or three Skyr with just as many Omnes, while some managed to fill up a cart with eight Omnes. Things must have been cramped, not to mention the stench.

The door opened once more and Jericho entered, sitting next to Miles so as to not impose on Mykael's personal space. Being in such tight quarters with two of the most powerful Skyr in Rompu was intimidating.

The wagon's wheels creaked to life five minutes later and sent Miles' small body lurching forward. He composed himself and looked out the window, trying to guess what direction their route would take them. With the hilly landscape and blank sky, though, everything looked the same. He watched Io saunter away, pulling the cart behind her with ease.

Despite nearing noon, it was still too early in the day for Jericho to be talkative. He gazed out the window, taking sips from his flask every so often. His beard had gotten longer and mangier. Meanwhile, the king was caught up in whatever information his sheet of paper held.

Sunlight trickled in through one of the windows and cut through the paper, rendering it translucent, which allowed Miles to make out bold lines drawn with black ink on the other side. It looked like a map.

Eventually they stopped to allow the Carriers a break for some rest and water. It acted as a break for the entire company too, as they all fumbled outside to stretch their legs.

"Aye!" someone shouted, pointing a knobby finger toward the sky.

What started out as a black dot, hardly visible, quickly began to take shape. Thick limbs, great lashing tail. Wings flapping heavily, jaw agape as it coursed through the air, roaring as it dipped lower.

The Veratt.

The Skyr scrambled to retrieve their weapons. Archers aimed their arrows at the beast as it grew closer. Others gripped their swords and maces tightly in case the monster landed.

Miles steadied his heartbeat and focused on conjuring the image of his father, just in case he was needed. His fists felt feverish.

But their preparations proved unnecessary. The Veratt swooped down, eyed the caravan, and evidently decided they weren't worth its time. It flew off toward the east, in the direction they had come from.

"Pack up!" Jericho yelled over the excited tones of the Skyr and Omnes. "We're movin' in ten minutes!"

In less time than that, they were on the road again. With nothing to do and nobody to talk to, Miles resigned himself to a nap.

But sleep didn't come easily. The road was uneven, and every time he was finally drifting off, he would be jolted awake by a sudden bump. He kept his eyes closed anyway; the relief they felt from the rest was incredible.

He opened them with his father's exclamation, "We're here!"

To Miles, it was a city street just like any other, with cars lining the sidewalks and streetlights shining the entire length of the road. They were sandwiched between a muddy black pickup truck and a tiny white-and-blue car with the words CAR 2 GO painted on its side.

The sky was a gradient of blue to purple. Miles held his father's hand as they walked along the sidewalk, around the block, to a restaurant on the adjacent street. It was a place called the Texas Chili Parlor that his father had been raving about for a few weeks. Miles wasn't much of a chili fanatic, but he was promised they served burgers as well, so he'd agreed to go.

The restaurant was dimly lit. People sat at wooden tables in dark corners, laughing and chatting. A family sat at one of several round tables in the middle of the room, reading their menus.

His father greeted the burly man to their left who stood behind a cash register, then they made their way over to a small table for two against the far wall.

"Take a look at the burgers," his father said, handing over a menu.

Miles turned to the page that listed their burger selection and quickly spotted one with ingredients that interested him: mustard, grilled onions, pickles, swiss cheese, and lettuce. "I want this one," he said, pointing. The name wasn't a word he knew.

"The Gringo Burger? Looks pretty good," his father smiled. "No mustard though, right? Ketchup instead?"

A nod, as well as a smirk.

After many minutes and iterations of the question "When is someone gonna take our order?" from his father, a waitress finally arrived with a wide grin on her face.

"Hey fellas," she greeted them. "What'll y'all have tonight?"

Miles was shocked he even had a choice. "Uh...zol, I guess," he told Jericho. He had eaten too much kreer at the outpost.

The company had stopped for the night and set up a temporary campsite. Each pair of Omnes had to share a tent, but every Skyr had their own, as did Miles. Another surprise.

In his tent was where he waited, curled up under a hefty blanket while dinner was cooked. A fire had been started in the middle of the camp and a majority of the travelers gathered around, soaking up its warmth and telling stories. Jericho returned to the chef and relayed Miles' order.

His stomach was gurgling angrily by the time Risath retrieved him. The Omne guarding the flap of Miles' tent must have been hungry too, because as soon as Risath relieved her of duty, she darted toward the cook.

Miles sat on a small square blanket next to King Mykael and Jericho, who both had foldable lawn chairs with glasses full of water in their cup-holders. He became astutely aware of how parched he was.

The zol was moist and delicious. The cook had sprinkled a seasoning of dried herbs on the meat while roasting it, which had absorbed into the crispy skin. It was the best meal Miles had eaten since the night he left Trafier.

Across the fire, Miles saw Kricket sitting cross-legged on the ground, talking to a female Skyr. She seemed to only have a mild interest in what he was saying; her food was much more appetizing than the Omne's conversation.

He noticed Jericho was eating zol as well. "What kind of seasoning is this?" Miles asked him. The Skyr shrugged and tore off a piece of skin, gnashing it with his sharp teeth. He bit into the tender meat and squirted juice onto his goatee.

Miles took another bite of his burger with a satisfying crunch from the lettuce. His favorite part was the onions, how they were soft but still a little crunchy.

His father was spooning some chili into his mouth when he reached into his pocket. He pulled out his cell phone, which was vibrating noiselessly against the din of the restaurant. "Yeah?" he answered.

Miles listened while he ate his meal. He placed another forkful of potato salad in his mouth even though it was colder and less flavorful than he had expected.

"No, I told you yesterday," his father said to the person on the line. His face shifted from a frown to a scowl as he listened. Miles could hear the high-pitched voice floating softly through the air, slicing apart the noise around them. He suspected it was his mother.

He bit down on a dense piece of potato, upset by his father's expression.

"We have about two days left," Jericho told Mykael.

The king handed his empty plate to a scruffy Omne at his side. As the creature scurried away to rinse it off, Miles caught him licking up the leftover scraps of meat.

"I know that," Mykael said. "I have the map. You know I have the map."

"Yes, Majesty."

"I don't need you telling me things I already know."

Despite his size and threatening nature, Jericho seemed incredibly small when interacting with King Mykael.

"Would you just relax? What is your problem?" Miles' father asked irritably. He placed an elbow on the table and held his head in his hand. "No," he said after a moment. The word was harsh. Biting.

Miles attempted to distract himself with whatever program was on the television above his father's head. Unfortunately it was just the news, but it was better than listening to his parents argue.

The anchor was a woman the same age as his mother, sporting long brown hair streaked with blonde. A square graphic floated to the right of her face, framing video footage of police officers standing around a destroyed car. Its windshield was smashed, its hood dented. The subtitles plastered on the bottom of the screen said something about a support beam falling from the roof of a building onto the car. No one was injured.

"Because I should be allowed to see him whenever I want," his father snapped.

Miles' eyes instinctively shot down from the screen to his father's face. The man's hand was still cradling his forehead with his eyes shut as he breathed a deep sigh. The voice of Miles' mother buzzed through the phone's receiver, loud and angry.

But his father cut whatever she was saying short. "Shut up," he said.

The words rang in Miles' ears. He blinked, staring at his father, who seemed oblivious to the fact his son was watching and listening.

"Would you just shut up?" he said, quieter this time. His eyes fluttered open, meeting his son's. In that moment, he looked broken.

"Sorry, Majesty," Jericho apologized, scarfing down his last morsels of food.

The king's snarl was becoming more pronounced.

Miles didn't like where the situation was headed. Mykael was breaking again.

"You think I can't read a map?" Mykael asked Jericho. Even Miles knew the question was the kind that wasn't meant to be answered. He hoped Jericho was aware too.

"I didn't mean to offend you," Jericho said coolly, swallowing what was left of his meat. "I was just informing—"

The king rose in an instant, gripping Jericho's throat. "I don't need you to inform me of anything," he hissed, raising his stinger to Jericho's temple. "I ain't an idiot, am I?"

"No, Majesty," Jericho stammered.

"Of course I ain't. How would I have summoned a beast as fierce as the Veratt if I were an idiot?" It was another question King Mykael did not intend to be answered, made abundantly clear by the tightening of his grasp.

Jericho tried to choke out words, but failed.

"Anything to say?" asked Mykael. The sharpened tip of his stinger was now pressed lightly against Jericho's head. A thin sliver of blood trickled down his cheek.

Everybody gaped at the spectacle. Kricket was no longer talking to the lady Skyr. Risath stood only a few feet away.

"No," Jericho barely squeezed out. His tan complexion was turning pale as he lost circulation.

"What?" Mykael asked.

Without waiting for a reply, the king's stinger swung downward and stabbed Jericho's side. It retracted and reinserted twice more, faster than Miles' eyes could even register.

Miles released a horrified yelp. Jericho was silent, gritting his teeth. He clenched his fists. Nobody moved.

Mykael's grip loosened and Jericho tumbled to the ground, clutching his side and screaming in agony. Three large holes were torn in his shirt and blood drizzled onto the grass. Risath was already at his side.

Miles held a hand to his mouth, his eyes wide and body trembling. His legs felt unstable.

There was a noticeable change in the king's demeanor as he surveyed his handiwork. His shoulders grew less tense and his body slouched slightly. He took two steps back and lowered his tail.

"Okay. Yeah. Bye," his father muttered curtly before hanging up the phone. He frowned apologetically at his son, offering a timid smile. "Sorry about that, buddy." He didn't receive a reply, so he ate some more chili and stared down at his bowl for a few moments. Miles took another bite of his burger, not really tasting it.

"Get him bandaged up," Mykael said softly as he ran a hand through his hair. His tail drooped and brushed against the swaying blades of grass, leaving behind wet, red marks.

Risath was kneeling down and applying pressure to the wound. Jericho had already passed out from the pain. Risath shouted for an Omne to fetch medical supplies from one of the wagons, and two scurried off into the darkness, away from the fire's flickering light.

Miles remained still, not uttering a word.

"I've got something I wanna show you," his father said warmly. "Are you finished?"

The young boy nodded, though he still had most of his potato salad and half a burger left. He daydreamed about being tucked in bed with Ollie, watching the dog's furry tummy bob up and down as he breathed.

His father paid the man near the door then took Miles' hand and led him outside. The sun had already set. They walked lethargically down the sidewalk and rounded the corner, heading straight past where the car was parked.

They passed through an illuminated courtyard filled with hedges, statues, and plaques. They crossed a tiny street and clambered up huge stone steps that led to an enormous brown stone building. They circled the building, following the curved path, until they reached its front, where they descended more giant steps and stood in the middle of a pathway, turning to face the building. The vast lawn had neatly trimmed grass that was a too-perfect shade of green. It was like a movie set. The yard was lit up by faint lamps lining the pathway that led from a city street to where they stood.

"This is the capitol building," his father said. His smile was more genuine this time around.

The capitol was one of the biggest buildings Miles had ever seen in person. Its base was a long brownish-white rectangle, stacked with a pillared dome in its center and a statue perched on the very top. The statue was too far away for Miles to clearly see what the figure was. More lights shone on the building, casting deep shadows on its countless pillars and recesses. Some of the windows were lit up on the inside, while others were dark and blended in with the rest of the building.

It was entrancing.

"Wow," Miles whispered.

A couple yards away, a college-aged couple had set up a checkerboard blanket on the grass near what appeared to be an old cannon. She leaned back against his chest, the both of them sipping from bottles, giggling about something.

"Pretty cool, huh?" his father said, approaching the steps again. Three sets of towering brown doors, each separated by stone pillars, made up the entrance of the building.

"Yeah," Miles said, craning his neck to look up at the dome. It was an impossible distance away. "What's on top?" he asked.

"It's a sculpture of the Goddess of Liberty," his father explained, resting a firm hand on Miles' shoulder. "She's holding a sword in one hand and a star in the other."

"Why's she holding those?"

His father shrugged. "Dunno," he confessed. "Never thought to ask."

Miles frowned at the unsatisfying answer. "I wish I could see it."

"We could come back soon, during the day," his father offered. "You can see her way up there, and we could even go inside and have a look around. Sound cool?"

The frown transformed into a grin. "Yeah," Miles nodded fervently.

"It's a plan, then."

They both stood for several minutes, admiring the elegance of the building, basking in its glow. Miles had to be torn away from it.

The car ride home felt long. The moon was shrouded in gray clouds.

CHAPTER TWENTY-ONE

LUKEWARM

It took a couple more days of uneventful travel to reach the newly-built outpost, which was nearly identical to the previous one. It was located underground, with a hatch hidden in the middle of rolling hills. The interior was laid out a bit differently, but the core buildings remained the same: dormitory, king's safe house, cabins for Jericho and the other generals. At least this time the ladder leading underground wasn't so terribly long.

Being away from home for so long was weighing down on Miles. Each passing day felt like another year without his parents and Ollie. He was also desperately craving pancakes. It was time to focus and get ready to take down the Veratt.

In no time at all, Miles was back to his routine of practicing spellcasting outdoors. The Skyr forbade him from crafting any lightning again, but just to be safe, he was positioned almost a mile away from the hatch in case any Rompuns caught sight of smoke or any other indicators.

Miles had grown accustomed to Risath being his personal bodyguard. He stood nearby, arm behind his back, observing the kid. A group of Omnes had come up as well, loaded with quilts and picnic baskets full of snacks.

The first order of business had been figuring out how to douse the flames without having to hurl them at something, which would be a bad situation when surrounded by grassy knolls.

Conjuring the magic was easy. All Miles had to do was picture his father's face—really intensely concentrate on the image—and just like that, he was holding fire. So his theory had been that the opposite would be true as well: if he simply ceased all thoughts of his father, the fireballs would dissipate.

He was wrong.

He'd tested this hypothesis by tossing two fireballs into the air, stepping back a few feet, and wiping the image of his father from his mind before they hit the ground. What resulted was a small patch of fire that Risath and some Omnes had to scramble to put out by beating it with their picnic blankets. They tossed dirty scowls at Miles as they examined the scorch marks on their quilts. From then on, they'd equipped themselves with water buckets in anticipation of dousing more flames.

With many failed attempts behind him, Miles plopped himself on the ground a good distance away from the many blotches of blackened grass and pondered what had gone wrong.

After almost an hour of thinking, he had another plan.

The test would be the same. He'd create two fireballs from the image of his father, throw them above his head, and try to make them disappear before they started another grassfire. But this time, he would focus on the night he shared with his father on the capitol building's lawn. His father's hand on his shoulder, looking up in awe at the immense building, trying to make out the Goddess of Liberty against a pitch-black sky.

It didn't work.

"What the hell are you doin'?" Risath shouted at him as the Omnes stamped out the last of the fire.

Miles had been positive his theory would work. Focusing on an angry image created the fire, so shifting to a happy image should've eliminated it. The concept was simplistic, but it made sense to him. He would need to try again.

Risath and the Omnes swore loudly as Miles cast two new fireballs into the air.

He didn't let the irritable words distract him. His father's face was boldly imprinted in his mind and his eyes followed the fireballs high into the air. As they slowed and subsequently began their descent, the image was still present.

Instead of cutting straight to the new thought, out on the capitol lawn, Miles attempted a smoother transition. Keeping the base image, but changing the context.

The irritation of his father's rough features shifted, taking on a new meaning. It was no longer anger conveyed in his eyes, but weariness. He was drained. He was drained as he placed a hand on his son's shoulder, searching for the sword and the star that the Goddess of Liberty held in her grasp. But he was sharing a moment with his son, and that was important. It was just the two of them together, sharing something that was theirs and no one else's. And they were both appreciative of that.

The fireballs were gone.

The next morning, Miles tried to accomplish the same goal with his water magic. Making sure he was capable of stopping water wasn't quite as urgent as fire had been, but it would still be beneficial to master.

Applying his theory to the water spell was a lot more manageable than the fire had been. Giving a new context to his grandmother's octopus hotdogs—the memory which he drew on most consistently to send water jets spraying from his palms—was fairly simple. It was barely even a transition, but it worked all the same.

He imagined his grandmother cooking the hotdogs, then slicing them down to their middles to create the octopus legs. But instead of letting the thought of never eating them again sadden him, Miles pressed on and remembered her putting the octopuses on a plate with some ketchup. They would sit together in the afternoons and watch television together while he ate.

Within seconds, the streams died down, leaving behind water droplets on his palms. He smiled proudly.

Miles recalled that the other two types of spells the book mentioned, aside from Lightning, were Earth and Healing, so he spent the afternoon after his lunch break trying to raise up a chunk of the ground, lift a rock, or even kick up a dust storm. None of his attempts were met with success.

Frustrated by his failings, Miles set to cheering himself up by continuing to practice what he knew he could accomplish. He quickly discovered a way to channel his energy in such a way to create jets of flame that shot out in solid streams from each of his palms like the water had, and pointed them upward, crisscrossing them. Embers licked his cheeks and he grinned with satisfaction. His hands felt hot and sticky afterwards.

By that time, the sun was beginning to set and Miles once again felt compelled to try casting new spells. He didn't feel prepared for Earth yet, but he wanted to give Healing a shot. He approached Risath with apprehension.

"Yeah?" Risath mumbled at the young kid. "Ready to go in?"

"Yes," Miles replied. Even before he had finished saying the single syllable, Risath snapped his fingers and the Omnes began packing up their belongings. Miles cleared his throat.

"Somethin' else?"

"Can we go see Jericho?"

Risath cocked an eyebrow. "What for?" he asked, more curious than annoyed.

"I wanna try to help him." The scene of King Mykael jabbing his stinger into Jericho's side flashed in Miles' mind. His eyelids fluttered and he shook the thought.

"Yeah, okay," Risath snorted. "Fine. *C'mon!*" he barked at the Omnes, who were carefully folding their blankets. All of their wicker baskets were empty. The day's lunch had consisted of apple slices and sandwiches with thick meat and white cheese on wheat bread.

The group climbed the ladder down into the encampment, with the Omnes wandering off while Risath brought Miles to Jericho. The injured Skyr had opted out of residing in the medical shack and was instead in his own cabin.

Risath rapped his knuckles on the door and took a step back. There was a grumble from inside, and a few seconds later Jericho opened the door. "What?" he asked, looking from Risath down to Miles. He looked like a wreck. In addition to the multitude of scars and blisters that covered his body, his whole lower torso was now wrapped in thick white bandages that poked out from under a ragged shirt.

"The kid says he wants to try helpin' you," Risath said, unable to wipe the smirk from his face.

Jericho grinned as well. "That so?" he asked, gently pressing a hand to his side. His shirt looked damp, like blood had started to seep through.

"I think I can," the boy said, feeling somewhat queasy at the thought of seeing Jericho's wounds. He was sure he'd be able to heal Jericho's injury once he unlocked the proper method; the tricky part would be figuring out that method.

This made Jericho burst out laughing, even snorting. It was a wildly unsettling sound. "Right," Jericho said, rubbing his nose with the back of his hand. "Whatever, come on in. Try whatever it is you wanna try."

Miles accepted the invitation and entered the tiny house. It was comprised of no more than a bedroom, bathroom, and den, the latter of which made up half the building. The place was sparsely decorated, which was to be expected since they had only just arrived at the camp. There was a tall table in the den, cluttered with loose paper and crumb-covered plates. Some bags lay near the door, unzipped and half unpacked. There was nothing else in the cabin.

Jericho sat down in one of the chairs at the table and pulled his shirt off with some grunts and groans. He tossed it to the floor, exposing his bruised and battered chest. The long bandage, now more pink than white, was carefully peeled away.

The sight underneath was not as grisly as Miles feared. It was quite tame compared to some of the things he'd seen in movies. "How's it look, doc?" Jericho asked. Miles was young, but he could still detect the sarcasm. Risath chuckled, leaning against the doorframe while he quietly observed.

"It looks okay," Miles answered anyway.

"Just okay?"

There were six two-inch slits in Jericho's side, just below the ribs, where the stinger had penetrated his skin. Mykael must have been moving even faster than Miles could see that night. They would have been nothing more than minor holes if the tip of Mykael's stinger had pricked him, but the king had lost himself and dug deep into Jericho's side. Someone had done a passable job at stitching him up, and the bandages covered all the cuts, but blood still managed to ooze out with any fast or extensive movement.

"There are more cuts than I thought," Miles confessed, having only expected three.

"You outta your element, kid?"

Miles frowned because he knew the answer was yes. But he needed to try anyway.

"I can put this back on if you want," Jericho said, waving the bloodied bandage in front of the boy's face.

"No," Miles shook his head. "Let me try first." He held up his right hand and let it hover over the incisions. Jericho laughed, obviously not expecting anything to happen.

Miles understood that he had to pinpoint one image. One thought. One idea. Something to fixate on and channel his energy through as a conduit into the real world. He also understood that he needed to make absolutely sure he avoided accidentally thinking about his father, or else Jericho would have yet another injury to worry about.

He drew a blank.

"Well?" Jericho drawled.

Miles ignored him and forced images into his mind. First was his mother welcoming him at the front door. He felt a slight tug, a spark, but nothing really tangible. Next was Mrs. Mendol asking him what he had done over the weekend, and the spark was snuffed out. He had gotten farther away. He went back to his mother. She was in the kitchen, heating up a pot of soup on the stove for him while he sat on the couch next to Ollie, petting the dog's smooth back. The smell of chicken noodle soup was intoxicating; it warmed his insides and excited his nostrils.

"Do you like Dad's apartment?" she asked from the kitchen.

Miles didn't turn to look at her over the couch's backside. He wanted to sit still and pet Ollie. "Yeah," he replied half-heartedly.

Ollie repositioned himself, turning from his side onto his back, exposing his pink belly for Miles to rub. The boy giggled and did so, furiously rubbing his palm back and forth, arching his fingers every couple of strokes to let his nails lightly scratch the dog's tummy. Ollie groaned with gratification.

Another spark. But just as quickly as it appeared, it was gone. He had nothing.

He lowered his hand in defeat.

Jericho and Risath both looked amused.

"Maybe next time," Jericho said as he reapplied his bandage. Its edge curled, the adhesive worn down. He stood and gathered his shirt from the dusty floor.

"C'mon, then," Risath said, opening the door. Miles' face was flushed with embarrassment. "See you at dinner," Risath said to Jericho.

As they marched past the medical shack, Miles asked, "Can we go see the king?"

"You're full of requests today, ain't ya?"

But Risath relented and they walked together to the safe house where King Mykael was living, which had been constructed with thick metallic walls and had no less than four armed guards posted outside its entrance at any given time.

The king wasn't preoccupied with anything when Miles entered his room. He seemed to have been just sitting around, eating a snack. "Want some grapes?" he offered.

"No, thanks," Miles said, feeling a little more comfortable. He went on, not wanting to overstay his welcome and have the other side of the king show its face. "I was just wondering if I could borrow your magic book again. I'm having trouble with some stuff. It might help me."

Mykael frowned at this. "Hate to tell you, but no. My whole library was lost in that assault."

Miles' heart sunk. His stomach tied itself up.

Outside the room, Risath was surprised to already see the boy strolling past him. "Quick visit," he muttered, trailing behind Miles as they left.

Miles lay motionless in his bed. He stared at the ceiling, pleased with himself for learning how to better control fire and water, but frustrated by not being able to pick up earth or healing yet. Not having the opportunity to hone his lightning was irksome as well.

He sat up as his mother placed the steaming bowl of chicken noodle soup on the TV tray. He stirred the spoon, knocking noodles around into the big chunks of chicken. Miles loved her homemade soup. His grandmother had taught her how to make it.

"It's hot," she unnecessarily warned him before she walked away. A clattering of pans and bowls emanated from the kitchen, drowning out what was being said on the television. Miles grabbed the remote and increased the volume.

Ollie stood on the couch and took a cautious step toward the TV tray, leaning as far forward as he could. His wet snout pointed upward, rapidly sniffing the air in the soup's vicinity. Miles laughed and pushed the dog back, saying, "That's not for you."

A moment later, Miles' mother joined him on the sofa, setting her own bowl of soup on a tray. She lifted a spoonful of soup to her lips, blew on it, then gulped it down. She stared ahead at the television as she spoke.

"Did you have a good time with Dad?"

"Yeah," Miles answered.

"Good," she said. Another spoonful.

Miles decided to give his soup a try, hoping it had sufficiently cooled. He blew on the little puddle of liquid and noodle resting in his spoon, but it still burned his tongue. He grumpily slid the spoon back into the bowl and continued waiting for it to cool on its own.

"What did you two do?" his mother asked.

He told her about everything: the creek, the blu-rays, the burger he ate at the Chili Parlor, going to see the capitol building at night. He left out the part about hearing their argument on the phone. There was something he wanted to know, though.

"Why doesn't Dad live here anymore?"

His mother gave him a hesitant sideways glance before eating another spoonful of soup. Then another. She was nervous, which made Miles nervous. He'd never seen her so shaken before.

"Well..." She tried to grasp the proper words. "You know how you've, uh, been going to talk to Mrs. Mendol at school? Do you remember that book she let you borrow?"

"Yeah," Miles nodded. "'Dogs Divorce.'"

"Do you understand what a divorce is?"

He shrugged. "Kinda." He felt a little nauseous. Even the homemade soup sounded unappealing now.

His mother neglected her own soup too. "Well, Dad and I are getting a divorce," she said. "It's kind of hard to explain."

"Is it because you don't love each other anymore?"

At first she didn't say anything. Then she whispered a word Miles couldn't hear.

"That's what the book said," he explained. Seeing his mother cry upset him, but speaking made it easier for him to maintain his composure. "Sometimes parents don't love each other anymore, or they don't like being around each other. So they get divorced."

"It's complicated," she said.

Miles didn't feel any tears coming on. He just felt nauseous. He looked at his soup and noticed it was no longer steaming. "Okay," he said.

"Even though he doesn't live here anymore, you'll still see him a lot," his mother assured him, wiping her eyes. She tried to smile. "He's not far."

"Okay," Miles repeated.

Her smile faltered. "Do you have any questions about this?"

Miles shook his head.

"You can ask me anything, bug. Dad will talk to you about it too."

"I don't have anything to ask."

She leaned over and kissed his forehead. "I love you," she said softly.

"Love you too."

Miles looked at his mother and saw she was crying again. Just watching her son and crying. The sight finally got to him. Tears dribbled down his cheeks, staining his shirt. Ollie evidently considered this the ideal moment to roll on his back again and request another belly rub.

Both Miles and his mother couldn't help but crack up at the dog, who simply wagged his tail expectantly. Miles scratched Ollie's stomach and shared a smile with his mother.

He began to think about his father, sitting alone in the apartment, and Miles wondered what he was eating for dinner tonight. What he was watching on television. What time he would go to bed. What he was thinking about.

"Your soup is getting cold."

Miles let her take over scratching duties while he ventured another spoonful of soup into his mouth. It was lukewarm and he ate it quickly.

CHAPTER TWENTY-TWO

THIEF-ANT

Breakfast was quiet. His mother cooked scrambled eggs, bacon, and buttered toast. Miles had always preferred his father's eggs, which were much creamier and cheesier than what his mother prepared. While his mother carried their plates to the sink for rinsing, she asked Miles how he had slept.

"Fine," he lied. In truth, it had taken him almost an hour to fall asleep, and even then he had woken fitfully throughout the night. School would be more of a chore than usual and talking to Mrs. Mendol would be a headache.

"Did you have any dreams?" his mother asked next.

"Nope."

She scrubbed away at the dishes, even though there wasn't much of anything to clean off. She let her hands hang under the warm running water, wiping nothing away with the bright yellow sponge. "Finish getting ready," she told him.

Miles got up from the table and entered the living room. The television was still tuned to Nickelodeon, which he had been watching while waiting for breakfast and packing for school.

On the floor beside the coffee table, Ollie was gnawing his own ankle.

"What are you doing?" Miles asked the dog.

As expected, he received no response or even any recognition. Ollie kept chewing with his jowls drawn back and fangs bared. He finally finished biting himself and curled up into a black, furry ball on the carpet. On the screen, Spongebob was talking to Squidward about something in the Krusty Krab.

Without him even noticing, his mother sat down on the couch and smiled. "Where's your ball?" she asked Ollie, startling Miles. He expected to be chastised for not being ready to leave.

The dog hopped to his feet, wagging his tail excitedly.

"Where's your ball?" his mother asked again.

At that, Ollie was gone, zooming into the hall. Moments later, he trotted back into the living room with his green squeaky ball clasped awkwardly in his mouth. Ollie obediently dropped it by Miles' mother. It had taken her a week to teach him the basics of fetch.

"Wanna throw it?" she asked Miles.

"I'll be late," he said.

She grinned. "We can skip today if you want."

Miles nodded happily and took the ball. All the while, Ollie's eyes never left it, locked onto their target.

The boy held the ball up and Ollie readied himself. Miles tossed the ball downward so that it would gain a nice bounce as it traveled down the hallway. Ollie raced after it at top speed, skidding to a halt at the end of the hall and swatting the ball in mid-air.

"I'm sorry you have to go through this right now," his mother said as they watched Ollie struggle to grasp the comically large ball in his mouth. "Especially so soon after everything with Grandma. I know it's tough."

"It's okay," Miles said absentmindedly. Ollie placed the ball at the kid's feet and sat, tilting his head. The dog vanished as Miles threw the green ball down the hallway again.

"Has talking to Mrs. Mendol been helpful?"

"Yes," Miles said.

They were quiet as Ollie brought back the ball. He kept it in his mouth and let out a low growl when Miles tried to take it, but eventually the dog relented.

He handed his mother the ball, and when she chucked it down the hall, Miles asked, "Why do you and Dad not love each other?"

It took a second for her to respond. "We still love each other," she said. "We're just not *in* love with each other."

"Why?" he asked. There didn't seem to be a difference to him. Love was love.

"It's complicated," she said.

By now Ollie had come back, but he was done playing. He lay a couple feet away, holding the ball steady between his paws as he licked and chewed on it. Every few bites, it let out a meager squeak.

"It'll make sense when you're older," his mother said. "I'll explain it to you then. Deal?"

The answer left Miles deeply unsatisfied, and the knot in his stomach tightened, but he conceded. "Deal."

He sat down next to her on the couch and scooted back so that his legs hung off the edge, dangling above the carpet. The two watched Ollie as Mr. Krabs shouted at his employees about money on the TV.

"You're being really mature and strong about all this," his mother said. Ollie sat up and stared as if she had been talking to him. Then she asked, "What do you wanna do today?"

Two full days passed before Miles felt confident enough to make another pass at manipulating earth. By the third day, he was relieved of all embarrassed and frustrated thoughts. He felt rejuvenated and motivated to solve the puzzle.

His audience was smaller than usual. He was now accompanied only by Risath and three Omnes, who were busying themselves with drinking games as they sat cross-legged on their picnic blanket. Each possessed a bottle of raspberry-infused beer. They cheerily clapped and sang songs in a foreign language, the words darting in between claps:

"Viry'n de mahl,
as'ror en bil,
falahl m'rir'ent'l
ioren dehl!"

With each iteration, the first and third lines changed and the rhythm grew faster and faster until one of the Omnes stumbled, the consequence for which was taking a drink while the other two guffawed and hollered. Then the process would start again.

The entire thing was terribly distracting for Miles, so he was already feeling sour about the day before he even started. He swung a foot, kicking up clumps of dirt. He sighed and figured the tiny clumps were as good a place to begin as any.

The dark brown clusters contrasted with the bright, picturesque green of the swaying grass, made all the brighter by the sunlight. They were easy to focus on, but Miles narrowed it down even further by concentrating on the largest piece.

"Pik a'drin,
as'ror en bil,
zash en yll'tr
ioren dehl!"

A great roar erupted from the boisterous group and the chubbiest of the three gulped down some of his beer. Miles scowled, returning his gaze to the clump of dirt.

First he needed to select a mental image to link with the earth. This was proving to be a lot more difficult than it had been before, though. He worried that because he was finally understanding how the magic worked, he was now overthinking things rather than allowing the link to occur organically.

His mind leapt to sharing Chicago dogs with his father. Biting into the end of the hotdog, mouth on fire from the peppers, crunching the pickle. They stood on a sidewalk downtown as people milled past, nearly brushing against him.

Peppers.

He transitioned his thoughts from the Chicago dog to sitting at home with his mother and father, eating a slice of cheese pizza while they watched an awards show.

His father had picked up a large, green-yellow pepper from out of the pizza box. The pepper was crinkled and bent. "Wanna try it?" he'd asked, grinning toothily.

"What is it?"

"It's kinda like the ones on Chicago dogs, but bigger," his father had said. "It's called a pepperoncini."

"That's not what you called the other ones," Miles had pointed out to him.

"Oh, I know. They're not the same, just similar." He had then taken a bite off the tip and juice squirted out onto the pizza slices inside the box. "Wanna try?"

After a second of thinking it over, Miles had declined. "The ones on the hotdogs are too spicy for me already."

There was a chuckle from his father before he took another bite of the pepper, not chewing it until he'd taken another bite of pizza as well. He had chewed the two together and moaned, *"Mhmm."*

Nothing happened.

The dirt didn't move an inch.

Miles wasn't sure what exactly he should be expecting earth to do when manipulated by his magic, but whatever it was, it wasn't happening. He had hoped to make it levitate at the very least.

The memory transition was probably too drastic. In the others, he had kept the same base image and moved it into a new memory. This time, he had used the peppers on the hotdog as a base and changed them into the pepperoncinis. It was entirely possible that the memory of the peppers wasn't a strong enough base to begin with, but either way, his context shift was faulty.

So he tried again.

He sat on the ground, crossing his legs and placing his hands on his knees. His brow furrowed, lips pursed. Images flashed in his mind one by one until the entire scene was reconstructed.

Father. Sidewalk. Hotdog. Peppers.

He remembered asking, "What—"

An explosion of noise from the Omnes disrupted his train of thought.

He cast Risath a conspiratorial glance, hoping the Skyr was just as aggravated by the game as he was. But Risath was watching the trio, laughing along with them as they kept drinking.

Miles resettled.

Father. Sidewalk. Hotdog. Peppers.

"What are these called?" he had asked his father, pointing at the tiny green peppers nestled between the wiener and bun.

They were thin, cylindrical, and came to a dull point. It was the year before, the first time he'd ever eaten a Chicago dog.

"Sport peppers."

He then hazarded another bite, reeling at the spiciness of the second half of the sport pepper.

Peppers.

It was obvious how he should shift his thoughts this time around. He nearly blushed at himself for not realizing it sooner.

The sidewalk fell away beneath him and his father, quickly replaced by a car. By a parking lot. By a restaurant. By neon signs.

Miles had been sitting in the front seat. A rarity. His mother had left earlier that evening to visit his grandmother in the hospital while he and his father stayed behind. The two of them had settled on Sonic for dinner.

Seeing a Chicago dog listed on the menu had immediately caught the boy's eye and he asked to order it.

"It's not as good as the ones we usually get," his father had warned him.

"I wanna try it."

So he'd gotten the Chicago dog with tater tots while his father ordered a cheeseburger and tots. His father had been right. It wasn't as good.

Still nothing. The clump remained solidly on the ground, tickled by the grass.

"How's it goin' over there?" Risath asked.

"Fine," Miles told his father as he climbed into the passenger seat. Without his mother joining them on rides anymore, Miles was allowed to sit in the front seat while he was shuttled between the house and apartment. It took the sting out of everything just slightly.

But only slightly.

"How's school been?" was his father's next question as he fired up the car. He looked over his shoulder as he backed out of the driveway.

"Fine," Miles said again.

Their conversation went on like this, stalling in sync with the car as they sat in traffic on the highway. They finally arrived at the apartment and Miles bee-lined for his room, closing the door behind him and pulling a book out of his backpack.

His father cooked a hefty meatloaf with mashed potatoes and green beans for dinner. While his mother always chose the path of boxed potatoes, his father preferred making them himself. He would peel most of the skin, boil the potatoes, drain the water, then mash them up while adding milk, butter, salt, and pepper. Sometimes he sprinkled in garlic as well. The process usually fascinated Miles, but he decided to stay in his room and read.

The meatloaf was warm and delicious, filled with chopped onions and green bell peppers. Miles took a bite then shoveled some potato and green beans into his mouth to chew them all together. They ate mostly in silence.

Near the end of the meal, his father said, "I heard Mom talked to you."

Even with the vagueness, Miles understood what his father meant. It took him a moment to nod. He wanted to delay the conversation as much as possible.

His father offered a brittle smile. Miles felt a pang of sadness for him, but it didn't make the situation any less uncomfortable.

"Do you understand what's going on?"

Miles only shrugged. It wasn't enough of an answer for his father, who urged him to say something. "You're getting divorced," he said, not fully grasping the meaning of the word. He knew enough based on the context and Mrs. Mendol's dog picture book to know what was happening.

"Right," his father said quietly. For a second it looked like he was about to go on, but he backed down. He picked up their plates and carried them to the sink. He ran the water for a moment then shut it off, returning to his seat.

"Why?" Miles asked.

The dining room was still. The question hung between them, suspended in the air like a bubble waiting to pop. But then his father spoke.

"It's complicated," he started, mirroring Miles' mother. "There's a lot going on between Mom and me right now."

"You two fight a lot," Miles said, recalling the shouting matches he'd heard his parents engaged in so many times. The arguments that had pushed him to tear apart his bedroom.

The sentence seemed to smack his father. "You're right," the man agreed. "We've been fighting a lot lately. That's part of it."

"What are you fighting about?"

The stilted conversation made time slow down.

"Lots of stuff," his father replied.

"Like what?" Miles insisted.

His father sighed. "It's complicated," he repeated. "We...I did something bad," he said, running fingers through his hair. "We still love each other, but I did something really stupid, and Mom is pretty mad at me for it."

"What did you do?"

"Now that's definitely not something we can talk about."

Miles could tell by his father's tone that pushing him down that road would be fruitless, so he asked something else instead. "Why don't you two talk about it? That's what we learn in school. When we get into an argument, we're supposed to talk about it instead of fighting."

"We tried, buddy. It's a bit more complex than just talking about it. That's where the fighting came from."

"So she's mad at you for doing something stupid and now you're getting divorced?"

"Yeah."

More silence.

Neither of them knew what to say to the other. Miles didn't have many questions, and the few he did have would surely be danced around. It was almost completely pointless to even try discussing the issue since everybody thought he was too young to comprehend any part of it. He was frustrated by his confusion and everyone else's unwillingness to clarify things for him.

"Why won't you tell me anything?" His voice was loud and firm, almost a shout.

It clearly stunned his father, but the man didn't skip more than a beat. "Because it's complicated," he said, repeating that favored word. "It's more than you'd be able to understand, and it's more than you need to know right now."

"Why is it more than I need to know?" Miles demanded, fed up with half-answers. "I'm not too young to be told."

"Yes you are, Miles."

"I'm—"

"You're a kid and I'm an adult. That's the way it is. I'm your dad, and if I think you're too young, then you're too young. I wish I could make things less confusing for you right now, but I can't, buddy. I'm sorry."

Miles wanted to scream at his father. He wanted to bang his fist against the table. As he glared at the man, he didn't see anger in his father's eyes. Or irritation. Or frustration. He saw that same tiredness he'd seen so many times the past few weeks. Suddenly he felt crushed.

"I don't want you to get divorced," he said. "I'm sorry."

"I know. But I think it's for the best. The only thing that's gonna change is Mom and I don't live together anymore, alright? Everything else will stay the same. I'll still see you as often as I can. Every weekend, if you want."

Miles nodded, willing himself to be less angry. Wanting to take it back.

"Do you wanna watch a movie tonight?" his father asked hopefully. "I could make us some popcorn. After our stomachs settle a little, of course," he grinned.

"No thanks," Miles said, refusing the piece of honey bread. The Omne shrugged and stuffed it into her own mouth.

Lunch went by quickly and Miles returned to work mastering earth while the Omnes resumed their drunken game. They were surprisingly resilient for such small creatures.

One of them led and the other two joined in:

"Li'lyr de y'ow,
as'ror en bil,
zash de myre
ioren dehl!"

Miles tried to shove the sounds of their howling out of his mind as he sat down next to his clumps of dirt again. But their screaming grew louder and louder as their rounds grew shorter and shorter, their inebriation slurring the song and rendering everybody lethargic and off-tempo.

Staring down at the dirt, the wailing of the Omnes suddenly washed away, as did everything else around him. The sound of the wind blowing, of Risath's scratching his stubbled chin, of distant birds chirping.

All he heard was him telling his father, "I'm sorry."

In an instant, he was in the air.

Miles looked down at Risath's incredulous expression. It took the boy a moment to realize he wasn't actually flying; an enormous circular patch of earth beneath him had shot upward. Dirt, grass, and bugs floated fifteen feet above the ground, with him standing on top. He couldn't recall the last time he had smiled so wide. He was giddy with how easily this magic was coming to him now.

Now that he knew what was going on, it was easier to take control of the situation. Miles made the earth he stood on drift toward Risath, whose eyes followed him the whole way over. The Omnes had even stopped playing their inane drinking game and stared slack-jawed at the boy.

Miles lowered himself and stepped off the uneven mound of earth, grinning delightedly.

Risath was on the cusp of congratulating him when suddenly there came a rumble from the newly-created hole in the ground. Specks of dirt began to spit out of the hole as a faint scratching became more prominent.

Then something crawled out of the hole, and Miles went pale.

It was roughly ten feet long and resembled a centipede, but with a hard outer shell that was a murky red hue. It had a razor sharp tri-horn jutting from what Miles presumed to be its face, though without any distinguishing features it was impossible to tell. Six skinny legs on each side of its thick body carried it out onto the field, scurrying to point its horn toward the five individuals staring at it. Below the horn, a mouth filled with hundreds of tiny fangs opened up to unleash a roar. It was an ungodly sound, splitting Miles' eardrums and almost causing the boy to fall to his knees.

Risath cursed. The Omnes abandoned their quilt and darted toward the hatch.

But the beast was swift on its many feet. In a flash it was before the three stumbling, diminutive Omnes, curling its body so that its end circled behind the trio. They were surrounded.

The fat Omne was immediately speared on the giant insect's horn and tossed aside like a doll. He didn't get back up.

The other two let loose terrified screams, and one of them was instantaneously silenced by the insect biting into his abdomen, effectively ripping the Omne in half. Blood sprayed onto the grass and stained the animal's shell.

While it was preoccupied, the last Omne scrambled over its back, hoping to still make it to the hatch. But the game she'd been playing for so many hours had made her clumsy and she practically toppled over the insect's shell, landing face-first on the ground. What happened next was not pretty or pleasant.

All the while, Miles stood motionless, horrified and unable to will his body to move. Risath muttered one swear word after another, furious with himself for not having a weapon.

"Kid!"

Miles was shaken out of his stupor and realized it was the fourth time Risath had tried gaining his attention.

"What?"

"You need to do somethin'," the Skyr said. "We can't out-run this thing and ain't no way I can kill a damn thief-ant with my bare hands."

This is what he'd been training for.

At that moment, the insect finished playing with its food and consumed the three Omnes it had maimed, leaving behind only a few limbs and scraps of clothing. It swiveled its head to face its new targets with machine-like agility.

Risath took off as the thief-ant charged forward.

No time to dawdle.

Without thinking, Miles directed all his energy toward the beast. Thoughts of his father made half of the thief-ant's legs catch fire, causing it to skitter in another direction. It rolled back and forth, flattening the grass as it tried to put out the flames. Miles took this opportunity to test his newest ability by thinking back to how he felt after yelling at his father. A rectangular patch of earth that held the thief-ant rose toward the sky.

The creature failed to notice it was now considerably high in the air and accidentally rolled off the edge, careening toward the spot where Miles stood. The boy jumped out of the way a split second before the thief-ant crashed into the ground, its horn stabbing deep into the earth. But the thief-ant was clearly built to burrow, so the animal wasn't impeded by this at all and slid its horn out with ease.

The first thing Miles took note of was that while the thief-ant's legs were no longer burning, they had been severely charred by his magic. It would either be severely difficult to walk, extremely painful, or both.

The second thing was that the beast was incredibly angry and gearing up to impale him.

To buy himself some time, Miles lifted the thief-ant into the sky again, but the creature was too fast and clever. It hastily jumped off the patch of earth before it ascended too much, propelling itself toward Miles again.

Another flash of his father's tired face and Miles shot the ground beneath him upward and away from the thief-ant, leaving the animal to slam into a hole where the boy had been a moment before.

From above, Miles began to shoot streams of fire, but the thief-ant barely reacted to the assault. Its tough protective shell made it impervious to Miles' flames. Without fire being at all effective, he was going to have to rely on earth. He didn't imagine water would do much damage to the insect.

He tried lifting up two slabs of earth on either side of the thief-ant to bring together and squish it, but even the thought of such a feat mentally exhausted the kid. He wasn't yet skilled enough to pull off such a feat while simultaneously keeping himself afloat.

So instead, he tried flattening the beast. The mound of dirt holding Miles up crashed into the thief-ant, whose horn pierced the ground and tore the patch in two, sending Miles flying backward and tumbling down the side of a hill.

When Miles tried to stand himself up, it felt like every bone in his body was broken. He was sure he could feel his ribs cracking with each cough, and he was suddenly aware of tears streaming down his face.

He had to be brave.

The thief-ant crested the hill. Its magenta exoskeleton was marred with dirt and grass and singed from Miles' flames. Yet it was still fighting.

Still fighting while Miles lay defenseless and unable to move at the bottom of a hill the creature could cover within five seconds. Maybe less. Probably less.

Nothing was working.

Not fire, not earth—he still very much doubted water would have an effect on the beast—nothing.

Only one option was left, and he was sure its use would make the king livid. But would he be more upset if Miles conjured lightning, or if he died?

He might as well find out.

Miles peered at the thief-ant. The sun behind the creature's silhouette was virtually blinding. And then the insect was off, scuttling down the hill, its legs a blur.

Miles would either be dead in two seconds or he wouldn't be. He didn't fight past the fear—he used it. He saw his grandmother's frail face.

Lightning struck, tearing the thief-ant in two. It gurgled out a violent scream as its two halves plunged down the hillside, bouncing along the grass and shooting past Miles' tense body. It slid to a halt behind him, legs twitching every couple seconds.

He finally exhaled.

Miles lay his head back on the soft grass and closed his eyes. Sunlight bled through his eyelids, casting an orange hue on the void. His breaths were long and deep and ragged. Aches ran through every part of him.

After twenty minutes, he tried to sit up, but couldn't. He opened his eyes and stared at the cloud passing by, trying to find pictures in their shapes like his mother did. He inhaled slowly, and as he breathed out, his mother's smile on his mind, his body began to tingle. His bones felt stiff, his muscles re-laxed. He looked down at his bruised arms and watched the spots fade away, his body encased in a green and blue glow.

He stood without a problem.

In his head, he sang a melody:

Viry'n de mahl,

as'ror en bil,

falahl m'rir'ent'l

ioren dehl.

Slowly, he shuffled up the hill back toward the hatch to tell King Mykael that he was ready.

CHAPTER TWENTY-THREE

SPEAKIN' OUTTA TURN

That night, a grand feast was held in celebration of Miles' mastery of magic. Or at least as close to mastery as he could get; he was no David Blaine, but he felt incredibly accomplished after killing the thief-ant on his own. It had been good practice for what was to come with the Veratt.

After he had tracked down Risath and told him what happened, the Skyr ordered a messenger to alert the king of Miles' feats. A short time later, Miles took a nice, long, warm bath to wash away the dirt and blood caking his body.

Now dry and smelling sweetly clean, Miles dressed himself in some fresh clothes that were delivered while he'd been bathing. It was lucky that Omnes were around the same size as him. He appreciated being able to finally wear some new clothes, which felt soft and light against his skin.

A knock interrupted his dressing, which he hastily finished by pulling on some socks and a crisp new pair of shoes he had just spotted by the door.

It was Risath. "Ready?" the Skyr asked.

"Yeah," Miles nodded, slipping the shoes on. They hugged his feet tight.

"Are those Hyron's hand-me-downs?"

"They feel new," Miles said, a little offended. New clothes were a luxury he hadn't really experienced since his time in Trafier.

"Don't look new," Risath grunted. He pointed at a green stain at the bottom of the shirt that Miles' eyes had missed. "That's where Hyron spilled stew on himself. The idiot. Anyway, c'mon." He turned on his heels and led Miles to the dining hall a few buildings away.

Everybody who mattered was in attendance at the dinner: King Mykael was, of course, at the head of the table, and near him sat Jericho and Risath, as well as numerous Skyr and a select few Omnes Miles had seen often around the camp.

It didn't take long at all for Miles to realize the king had slipped into his dark, vicious form. When a servant brought a glass of wine that was different than what Mykael had wanted, the king slapped the silver tray out of his hand. The glass tumbled to the floor, its stem snapping in two, and wine spilled all over the Omne's shoes.

Mykael angrily ordered the Omne to clean up the mess and bring him the glass of wine he had requested. Humiliated and probably a bit frightened, the Omne nodded fervently and shuffled out of the dining hall, his wet feet smacking against the ground.

Despite the king's ill temper, Miles found himself enjoying being a part of the festivities. Having such a luscious meal prepared in his honor made the boy feel excited and proud. He had accomplished a lot that day, as his gurgling stomach reminded him.

The appetizer was a simple salad with grapes, cherry tomatoes, cucumber, and feta cheese. Miles was not overly fond of feta, but it would be a hassle to pick out the white crumbs one by one, so he dealt with the taste by drowning the lettuce in a light brown, translucent dressing. Little dark flakes floated in the concoction and gave it a kick of zest that Miles found to be quite delicious.

He had barely finished his salad when a female Omne whisked the bowl away. Without even five seconds to ruminate, a plate filled to its perimeter with food was placed in front of Miles by another Omne. The servants were dancing in and out from between the guests, half of them lifting plates while the other half set them down. Miles was impressed by the grace and agility of the stubby creatures, considering his only real experience with Omnes involved Kricket and Gryff bumbling around foolishly.

"Thank you," Miles tried to say, but before his words could reach their ears, the Omnes had already disappeared behind the kitchen doors.

The main entree was a rack of ribs slathered in brown, sticky sauce that smelled like honey and burnt wood. They reminded Miles of the pork ribs his father used to grill, but the meat and sauce were vastly different. It was a lot tougher to chew, and the sauce much smokier. That said, the meat was spectacular. Miles wanted to know why they had been eating like scavengers for the past several weeks if this sort of food was at their disposal. He felt cheated by Mykael keeping meals such as this to himself.

Miles' plate also housed familiar sights, including a warm buttered roll and green beans that were liberally salted and peppered. He fiendishly scarfed down the roll and minutes later an Omne carrying a bread basket brought him another.

When he finished his ribs, a different Omne brought him another rack.

And the same with the green beans.

So he continued to eat.

Miles ate more than he even knew he was capable of. Since the food kept coming, he kept shoveling it in. The battle with the thief-ant had given him an exceedingly strong appetite and this food was hitting the spot.

"Thanks," he finally managed to tell an Omne while she refilled his water glass. She didn't smile or speak, simply nodding.

All the while, King Mykael was barking out orders at every Omne unfortunate enough to appear in his line of sight.

Miles couldn't help but wonder if King Mykael, who was a powerful, brilliant Skyr, could be torn apart so savagely by opening a rift, then what would happen if he attempted to open one himself to go back home? He was just a small, frail child. He would be decimated.

He admitted to himself that he had consumed far too much food already, especially where bread was concerned. Combined with the meat, vegetables, and multiple glasses of water, everything sat heavy in his tiny stomach. But there was more.

As half the Omnes cleared away the guests' plates, the other half handed everybody a smaller one with a petite piece of cake at its center. It was a creamy yellow color, topped with fluffy whipped cream and drizzled with a blue glaze.

Miles cut off the tip of his piece and speared it with his fork, eagerly stuffing it in his mouth. He chewed, considering its flavor for a few blissful seconds. It was cheesecake with blueberry syrup.

He ignored his stomach's aching pleas and began devouring the cake. It was exactly like the cheesecake at some fancy restaurant his father had taken him to one night as a surprise.

"I think we both deserve a nice meal, don't you?" his father had smiled from the driver's seat. Miles just shrugged.

And now they were eating dessert, both of them having ordered their favorites. Miles had gone with a plain piece of cheesecake with blueberry syrup on top. The thick, blue sauce was squirted along the rim of the plate, arcing and swooping in an elegant design to encircle the cake.

His father had gotten key lime pie. The shade of green always grossed Miles out, so he upheld his tradition of refusing to try a bite when his father offered. "More for me," the man said, diving in. His eyes rolled back in his head after the first bite, moaning about how scrumptious it was. He flattened the mountain of whipped cream on top, covering the entire surface of the pie.

The king looked annoyed as a messenger scurried into the dining hall, bee-lining toward him. The Omne was visibly shaking as he stood before Mykael, waiting for permission to speak.

"What?" the looming Skyr asked coldly.

"Your Majesty, you requested constant updates on the Veratt's whereabouts?" The Omne's inflection made it a question.

"Spit it out, then."

"The beast is flying toward Trafier, Majesty."

Miles stopped eating his cake, staring at the head of the table with his mouth agape.

The king grinned, exposing his sharp, crooked teeth. Miles suddenly felt sick, and he wasn't sure if it was because he knew

Mykael was excited or because of the excessive amount of food he had consumed.

"Fantastic," Mykael laughed.

"Do you want me to send some men to Trafier, Your Majesty?" asked Jericho, suddenly at attention. "To track the beast?"

"No. Well, yes," the king corrected himself. "But not yet. Round up some troops, but wait til I say to send them off. Maybe just one can be sent ahead to ensure the Veratt is on course for Trafier, but otherwise let them wait until it's leveled the city. No need letting them get caught in the crossfire." His eyes glinted with the thought of Trafier crumbling to the ground.

Buildings collapsing, fire raging.

Jaselle lost and injured in the marshes, Mortimer squeezed by the Veratt's claws until he burst.

Mykael was still giving orders to Jericho and the messenger when Miles blurted out, "Let me go!"

The king's glare could cut flesh. "You speakin' outta turn, boy?" he hissed, his voice a low rumble echoing through the room.

"I can control my magic," Miles said, hoping the statement was fully or at least mostly true. "You kept me here so I could fight it. So I could capture it and let you use it. Let me go do that." The Skyr lining the table could see the boy's desperation fogging up the room. He swallowed loudly.

"No," Mykael said simply. "If the thing wipes out Trafier and all those idiot Rompuns and traitors in there with it, then it's doin' half my job for me. You can go with Jericho and his men when they leave."

"There's no time. The Veratt might be gone by the time we reach Trafier," Miles pleaded, hoping it would sway the intimidating Skyr.

"No. And if you speak out again, Miles, you can bet your ass you won't like what happens next."

Miles could feel the frosty stares cast at him from every other person in the room.

So he bolted.

In seconds, Miles' chair was lying flat on the ground and he was out the door, rushing through the hallway toward the exit. Behind him, he could hear the Skyr scrambling out of their seats, the king screaming orders at them to *"catch the damn kid!"*

The dining hall wasn't far from the front door, so Miles was outside in mere moments, standing twenty feet away from the campfire that was surrounded by Omnes and low-level Skyr.

Miles had always been fairly quick on his feet, but the Skyr were both fully grown and much more agile than him anyway. He was nowhere near the ladder's base when the Skyr chasing him pushed their way out into the open.

"Grab the kid!" an anonymous Skyr yelled.

For a moment, nobody moved. It took them the space of that moment to process what was transpiring. After that moment, movement flooded Miles' vision. Every living being in the underground camp was honing in on him like guided missiles.

Thankfully, a majority of them were gathered around the fire for dinner, so the pathway to the ladder was clear save for two lagging Omnes that waddled toward him, arms raised and forked tongues lashing wildly.

It took little effort to duck out of their way. While doing so, Miles accidentally caught a glance over his shoulder and was horrified to discover a huge number of Skyr were gaining on him. To buy as much time as possible, he lobbed a sizeable fireball backward. He didn't see the results, but he heard pained yelps and knew that some damage was done.

Miles leapt onto the second rung of the ladder and moved all of his limbs faster than he ever had before. Halfway up, he stopped and turned to face the mob running after him. He let go with his right hand and pointed the sweaty palm at the mixed group of Skyr and Omnes below, concentrating on the mental image of his grandmother.

A torrent of water exploded from his open palm, its end growing wider as it cascaded toward the mob. He moved his hand side to side, the spiraling stream of water thrashing violently like a fire hose, sending waves of Skyr and Omnes tumbling backward. Many lost their balance and fell, shoved along the dirt floor by the water, which was making the ground soft and muddy. Even more began to slip or get their feet stuck.

Satisfied, Miles turned off his magical water jet and continued his ascent.

He pushed open the hatch which was a lot heavier than he had anticipated. With a great amount of trouble, he managed to slam it shut again when he was on solid ground.

He darted in the direction of the Carrier stable, which were secluded in the middle of the hillside near the hatch, hidden to any passersby. As he crested a third hill, he could finally make out the silhouette of the wooden stable in the clouded moonlight.

At the bottom of the hill, he spotted Io and made his way toward her. He winced at the sight of the stumps where her wings once were, their tips still encrusted with dry blood.

"Hey, what are you doin' here?" came a voice in the dark.

Miles turned and saw Kricket staring at him, a bucket of water held against his puffy chest.

"I need to leave," Miles said. "Please don't stop me. I know magic."

"I know you know magic, you dolt," Kricket said, setting down the bucket. Water sloshed and splashed onto the cool grass. He took a step forward.

"Stay back," Miles warned him. "I'll just take Io and go." After a second of deliberation, he decided to ask, "Why are you over here?"

"I'm stuck doin' this crappy job cause I took you to that resort without telling anybody. Why are you leavin'?" Kricket asked. He had come to a halt, not wanting to incite another fiery beating.

"The Veratt," Miles replied. "It's flying to Trafier. I need to stop it from hurting everyone there."

Kricket's face went pale. As pale as his scaly, grey face could become, anyhow. "Can you even do that?" the Omne asked, skeptical. "You that strong?"

Miles shrugged.

"Well," Kricket said, after taking a deep breath, "can't hurt to try." He picked up the bucket of water again and carried it over to Io, who began to lap it up happily. Kricket looked at Miles. "Why would I stop you?"

"Because you work for the king," Miles said slowly.

"True. And I also want that damn Veratt dead," Kricket spat. "That thing killed my mother and my sister." He patted Io on the nose. "Let her finish drinkin', and we'll go."

Relief poured through Miles and his muscles instantly relaxed. The past five minutes had been such a whirlwind, he hadn't noticed how tense his body had become. For a few seconds he fell into a daze listening to the soothing sound of Io's tongue lapping up the water, but he quickly regained his composure.

"We can't wait," Miles told him. "The entire camp is kind of after me."

"All of 'em?" Kricket asked. "Wow."

"Not all of them," came a voice from behind them.

Miles flipped around, his hands up and ready to cast whatever spells he needed to ward off his attacker. It was Mykael.

The king also put up his hands, waving them in surrender. "It's okay," he said. "It's just me. I told the rest to stay behind, that I'd handle you."

"I have to go," Miles said.

"I know," Mykael nodded. "I'm sorry I couldn't help you more. It gets harder and harder to push through."

"It's okay," Miles told him, his voice soft and gentle.

Mykael's gaze shifted to the ground, then locked onto Miles. "Please kill it. Kill that thing. Bring us peace."

Miles nodded and said nothing else.

Kricket broke the silence. "Some of the others have already had their water for the night, so let's hop on and get outta here," he said.

"No," Miles refused. "I want Io."

Kricket shrugged. "Alright," he conceded.

They let Io drink until the bucket was just over half-depleted, then Kricket saddled her up and assisted Miles onto her back. Kricket climbed on and adjusted himself behind Miles, scooting the boy closer to the Carrier's neck. "Ready?"

"Ready," Miles said. He looked down to Mykael, who shivered in the night's cool air. The king looked up pleadingly at the young boy.

"Please bring me peace," he said.

Kricket uttered a command, and Io was off.

Miles thought he could see the outline of the Veratt against the full moon as clouds shifted in the skies, but it was too far away and he couldn't be sure.

For all he knew, the Veratt had already destroyed Trafier.

CHAPTER TWENTY-FOUR

THEN HE HEARD
THE SOUNDS

The air was cold. Dry. Miles had forgotten how cold it could get in Rompu's open fields at night. The sickly green moon illuminated the trio as they raced through Rompu's countryside.

Io's running speed was a pleasant surprise; it was nearly comparable to her flight. She and the other Carriers had been forced to keep their pace at a mild trot so as to not disrupt any passengers or baggage during transit between camps, but now that she only held two bodies rather than a packed cart, she was eating away at the distance between them and Trafier.

Which was good, because Miles could no longer spot the Veratt's disfigured body in the gloaming.

Not that he had many opportunities to search the skies. Io ripped across the plains with veracity and Miles had to clutch tufts of fur in his hands in addition to wrapping his arms around her neck to not be bucked off and sent rolling.

"How long until we get there?" Miles shouted at Kricket over the wind blasting at their ears.

"How should I know?" the Omne retorted, shifting the reins he held in his tiny claws so that Io curved slightly left.

Seemingly in no time, the edge of the marsh was in view. Farther away, they could see the looming towers of the Skyr outpost that guarded the entrance of the main road through Jesieu. The peaks of the towers were jagged, almost impossible to see against the swiftly darkening sky. The image felt peculiar to Miles. It gnawed at him as Io raced toward the edge of the swamp, keeping a good distance away from the towers.

And then it hit him. Their tops were jagged because they had been broken off. The Veratt had already arrived, and despite their record-breaking travel time, it had beaten them by a large margin.

Io came to a startling stop when she reached the outskirts of the marshes. The change in velocity almost threw Miles over her head. She began to back away slowly, uneasy at the prospect of sinking her legs into the murky waters.

"Don't worry, girl," Miles cooed, rubbing the back of her neck affectionately. "It's just water. We need you to help us get there faster." He knew his words held no actual meaning for the animal, but he assumed she would respond to the tone of his voice like Clint and Ollie did.

Kricket gave Io another order in the thick accent of his language while slapping the reins against either side of her. In reply, she let out a low whine that vibrated her whole body. Miles felt the vibration move through his legs, into his chest.

"What's wrong with you?" Kricket wondered aloud, knocking the reins against her matted fur. Her captors had not bothered to groom her in a while, if ever.

Miles was wondering the same exact thing, but then he heard the sounds. They were faint at first. So quiet, they had just been background noise that bled into all the other nighttime eccentricities that one hears when the sun disappears. Crickets, the wind's howl, midnight birds singing soft songs.

But when he listened, he heard.

It was screaming. Some shouts of pain, others of orders. All of them chaotic. Fire burning. People running, their feet hitting the wet ground, splashing through the swamp water and brushing past the graying trunks of the cypress trees. Deep, horrifying, animalistic roars. Carriers must have had superior hearing, and the sounds were piercing Io's ears, frightening her. Urging her to turn around and seek safety.

After Kricket egged her on with his reins a third time, Miles silenced him. "She can hear the Veratt," he explained. "She hears it tearing Trafier apart already. That's why she's scared."

"How do you know that?" Kricket cocked an eyebrow.

"I can hear it too. It's not very loud."

The Omne stuck a long fingernail in the miniscule hole on the side of his head, digging out a wad of amber earwax. "My hearing ain't as good as it used to be."

"We need her to go," Miles said anxiously. He rubbed the back of the Carrier's neck some more, hoping the action would calm her nerves. He was terrified too, but he knew the guilt would be unbearable if he didn't even put up a fight and just allowed Mortimer and Jaselle to meet the same fate as their son. He imagined this was how vulnerable and useless Kiko must have felt when he was faced with the Veratt. How could someone as small as him have any chance of putting a dent in a creature so formidable and destructive? In that moment, Miles had the sinking feeling that he wasn't as prepared as he'd thought.

But still, he had to try. He had to be brave.

"You've helped us so much, but we need you to keep going," he said to Io, running his thin fingers through her shimmering fur. "I won't let anything bad happen to you." He felt a tingling in his fingertips and there was the familiar bluish-green glow. Io stopped fidgeting and whining as the effervescent light glided across her body, twirling around her scabbed stumps. They began to pulsate, the scabs falling off as new flesh began to grow from the wounds.

Then they were in the air.

"Oh, wow!" Kricket screeched, except instead of "wow" it was a word Miles was not allowed to say.

Io flapped her new wings, lifting them higher and higher until they oversaw the treetops of the Jesieu Marshes. Near the back of the swamp, lights from several small fires fought against the darkness.

Suddenly the Veratt shot upward out of the marsh and into the sky, coiling through the air and casting off bits of flame that peppered its veiny, muscled body. Its purple skin shone in the flattering moonlight. Without any hesitation, the beast arced backward until its face pointed down toward Trafier and jettisoned itself back into the skirmish.

Miles gulped.

Kricket swore again.

Io did not whine.

She remained mid-air, flapping her wings at a steady pace to keep them stable. "Good girl." Miles could barely get the praise past his lips. Forming words was an arduous task when coupled with the sensation of his enormous meal rising up from his stomach into his throat.

Luckily he leaned over in time to vomit without getting any bile or chunks of food on himself or Io. When he was finished, he spit the last bits of puke out of his mouth as he watched the rest of it careen toward the earth.

Kricket asked if he was okay. "Yeah," he said, "I just ate too much at dinner, I think."

"I don't think I ate tonight, actually," Kricket mused. "Hmph." He then gave the command and Io flew toward the commotion.

They had cut the distance between them and Trafier in half before Kricket gave Io two taps with the leather reins. She lurched forward into a dip, sending them nose-diving toward the treetops. Before impacting, she gracefully pulled herself back up and skimmed above the somber green leaves, some of which nicked Miles' feet.

Trafier was close now. The sounds had gotten louder. They must have been overbearing for the poor Carrier as they grew nearer.

"I'm gonna bring her down right in the thick of it," Kricket said. "You hop off and get to doin' what needs doin'. Don't worry about me and her. We'll be fine."

"I need to go to the apartment," Miles said. It hadn't even been a conscious thought before he said it out loud. "I need to see if Mortimer and Jaselle and Clint are alright."

Miles could feel Kricket nodding as the Omne's rough chin scraped against his back. "Okay. I'll try to meet you there, if I can find it again."

So, as loose as it was, they had a plan:

1. Make sure the people Miles cared about most were still alive and unharmed.

2. Kill the unearthly creature that had spent the past who-knows-how-long terrorizing an entire kingdom.

Simple. Straightforward.

And then they arrived.

Io elegantly swooped through a break in the trees, only to be immediately startled by the Veratt crying out in fury and swiping a claw through one of the two remaining palace towers. The Carrier instinctively tucked her left wing under herself and curved her right one, resulting in her body turning on its side as she tried to distance them from the angry, thrashing beast. This sent Miles and Kricket soaring off her back and onto the battleground.

They had still been ten feet in the air when Io implemented her countering maneuver, so the fall was both impossibly long and impossibly short all at once. Miles crashed into the mud, landing on his right shoulder, which he could have sworn he heard crack. He let out a scream of pain, writhing in the slush as he grasped his shoulder.

Kricket landed five feet away on his back. He didn't scream as he hit, the impact knocking the breath out of him.

Miles stopped wriggling like a worm and instead lay motionless in the muck, his eyes staring up at the treetops. Frantic Rompuns ran past on every side of him and it was a miracle he wasn't trampled by their large, stumpy feet.

"Kricket?" Miles managed to get out. He couldn't be sure how audible he had been.

Either the answer was not at all or Kricket had been knocked unconscious, because there was no reply from the Omne. Nothing but a distressed groan. "Kricket?" he tried once more.

"What?" Kricket grunted, squirming in the mud.

The Veratt flapped its terrible wings and brought itself into the air, clenching a tree in each hand and ripping them out of the ground as it ascended.

"I think I broke my arm. Or my shoulder, I mean," Miles said, louder this time. He ached far more than he had after the bout with the thief-ant.

"Can't help you there, kid."

Miles tried to focus his energy on himself like he had earlier in the day, but there was a familiar pounding in his head. He knew that it had to be partly because of the unexpectedly rough landing, but part of it was more distant than that. It was like a low rumble. It felt as far away as the sounds of Trafier had, up in the sky on Io's back.

With all his strength, Miles stood and was disgusted by the amount of mud covering his clothing and the side of his face. It dribbled down his cheek, almost touching the side of his mouth. He ambled toward Kricket.

"Go to the apartment," the Omne told him. "I told you, I'll be fine. I'll meet you there."

"Are you sure?"

"Shut up and just go, kid."

Miles turned on his heel, which was a much more painful operation than he had thought it would be, and began limping in the direction of the palace's entryway.

He weakly looked side to side, trying to make out Io in the discord, but the Carrier was long gone. Miles wondered if she had somehow gotten herself killed or if she had simply flown away, back to Ruhig where it was safer.

A couple Rompuns and one Skyr accidentally knocked him down as he sluggishly made his way across the battlefield. None of them stopped to apologize or even noticed that he had returned, considering the much bigger things they had on their plates. Each time, Miles carefully lifted himself back up and continued his march.

Inside the palace, the situation was no better. The Veratt's assault had destroyed a large portion of the building, blocking off the fastest route to Mortimer and Jaselle's apartment. A maylan sniffed at a burly green hand sticking out of the rubble, some of its fingers snapped and dangling at the joints. But Miles could tell by the ridges on the animal's back that it wasn't Clint, so regardless of how guilty he felt for abandoning it, he had to move on.

In his time living here, Miles had learned numerous routes through the palace halls to reach the apartment, and though the second one he tried was also barricaded by debris, the third was mostly clear. What he found most troubling was that with the exception of the mourning maylan, he had not yet seen another living soul in the building. He had stumbled upon a lifeless Rompun corpse, which he hurriedly rushed past, blinking away the grisly image.

At last he turned into the hallway that held the entrance to the apartment only to discover that halfway down, the building had been smashed to bits, leaving nothing but wreckage and an oversized exit to the madness outside. Miles couldn't remember how far down the hall the apartment was, and his gut began to twist. He threw up again.

When that was over, Miles wiped his mouth with his sleeve and walked as far down the hallway as physically possible. Among the bloodstained chunks of stone and tile was the nameplate that read Mouton, broken into three pointy pieces.

Then there was a bark, and Miles was pushed to the floor.

Clint licked eagerly at the boy's face, his tail nothing more than a blur as it wagged. Miles winced at the pain in his shoulder but laughed a deep, relieved laugh.

"Clint! Clint, get back in—"

Jaselle's voice was cut off as she saw who the maylan had pounced on. She pulled the apartment door open the rest of the way and practically sprang to the floor, encasing Miles in her arms.

"Ow, ow, ow," he squealed, and she backed off.

"Oh, I'm sorry, dear," she said with worry and dry blood on her face. "What's wrong? You're hurt?"

"It's my shoulder," Miles said. "I think I broke it."

Jaselle ushered him inside and Clint happily followed them in, trotting alongside Miles.

Most of the apartment's floor was littered with various objects that had fallen off shelves and tables in the quake of the Veratt's attack, including Miles' favorite orange bowl. Jaselle had propped up the kitchen chairs and instructed Miles to sit down at the table.

"Let me take a look," she said, lifting off his shirt.

Miles glanced at the injured shoulder, which sported a severely dark blue bruise mixed with a dash of purple and green. It was almost black. Jaselle inhaled, the air making a coarse sound against her gritted teeth.

"That doesn't look good," she said needlessly. She wiped the mud off his face with a rag. Miles didn't say anything, but he was grateful.

She pressed a finger to the top of his shoulder, where the coloring of the bruise ended. He jolted back with an intense pain rippling through his arm. He began to silently cry.

"Sorry," Jaselle said, "but I need to check some more." She continued feeling different parts of his shoulder and arm, all of which filled the boy with an unimaginable pain. Once she finished, she gave him her diagnosis. "I don't believe it's broken."

This shocked him. It was the worst pain he had ever experienced in his entire life.

"It's not broken, but it's obviously badly sprained. Either way, you won't be able to use it much. Try not to move that arm."

Miles rubbed the tears from his face, and the pain had given way to restlessness. It would be a lot harder to take down the Veratt with one of his hands out of commission.

Clint yipped at his side, wanting to be petted. Miles rubbed the top of the maylan's head, dampening it with his tears. The boy began to weep again, flooded with happiness that Jaselle and Clint were both still alive.

Then he asked between sobs, "Where's Mortimer?" He was suddenly astutely aware of the blood caking Jaselle's round face. Her red hair was pulled up in a messy ponytail. Before she could answer, he asked, "Is Mortimer dead?"

"No," she smiled, helping Miles put his shirt back on, delicately snaking his injured arm through the sleeve. "He's okay. He left to help defend the city. Miles, dear, how in the world did you get here? The queen sent a band of soldiers to retrieve you from the Skyr, but they said—"

"I need to find Mortimer," Miles interjected. He would've loved for the reunion to last much longer and include tea and snacks, but he needed to get moving. "Where did he go? Which way?" He tried to get out of his chair, but Jaselle firmly sat him back down.

"Absolutely not," she said fiercely. "You're not leaving my sight again. We were just about to head for—"

Miles didn't have time for her to finish her sentence just so he could refuse whatever she was suggesting anyway. He ducked under her arm and darted for the open door. Clint zipped past him into the hallway, ready to follow wherever the boy led.

Jaselle called out to him, but Miles was much speedier than the admittedly heavyset Rompun, and he easily eluded her. He shot out the doorway and veered to the right, hopping onto the steaming rubble, jumping from stone to stone until he landed with a *plop!* in the soggy grass. Clint didn't miss a beat.

"Miles!" Jaselle yelled, but he was off.

Distant thunder still crashed inside his head, the ache growing stronger with every passing minute. Meanwhile, he had slightly modified the plan:

1. Make sure Jaselle and Clint were still alive and unharmed. *Check.*

2. Find Mortimer somewhere in the unending chaos to make sure he was alive too.

3. Figure out what happened to Kricket.

4. Kill the unearthly creature (hopefully with help from an alive Mortimer and Kricket) that had spent the past who-knows-how-long terrorizing an entire kingdom.

A little less simple. A little less straightforward.

But still somewhat manageable.

The Veratt was still in the same spot Miles had last seen it, tossing screaming Rompuns and Skyr into the air while it tore trees out of the ground and hurled them like javelins. As long as it stayed occupied, Miles could keep looking for his two closest allies. In the back of his mind, though, he knew he would have to battle the Veratt sooner rather than later.

Up ahead, three Rompuns had carted out three cannons from a massive hole in the palace wall and were moving them toward the Veratt.

Miles increased his speed to a light jog and soon caught up with the three Rompuns, who were pushing the massive pieces of artillery at a glacial pace. He squeezed past two of the cannons and was about to start running when one of the Rompuns sputtered his name. "I can't believe it's you!" the raspy voice then said.

Miles looked over his injured shoulder. It was Mortimer.

The Rompun stopped pushing and they embraced while Clint panted wildly.

Mortimer looked the boy in his eyes, holding him by the shoulders. "How'd you get here?" he asked, sounding tired and hoarse.

Miles almost screamed. "My shoulder, my shoulder," he slurred. Mortimer quickly let go.

"C'mon, Mortimer!" one of the Rompuns urged him, pushing their cannons along.

"Give me a damn second, will you?" Mortimer snapped. To Miles, he repeated his question.

"Doesn't matter," Miles replied, once again wishing he had more time for their reunion. "I need to kill the Veratt."

"Don't we all," Mortimer grunted. "Well, I've got a cannon. What've you got?"

Miles held out his palm and ignited a fireball in it, letting the ball grow larger and wilder until it was the size of a basketball before dousing it in a relatively weak jet of water. The small feat wasn't nearly as affected by the pounding in his head as his healing.

"I've got magic," he said.

"Oh," Mortimer muttered. "Well, that'll come in handy, I guess."

CHAPTER TWENTY-FIVE

THE TRICK

By the time Mortimer and the other Rompuns had gotten their cannons into position, the Veratt was finally on the move. The creature hoisted itself into the air, screeching as it swung its claws at the treeline, sending leaves scattering across the muddy battlefield and tree trunks splintering, crashing into the side of the palace.

"Where's the queen?" Miles thought to ask.

"She's gone, she's safe," Mortimer grumbled, struggling to rotate the cannon to point it farther to the left. The Veratt was hovering over the palace, roaring brutishly at the frantic Rompuns and Skyr below.

Trees had collapsed on a group of soldiers a short distance away. Miles tried to drown out their screams with another question. "Have you seen Kricket?"

"Who?" Mortimer asked. The word was hardly more than a guttural sound as he put all his energy into moving the iron cannon.

"He's an Omne. He's one of the ones who attacked us in that tunnel."

"Why would he be here?"

324 · TRAVIS M. RIDDLE

"I brought him."

"Miles, I don't have time to figure out why you woulda done something like that," said Mortimer, letting go of the cannon. He took deep breaths, in and out, leaning against the weapon. The Veratt perched on top of the main palace spire. It appeared to be resting and surveying the carnage it had caused, sure that nothing below would be able to bring any harm. Clint stared intently, not tearing his eyes away for one second.

Miles kicked one of the heavy wheels, which caused Clint to bark at him. "Are these even strong enough to beat it?" he asked.

"Probably not," Mortimer admitted, still out of breath. "But the Ruhigans should already be on their way to help us. We just need to hold it off until they get here and try to make sure it don't do too much damage."

Taking a look around, Miles didn't think that plan had been very successful. He then stepped around to the back of the cannon and examined it. "How does this work?"

"You just open up the cascabel here"—Mortimer demonstrated lethargically—"and light the fuse that's inside. Then boom goes the cannonball."

The Veratt was still taking its break. Soldiers on the ground threw spears, fired guns, did anything they could while it was motionless atop the palace, but nothing had any real effect on the monster. It looked satisfied with itself, hunched over like a great big ape.

Miles nodded. "Sorry, but can you all face those the way you had them before?"

Mortimer let out a weary, incredulous sigh. "Why would we do that?" he asked.

"I can use my magic," Miles said. "Just trust me. But it'll be easier if you turn them before I try."

The Rompun grumbled something under his breath then motioned for his allies to turn their cannons back, to face the ravaged clearing the Veratt had previously occupied.

The whole process took another couple minutes, and by that time the Veratt was getting antsy, shifting back and forth on its perch. It scraped its claws along the stone roof of the palace, producing an irritating sound that pierced the eardrums of everybody in the marshes.

"Hurry," Miles ordered the Rompuns. "It'll be harder if he's on the move. Especially if he's in the air."

"It ain't exactly easy," Mortimer said snippily, his green palms pressed firmly against the barrel. "You know how much this joker weighs?"

"But what about the mighty strength of Mortimer?" Miles joked, keeping a vigilant eye on the Veratt, just like Clint.

Eventually, Mortimer and the unnamed Rompuns got their cannons facing the original direction again. "Now what?" Mortimer sighed.

"Everyone open up the—" Miles paused, trying to remember the word Mortimer had used just a couple minutes prior. "—open up the lids," he resigned, taking a few steps back so that the whole row of cannons was in his line of sight.

Mortimer and the other Rompuns followed his order. "Now what?" one said.

"Now get away."

Miles raised his hands, pointing his palms toward the line of cannons, each with their cascabels raised and ready for war. He curled his fingers and conjured the memory of apologizing to his father.

With hardly any delay, the stretch of earth beneath the cannons rose into the air, carrying the heavy weapons up with it. Most of the Rompuns gasped in amazement, but Mortimer remained silent, watching the young boy at work.

In the air, Miles made the piece of earth turn so that the front of the cannons faced the Veratt, who was still sitting in the same spot and was now curious as to what was happening.

The next part would take twice as much concentration, but Miles was prepared. While he kept the earth floating, Miles also began to focus on his father's face.

But his head ached. The dull rumble thumped away in his mind, taking on familiar cadences and inflections. He faltered.

The strip of land began to plummet downward, but Miles recovered and caught the cannons, lifting them back into the sky. He was worried the sudden movements would startle the Veratt, but the creature remained still, more curious than ever about what was transpiring.

Miles knew he didn't have long, though. The Veratt was definitely anxious.

He tried again. The trick was to concentrate on both images, but still manage to keep them separate, which was a lot harder than he'd expected. If either image began to flicker out, it would ruin the spell. He needed to craft two clear, perfect images in his mind and sustain both of them for as long as necessary.

The heat, the screaming, the increasing headache, and the pressure of defeating the Veratt were not the greatest combination of things to help him accomplish the strenuous task.

He inhaled then exhaled slowly.

The Veratt screeched.

He saw his father.

All three cannons lit simultaneously, and within seconds cannonballs jettisoned toward the Veratt. Clint howled.

The Veratt tried to dodge the blast, but it wasn't quick enough. One of the cannonballs sunk into its thick, purple chest and another tore through its wing—the third missed, bursting through a palace wall—and the creature shrieked in what was either dismay or aggravation.

Miles carefully lowered the strip of earth back down to the ground. *"Reload!"* he yelled as the Veratt lifted itself up into the air. *"Fast! Fast! Fast!"*

Mortimer and the two Rompuns rushed toward the cart that held the rest of the cannonballs and proceeded to stuff them into the barrels as hastily as possible, but the Veratt was too agile. It dove toward the earth, reaching out its blistered claws and snatching up two of the cannons, only one of which had been reloaded. The Rompuns standing nearby were blown back by the wind as the Veratt swooped upward.

It was a longshot, but Miles had to take it anyway. He fired off the loaded cannon held in the Veratt's hand, but its barrel was pointing toward the sky, so the cannonball shot up into the clouds and fell somewhere far away in the marshes. In retaliation, the Veratt threw the two pieces of iron as far as it could and they disappeared on the horizon.

"Miles, hurry!" Mortimer shouted in the distance.

So Miles did as he was told. He lifted up the same patch of land, which now held one lonely cannon. Complicating matters was the fact that the Veratt was hovering directly overhead.

Not having enough time to think things through, Miles tilted the piece of earth backward so that the barrel slanted up toward the Veratt. The cannon no longer had any support beneath it, and it plunged toward the ground. He was still able to fire the cannon before it rotated too much in midair and the cannonball made contact with the Veratt's lower leg.

The cannon crashed into the trench where Miles had lifted up the layer of earth, tumbling down and sinking into the newly exposed dirt. Overhead, the Veratt unleashed another unearthly shriek that amplified the pounding that was still raging through Miles' skull.

His parents' angry voices were bouncing around in his head and he couldn't make them stop. The headache was starting to cloud his mind and make him feel weak. He feared he might throw up again.

"Miles!" Mortimer yelled again.

But the boy's headache was overpowering now. He dropped to his knees, clutching at his head, not even noticing how dirty he was making his already greasy hair. He sunk half an inch into the mud. Clint raced to his side and began to lick his cheek.

"Stop, Clint," he whispered, and then again more loudly when the maylan disregarded him.

Clint yelped at the boy, and Miles was forced to look up at his slender, black face. His tail began to wag as they made eye contact.

"What?"

Another bark.

With what felt like thunder crashing inside his skull, the only thing Miles could focus on was Clint. The maylan let out another bark, this one more aggressive, followed by a short whine.

"What?" he asked again.

Out of nowhere, Miles was thrown backward by a hulking green mass. When he was able to force his eyes open again, he saw that Mortimer had leapt onto him and shoved him into a tree. Clint was at his side once more, and now in addition to his head and shoulder, his back was killing him. At that instant, the Veratt slammed head-first into the ground where Miles had been collapsed. Mud and grass exploded in a wide radius around the monster, splattering against their faces. The creature stood woozily, stumbling around for a moment before regaining its composure.

"Thanks," Miles said.

Mortimer patted him on his good shoulder, which the boy didn't want to confess hurt a great deal as well. "Told you I'd keep you safe, didn't I? Speaking of, sorry about letting you get kidnapped and all," he amended.

"It's fine," Miles said, trying to stand. Mortimer had to help him up. Clint continued to bark at the Veratt, which was now less than ten feet away from where they stood.

"We need to move," Mortimer said.

The trio retreated deeper into the marsh, splashing through puddles, crushing helpless forn in the process. They stopped after traveling only twenty or thirty feet, which was all Miles could muster in his given state.

They stopped at the edge of a pond, its surface aglow with the dim light of forn swimming mindlessly, blissfully unaware of the horrid event taking place in their home. Miles was too tired to continue moving. His body screamed at him. All he could do was focus on breathing regularly as he watched the Veratt rise into the air once again and come smashing down into the palace.

The creature swiped its meaty claws, tearing down the remaining pillars as it whacked its massive tail into the walls, bringing them down with ease, as if they were built out of tooth-picks. Stone and glass shattered, crumbling in the Veratt's wake.

Miles let out a cry when he realized Jaselle might still have been inside. Clint continued to whine. Mortimer didn't make a peep. The violent storm that was the Veratt continued to rage.

CHAPTER TWENTY-SIX

MESS

"We need to get outta here."

Mortimer's words fluttered through Miles' ears, failing to latch onto them. He blinked out of his stupor when the Rompun shook him by his injured shoulder and said it again.

"We need to leave. We need to start evacuating. This is hopeless." He took a step forward before turning and saying, "Stay close."

Miles nodded and followed, returning to the trench where the cannon lay uselessly. His Rompun companions were struggling to drag it out while the Veratt tore apart the palace.

"Leave that," Mortimer told the two Rompuns. "We gotta leave Trafier. Now." There was rigidness to his voice, a grave seriousness, that Miles had never heard before.

The bearded Rompun scoffed and asked, "Where we goin', then?"

"Anywhere," said Mortimer. "No time to argue 'bout it."

"My family is here somewhere," the Rompun snarled. "I'm not leavin' them behind."

"I didn't say to, you fool," Mortimer sighed. "Go find them. Leave this piece of junk here and find your wife, Vick. Find your kid, get the hell outta here."

"Where are we meeting?" asked the other Rompun, a woman with long, tangled straw-colored hair and more muscles than Miles had ever seen on a Rompun.

Mortimer pondered this for a second. "Go east," he answered. "Head toward Claire. No outposts over there, plenty of water to quench anyone's thirst. Go."

Vick and the woman nodded, taking off in different directions. Mortimer faced Miles and Clint, who paced around the boy's legs.

"Have you seen Jaselle?" he asked. "I guess you must've, if Clint is with you. Where is she? Where'd you see her?"

Miles pointed at the rubble the Veratt was rummaging through. It was almost half a minute before Mortimer could tear his gaze away from the scene. "Right," he said in a surprisingly reserved tone. "How long ago?"

Miles replayed the recent events in his head, calculating. "I think five minutes. Maybe almost ten." It felt much longer.

"She might've gotten to the panic room, then," Mortimer said, running his rubbery hand over his bald head. "That, or she ran outside trying to find you. Either way, I don't think she's in that mess."

"So where are we going?" Miles asked. He then ordered Clint to stop walking in circles around him.

Instead of replying, Mortimer cupped his hands to his mouth. *"Listen!"* he roared, his voice carrying through the wind and across the swamp. Nearby Rompuns and Skyr stopped what they were doing and looked at him, while others farther away turned to hear what he had to say while they kept running.

All the while, the Veratt played with bits and pieces of the fallen palace as if they were LEGO bricks. Nobody bothered shooting at it anymore. They knew it was an act of futility.

"We evacuatin' Trafier," Mortimer shouted, his voice somehow even louder than it was before. *"Gather up who you need and whatever other supplies you can carry. Help the injured if you able. Head east—the roads are damaged, but they're good enough—and get to Claire River. We'll all meet there. Go!"*

There was a wildfire of movement as the citizens of Trafier began to rally. Some took off straight for the river while others bundled up barrels of what Miles presumed to be vegetables and fruits. Many lay on the ground, bloodied and moaning, waiting for assistance.

In the distance, through thick smoke, Miles saw the outline of what could only be Io. The boy tugged on Mortimer's shirt. "Call Io!" he said, knowing his voice would never in his life carry as far as Mortimer's could.

Mortimer did so, and the silhouette perked up at the mention of her name. She turned her head and darted past the hysterical Rompuns trying to salvage their city, yipping in delight when she saw Miles. Kricket wasn't with her.

She came to a skidding halt in front of them, kicking up mud that slapped against their legs. "Whoa," Mortimer murmured, fixing his eyes on Io's dirtied face. He ran his fingers through the fur of her cheeks, and the animal purred happily. "Where'd she come from?"

Miles ignored the question and asked one of his own. "How are we going to find Jaselle?"

Mortimer shrugged, his expression troubled. "If she's with the queen, she's safe, and there's no way we could get to 'em anyway."

"But we can't be sure that she's there."

"Nope." He continued petting the Carrier's shaggy fur. It was covered in dirt and torn sedges. Then the Rompun suddenly screamed, *"Jaselle!"*

There was no answer. He called again.

Nothing.

"Maybe she's too far away," Miles offered hopefully.

"Maybe," Mortimer nodded, climbing onto Io's back. He held a hand out to lift Miles, but the boy handed him Clint first before being yanked up.

Mortimer grasped the reins that were still wrapped around Io's neck. "We'll fly up, keep telling people to evacuate, and search for Jaselle while we do it. Sound good?"

"Sounds good. We need to find Kricket too," the boy quickly added.

"Okay." Mortimer sounded unsure about that part.

Io ascended unsteadily. Their landing earlier had undoubtedly taken a toll on her wings, which were new and likely sensitive. Miles held Clint tightly to his chest so the maylan wouldn't fall off.

The chaos became more unreal and even more terrifying as they floated higher into the air. The point of view made every Rompun and Skyr look like nothing more than green- and tan-colored pieces of a board game, but at the same time it magnified the extent of the Veratt's power. From this perspective, Miles noticed how many of the figures below were actually motionless.

Thankfully the Veratt's back was turned to them, so it had not yet noticed the Carrier flying upward. It was impossible to know how the creature might react if it saw them, and neither Miles nor Mortimer were particularly eager to find out. Io soared ahead, with Mortimer stopping her every ten feet or so to yell out his instructions to the people below. They all responded accordingly, getting to work preparing for the mass migration.

They couldn't find Jaselle in any of the crowds. Kricket was nowhere to be seen as well.

And Miles' headache was getting worse. It felt like his parents screaming inside his skull while taking a buzzsaw to it. The pain pulsated, taking on the irregular rhythm of words. It was becoming harder and harder to keep under control. With the pain smothering his thoughts, it was impossible to fight through and focus on anything to conjure his magic. He needed to do something about it or else the Veratt wouldn't be stopped.

They covered as much ground as possible without disturbing the Veratt, who was still content scouring through the debris it had created, searching for who knew what. When Mortimer was satisfied with the amount of people who had heard his message, he said mournfully, "Alright, let's go."

"We can keep looking for Jaselle," Miles said. He thought back to Jaselle's story about losing Kiko to the Veratt, and his stomach churned at the idea of her joining their son.

"No," Mortimer said simply.

"We—"

"She's not out here, so she's probably with the queen." He put on an unconvincing smile. "It's deep underground, and there are tons of tunnels leading out to Rompu. One of the exits is near the river. That's why I sent everyone there." He shifted his weight, eliciting a whine from Io. "We should join 'em. We'll beat everyone by a longshot thanks to Io here."

Miles asked, "Do you think the Veratt will follow us?" He stroked the smooth ridges on Clint's back. The maylan was still at attention, peering over the side of the Carrier at the commotion below.

"Hope not," Mortimer chuckled. "Everything's bettin' on it not and instead flying off somewhere else. We'll be in more than a pickle if that don't happen." He tugged at the reins and Io rose higher into the air, above the treeline.

And then the screaming began to intensify by the second, joined by the clanging of swords and metallic blasts of gunfire. Miles looked down to see what was going on. Right as he processed the scene, a sharp jab shot through his head and he had to clasp his eyes shut. He clutched at his hair, pulling on it, the sensation distracting from his pain.

You have to run these things by me!

Clint barked madly and Mortimer looked down as well. He whispered something unintelligible before making Io swoop toward the surface. As the pain dulled marginally, Miles opened his eyes and looked at the erupting chaos they were flying toward.

The king's Skyr that had pursued him finally navigated through the Jesieu Marshes and were now riding their amputated Carriers around, slashing and firing at the weakened Rompuns.

"Mykael's really going all out, ain't he?" Mortimer muttered angrily to himself.

They had almost reached the ground. Mortimer had a ferocious gleam in his eyes, his teeth bared and ready to rip somebody apart. In the shuffle of bodies, Miles immediately spotted a familiar one-armed Skyr among them. Risath leapt off his Carrier, allowing the animal to charge onward into the fray, desperately trying to escape the carnage and seek refuge in the trees.

Miles wanted to tell Mortimer to go easy on the Skyr, to try to subdue rather than kill them, but he knew it wouldn't do any good. There was no time to explain what was happening with King Mykael, and the conflict had begun to boil over before he had ever set foot in the kingdom, with histories and implications he could not begin to understand; it was no use trying to solve it himself. All he could do was eliminate the Veratt and hope it helped fix things.

If his headache would just go away.

Io slowed into a graceful landing and Mortimer jumped off her back to charge into battle, leaving Miles and Clint sitting helplessly on top of the Carrier.

Jesus Christ, would you calm down?

"Miles!"

The boy turned halfway around, twisting his torso to spot a short, gray lizard-person with an eye patch running his way.

"Kricket!" he called back.

The Omne waved his stubby arms in excitement as he neared Io. He came to a halt at her side, gazing up at Miles on her back. The left side of his head was caked in a dark mixture of what appeared to be dirt and blood. His clothes were scruffy and soaked in red. He looked like an absolute mess.

"Are you hurt?" Miles asked.

"No—well, kinda, but no, I'm fine," said Kricket hurriedly. He began to hike himself up onto Io's back and grumbled, "Alright, let's go! Headin' east! Kick it!"

"We can't," Miles said. "The Skyr are here and it's my fault. They were following me. I have to stop them from hurting everyone."

"They were comin' here whether you came or not, we both know what Mykael's capable of. And the Veratt's gonna hurt them anyway," Kricket said. "But that's exactly why we need to bounce. Remember how I'm your accomplice in getting here and all? Pretty traitor-y. They ain't gonna be thrilled to see me."

Miles stood his ground. "I can't," he shook his head. "Sorry."

Kricket stopped trying to scramble up the side of the Carrier. To her credit, Io had politely ignored the Omne's attempts as he dug his claws and boots into her side, remaining perfectly still and obedient. "Well, hell," Kricket pouted.

"You can help us fight, though," Miles offered. "I've seen you in a fight. You're not bad."

"Kid, you pummeled me the first time we met."

Miles grinned. "Yeah, but the Skyr don't have a bunch of cool magic like me."

"Nah, they don't," Kricket agreed. "Just huge, meaty claws to cut me in half with."

"Yup, that's all," Miles laughed.

The Skyr were still brawling with the Rompun knights near what had once been the entrance to Trafier's palace. Miles shuddered to think that the wrathful side of King Mykael might prevail after all. The Rompuns weren't prepared for an attack from the Veratt, let alone an assault from the king's Skyr at the same time. Miles cried out as a particularly bulky Skyr with four claws—no hands—snapped at a Rompun, cutting off his arm at the elbow. The Rompun shrieked and stumbled backwards, the sword in his hand accidentally plunging into the gut of a confused Carrier. Its howl was unbearable. Io whimpered and lunged forward to aid her comrade, but Miles quickly pulled on the reins to stop her, almost causing Clint to tumble off. There was no way to help.

Watching the dismal events unfold, Kricket let out a lengthy sigh. "Alright," he said. "I'll fight. I guess."

Silently, Miles extended his hand and helped the Omne onto Io's back. He scurried up and positioned himself behind the boy, just as they had sat while riding to the marsh.

Miles handed the reins back to Kricket since the Omne knew more about handling the Carrier's movements. It would also make it easier for Miles to keep a firm hold on Clint, who grew more restless by the minute.

Noticing this, Kricket said, "You should just let him run. Maylans love this kind of stuff. They're bred to be fighters, y'know."

Miles adamantly shook his head. "No way. I'm not letting him get stabbed by a stupid Skyr or stomped by the Veratt. I'm keeping him safe."

"Honestly, kid, he'll be plenty safe out there. Maylans are resourceful little things."

"When I found him he was injured in an empty tunnel," Miles pointed out. "And Jericho tossed him around like a stuffed animal when you two came to take me. I don't know if Clint is really the fighting type."

"Point taken," Kricket said. "His name's Klipse, by the way."

"Nope."

Miles peered into the battling crowd, trying to make out the shape of Mortimer. With the dizzying movements of so many bodies dancing around each other, plus his unending headache, it was impossible to spot Mortimer. After everything the Rompun had been through, however, Miles was no longer very concerned about him becoming one of the growing number of bulky green corpses that littered the ground.

"Look," Kricket said, "he's gonna get in the way. That's all I'm saying."

"I don't care," Miles told him. "I love Clint and I'm gonna keep him safe." He clutched the furry animal to his chest, Clint's hot breath on his neck as he panted.

Kricket decided to drop the issue and yelled out a command to Io. He had to repeat himself since she was still distraught over the stabbed Carrier, but eventually she flapped her incredible wings and brought them above the battlefield.

Suddenly, blurry figures shot downward through the treetops and into the earth, landing with a wet slam. They only stood still for a split second before jumping into action. There were easily fifty of them, if not more.

Now that the figures were moving slower, Miles smiled. It was the Ruhigans. Armed with crossbows and rapiers, they began slicing away at the aggressive Skyr, who were caught off guard by the newcomers. The Rompuns cheered heartily to welcome their allies.

"So what's the plan?" Kricket asked, surveying the chaos.

The arrival of the Ruhigans had captured the Veratt's attention and it was no longer digging through the palace rubble. It had turned around again, whipping its massive tail back and forth like an excited puppy. The monster grinned a harsh, bloody grin and lumbered forward.

"Well," Miles sighed, "I guess I should deal with that."

"*Fen dyria,*" Kricket muttered. "I was afraid you'd say that."

CHAPTER TWENTY-SEVEN

WINGS

First, Miles tried using his earth magic to lift the individual slabs of concrete and metal that once comprised the palace, but his attempts ended in failure. It was what he'd expected, but he still felt the need to try. They would have damaged the Veratt much more than anything else he could pick up, since there were very few boulders littering the swamp.

The monster bellowed as it swung at the Ruhigans, who glided through the air gracefully, dancing around its car-sized fists. They fired their crossbows at the Veratt's face, the iron bolts jamming into its cheeks and forehead. It let out a gravelly yelp and pounded its fists on the ground like an aggravated gorilla.

Kricket picked a bow up off the ground and scrambled around looking for some arrows to shoot.

"I don't think that's gonna work very well," Miles said, gesturing toward the Veratt lumbering around with crossbow bolts already lodged in its head.

"Right," muttered Kricket dejectedly. "Well, I'm screwed, then. No fight for me."

Miles pointed to a broadsword lying on the ground a couple feet away.

"Do you honestly think I can pick that thing up?" the tiny Omne asked sarcastically, flexing his non-existent muscles.

The boy then kicked the hilt of a dagger at his feet.

"You want me to use that?"

A shrug.

"Against *that*?"

"You could stab its foot."

Kricket stared at him. "I can't do much here, kid," he said. "That's just the way it is."

Miles nodded. Kricket was right; if an iron bolt piercing its face had little to no effect on the Veratt, surely a dagger to the toe wouldn't even register.

"Take Clint," Miles said.

"Where?" Kricket huffed.

"Everyone is meeting in the east," Miles said. "Near the Claire River. Do you know how to get there?"

"I can figure it out," Kricket said. "I'm feelin' like the people there aren't gonna be fond of an Omne amblin' through, though."

"You're probably right," said Miles. "Just get there and hide, then. Get safe but don't let them see you. If Mortimer comes, go to him. I told him you're my friend."

"I dunno who Mortimer is, kid."

"The Rompun who was with me when you attacked us in the tunnel."

"Miles. That was a long time ago and I've only got one eye. You think I remember what that fat, green blob looks like compared to the other fat, green blobs?"

"You're being very sassy."

"Sorry."

The Veratt was still bellowing behind him; he had no time to give simple orders to Kricket. "Just go there, hide, wait, whatever. Keep Clint safe. Okay?"

"Okay," Kricket nodded.

Miles picked up the dagger by its hilt and handed it to him. Its blade was dull and dripping with blood. Kricket took it without saying a word, then snapped his fingers at Clint.

"Klipse!" he hollered.

"It's Clint."

Kricket scowled. "Clint," he said begrudgingly. "Let's go, pal. You remember your old bud Kricket, don't ya?"

The maylan was hesitant and looked to Miles for advice. The boy pointed to Kricket and snapped his fingers too. "Go," he commanded.

Clint obeyed. As Kricket jogged off into the thick fog of the marshes, the maylan trotted by his side and soon disappeared.

Miles watched Ollie run off into the hallway toward the shouting. The dog had heard the clanging of food being poured in his bowl and he was hungry for dinner. Miles sat in his bed, still waiting for his own to be ready.

He tried to drown out the words of his mother and father in the kitchen. He held his *The Wild Bunch* blu-ray, scanning the paragraphs on its back cover. The blu-ray player was at his father's apartment, so he couldn't watch it here, but he could picture the opening scene in his mind. He saw Pike Bishop riding horseback past the huddled group of children who all watched with admiration as he sauntered by. They didn't know that shortly he would be robbing the railroad office with his crew.

"You have to run these things by me!" his mother objected. "I don't want you coming through here, in and out, in and out, whenever you feel like it!"

"Jesus Christ, would you calm down? It was just dinner."

"It's not *about* the dinner," she retorted.

They continued arguing. Miles didn't want to hear it. It was giving him a major headache. He wanted Ollie to finish eating and come back so he could continue petting him.

With Clint gone, it was time to step up. It was time to really start fighting. But the pounding in Miles' head was still crippling him, and his concentration was feeble at best.

Miles turned on his heels and cast a dozen fireballs from his palms. The beast was over fifty feet away, but the projectile fireballs could cover a hefty distance.

In his weakened state, though, all but three of the fireballs fizzled out before making it halfway to the Veratt, while the remaining ones lashed against the creature's legs and torso. The only indication they'd had any effect on the creature at all was the fact that it turned its ugly head to seek out the source of its irritation.

Spotting Miles, it lifted itself into the sky, accidentally crashing into a few stray Ruhigans with its massive wings. The falcon-esque creatures tumbled through the air, smashing into branches and mud. The Veratt unleashed a deafening roar and propelled itself toward Miles.

Lightning crackled into view and struck the Veratt in the center of its back, making it fumble and crash head-first into the ground, crushing many Rompuns and Skyr under its weight. There was a splatter of blood like squeezing a handful of Gushers. Miles' scream mixed with the victims' and he nearly dropped to his knees. Two more lightning bolts he had not intended to create shuttered downward and struck the fallen palace as well as a tree, igniting a fire just like he had done in the Skyr camp when he first arrived in Rompu. Lightning was far too dangerous to cast around so many people while his head was filled with cotton. Just that one instance had already hurt and killed far too many of them.

While the Veratt was down for the moment, Miles shot a stream of flames at the beast's face. There were still crossbow bolts protruding from it, which had been pushed even deeper into its head upon impact. Only an inch or two of the long, cylindrical pieces of iron could be seen sticking out of the Veratt now.

But the fire flickered out no more than two feet away from Miles. He shut his eyes, his head on the brink of exploding. He desperately pushed at the rhythmic pulsing that wracked his brain. He needed to—

"You're impossible," his father spat from the kitchen. The words carried through the entire house, coming to rest at Miles' bedside. He clenched *The Wild Bunch*. His knuckles turned white.

His mother let out a sarcastic laugh. "Okay," she said. "You should leave. Go to what's-her-name's place."

"You know it wasn't—"

—think, to concentrate, to focus. His mind spun, images of his parents and of Clint and of Austin and of the king and of Mortimer and of Ollie and of the queen and of—

"Miles!"

The yell came from his left. Miles opened his eyes and saw Mortimer limping his way, clutching at a wound on his arm.

"Come on!" the Rompun shouted. "Let's go!" The fire reflected in his wide yellow eyes.

In response, Miles stood and raced toward the Veratt, shooting fireball after fireball from his palms, only one out of every five fully forming and colliding with the monster. The vast purple creature began to push itself up off the ground, its claws squishing bodies beneath them, bursting with blood and mud. Miles ignored the image and kept running. The Veratt lifted its arm to attack.

At the last second, Miles lifted a wad of mud off the ground beneath him, carrying himself into the air toward the monster's face. His legs began to sink into the wet mixture. The Veratt's claw slammed into the space where Miles had just been, its nails digging into the earth.

Miles could already feel his grasp on the piece of earth slipping, and it began to waver and skitter back toward the ground. He then instantly lost the connection. Both he and the ball of mud hurtled downward and he landed on his back, staring up at the Veratt's torso from between its legs. Miles wasn't sure if the monster shared the same kind of weakness as humans, but he decided to take a leap of faith and sent a stream of flame directly upward into its groin. The Veratt screeched and flew into the air, so the heat must have somewhat hurt it. Miles grinned devilishly.

The remaining Ruhigans had regrouped and now surrounded the Veratt, firing more bolts into its side. They were joined by Io, who howled while circling the Veratt.

One lone bolt tore through the monster's wing, creating a tiny hole, and its throat nearly ripped as it screamed in genuine pain.

So their strategy changed.

Every single Ruhigan reacted immediately by aiming their crossbows at the Veratt's wings while it lifted itself higher and higher. It twisted during its ascent to ward off the assault, but three or four managed to hit their mark, all of which were accompanied by the Veratt's pained roars.

Suddenly the purple monster's battered wings shot out as wide as they could stretch and it thrust itself upward. The subsequent gust of wind pushed the Ruhigans and Io back into the muck, but they were quick to recover and fluttered back into the sky with haste. Io remained grounded, trying to shake off her filthiness.

High above the Jesieu Marshes, the Veratt suddenly propelled itself in the same direction Kricket had headed with Clint. Toward the evacuees.

Just then, Mortimer appeared beside Miles. "Let's go," he repeated, reaching out for the boy.

But once again, Miles ignored the Rompun's request and raced for Io.

"Miles!" Mortimer called again. "Miles, you've—"

The boy scrambled onto the Carrier's back, grasped her reins, and ordered her to fly.

She took off, flying through a hole in the treetops the beast had created. She came to a stop alongside the Ruhigans, who all hovered, watching with relief as the Veratt appeared to retreat.

Miles urged Io to proceed. They shot past the Ruhigans who shouted with surprise, pleading for him to turn back. He ignored them just as he had Mortimer.

His head was filled with screams and pain and fear, but Miles now knew where the Veratt was weakest, and it would never be more vulnerable than it was now. He needed to finish things. He needed to follow the Veratt and finally kill it.

CHAPTER TWENTY-EIGHT

REGARDLESS OF WHAT HAPPENED

Clouds blanketed the sky and smothered the green moon. Lightning flashed overhead and rain began to drizzle. Miles was losing control of himself.

Keeping an eye on the Veratt was a challenge since its purple skin blended in with the dark backdrop of the sky, but Miles was able to lock onto it and steer Io in that direction. He glanced down every minute or two to check where they were, and he was relieved to see that they were completely passing up the Claire River.

The Veratt was not headed for the people who had evacuated already. They were safe, for now. But that meant Miles had no idea where the Veratt was actually going.

Within an impressively short amount of time, they were already soaring over Lake Maulage and Garn. Miles could barely make out the resort nestled in the hillside. He wiped raindrops from his brow and looked back to the Veratt up ahead.

"Good girl," he cooed to Io, though his words were masked by the rumbling of thunder. He knew it would be useless to try calming himself down. His body was too tense, his head was splitting, and he could very well be flying to his death.

You're impossible.

You know it wasn't anything like that.

They pressed on through the storm, trailing the Veratt by sixty or seventy feet. Carriers were incredibly fast flyers, which Miles had already known, but he was doubly impressed by how agile Io was in the horrid weather. He didn't doubt she could cross the entirety of Rompu in half an hour.

Which is precisely what they did. The Veratt closely followed the coastline, gliding high above the very edge of Rompu where it met the Gulf of Lasir. Before too long, they had reached the treeline of the Violet Woods, where Miles had met Mortimer so long ago. The beast ducked into the purple forest.

Miles brought Io down near the edge of the trees. He climbed off her back and gently petted her cheeks. Her fur was dirty and matted, not to mention damp with rain, but he continued anyway. "Thanks," he said to her, knowing there was no way she could understand his words. "You've been a great friend."

The Carrier purred contentedly, though she shifted back and forth anxiously. She could sense the danger close at hand within the woods.

"Stay here," Miles told her. "If I make it back, I need a way to get to Trafier. If I don't come back, fly home to Ruhig. They probably miss you in Windheit."

Io stared blankly at him.

"Or you can just fly away when I go into the woods, I dunno, I'm not your boss," Miles sighed. "Just don't follow me. Okay? It's dangerous in there." His voice was shaky. "But I have to go in anyway. For Kiko," he said. It hadn't even occurred to him until he said it out loud. "And for Mortimer. And Jaselle. And Byrn, and the queen, and for the king, and for Rompu."

He rubbed Io's nose. She huffed, which turned into a violent sneeze.

"I've gotta go now," he told her, knowing that he had already stalled too much, standing around talking to an animal. "See you later."

Io leaned forward and dragged a rough, dry tongue across his face. It was like being licked by a giant, overweight cat. Miles chuckled. He thanked her again then gave her one last pat on the nose before marching into the Violet Woods.

Judging by where he'd seen the Veratt land, the creature couldn't be more than a fifteen minute walk from his current location. It might take a little longer due to navigating through the bushes and tangles of roots, but he'd be facing the monster shortly.

I'd also appreciate you not bringing it up around him, okay?

The rain was falling harder now. Miles rubbed his forehead feebly. The thunder and rain made the whole situation even more dramatic, like something out of a movie. He felt like an action hero, like Clint Eastwood. He tread quietly through the brush, though any snapping of twigs or rustling of leaves was being drowned out by the storm. It didn't hurt to be careful.

He was faintly starting to hear the anguished roars of the Veratt. It was definitely hurt and susceptible to an attack. It hadn't noticed Miles following it in the storm; if it had, surely it would've assaulted him already. He was a small target and there were no other threats around. Miles just needed to gather his strength so he could properly cast his spells and put up a proper fight. But his head was pounding—

Of course I'm not, do you think I'm crazy? I don't want him thinking of his dad as some—

You're doing it right now! Lower your voice!

Miles got off his bed and snuck into the hallway, not making a sound. He peered around the corner and looked into the kitchen where his mother watched over a silver pot on the stove while his father stood cross-armed by the refrigerator.

"Sorry," she said, softer this time. "And sorry for snapping at you."

His father didn't react. He just watched her overlooking the large pot. Miles could smell Andouille sausage cooking with onions, bell peppers, and some garlic. A plastic container of rice and a can of kidney beans sat on the counter beside the stovetop. Jambalaya was for dinner.

"All I'm asking is that you don't punish him for what I did," his father then said as she stirred the contents of the pot. His voice was quieter now too. Miles remained in the hallway, peeking out at the conversation.

From where he stood, he could now spot the Veratt a good distance away. It was sitting down in a small clearing, barely big enough to fit the beast. Its wings were outstretched as it inspected the damage inflicted by the Ruhigans. The Veratt's fists were clenched, pushing against the leaf-strewn ground. One arm lifted and in half a second the Veratt pummeled a tree trunk, toppling it.

Miles edged forward, staying hidden behind the trees as he pushed ahead. The Veratt hadn't noticed him yet. He was certain the creature wouldn't feign ignorance and pretend it couldn't see him; the Veratt was not a subtle beast.

It's not punishing him, it's punishing you.

Well, either way, it's not fair.

His mother tore her gaze away from the jambalaya. *"Fair?"* She choked out a laugh.

Miles stopped advancing. The angry pounding in his skull was worse than before. Without his full capabilities, he didn't stand a chance against the Veratt.

Right now, the monster's wings were wide open, inviting an attack. He needed to take advantage of that. In his current position, Miles faced the Veratt's left side. If he circled around, he'd have a better opportunity to launch an attack at the creature's weak spot before it was even aware of his presence. It probably wouldn't be enough to take the monster down, but it was a start.

It was the best plan Miles had, so he climbed haphazardly over a fallen log and made his way over to a good vantage point he'd picked out, about twenty feet behind the Veratt, where he could hide amongst a cluster of bushes flanked by two thick trees. After conjuring his magic, he could duck back down and the Veratt would be none the wiser to his location. For a couple seconds, anyway, until it ripped the forest apart and discovered him. But any extra time bought was valuable, given the weakness of his magic in his current state.

It took a couple minutes for Miles to reach the collection of bushes, all of which were decorated with streaming orange tendrils that drooped low to the ground.

He slumped down to the floor and leaned his head against the wall, not wanting to actually look at his parents anymore. While they talked, he could hear Ollie chewing his dry food and knocking his metallic bowl around. His parents made the pounding in his head grow worse.

"It isn't," his father said.

"You have a lot of nerve talking about—"

I know—God knows I'm aware of that. But it's true. He's my son too, regardless of what happened. I deserve to see him.

He eyed the Veratt, which was still overlooking its tattered wings. Tiny holes acted as makeshift peepholes to show the other side of the clearing. With his head still aching, Miles stood and raised his hands toward the beast. He needed to choose a spell that would travel the required distance even without his full concentration. If he missed and accidentally lit a tree on fire, the Veratt would immediately know he was there. No room for screw-ups.

He decided his best bet would be fireballs. They seemed to fly relatively far in Trafier, and they had a good chance of either enveloping the wings or tearing right through them, both of which would be beneficial. It hadn't been raining back in Trafier, though. If the fireballs were too slow-moving, they would be extinguished before ever reaching the Veratt. But stream of water wouldn't be powerful enough to tear a hole in its wings, and there were no heavy boulders around to lift.

It would have to be lightning.

Miles accepted the fact that he couldn't—purposely, anyhow—conjure two lightning bolts at the same time, let alone divert their strike paths to both of the Veratt's wings. He'd have to settle for one and hope it would disorient and weaken the creature enough for him to cast more spells.

You will see him. Don't be ridiculous.

Miles imagined his grandmother's face, smiling at him as she drifted off to sleep in her rocking chair on Christmas night. The bolt of lightning shot down from the sky and pierced the Veratt's left wing, almost tearing it in two. Part of it clung to the other half on strings of sinewy muscle. The Veratt screamed in agony, leaping to its feet and stumbling backward, clutching at trees and crushing their trunks in its fists. It spun in a half-circle but the motion was too fast; the rest of its wing tore from the momentum and collapsed onto the dead purple leaves that littered the forest floor. Another scream.

Miles hid behind the bushes, not making a sound. The Veratt was on high alert now. Everything was a threat.

He cautiously craned his head around the corner and watched his father, who was now kneeling down and petting Ollie as the dog licked up crumbs of food in his bowl.

"This doesn't have to be hard," his father muttered.

His mother nodded. "No, it didn't have to be hard, but you made it hard."

Miles needed to land another attack before the Veratt regained its footing, no matter how crippling his headache. He jumped out from behind the bushes and raced forward into the clearing, lobbing fireball after fireball from his palms. Most either dissipated on their own or because of the rainfall, but some hit their mark and singed the Veratt's flesh as well as what remained of its left wing. Nothing except contact with its wings seemed to have any impact whatsoever.

Now that it could comprehend what was happening, the Veratt leapt toward Miles with its claws outstretched. Miles sprang to the left and the monster's fingers dug deep into the soil. The resulting quake made Miles stumble and fall to the ground and he hastily crawled away, tossing a useless fireball at the top of the Veratt's hand.

He got to his feet and darted back into the treeline, maneuvering through tree trunks to position himself behind the Veratt again. He readied his mind and focused on the other wing—

He saw his grandmother resting in the hospital bed, her face wrinkled and tired. A pale blue sheet covered her body, bobbing up and down steadily with her breathing.

The image began to change, began to instead show her resting on the rocking chair again, back and forth, back and forth, peaceful, quiet. The fireplace crackled, embers dancing on burning logs and falling into ash. Miles sat on the*lower your voice*rug nearby, playing with the new toys his parents had given him that morning, as well as*well either way it's not fair*the ones Santa had left behind along*you will see him*with a note for*don't be ridiculous*him beside the empty plate that held milk and cookies. He cast a sideways glance at his grandmother as her eyelids*this doesn't have to be hard*drooped, then closed, but the*no it didn't*rocking continued. Her foot gently*have to be hard*pushed off the carpet. He*but you made it hard*smiled.

The pounding in his head was too much. The angry voices muffled his concentration. He let out a scream. The Veratt yanked its arms out of the ground and turned to face him, maw agape, teeth like spikes and glistening with blood.

It reached out and grabbed a tree on either side of Miles and tore them from the earth. Dirt came loose around the roots and rained down on Miles' head. The Veratt casually tossed the trees backward as if they weighed no more than pillows.

Miles tried igniting his palms to send a torrent of flames at the creature's face, but nothing happened. He was powerless. The words and images of his parents kept mixing in his head and nothing felt normal.

All he could do was turn around and run. He zipped past trees, tripped over rocks and weeds, cried as raindrops hit his face and bark scraped his arms. The Veratt could be heard stomping behind him in pursuit.

Miles stopped running, breathless and unable to continue. For a second, he regretted leaving Io behind. He slouched with his hands on his knees, wheezing and staring at the ground. When he looked up, he saw he was in an even bigger clearing. There were charred pieces of fabric, scraps of meat, and various trinkets scattered about the clearing. An empty cage sat open several feet away from where he stood. It was the outpost.

CHAPTER TWENTY-NINE

TOO MUCH

Miles huddled under blackened scraps of tent, hidden from view. Rubble was scattered all over the abandoned camp and there was no way to distinguish between the lump of a broken chair and the lump that was him underneath the fabric. He leaned against a closed red chest, staring at the dark orange fabric covering his face, almost black.

A little ways away, the Veratt screeched and slashed through a tree. It toppled to the ground and sent a shockwave through the earth that rattled Miles' bones.

His father remained quiet after that. Miles watched as his mother dipped a spoon into the pot and pulled out a soft mound of rice with a piece of sausage nestled on top. She tasted it, nodded, and sprinkled a dash of cayenne powder into the mixture then stirred. After three or four rotations, she clicked the stovetop off. She didn't call Miles to come eat.

"I think you should go," she said to his father. "Dinner's ready and it would just confuse him if you stuck around for it."

Miles leaned his head against the hallway wall, looking up at a framed photograph of himself on his first day of kindergarten. His younger self sat at a short, round table, staring directly into the camera with a dazed expression, not particularly thrilled to be there.

"I'm not done talking about this," his father said curtly.

"Neither am I. I'll call you later tonight or we can talk about it in a few days. But right now, he needs to eat."

Miles lightly tapped the back of his head against the wall. He leaned forward and looked at the chest he was sitting against and recognized its distinct color. A deep red. It was Vinzent's chest, where Mortimer had found Kiko's drawing.

The Veratt stomped into the clearing, its breathing heavy and audible. The beast carried with it a carrion stench that invaded Miles' nostrils and nearly made him retch.

"*Miles!*" his mother called.

He stood and waited a couple seconds, to strengthen the illusion that he was coming from his room, then rounded the corner and entered the kitchen, sniffing the air. "Jambalaya?" he asked innocently.

"Yep," she smiled, scooping a portion of the food into a bowl for him. "Say bye to your dad then wash your hands."

"Bye," Miles said to his father, not looking the man's way. Out of the corner of his eye, Miles saw him initiating a hug and he knew he needed to reciprocate.

"Love you, buddy," his father said as they embraced.

"Love you too."

His father gave him a firm pat on the back then addressed his mother. "Call me later, please," he said. She nodded and he departed without another word.

Miles could hear the Veratt searching through the camp, but he wasn't sure exactly how far away the creature was. Based on the rumbles of each footstep, it seemed it was on the fringes of the encampment. Still relatively far away. Far enough for Miles to surprise it.

The recuperation had been extremely helpful, and Miles' head was feeling considerably less cloudy and muddled. He was finally able to concentrate on his own thoughts without the distorted yelling in his mind blocking anything out. He could finally focus and start fighting back. He just hoped it would be enough.

Miles got on all fours and crawled painstakingly slowly to the edge of the flattened tent, being cautious so as to not draw any attention to himself. The flap was stuck to the muddy ground, creating a wet slap as Miles pulled it free. He looked out into the clearing and saw the Veratt lumbering around on the opposite side, its back turned to him. Its remaining wing was tucked away, closed off to another assault. The thin, bloody tissue that was once its other wing twitched sporadically.

This was the moment.

Miles concentrated on two of the trees near the Veratt; on their trunks, their roots, the mushy soil covering the roots. He imagined the separate particles pressing together, latching onto the roots, keeping the tree from falling over, from shifting in place. He lifted them. The trees floated into the air, with huge mounds of dirt clinging to the ends of them.

Before the Veratt could turn around and see what was going on, Miles threw the trees against its back. The monster roared in shock and fell forward into the mud, the two trees pinning it to the ground. It hastily shoved them off and rose again just as a third tree hurtled through the air and slammed into its face. The Veratt stumbled backward, nearly tripping over its own tail.

Miles ate his dinner in silence, messily shoveling the jambalaya into his mouth so he could finish and get back to his room. He didn't want his mother to ask if he had heard the two of them yelling because he didn't want to lie to her, but he would. Ollie sat politely at his side, awaiting any morsels of food that fell into his domain.

The Veratt still couldn't ascertain where the boy was, so Miles used that to his advantage. He could throw tree after tree at the thing without ever revealing his hiding spot, and that was exactly what he did. But the Veratt had adapted, making sure to keep its fragile wing hidden away from the dangerous outside world. No matter how many trees collided with the beast, it would not be put out of commission unless its other wing was torn to shreds.

Miles couldn't use any of his fire spells without revealing himself, so he needed to improvise. He held another tree in the air and sent a lightning bolt striking into its purple leaves, igniting the entire tree. He threw it and it impacted with the Veratt's torso, but failed to do any significant harm.

While the trees had been a good distraction, he needed to start doing some damage to the wing. He sent down a couple lightning bolts, all of which missed their mark and either hit the earth or struck more trees, starting more fires that quickly began to spread. To compensate, Miles made the rain fall even harder in an effort to douse the flames.

The problem was that the Veratt barely ambled into Miles' line of sight anymore, and it was simply too difficult to hit his target without seeing it. He had to move.

Miles cast the fabric aside and leapt to his feet, sprinting toward the Veratt. It was stumbling around stupidly, still trying to figure out where the kid was. It finally spotted him and unleashed a threatening roar before racing forward.

The boy veered to the left, narrowly avoiding a swipe of the Veratt's claw. Its sharp nails sliced through the air and tore into the ground, crashing through left-behind crates and coals. Ash fluttered, swirling into a small vortex before languidly drifting back to the ground.

Miles cast another lightning bolt at the Veratt's back, but the bolt angled poorly and scorched the earth near the creature's feet instead. Miles yelled out in frustration.

The Veratt turned and swung its claws again, but the boy was far out of its reach. Miles withdrew to the treeline, shooting a few meager fireballs at its arms as he did so. It shrugged them off like delicate snowflakes.

"Could you hear any of that?" his mother asked. She looked at him from across the table with concern.

"No."

Her face contorted, then relaxed. "Good," she said. She pushed her food around with the spoon, the metallic utensil clinking against the ceramic bowl.

The Veratt tried lifting itself into the sky, but with a missing wing it was impossible and all it could accomplish was a meek jump which resulted in a minor earthquake upon landing.

But now its wing was exposed.

"You're going to be seeing less of your dad for a while, I think," she then said. Her voice was hesitant.

Miles tried to think about something else. He didn't want to think about his parents. His mind went back to the image of his grandmother gently rocking in her chair.

His lightning bolt struck the tattered remains of Vinzent's tent where he had been hiding minutes before. Not even close to the Veratt's wing, which now curled back up.

"Why?" he reluctantly asked his mother.

"It's kind of hard to explain, but you probably won't be seeing him every day anymore. But you'll still spend lots of time with him on weekends."

Miles nodded. He didn't know what else to say.

The Veratt lunged forward, reaching out its ape-like hand to grab the boy. Miles jumped out of the way, but one of its nails scratched his leg. A large gash opened and blood spilled onto the wet grass.

He landed with a thump a few feet away, slamming his already injured shoulder into a decaying log. He screamed in pain, tears filling his eyes. It was all too much. His shoulder, his leg. His parents. The Veratt. The divorce. His grandmother. Everything. It was all too much.

He had blown his opportunity.

He was done.

This was it.

The Veratt upended trees as it lumbered toward him, dirt and insects exploding onto the surface as it tore the roots from the ground. Miles looked into its face. Its sharp ridges, the ugly teeth dripping with saliva and blood. Piercing black eyes and magnificent horns jutting out from either side of its head, one of the tips chipped and scraggly. The Veratt stared back as it approached one devastating step at a time.

"Are you okay?" Miles' mother asked him. Ollie had gone to her side of the table, expecting better luck over there.

A mild vibration began to ring out in Miles' body, and it became more intense as the Veratt grew closer. The stench emanating from its body was overpowering. He gazed at the Veratt's eyes, trying to find any semblance of anything there besides darkness. Besides black.

"I don't know," he told his mother. Tears streamed down his face and he set his spoon down. His body shuddered as he cried.

His mother pushed her chair out and was instantly at his side, wrapping an arm around his shoulder. He winced away, but settled back down.

"It's alright," she said. "It's alright."

There was nothing in the Veratt's eyes.

Miles shot out a hand and a bolt of lightning burst from his palm, hitting the Veratt in the center of its abdomen. It took a step back in astonishment and extended its wing.

Without a second to waste, Miles lifted up a tree behind the Veratt with one hand and shot a stream of fire at it with the other. All of its violet leaves erupted into violent flame and Miles turned the tree onto its side, its top facing the Veratt.

The tree cut through the air like a javelin, slicing through the Veratt's wing.

It tore an enormous hole in the thin patch of skin, the edges seared by the fire.

The flaming tree careened through the air over Miles' head and crashed into the treetops behind him, collapsing into a fiery blaze several yards away.

The Veratt screamed in terror as embers flickered against its wing, burning additional smaller holes that made the creature's wing look as mangled as a piece of swiss cheese.

"It's alright," his mother said a third time, rubbing his shoulder.

He could see tears in her eyes too. She was crying just as hard as he was.

"It's alright," she said again, and then softly, "I love you. It's alright."

He pushed himself up off the ground, putting all of his weight on the uninjured leg. The vibration in his body was flooding his senses now and everything was turning to white.

He saw in his mother's eyes her anger, her sadness, her fear, her guilt, and he told her, "I love you too."

Everything popped back into color as the world behind the Veratt ripped away in a bright blue and green void. The colors shimmered like they had when they hovered around Clint's leg, around Io's wings.

Miles held out both hands and shot one bolt of lightning from each, shoving the Veratt back with each impact. The monster screamed with fury and fear.

After a third strike, the creature's tail dipped into the swirling void, and in a blink the Veratt was torn away. Its howl was nothing more than an echo in the Violet Woods.

For several excruciatingly long moments, the colorful void continued to swirl rapidly, sucking up ash and dirt and leaves before it shrunk in size and disappeared.

Miles sunk back to the ground, casting a sideways glance at his bleeding leg. The skin was almost completely covered in red. Fire raged around him. The strange vibration had left his body and was replaced with unbelievable soreness. His mother kissed him on the cheek and the tension left his body. He felt like he could finally rest. He could finally stop.

He closed his eyes and was consumed by sleep.

CHAPTER THIRTY

EVERYTHING BLURRED TOGETHER

A light knock on the door woke him. Miles readjusted and found himself tightly tucked in a stiff bed with thin, cream-white sheets. The room itself was the same color, with generic paintings of oceans and sailboats adorning the walls.

The door slowly opened and Mortimer's large green face filled the crack between it and the frame. When he saw Miles was awake, he opened it the rest of the way and proclaimed, "Hey, kid!"

The Rompun jolted to the bedside and grinned the widest grin Miles had ever seen. It was contagious.

"How you feelin'?" Mortimer asked, unable to contain the joy in his voice.

"Fine," Miles answered. "Pretty sore."

Mortimer nodded. "Yeah, doctors said you prob'ly would be. You took a pretty good beating the other night, kid. We weren't sure you'd made it."

"Where am I?" Miles asked, looking around. The room was unfamiliar. It smelled like the sea, and he thought he could hear the distant sound of waves lapping against a shore.

"The hospital in Merrikar," Mortimer replied, taking a seat in a nearby chair.

"Merrikar?" Miles parroted. He chuckled, thinking back to the first day he met Mortimer and the Rompun had asked him if he was from here.

"Yep," Mortimer said. "Closest town to where we found you in the woods. Had to get you to a doctor fast."

"How'd you even find me?" Miles asked.

"Followed the lightning, just like when we tracked you to the king's camp. Was a little harder to pinpoint exactly where you were, though. The Violet Woods are pretty huge. The enormous forest fire you started helped, though."

Miles tried sitting up, but the effort was more than he could handle. His body practically screamed at him to stop, so he obeyed.

"Oh, hold on," Mortimer said, getting up. He shuffled out of the room and returned a minute later with Jaselle and Clint.

The maylan tried hopping onto the bed but Mortimer caught him in midair. "Nah, nah, nah," he told Clint. "Don't imagine him pouncing on your leg woulda felt too nice," he said to Miles. The boy definitely agreed. Mortimer set Clint down farther up, where he could cheerily lick Miles' face.

"Hi, Jaselle," Miles greeted her, scratching Clint's neck.

"Hey," she smiled back.

"I'm glad you're okay."

"I'm glad you are too," she said, sitting down in the chair Mortimer had procured. "Though I am very upset that you didn't listen to me."

"Sorry," Miles said sheepishly.

Jaselle chuckled and waved off the apology. "I think it all worked out in the end."

As Clint gave him another lick, Miles asked, "Where's Kricket?"

Mortimer wasn't sure how to respond. "Dunno," he said. His large yellow eyes blinked.

"I gave Clint to him," Miles said. "They were heading for the Claire River."

Mortimer gave the boy a pitying look. "Sorry, kid," he said. "I didn't see no Omnes at the river. When I got there, I was checking to see who made it out and I saw Clint runnin' around like a maniac."

Miles said nothing. He rubbed Clint's head and gave the maylan a kiss on his furry cheek. He wanted to know what else had happened in Trafier, but he didn't have the strength to be told such a stressful tale. Right now he just wanted to relax and bask in the happiness of his friends, thankful that they at least had made it through the ordeal. Thankful that it was all over.

"So the Veratt is gone?" he finally asked Mortimer.

The Rompun chuckled. "That's the question on everyone's tongues," he said.

"Oh, right," Jaselle muttered, standing. "Alys wanted to talk to him."

"Right," Mortimer nodded. The two of them headed for the door. Mortimer looked back and asked, "You wanna keep Clint in here?"

Miles nodded. The maylan's warmth was comforting.

Mortimer gave him another smile and closed the door.

It was almost an hour before the queen finally entered Miles' room. She had spent every waking hour the past two days working to reconstruct Trafier as well as all the other towns the Veratt had ravaged.

By that time, Miles had managed to focus his energy long enough to mend his aches and wounds. The recovery didn't stop him from enjoying some relaxation in bed, though.

"I apologize for the delay," Queen Alys said as she took a seat in the chair at his bedside. She smiled warmly at him. "Are you feeling better?"

"Yep," he answered.

The wrinkles on her face seemed deeper than before. She shifted uncomfortably in her seat, considering how to broach the next subject. "So," she started, "there's something I need to ask you about."

"The Veratt."

"The Veratt, yes."

He let out a sigh. "I was in the woods, I was fighting it, it cut my leg, then..." Memories of that night were foggy. Only bits and pieces were able to fight through the haze. It was like someone had erased writing on a white board, only leaving behind random stray marks.

"We haven't found a trace of it anywhere," Queen Alys informed him. "Did you kill it? I'd think a body would have been left behind if so."

Miles shook his head. "A rift opened up," he said. "And then it was just gone. Then I woke up here."

A smile flashed across the queen's face. "Really?" she asked. "A rift? Pink and yellow, swirling together like ice cream mixing?"

"I guess," Miles murmured. "No," he then said. "Not pink or yellow. Blue and green."

"Well, that still sounds almost exactly like the rift that opened when the creature was summoned. I believe you've done it, Miles. I don't know how, but you did."

A rift. He had opened up a rift somehow.

"I don't know how I did it," he admitted.

"That doesn't matter," Alys waved him off. "What matters is that the Veratt is gone now." She planted a sloppy kiss on his forehead and thanked him. "This is glorious news for Rompu, Miles. We are in your debt."

Miles wondered if the king had been cured when the Veratt was sent away or if he was still suffering for what he had done to the kingdom. He asked, "Is King Mykael okay?"

The queen's smile faded. "He's...he will be, I think," she said.

"So you found him?"

"Yes, he's back in Trafier. On their way here to retrieve you, some scouts found him lying unconscious in the hills."

"Have you talked to him?" Miles asked. "Is he back to normal?"

Queen Alys shrugged. "It's hard to say," she answered. "I briefly spoke with him before I came here, yes. It was not a long conversation—he was exhausted and quickly fell asleep again—so I'm not sure, but he seems better. Not fully himself, but I hope he will continue to recover."

Miles' face brightened. He then asked, "What now?"

"Now we rebuild," the queen said, her tone light and melancholy. "The Veratt inflicted a lot of damage on our kingdom.

The countryside was torn apart and towns were flattened, including Trafier—frankly, it's almost inconceivable, the amount of destruction.

"But we'll push on; we'll make things better again. They might not be quite the same as they were before, but they will be wondrous again, in a new way. Trafier will be re-established. Roads will be repaired and several new ones will be built to better connect all of our villages. Seeds will be planted in the Violet Woods. The Skyr outposts will be torn down. I've not yet decided what will happen to those who betrayed the kingdom in favor of the king, but they will be integrated back into society. It might be slow progress, but it will be progress."

Miles looked out the window and saw nothing but sky. It was a cloudless day and all that filled the pane was a light blue.

"I hope things get better soon," he said.

Queen Alys smiled again. "They will," she said confidently. "Soon Rompu will be beautiful again. All of those silly Ruhigans up north will finally want to come down *here* on vacation," she laughed. "And some might even stick around." She rose, then said, "You don't need to worry. We'll be perfectly fine."

As she left the room, she turned to Miles and thanked him. He smiled.

The next day, the doctor instructed Miles to get out of bed and start walking around. His leg was incredibly stiff at first, but he soon got the hang of bending it again.

One of the queen's Skyr guards brought him to the local inn where Mortimer and Jaselle were staying. He found the two of them in the lobby, sitting in puffy armchairs by the fireplace.

Jaselle was reading a book while Mortimer watched Clint chase his own tail.

"Hey!" Mortimer greeted the boy as he stepped inside. "Up and about!"

"Yep," Miles grinned. He kneeled down, which was quite a feat, to pet Clint. The animal bounded toward the kid the moment he saw him.

The three sat and talked the morning, eating some sandwiches for lunch. Miles still didn't have much of an appetite, so he only had three or four bites before setting his plate on the floor for Clint to munch on. The maylan had a taste for provolone. By the time afternoon rolled around, Miles had mustered up the courage to tell the Moutons he was planning on going home soon.

"When?" Mortimer asked, visibly upset by the news.

"This evening, if I can," Miles said. "I miss home."

The Rompun and his wife smiled, though a tear marred her cheek.

"Of course," Mortimer said. "Back to *Texas* and your *westerns*, right?"

Miles grinned. "Right," he said.

"We'll miss you," said Jaselle.

"I'll miss you too," Miles said, unable to help himself from crying a little. "Will you take good care of Clint for me?"

"Agh!" Mortimer grimaced, jokingly disgusted. "I didn't even wanna take the mutt with us at all, and now you saddlin' me with him?" He grinned again. "Sure I will, kid."

"Thanks." Miles gave him another hug.

They spent the rest of the afternoon talking, joking, telling stories about Austin and Rompu. They took Clint on a walk and played fetch with him. They ate tartlets and drank endalain tea and consumed countless other treats.

As the day neared its end, they gathered outside the inn to say their goodbyes. Mortimer wrapped his arms around Miles, enveloping the boy in his blubbery mass. Jaselle followed suit.

As Miles pulled away, Mortimer gave him a pat on the back. "I'm glad to have met you, kid," he said, his large yellow eyes welling up.

"I'm glad too," Miles told him.

"Even though you lost my favorite sandals."

Miles punched the Rompun on the arm and Mortimer guffawed.

It was a pleasant day.

Miles walked twenty minutes east of Merrikar into the Violet Woods. The sun was setting behind the trees and the forest was already shrouded in the faint light of dusk.

He found a tree stump that was more or less free of bugs and took a seat on it. Blades of grass tickled his ankles as he adjusted himself, taking in the beauty of the woods.

It felt like a lifetime had passed since he'd woken up here, confused and afraid. The old version of himself would be amazed and baffled by his ability to sit on a *dirty tree stump* without shifting about anxiously. He remembered Mortimer telling him that first night that in the Violet Woods, everything's dirty. He realized he would miss the dazzling purple leaves that gave the Violet Woods their name. And that despite all the bad that had happened here, a lot of good had too. He had grown to love Rompu. He wished Mortimer, Jaselle, and Clint could come back home with him. Maybe Kricket could come too, if he felt so inclined.

Miles stared straight ahead, unsure of how to summon a portal back to Austin. When it had happened with the Veratt, it had been a complete accident. An extraordinarily lucky one, but an accident all the same. That was also true of his arrival in Rompu in the first place.

He thought back to his mother, looking into her eyes, seeing she shared the same trepidations he felt. Telling her he loved her. And he knew that what the queen said was true: everything would be wondrous again.

With his mind clear, a void opened ten feet in front of him. Blue streaked with lime green. He took deep breaths. In. Out. Then he stood and walked forward.

Nothing could be seen on the other end of the rift, if you could call it an end at all. Yet somehow Miles knew that it would take him home. He felt his mother's embrace. He knew it was safe.

He stepped into it and everything blurred together, blue into green into orange into yellow into brown into red into black.

ABOUT THE AUTHOR

TRAVIS M. RIDDLE lives with his pooch in Austin, TX, where he studied Creative Writing at St. Edward's University. His work has been published in award-winning literary journal the Sorin Oak Review. He can be found online at www.travismriddle.com or on twitter @traviswanteat.

CPSIA information can be obtained
at www.ICGtesting.com
Printed in the USA
LVHW111537141119
637372LV00003B/632/P